Book of Shadows

MATHILDA, SUPERWITCH
BOOK ONE

KRISTEN ASHLEY

ROCK CHICK
PRESS

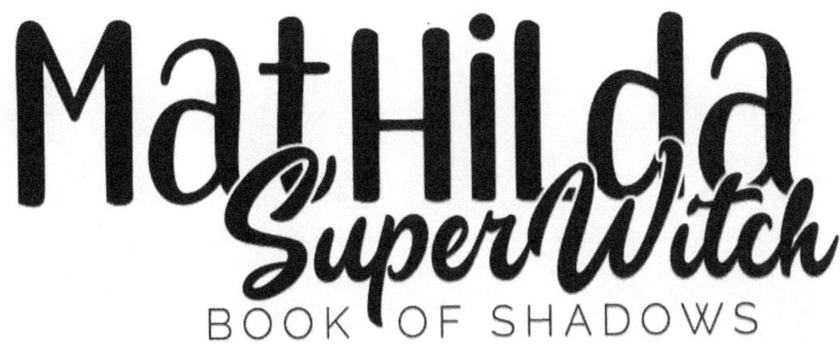

KRISTENASHLEY

NEW YORK TIMES BESTSELLING AUTHOR

Years ago, when I started writing this book, I did it to entertain my beloved friend,
Lucinda Ferguson, after she was diagnosed with cancer.

In the book, I introduced the character of "Lucy," a loyal friend, a down-to-earth
person, a movie lover, a great cook, a fabulous wit and a complete love.
Just like the real Lucy, my Lucy.

But my Lucy never read a word.

So now I'm dedicating this book to her memory.

I make your recipes all the time, my darling Lucy.
In the War of the Wooden Spoons you'd win.
Hands down.

Hope you've got a decent KitchenAid mixer up there.

The Month of November

The *Journal of Mathilda* also known as *My Book o' Shadows*.
(Witch. Apparently)
(Note: Now understand scariness of own name.)

2 November

Aunt Mavis told me I'm supposed to do this, start a journal, so here goes.

I am Mathilda Guinevere Honeycutt. I am thirty-three years old, single (thank God)(-dess apparently) and currently unemployed (kinda).

Oh yes, and I'm a witch.

Not kidding, I have magic. I saw it last night shooting right out of my fingertips like pixie dust. Well, actually more like sparkler fireworks mixed with a bit of pixie dust *à la* Tinkerbell without the wand. Anyway, it scared the bejeezus out of me, but what could I do but watch it fly?

Yesterday morning I thought it was all a drunken hallucination from too much vodka and sugar consumed at the Hallowe'en party. Mavis says it wasn't and told me to chant something, say, "So mote it be" and flip my finger out and there it went; hot pink pixie dust hit the cat right on its backside and…yikes!

Mavis tells me that the Honeycutt family has been witches since before recorded time. Even going so far as saying we were rumored to have something to do with Stonehenge, but then she said, "In the end, Stonehenge was just one big joke and not very funny, and now they're going to spend millions of pounds building underground roads and the like to protect it. Inconvenient and a waste of taxpayer's money! I wouldn't claim any part of that for the Honeycutts." And so on, but I wasn't listening anymore because pixie dust just shot out of my finger and I was still trying to cope.

She gave me some books and now I'm up in the Tower Room. I'm supposed to be reading. *History of Great Wytch Families* (it has a whole chapter on the Honeycutts!) and *The Honeycutt Book of Shadows, Unabridged, "D" (Dark Dabbling Spells – Dwindle Potion)* and *Celebrated White Witches, Vol. I, Calliope Agglethorpe – Desdemona Honeycutt* (952 pages!).

Witches are supposed to have journals, keep notes, track things like spells and the best directions when using a broomstick and the like. They call them their *Book of Shadows* (which is kind of a cool name I have to admit).

At least she's given me this yummy, leather-bound notebook (Aspinal of London, very posh, hot pink too, giddy up!). The journal is the best part about being a witch as far as I can tell from what Auntie Mavis has to say.

～

Some background:

Honeycutt family has been witches since recorded time.

As generations study magic, magical flow through bloodlines increases, therefore Honeycutts are very powerful.

History does not like powerful witches, so Honeycutts have been hunted for many years(!) and only survived because Auntie Mavis explained we were, "Wise, talented and well-protected." (Seems to me not enough to go on there.)

Have not known of my own witch-hood because am prophesied as being SuperWitch(!!) and therefore had to be protected by covens and secret societies(!!!) until reached an age where I could handle my power (which is now, though I may not agree).

Have been personally watched and/or hunted by bad guys all my life (unknown to me) who want, a) to murder me so they can steal my power (Auntie Mavis says that unless they are warlocks this can't happen, virtually impossible, even hard for warlocks, although there are many out there who don't know that…great), b) to murder me because of the people I'm prophesied to help are meant to go on to do important things (maybe) or, c) to murder me so I will just be dead because witches scare people.

Must say, I'm not too certain about any of this. (Understatement.)

~

3 November

I have not shot pixie dust out of my fingers yet today or yesterday, so I feel a little better about that at least.

But have been given more background and history about family and myself, and talked with Gran and Mom and am feeling a bit strange that they're so excited to be "out" about "The Craft" and, "Oh Honey, we just can't wait until you realize your full potential."

Blah, blah, blah.

So, I have to tell you that I already have a great deal of pressure in life in general considering current state of affairs with the revamp of the café before Day of the Dead announcement, so now have SuperWitch/savior-of-world onus on me.

Perhaps I should fill in journal just in case get hunted by bad guys and killed pre-realizing-full-potential so can have my own paragraph (sentence?) in the next version of *History of Great Wytch Families*.

~

History of Mathilda, SuperWitch in Training

Born in Denver, Colorado to hippie mom and absentee dad (also mysteriously absentee granddad, hmm).

Grew up living in family unit that included Mom (health-food store clerk and candle maker for most of my life but recently started own line of hand and body lotions). Often stayed with Gran (yoga guru even before it was popular and now very rich and sought after) and two sisters (one older, Viviana, one younger, Ursula—both practicing witches and kept it from me as am The Chosen One, explains some sibling rivalry issues I had heretofore not understood—so currently not talking to either of them).

Ate lots of granola and took it on the chin with many outfits before got a job at thirteen so I could buy my own clothes and leave tie-dye behind forever.

Did okay in school, went to college and majored in drinking and soap operas (yet finished in four years, now understanding some early magical powers) and graduated and landed a job in retail so could be close to greatest love, Ralph Lauren.

Had many boyfriends all of whom were, a) cheats, b) cheats and thieves, c) just thieves, d) confidence suckers ("You're going to wear *that*?" etcetera) or, e) self-involved, egomaniacal assholes (maybe E is independent trait that applies to all the rest).

Struggled with diet and workout regime for many years until made note of important fact that men actually like ass, it's fashion designers who don't (and they're usually gay, so why?). This was obviously a relief.

Embraced café society when Starbucks took over the world, as life is much better with vanilla lattes in it.

Talents: Can cook and am perfectly willing to tell you if an outfit suits you (or not).

Could use help with: Choosing men and dealing with SuperWitch predicament.

~

The Aunt

Mavis Lilian Honeycutt-Frost.

Married to Uncle Otto, but I never met him as he left years ago and is not talked about.

Ever.

I've known Mavis since I could remember. She is one of those very cool aunts, the kind who brings you chocolate and tells you not to worry about chocolate causing zits because that's a myth (probably zapped 'em...mm, Zapping Zit Spell may be useful). She's also the kind who thinks all your boyfriends are great and then hates them after you break up with them.

She's English and lives in a small seaside town in Somerset called Clevedon (where I currently live but am now thinking work visa procured for me by Mavis might be magical and may go up in puff of smoke).

Being English made Mavis even cooler because she's foreign and has a posh accent, and my sisters and I could go out and visit and feel cosmopolitan after we came home.

She reminds me of Merryweather from the Disney *Sleeping Beauty* cartoon: dark-haired, short and round (and prefers very tailored, sleek clothing—shame that, would benefit with embracing the Earth Mother Look).

She lives in this big, weird castle-esque type thing on a cliff called The Gables (a Honeycutt piece of property).

There is only one place that I've known that gives me the same feeling as The Gables—New Orleans. Strange, eerie, dreamlike, once you get there, you never want to leave. It is almost like the place caresses you, yet it feels like it is very warm, comfortable, cozy, safe... and closing in on you, smothering you...and you love every minute of it.

Anyway.

~

Mathilda's Move to England
(Enter yummy Sebastian who is off-limits because too much my type and thus must beware.)

So, last summer I won a competition I'd entered for the hell of it: Best Brownies at the Taste of the Rockies. (I dabble in baked goods—but Taste of the Rockies! That's big.)

After e-mailing the news to Mavis, she wrote that she was having some troubles with the café she's run for years as café society was beginning to take over England and no one wanted cream teas and Victoria sponge anymore and everyone wanted espresso and brownies.

She asked for my help with a new menu and updated "happening" (wince) decor.

Had just broken up with Penishead Number Who Knows in Disastrous Love Life of Mathilda and was currently feeling that I'd gone as far as I wanted to go in retail, so felt that maybe a look-see into the invitation to change of life wouldn't be a bad idea. I could rent my condo easily and Auntie Mavis told me a work visa wouldn't be that hard to obtain (hmm) as she could pull some strings (hmm, hmm).

Life could be worse than living in a seaside town in the Southwest of England and serving cappuccinos to boys with accents.

So I did it.

(Craziness! as not normally risk-taker but maybe had a spell cast on me?)

Auntie said she'd give me the top floor of The Gables and fix it up so I could have my own little flat (is very nice, with fab view, curlicue iron bed and claw-footed tub, yay!).

I had arrived at Heathrow and was struggling out of customs due to overzealous duty-free shopping when I noted that I could not spot Mavis.

What I did spot was this man coming at me (surely not *at me*, just toward me to pass me in order to passionately embrace stick-thin, sunken cheeked, freakishly tall, supermodel-esque woman behind me carrying $5,000 Louis Vuitton bag).

Oo la la. I think parts of me started quivering just from looking at him. He was yum-a-licious—tall, great hair and attitude.

He was either a fashion-conscious dickhead or gay, both of which I was deathly attracted to (alas).

Please note bizarre alternate universe of American/English fashion: In America many (not all) women have a clue about fashion and/or make an effort and majority of men are slobs (unless have girl-friend/wife who dresses them, are gay, players or are freaks). In England, the opposite is true as many men have natural fashion sense that is quite luscious and most women (not all) are either scary fashion kamikazes (which is actually very interesting) or don't care at all (eek!).

Though, this doesn't matter seeing as every single woman in this country has utterly perfect skin.

Not a joke.

Since I'd been here, I'd not seen that first blemish.

I should have known, totally, this sceptered isle was *steeped* in magic.

He was looking at me so I was pleased that I had strict life philosophy of never wearing knockabout clothes when could be stylish with a bit of effort even if it meant sacrificing comfort.

When I was just about to pass him, he said in a fabulous, deep, English-accented voice, "Mathilda."

It wasn't a question, it was a statement, and even if I wasn't Mathilda I would have said, "Yeah?"

Which is what I said.

"Yeah?" (Smooth.)

He told me his name was Sebastian something-or-other (had stopped listening at "Sebastian" because no one is actually named Sebastian, that's a bad name, there's no way to make it a nickname and sounds very romance novel-y/soap opera-ish) and by the time I started to listen again he was telling me Mavis had been called away on urgent business and he was asked to pick me up.

I'd never heard of him before so I was looking at him for signs of inherited Mavis traits as he could be secret love child (and thus related to me which would be disappointing). He handed me his mobile phone (which by the looks of it he stole from James Bond) and told me to call Mavis…bleh!

Ack!

Ack!

Wait! Wait!

Must…talk…to…aunt…

~

Later…

Had scary flashes of lights happening in eyes and lightheadedness. Went to talk to Mavis and she told me I was having a vision and to go with it (she was very excited).

Found out ('cause saw it in very own head) that urgent business that took her away from meeting me at airport was her waylaying baddies who knew I was coming to England and so were going to try and get me.

Further knowledge-sharing included information that Sebastian was member of millennia-old secret society and currently assigned as my very own personal bodyguard. He's been watching me since I arrived in the UK.

Hand hurts.

Head hurts.

Baddies after me.

Need drink.

~

7 November

I'm still alive, which feel is a good sign.

Designing interior of café with person (Wesley, bleh!) who doesn't understand my, "I want it to look Steven Tyler rock 'n' roll cool meets Madonna in-your-face hip."

Auntie very open about uncertainty re: how she feels about my vision.

Currently in witch training, which is very intense with meditation, herb study, chalices, pentacles, cauldron, etcetera, etcetera, etcetera.

Coven meeting tonight, a little nervous. Not sure I'm up for dancing naked in garden (especially since Sebastian is supposed to be watching over me and naked-dancing not my top choice for what I want him to see me doing).

Have talked with Sebastian twice since finding out he is my personal bodyguard. Have also had about twenty thousand Whitney Houston/Kevin Costner themed fantasies since finding out.

First time he came into kitchen while I was having early morning coffee (not fair time to visit anyone).

By the way, he has very sexy walk that starts at hips (mm).

He stopped close to where I was sitting at big, battered kitchen table, looked down at me and said, "You know?" (Man of few words.)

I said, "Yes."

And then he did a strange thing and gave me a picture of a scary-looking black dragon and said to memorize it, and whenever I was in trouble I should think about it and he'd be there.

I thought maybe there should be a beeper number or panic button just in case black-dragon-thinking didn't work, but it didn't seem I had a choice.

So I did as he told me and looked at it (*a lot*) and memorized it and the next day he came to the kitchen while I was drinking early morning coffee and stood by big, battered table, looked down at me and said, "Forget about the dragon. Don't think about the dragon anymore. At all. Ever." And then he left (somewhat rude, I think).

Auntie Mavis started laughing.

Perhaps too enthusiastic re: dragon-thinking-telepathic-panic-messaging practice.

~

Please note that things become clear to you when you look back.

After picking me up from the airport, when Sebastian took me to his place to wait for Mavis, I was worried I'd see his boxers thrown on floor and dishes not cleaned and beer cans not thrown away. Or worse, very tidy chrome and leather-esque abode.

Instead it looked like Indiana Jones's house from the *Raiders of the Lost Ark*. Very scholarly, cozy and masculine with books and interesting junk lying about.

He left me there as had something pressing to do (also fighting baddies with aunt?) and upon some (minimal) poking around (anyone would do it), noted he had Vonnegut, Hemingway and Hiaasen but also had three bookshelves dedicated to Arthurian Legend (little scary) lots of stuff on occult (scarier) and had a bowl of stones (now think may have been runes) and other stuff, didn't know what it was until now (crystals, various talismans, etcetera).

Don't know what his secret society's name is as is very secret and Mavis says I need to think about harnessing my power and not so much about Off-Limits Sebastian. I say that need something to think about that is pleasant instead of bad guys out there trying to kill me.

She saw my point.

8 November
(Early, early morning.)
(Wow.)

I was trying to get to sleep in curlicue bed when thought I saw something out of the corner of my eye. Auntie has a gazillion kitties so thought one had come to visit, so looked around but no kitty, then saw thing again.

Was light and floaty and I started to freak out because I remembered I was being hunted by bad guys and may be bad guy trick, so thought of black dragon immediately. Kept going around in circles (now on knees on bed) and trying to see floaty thing and thinking black dragon, black dragon, *black dragon* and was pointing randomly and pink pixie dust was flying everywhere…

And then thing stopped right in front of me and there she was!

A faerie!!!!

She had spiky ears and curly, long, light-brown hair and long, long fingers and gossamer wings that sparkled.

Yay!

Faeries!

I was so excited I kinda screamed a little bit, and the door flew open and then all this lilac and powder-blue pixie dust was all over the place with little explosions of it everywhere and the faerie disappeared.

"A faerie! Faerie, faerie, faerie!" I shouted.

Mavis had come to my rescue and she started running around chanting and so-mote-it-being with me jumping up and down on the bed shouting, "Faerie, faerie…stop it, you'll hurt the faerie!"

Then Sebastian came running in and slid across the plank floors to stop right at the foot of my bed and looked around at the place dripping with pixie dust and two women running and jumping around shouting.

He was so, well…normal with pixie dust landing in his hair and on his shoulders with this kinda angry-esque expression that I stopped and so did Mavis.

"I swear, there was a faerie just at the corner of my eye, and then she stopped and I saw her clear as day. I swear it!" I said when everyone had quieted down.

Sebastian looked at me for a bit and then muttered, "For fuck's sake," (very lush accent even when cursing…mm) and walked out.

Auntie is pleased I had a visit from a faerie though she said to beware because some faeries aren't great but most are, so…yay!

Mavis said I'm coming along if I'm seeing faeries (though don't know how I feel about that) then cleared the pixie dust with a flick of her wand and went back to bed.

Am very tired after pixie-dusting straight from finger (is taxing, that's why witches use wands as direct pixie-dusting takes too much power and energy and leaves you weak).

Must go to sleep but wanted to write down in my journal that I saw my first faerie.

Yay.

(Wonder how Sebastian got here so quickly. Hmm.)

～

Later…

Have not seen faerie again and fear may have scared her with all the pixie dust and shouting. Or maybe they just come at night.

Mental note: must research this or ask Auntie.

Mavis will not tell me where Sebastian lives and I do not know if this is, a) because she doesn't know either or, b) because she fears me showing up on his doorstep in the middle of the night wearing lacy peignoir set *à la* Alexis Carrington Colby Dexter and making a fool of myself or, c) because she thinks I may stalk him.

Doesn't matter, too busy to worry about yummy-yet-off-limits Sebastian right now.

Coven Meeting was not what I expected, very boring. Spent forty-five minutes discussing who should get annual scholarship (Penelope Custard (unfortunate name) studying midwifery), then Octavia Blackwell talked on and on (and on) about how her daughters don't take The Craft seriously and all they want to do is party in Ibiza and make love potions (poorly).

No "bubble bubble, toil and trouble."

No naked dancing.

Nothing.

Have meeting with plumber to discuss the floor tile in bathrooms of the café. My choice was four times more expensive than regular tiles, so Mavis wants compromise. Ack!

Later…

Went to meeting with plumber thinking of plumbers with pants hanging down in bad ways and filthy T-shirts. Walked into meeting at café having already decided to give in on tile in favor of velvet couches.

Stopped short in door as saw Mavis with man who looked like a much less scruffy, but still incredibly sexy Sawyer from *Lost*.

Dee-lish-us!

And he was the plumber.

How could he be the plumber?

He's named Aidan.

Aidan the plumber.

Am on my guard as there are no plumbers named Aidan who look like Sawyer from *Lost* in whole wide world who are not bad guys in disguise.

Decided to hold my ground about tiles.

(Pleased I wore spike-heeled, pointy-toed, killer boots with jeans that show my ass to best advantage, even if possible baddie.)

~

17 November

Am tired and cranky.

Had day of reckoning today, which went very well but ultimately annoying. Want to rest, forget I am SuperWitch and go to a beach, somewhere…anywhere.

First, Wesley does…not…share…my…vision! He does not understand that glamour and style are actual draws. That people will want to be somewhere just because it's cool.

He says velvet couches and curvy, hidden booths in back may be bad when coupled with significantly caffeinated beverages and teenagers.

He fears no span of the generation gap.

He doesn't understand essence of coffee house culture!

I told him there were places all over America filled with black-haired, scarily-made-up goths or grunged-out neo-hippies drinking copious amounts of coffee and scarfing down lemon scones beside power-brokers, soccer moms and trendy senior citizens who prove him wrong.

He says maybe so but this isn't America.

Duh!

Like I'm not (somewhat painfully) reminded of that *every freakin' day*!

Nearly mentioned that it has been working pretty well for some time in France too, but find that English have weird thing about France and figured this would not help my cause.

Feel that Wesley is trying to turn Mavis against me.

Stupid Wesley.

Then Mavis made me spend hours with Aidan (the plumber!) going over tile samples to try to find a happy medium.

Found out through Mavis being huge, embarrassingly obvious busy-body that Aidan went to Cambridge and studied history to ultimately be professor (which explains posh accent) but quit because was getting bored of history and didn't like academia (but apparently does like pipes and toilets, hmm).

Spending the afternoon with Posh English Sawyer from *Lost* looking through tiles is some kind of agony, as constantly should appear witty and vivacious or subdued and mysterious and was too tired to be either, so was just myself, which I try never to be.

And then Auntie came up with idea of "tasting party" to "get a lock on the menu." (Ack!)

So I spent ages preparing and baking for tasting party as whole coven, and as Mavis put it, "a few friends" (over forty people!) were coming to taste test my cooking!

All of this with magical training and study (books, books and more freaking books). There is much pressure to learn and realize full potential (Mom and Gran calling requesting progress reports, Viv and Su e-mailing constantly. Ack!)

Then, faerie has been visiting me at night and talking to me, but she doesn't speak English. Instead she talks like a dolphin on speed and whizzes around the room (and me) while I get ready for bed or when I'm trying to read *The Witch Familiar* by Balthazar Muldoon (over three hundred pages on cats!).

I think my faerie's name is BecBec because she keeps pointing to herself and saying that and then pointing to me and saying something that sounds (a little bit) like Mathilda.

Taste testing day today and I laid out three different types of brownies, six different cookies, five cakes, three scones and four muffins ready for people to consume and then cast judgment (ack!).

Mavis said it is good practice as will be doing it every day in the café, but still.

The "friends" included Aidan (the plumber) who was only other young person there, except me, and only man there at all (as Sebastian, at this point, suspiciously absent).

Aidan seemed to be trying really hard to be nice while figuring out why he was there and who all these alarmingly-dressed women were. (Mental note: must suggest a coven-meeting-makeover and soon!)

He didn't stay long but did stop and say he would definitely come to coffee house and sit on a velvet couch (ha!) and drink espresso with one of my "very nice" oatmeal cookies.

I thought that was sweet of him.

Near end, Sebastian deigned to honor us with his presence. I do not know why he was so late, but hope it was not because he was keeping baddies at bay but instead hanging in his lair and working out with free weights while wearing only shorts and sweating a lot.

He had a word with Mavis and then started to leave and grabbed a blond brownie with chocolate chips almost like it was a handful of peanuts from a bowl. I was about to get angry at how nonchalant he was with my brownie but then he took a bite and stopped and started to look around.

I feared he was trying to find a place to vomit as I figure he normally eats only skinless chicken and power bars and impurities in brownies were going to put him in anaphylactic shock.

Instead he saw me, and I think that he may have looked at me for first time with a smidgen of respect.

Very pleased with that, to be honest, but would only ever admit that to journal.

In the end, everyone liked everything, so taste testing was huge waste of time and energy (except, of course, found way to Sebastian may be through stomach…mm…but thinking (trying to convince myself?) that may not (shouldn't) care).

19 November

Feel very witchy at the moment.

Last night I was sleeping when felt someone shaking me gently. When I opened my eyes, the room was filled with candlelight as entire coven was surrounding my bed holding candles.

Mavis was the one shaking me and told me to be quiet and just do as I was told.

They gave me some clothes and this rather gorgeous, hooded, heavy, black cloak to throw on (lined in *real* black satin—fab!).

We walked together, single file out of the house. The witches blew out their candles when they walked out the door and we wandered along Poet's Walk, up and around, then down and through the wood. All of a sudden, I felt tugged away from the footpath and Mavis saw and told me to go with it.

I stopped at a tree, big and dark and scary at night, but I felt like it was something else, like it was human, breathing, warm. I can't explain it except that it seemed to be speaking to me without talking. (Spooky.)

I touched it and could swear it was vibrating.

Auntie Mavis gave me a knife and told me to cut a branch about a foot long but not until I asked the tree if it was okay. (Very weird talking to trees.)

I stood there in front of the coven (who were eerie silent) and felt like a total idiot but said out loud, "Tree, would you mind terribly if I took a bit of your branch?"

I kid you not, at that very moment the wind started blowing and the tree branches rustled and a few leaves fell off, floating down gently and scattered around me.

This seemed like a yes to me, but I looked at Mavis to be sure and she smiled and nodded her head.

So I carefully took hold of the branch and felt like I should take my time, so I stroked it a bit and then when it felt right, I took a deep breath and quickly cut the bit loose.

I don't know what happened then, but it felt wild. A sensation like a mild electrical shock coursed through my body quickly and then was gone.

When I looked around, the coven was surrounding me—all in their cloaks like mine—silent and watching.

Mavis gave me a tea towel and told me to put its contents at the foot of the tree as an offering.

In the tea towel was a leftover scone from the taste testing. I set it down at the tree, put my hand on the trunk and whispered my thanks.

Later, Mavis told me I had my wand.

And it was a powerful one too.

Current state of mind (FYI): Don't know how to feel about the wand, unannounced midnight coven meetings and trees talking to me.

28 November

Very pissed off and very sad and very freaked out, and do not want to be a witch anymore, because what is the fucking point?

Don't know what to do.

Last night, was sleeping (feel I am destined never to sleep full eight hours again in lifetime) and felt something strange happening to my hair, and then heard BecBec's mile a minute babble speech.

Opened my eyes to see BecBec pulling my hair and seeming excited about something (BecBec always seemed excited about something). Most annoyed, could not believe faerie wouldn't let me sleep.

I told her to go away, turned around and buried my head in the pillow.

Next thing I knew, covers were pulled slightly back and hair was being tugged!

Wasn't just BecBec but about five other faeries with BecBec! All were babbling in faerie-speak and seeming very excited and pointing to the door.

Thought maybe baddies were coming, but decided definitely I should wait to make sure before I thought of the black dragon as I didn't want a repeat of last time. (Mm.)

Faeries (these were both boy and girl faeries, all with diaphanous wings and pointy ears—one looked kinda not faerie-esque but more like a cute, bald alien with long fingers with knobs on end) were pointing at my closet and at the door and seemed very anxious.

Thought I'd go with my intuition (witchy thing to do, right?), which was telling me to follow them.

So I got dressed and put on witch cloak and grabbed my wand (at BecBec's worried motioning) and followed them out of my rooms, out of the house and onto Poet's Walk.

Then went round and down the side of hill, through woods.

I couldn't believe my eyes. There were faeries and alien faeries and then other tiny weird creatures all over the place(!) with wings, without wings, hopping along or jumping from tree to tree. All of them gave off little lights, mostly white but some green, orange or yellow (pretty).

We got into town and faeries guided me down a path behind a house where BecBec stopped and pointed impatiently at a window.

I wondered what would happen if anyone saw us but no one was about as was very, very early in the morning.

Light was coming through the window, so even though it was late, someone other than me was awake.

I looked through the window into a kitchen.

In the room was a woman of about my age, a boy of about six or seven and the sweetest little chocolate lab puppy.

"Cute puppy," I whispered to BecBec.

She put her finger to her lips and shook her head for me to be quiet.

When I looked back, the woman was shaking the boy so much his head snapped back and forth.

Ack!!!

I was frozen in horror, it all happened quickly as woman pointed at puppy wee on floor, grabbed boy and puppy and practically threw the both of them out the back door.

Ackity Ack Ack!

The boy was crying uncontrollably and the puppy was whining. It had to be near freezing, way past midnight and the child was wearing nothing but pajamas — no shoes, no coat, nothing.

What a fucking bitch!

What was she thinking?

"Come on, Cosmo, go pee, go pee, Cosmo," the boy pleaded through chattering teeth to the dog and started to pick his way through the yard, guiding the confused puppy around on his leash.

I didn't think about it except that I realized I had no time for opening sacred circles, etcetera. I had to work fast.

So I turned around once, twice, three times (my favorite number, figured it would do) and stopped at what I hoped was north.

Then whispered,

Banish the cold, take fear from the night.
Bring on warmth, give a feel of the light.
Protect the child against chill and shudder.
Keep him warm with no heart aflutter.
In no way will this spell reverse, or place on the boy any curse.
Calling on the power of my blessed tree, as I will, so mote it be!

(Hard to rhyme when flipped out.)

And then I pointed my wand at the child and to my shock, out flew pink pixie dust making a beeline to the boy, slamming him straight in the back, it exploded up and over him and the puppy in a shower of fuchsia light.

Then, nothing.

The boy didn't react at all. It was like he didn't even see the pixie dust. (Bah!)

But as I watched, he stopped shivering and quieted his tears and the puppy quit whining altogether, so I had a feeling that maybe it worked. (Yay!)

I didn't have a lot of time to feel pleased with myself before the door opened and the bitch started shrieking at him to get inside.

(What? The neighbors can't hear this? Whatever happened to "it takes a village?")

He hurried in and I turned again to watch through the window and saw her draw her hand back and…

Ack!

I'd had enough.

I lifted arm, fury surging through me, and I brought my wand down to whack the woman with all I had…

And *slam*, my wrist ran into something solid that forced my wand straight into the air and my magic shot out of the wand and flew up high over the house like a firework.

"Banish it!"

It was Sebastian behind me, holding my arm and hissing at me in my ear.

"Banish it, now!" he ordered again as the pixie dust started to come down but it wasn't pink, it was blazing blue.

"Mathilda!" he clipped.

I snapped out of it and said quickly,

> *Back to my wand, dark magic flee.*
> *As I will, so mote it be!*

All the sparks flew at me with what seemed like great velocity, plunging back into my wand, driving my wrist against Sebastian's hand as we both (with some difficulty and not a little pain) held my wand straight upwards.

When every flash, twinkle and glimmer was absorbed into my wand, I felt the heat in it burn me and I cried out, opening my fist and letting it go. It fell to the path between Sebastian and I, and we jumped apart just as it exploded in a flash of blue and white light.

I didn't have time to react or even think as Sebastian grabbed me and pulled me out to the street. He stopped the both of us, pulled me close to him and did this thing with his arm like Batman would do with his cape, except he didn't have a cape.

I saw the world turn to a shimmer around us and then he grabbed me again and pulled me toward Poet's Walk.

"Stop!" I shouted, but he didn't say anything and kept going, dragging me with him. "Stop right now!" I kinda repeated, still shouting.

He stopped all right, and I slammed right into him. And before I could step away, he took my upper arms and hauled me right up against his (very hard) body (yikes). He wasn't looking at me but over my shoulder.

Then he told me, "We have to go, the glamour won't last long." (Er, wha'?)

And off we went again.

I didn't say a word, just ran after him all the way up the Walk and into The Gables and right to my rooms where I figured I'd be safe to let him have it.

We both flew into the room, he closed the door and flipped on the light, and before he could get out a word or even close the door—

"What the fuck was that about?" I shouted.

I was angry, really angry. I don't think I've ever been that angry.

"Mathilda, you know better than that," he replied, and I could tell by the tone of his voice that he was pretty angry too, which pissed me off more because what did he have to be angry about?

"Know better than what? That woman is beating that boy right now. God only knows—"

He interrupted me impatiently, "A witch never meddles unless she's invited, never. It's elementary Wiccan Creed. At the very least, you should know that."

Ack!

Okay, so, I'd read a lot in the past month (a lot, a lot) and been told a lot (a lot, a lot) about not ever doing magic to others unless I'd been asked. A non-magical person or an innocent must always seek magic before it's performed. That was Canon Number One in the Magical World.

Fuck.

"So what do you do?" I asked. "Walk away? Watch? The faeries took me there. I couldn't stand around and do nothing!"

"You don't have a choice," he stated, like it was as simple as that.

"Well that sucks!" I told him. "That really sucks."

And then I let it all hang out, about the café and Wesley and velvet couches and expensive tile (though didn't get into Aidan, the plumber), and boring coven meetings and faeries never letting me sleep and trees talking to me and now my wand had exploded and that little boy was being beaten by his mom, and I didn't even want to think about that poor, cute puppy.

Then I started talking about being homesick (ack! where did *that* come from?), and my nightmares of never entering another Saks Fifth Avenue for as long as I live and how aggravating that I can't find a MAC counter within a fifty mile radius and no matter how cool,

Topshop…just…does not…cut it (I mean, we all aren't Kate Moss and can't pull off that rock 'n' roll waif look).

Then I finished with, "What's the point of being SuperWitch if I have to flit around making brownies and mochaccinos and wait for people to ask me for help? That's just stupid. Batman doesn't wait for people to ask for help! What do I do, get a big red phone and hope it rings?"

He was quiet through my tirade, and after he studied me for a bit, he then said, "You look exhausted."

Ack!

"Great, that helps a lot, Sebastian. Thanks. I *am* exhausted. No fucking duh."

I was too mad to be any good with a comeback.

He looked impatient. "You're doing too much with the café. You should be focusing on The Craft. I'll talk with Mavis."

"Good! While you're at it, tell her I'll take the brownies and mochaccinos over faeries guiding me to abused children I can't help, and if she says no then I'm just going to go home because having to wait to be *asked* to fulfill The Prophesy of The Chosen One really sucks."

And then, unfortunately, I burst out crying.

Fuckity, fuck, fuck.

Like all men faced with intense, unheralded female emotion, he just stood there staring at me

Brooding, sexy Sebastian all of a sudden faced with a crying woman became impatient (or more impatient) and uncomfortable.

Fucking men, they have no idea how to deal.

Then he came up, wrapped his strong arms around me and hugged me (which I have to admit was kinda nice). Then he walked me to the couch and sat down with me. And I didn't care if he was uncomfortable, I just sat next to him and pushed in close and cried and cried and cried.

Somewhere in the middle of crying and/or snuffling, I fell asleep and when I woke up a while ago, Sebastian was gone, morning had broken, my hand hurt, and I felt like hell.

And I miss home, I miss my friends, I miss Oreo Double Stuff cookies and Banana Republic and…

I lost my fucking wand and I have the strange feeling that the tree is mad at me.

30 November
(Have plan.)

Had long talk with Mavis and she explained Life of Witch containing:

    A) Frustration (want to do good deeds, people scared of you).

    B) Frustration (hunted, hiding, protected).

    C) Frustration (myths o' Satan worship, dark lore).

"Silly really," Mavis said. (Understatement.)

It was explained that rules were rules, tinkering with the innocent without their permission rarely leads to good things (yadda yadda yadda —what about the not-so-innocents?).

No matter, seriously frowned on in the magical world, no ifs, ands or buts.

In the end, she told me to get used to frustration and persevere, I had my calling and that was that.

She explained, "We have to be careful, history has taught us the art of cloaking our powers. Those that can find us, who open their hearts and minds, will find us."

Blah, blah, blah.

And then she said (and this was good), "It's not like we can put out a shingle."

(Mm.)

I thought that was interesting.

I took the rest of the day and went to Glastonbury and poked around a bit and noticed something important.

Auntie Mavis is wrong.

You *could* put out a shingle.

Others had done it, right out in the open. Sure they were new-agey and reeked of patchouli, but they weren't hiding, that's for certain.

Last night, I set my alarm for 2:30 a.m. and woke myself up (crazy, now waking myself up in middle of the night).

I got dressed, put on my witch cloak and went to the tower room to get the boline, which I wrapped in my black velvet alter cloth.

I then headed straight to the kitchen and cut off a huge chunk of chocolate maraschino cherry cake (one of my favorites) and wrapped it in a tea towel (feeling this had better work as would be serious waste of chocolate cherry cake).

Then I went to my tree.

On my knees next to my tree, I put my forehead against the trunk. I could feel nothing. It wasn't talking to me tonight (probably still angry I'd blown up its branch in a fit of (justified) rage).

I wasn't giving up.

"Please, Tree, can I have another branch? I promise to take better care of it and learn to be a good witch."

Nothing.

"Cross my heart."

More nothing.

Didn't want to promise to hope to die because, well, too close for comfort.

So I brought out the big guns and took the cake and set it at the base of the tree.

"Please. If you know me at all, you know that's a lot of chocolate maraschino cherry cake and that's quite an offering from me, let me tell you."

I heard the wind, the branches swayed halfheartedly.

"It's a really big slice. Look at it."

More swaying, stronger now.

"And yummy. Really yummy. Trust me."

More swaying, definitely getting something…

And then a branch came down and scraped my face.

I grabbed it on the upswing and sliced it off.

It was thicker, slightly more gnarled than my last bit.

I threw my arms around the tree, hugged it and said, "Thank you, thank you, thank you," and carefully wrapped my new wand in the velvet with the boline.

~

The next morning, I came down to the kitchen and Mavis was sitting at the big table, drinking coffee and staring at the sea.

I got my cup and walked to the table then tossed out the velvet with a flourish so that my new wand and the bolline flew out and slid across the table. (Dramatic, I know, but I was making a point and I didn't want it to be missed.)

I sat down and said, "I want to name the coffee house 'The Witches Dozen.'"

Her eyes were glowing with a strange light as she looked at the wand and me. It scared me a little bit, but I held my own in the freaky Wiccan staring contest.

Then my wand started to vibrate and clatter on the table. We watched it as it jumped around and then it whizzed across the table and into my hand just like I was Luke Skywalker and it was my light saber.

I have to say it was totally fucking cool!

"So," I said, "'The Witches Dozen?'"

And Mavis looked over my shoulder, and as I turned to see what she was looking at (Sebastian leaning in the doorway with his arms crossed on his chest, the usual impenetrable look on his face), I heard Mavis say (sounding all pleased with herself like it was her idea), "That has a nice ring to it."

Yee ha!

The witches were in business!

The Month of December

11 December

Too busy to write much.

New lease on Wicca and am busy training. Mavis and coven have been very supportive.

Yay!

Plans in full swing for Grand Opening of The Witches Dozen Coffee House on New Year's Eve.

Yay!

New Year's party is posh dress, so going to London to buy myself a new outfit.

Yay!

Harvey Nichols, here I come.

Yayayay!

Was Mavis's idea and although lots of work, will be very fun.

Wesley threw hissy fit last week when I told workers to cut half star shape into hardwood floor/all-weather matt at front door, and then to embed carpet sliver moon shape in middle of café.

Told Wesley was sick of his attitude and would be happy to allow him to move on to new client if I was being too difficult. Seemed to quiet down and no more hissy fits since.

Yay!

Hired staff member/baker/barista and she is lovely. Her name is Lucinda and she may be first new friend in England.

Yay!

Called Aidan on mobile and asked him if he'd like to go to Grand Opening (as was project's plumber and entitled to see finished product in action). (Ack!)

He paused for a (very) long time and then said this: "A bit short notice."

I said: "Oh, sorry."

(Cambridge-educated plumber Aidan probably going to big party with Princes William and Harry or something.)

He paused again and then said, kinda quiet and very sexy: "I'll change my plans."

Yayayayayayayay!

No William and Harry—just me! (And all the other people at the party, but still.)

Yay!

(May be baddie but can use him for personal sexual pleasure then vanquish him or something.)

Had espresso machine lesson and although Pandora (another member of our coven) had a bit of trouble with it (her curse caused a minor delay when espresso machine only gave out burgundy sludge with gold flecks in—Octavia had to mindwash espresso machine teacher man (don't worry, mindwashes not done very often, only in urgent situations like said espresso machine mishap) while Mavis released machine from curse—was sort of amusing, only after curse was lifted and I wasn't having silent conniptions at maybe having to buy another £3,500 espresso machine!), rest of coven showed signs of being natural-born baristas (with Fay and Beatrice being obvious standouts).

Only bad thing is Sebastian has taken to having breakfast in the kitchen.

He is always there when I arrive in morning, sitting with his long legs stretched out and reading *The Times*. Does not say good morning and did not appear to recognize or appreciate my early attempts to look attractive once I realized he was going to make a habit of breakfast sharing. So have given up and come down in fluffy slippers, flannel pajama bottoms, sweatshirts and no makeup.

Screw him.

(Mm.)

PS: No sign of the boy.

PPSS: Or his dog.

The Month of January

2 January

Witches Dozen a Huge Success!!!!!!!

First, must report that I found a great outfit for Grand Opening, simple little black dress: sexy cleavage, showed good leg and clingy but without being slutty. Nice.

The shoes were (I must say) kickass. (Tad expensive but never feel guilty when buying expensive shoes as always prove to be totally worth it.)

The *pièce de résistance* was the fab wrap that was all webby and lacy in way of Stevie Nicks ("Stand Back, Stand Back!").

Second, had so much fun cooking with Lucy pre-party. She is a total giggle and a great cook so feel some pressure taken off me. Food at Grand Opening was very big success with Lucy and me at the helm, so am relieved.

Third, Mavis told me to be ready early (early? nutty) as had some important things to go over with me. We took taxi to coffee house (is walking distance but not in four-inch heels).

When we got there the coven was already there. All the ladies dressed to the hilt and made up, I was proud of them as a few had taken some of my subtle (ahem) hints.

The blinds were closed, the decorations up and all was ready to be laid out for the party.

The coven had lit tons of candles, incense and there was soft music.

We had a glass of champagne and toasted The Witches Dozen (yay!).

Then they formed a circle around me while I stood in the middle of the sliver moon carpet and they told me to close my eyes and hold out my hands.

There was some chanting and when I opened my eyes again there was a big broomstick laid across my palms.

It was gorgeous.

Yay!

The handle was laced with satin and velvet ribbons in a bunch of bright colors with the ends hanging amongst the bristles (so pretty).

With great ceremony I hung it on the front door, and I felt happy thoughts about being a witch and a part of my coven who had woven good charms into broom (and thus whole coffee house).

Felt powerful and warm and loved.

∼

Grand Opening
All things going well as:

Complexion had decided against stress-induced breakouts (!);

Regardless of loads of testing of culinary delights, dress still fit (!!);

And shoes were miraculously comfortable even though they were drop-dead gorgeous (!!!).

(All magic?)

Guest list was huge and most everyone came and were very complimentary on décor (ha! take that Stupid Wesley!) and food (yee ha!).

Lucy and I decided we deserved to get a little drunkie-poo, and Lucy had very nice boyfriend who didn't mind making sure our champagne glasses were always full. (Good boyfriend.)

Began to worry about Aidan as night was no longer young. Also surprised by Sebastian, for as far as I could tell I still had a body and he was meant to guard it but was nowhere to be seen. (Shirking duties?)

Would not let apparent abandonment of male units in life ruin my evening. (Humph! Why did I spend so long finding perfect dress, fuck-me shoes and Stevie Nicks wrap when no one to appreciate it but Lucy?)

Then felt a hand on my waist.

Turned around, thinking it would be Sebastian there to be wet blanket, but it was Aidan.

He looked delicious with nice suit and tie replacing usual jeans and T-shirt.

"Sorry I'm late," he said.

Mm.

Was not upset, was drunk and happy and had successful café and many friends and pretty broomstick and very lovely man standing next to me.

Mm.

"Congratulations," he went on (meaning hit of café, not successfully finding perfect not-too-tarty outfit, although the way he was looking at me made me think it was more the outfit).

Rest of night dreamy as Aidan was gentleman to Mavis and other once alarming coven members he met at tasting party, funny and charming to Lucy and boyfriend and all-around perfect date (as was clearly date—yay!).

Peculiar feeling of being all tingly because was really happy (forgot how it felt) that all the hard work and my vision were to be appreciated and…

Then everyone started to get very excited as New Year was coming and ten, nine, eight…

And all of a sudden I was kissing Aidan (oh my *and* yowza) and then…

Aidan backed off looking really annoyed, and all of a sudden there was Sebastian.

And then (bah!)…

Sebastian kissed me!!!!

Ack!

Not the yowza kiss of Aidan, instead brushed his lips against mine and then leaned in and semi-whispered, "Happy New Year," in my ear.

And then he was gone.

Can you believe?

(Must admit, lips all tingly and not sure if it was from intense-plumber-kiss but may have been from whisper-soft-bodyguard-kiss but don't know…hmm.)

Later, during girlie bathroom break, Lucy said this: "What was that all about?"

As am woman and women speak the same language, I knew what she was talking about without asking, but she explained anyway.

"One second your snogging Sexy Posh Sawyer, the next George Clooney-slash-Colin Firth is having a go."

I replied, "George Clooney-slash-Colin-Firth? Hardly! More like Russell Crowe-slash-Sean Connery as is arrogance on top of arrogance."

Then Lucy and I had very long, intense discussion about this when decided Sebastian was Clooney *Ocean's Eleven* (for the dash, wardrobe and sexy glower), Crowe *Gladiator* (for the brood, deep voice and taciturn communication style) and Firth *Pride and Prejudice* (for the arrogance, height and, as Lucy put it, "Lanky 'Piss-off-all-you-little-people' walk"...mm).

Back to Aidan who persevered regardless of bad-mannered bodyguard. He put Auntie and I in a taxi and said he'd be back for an oatmeal cookie. (Yay!)

Nearly floated home—may have new boyfriend, definitely have new girlfriend, proved Wesley wrong and The Witches Dozen is out there and we were soon gonna kick ass and take names.

Arrived in rooms all blushing and happy...

Only to see Sebastian sitting (more like lounging nonchalantly for all the world like he lived there!) on my couch.

He stood up and announced, "I don't trust the plumber."

And walked out of the room.

The fucking cheek.

Haven't seen him since.

May ask for different bodyguard as Sebastian is most provoking.

4 January

Boy is here! Boy is here!

Oh wait, must go serve him.

~

Later…

Boy came into The Witches Dozen with his mom (she looked like hell, all shadows-under-eyes, gray skin and tousled clothes like she picked them up off the floor, bleh!).

He ordered hot cocoa and one of my Giganto Chocolate Chip Cookies (excellent choice).

I watched as he took a bite and his eyes got really round and happy (pleased with myself for that one), so I said from behind the counter as if just happened to notice his reaction, "You like that? You should taste my M&M's cookies. Come back tomorrow and I'll make you some."

His mom smiled one of those mother thank-you-for-being-nice-to-my-offspring smiles and bent over and kissed his hair.

Bitch.

Lucy whispered, "M&M's aren't on the schedule for tomorrow."

I said, "They are now."

Must go to Tesco for M&M's.

Very Much Later—near 5 January!

Am in Tower Room trying to scry but it isn't working. Having serious troubles with divination…no visions since my first came after finding out I was a witch.

Very annoying.

Very much want to look into boy's house but can't seem to focus.

Am doing it on the sly as Mavis has been pretty clear I'm not allowed to try scrying until I've had more practice with her around. Last time accidentally hooked into the radio studio during airing of BBC4's *Today* program and didn't realize I'd beamed myself in. I think I scared the bejeezus out of John Humphries as he lost track during brow-beating some poor Red Cross person when I said, "Let him finish, you pompous ass."

Sebastian heard it over the radio. I got in trouble. I didn't mean to astral project myself. It really pissed off Sebastian as he said it was hard enough looking after my physical self but would be impossible to protect astral self if I went around astral travelling as an amateur.

Amateur!

Am I The Chosen One or not?

5 January

Boy came in.

His name is Rory McShane and he likes M&M's cookies.

He likes them a lot.

He has a dog named Cosmo (knew that already but pretended I didn't).

He is eight years old.

He isn't sure that he'll like peanut butter cookies but he said he'd stop by and try them sometime (this after carefully glancing at even less together than yesterday Bitch-Mom-from-Hell).

Tried, while making a double espresso with room for cream, to focus on him but got his mom instead (!). She was on phone sounding very pleading while crying.

She's a total mess.

Maybe should give up attempts at magical intervention and call Social Services.

On another subject:

Aidan is MIA.

No call, no show, no nothing.

Am not going to call him as I made first move anyway and is his turn.

Lucinda says I should call him if I want to call him, and fuck "turns."

World of Lucinda is better than World of Mathilda as everything seems quite clear and straightforward and she is not scared of anyone or of what anyone thinks of her.

Want to be Lucinda when I grow up.

9 January

Last two days have been hell. As much as I love my Aspinal Book o' Shadows, wish I had computer journal as will kill me to write all this down.

Is important (or so Mavis says).

First, didn't see Rory for two days. Was worried and kept trying to see him, even going so far as breaking into Mavis's Magic Room and trying Mavis's crystal ball (very risky but I didn't get caught, thank goddess).

Aside: Mavis's Magic Room is awesome, it's where I have lots of my lessons and I love it in there. It's all red and mauve and purple with tassels and etched-globe, dangly Victorian lights and toss pillows everywhere.

It isn't exactly my style, I prefer light, airy, uncluttered, feng shui, etcetera, etcetera, but it is lovely to visit and very snug and comfy.

Anyway.

No visions of boy.

Nothing. Nada. Zilch.

Saw the mom in visions, lots of crying, looking over shoulder and tearing of hair as she is clearly insane, but nothing of the boy.

Then, yesterday, was standing in window frosting a carrot cake when I felt something weird crawling up my back.

Premonition (or Mavis told me later).

Ack!

Then saw Rory running but didn't see him with my eyes, saw him in a vision!

I left cake half-frosted and told Mavis to hold the fort, and I took off out the door.

Found Rory running toward café and crying very hard, slobbering on and on about his mom and grabbing my hand and dragging me toward his house.

Got in his house and was confronted with vision from *About a Boy* as mom was on couch, unconscious with vomit on floor next to her.

Ackity ack ack!!!

I hate vomit. I hate the sight and smell of it. I started to gag immediately in automatic response but then heard Rory crying and Cosmo whining. Realized I was the adult in this situation and had to act.

I walked up to the woman and put my hand on her forehead while telling Rory to call 999.

I lifted her up as best I could and shook her a little. She was warm and breathing (thank goddess) but she was dead weight, and I kept wracking my brain but in spite of superwitchdom and Chosen One Prophesy, in all honesty I didn't know what to do.

Furthermore, didn't have my wand.

Furthermore, was uncertain about magic in front of Rory as didn't want to screw up and levitate mom only to drop her on the floor or something. I doubt SuperWitch is supposed to tinker with the undeveloped psyche of eight-year-olds.

So, I thought about the black dragon.

Then I took my cue from movies (don't they spend a lot of time researching these things?) and continued shaking her and started slapping her gently around the face and talking loudly to her.

When Rory got back I said, "Rory honey, go get me a glass of water…hurry."

Then I thought about the black dragon again.

(I know what you're thinking but what else could I do?)

Rory brought the water, I threw it in her face, she groaned, moaned and her head lolled around, and then nothing.

I thought of the black dragon again. (Bloody Sebastian was taking his time.)

I got a big pan of water and threw it in her face and this time she began mumbling with more lolling.

I asked Rory where the bathroom was, and with a herculean effort (I thought) I dragged her off the couch and halfway across the room when Sebastian strolled in. (Yes, *strolled*, ack!)

He took one look at me dragging the woman across the floor and asked, "What's going on?"

I wanted to say, "We're dancing," but instead I just bugged my eyes out at him and then gestured to Rory and thought, "Suicide," in my head hoping he'd catch my drift and then…

"Fuck," he muttered.

No kidding.

"Did you call 999?" he asked as he pulled her out of my arms and picked her up like she weighed about five pounds.

"Of course I did."

What does he think I am, a moron? (Don't answer that.)

He dumped her in the tub, turned on the shower and gently slapped her about the face. I could have told him that water and slappage were not really working but then she mumbled some more and opened her eyes. (Of course, Sebastian dousing and slapping her would work.)

She took a while to focus on Sebastian then looked at me and then said, "Help me."

Straight out, she said it.

"Help me."

Yay!

If that's not permission to meddle then nothing is.

Then she said, "They're trying to kill me. You have to take care of Rory."

Sebastian looked at me, I looked at Sebastian and the mom started sobbing.

Then the ambulance people came and took her away.

~

Sebastian and I took Rory (in Sebastian's lush platinum-colored Jaguar XJS) to hospital.

~

Her name is Josephine McShane (I grabbed her purse before getting in Lush Jag and I looked through her wallet), and hospital people told us she'd taken a whole load of pills.

Stuffy person arrived and asked if we were family (while glancing indiscreetly at Rory).

I pinched the back of Sebastian's arm and said yes, we were his Auntie Mathilda and Uncle Ash (good nickname, eh?—took me a while to come up with that one but one cannot keep saying (or writing) Sebastian all the time, too much) and we'd most certainly look after Rory.

Sebastian did not appear too happy (but may have pinched pretty hard, er…accidentally).

Hospital people came back out and told me Josephine wanted to talk to me.

When I arrived in her room, she looked exhausted, pale and terrified.

She waited until I sat by her bedside and leaned in. Her lips were all chapped and looked sore and I made a mental note to bring lip balm on my next visit.

"I've been poisoned…" she started.

Ack!

"Hunh?" I asked.

"Poisoned. I know it sounds crazy but please believe me. I know who you are, what you are…I, um, don't believe in that stuff but I'm at my wit's end."

I gathered she was talking about Magic.

"That's why I came to town, I'd heard about what happens here… that people could find help here. I'm so tired…scared for Rory. And he's been so good. I got him that puppy and…" She trailed off, possibly remembering she's a psycho, then she asked, "What did I do to make them come after me?"

I had no answer for that and thought maybe I should go tell Stuffy Social Services Person that Josephine had lost her mind, before she said, "They said your name, 'Mathilda.' They said it the first time they tried to get him. They said, 'He's on the Mathilda Register.' When Aidan told me…"

Aidan!

Ack!

Mathilda Register?!?

Ack! Ack!

"…he was working with a lady named Mathilda I couldn't believe it. I didn't know if it was good or bad. But I went in your café, The Witches Dozen, right? Witches. Yes. And you were so nice and Rory hasn't talked to anyone like that in so long."

"When you say 'they' who do you mean?" I asked.

She didn't know, but "they" were always there…she has moved and moved, everywhere, to France, Amsterdam, Ireland, bladity, blah, blah, and she can't get away from "them."

She has no money, she's working two jobs, taking in laundry (do people still take in laundry? can't believe that!), cleaning houses. She can't let Rory out of her sight (except school and is even terrified of that, every day is a nightmare she said) for fear they'll get him.

"I'm trying to protect him, be a good mum and…"

She was working herself up so I patted her hand and said, "He's staying with Mavis and I tonight. Don't worry, Josephine, he's safe with us. You just rest. I'll be back tomorrow."

It took a while to get her calmed down, but she finally slept.

I watched her for a moment and then it came, lightheadedness and flashes in eyes and I was back at the window that night with BecBec, looking in, watching Josephine about to hit Rory and then she collapsed to her knees on the floor. She grabbed him to her and hugged him, sobbing sloppily and apologizing, and then they walked together out of the room with little Rory trying hard to be a big man and take care of his mama.

Jeez.

Thank goodness Sebastian stopped me from zapping her.

I grabbed the phone in the room and called Mavis. Gave her a quick briefing and told her we needed to activate the coven and get a protection spell put on the hospital room.

"Oh, my darling, your first Spellbound!"

She's very excited.

Personally, I'm scared shitless.

~

Sebastian and I gathered up Rory, his stuff, his dog and headed to The Gables.

I settled Rory and Cosmo in the Trunk Room, gave him a little potion to help him sleep (don't get excited, it was a child's dose of Night Nurse), tried my hardest to tell him everything was going to be okay (I don't think he believed me) and explained that I was just a moment away, he only had to call and I'd be there.

Broke my heart the way he looked in that big bed. Scared and alone.

Poor Rory.

I found Sebastian in the library.

"Don't even start," I warned before he could speak.

But then this was Sebastian, he had no intention of speaking just scowling at me and making me feel like an idiot.

I glared back at him for a second then muttered, "Right."

Then he asked, "Ash?" with an eyebrow raised and in a voice that pretty much said he didn't like his nickname.

I ignored that and said, "You ever heard of something called 'The Mathilda Register?'"

That brought the first shock of many that night.

Sebastian reacted.

I could see it in his eyes, the way his body tensed. One minute he was oh-so-nonchalantly leaning against the desk with legs stretched out and his arms crossed on his chest and then he was not-so-nonchalantly leaning.

"Where did you hear that?" he asked.

"Josephine."

"Who?"

Of course, he didn't know her name. In the World of Sebastian, she was unimportant. (What is, I wonder?)

"Rory's mother."

He just looked at me.

"Well?" I prompted.

"Well, what?"

Ack! The nerve.

"The Mathilda Register?"

"Don't worry about it."

Sebastian is most provoking.

The library is huge and very Professor Higgins in *My Fair Lady* but bigger.

There are two spiral staircases on either side of the room leading to wrought iron railed landings. Books piled upon books shoved here, there and everywhere (even, in some cases stacked up in piles on the floors and tables).

There is a huge fireplace *à la Citizen Kane* (okay, not that big) faced by a couple of worn, comfy couches and lazy, lovely velvet chairs with ottomans with tassels and in front of the window a big, heavy, carved wooden desk with some wing-backed leather chairs around it.

In short, the library was like everything in The Gables, huge, preposterously imposing yet relaxed and welcoming.

Freakish, I know.

There was an enormous book on a podium, handwritten (unbelievable) that held the list and location of every book in the library (including the ones stacked on the floors and tables and those that had been "checked out"—crazy, what's crazier is that it rewrites itself every time you take a book or move a book, I'm not kidding).

I walked to it and looked up my name. (Should have done this ages ago, maybe, but who has time?)

There it was, *The Mathilda Register, The Myth of* by Hamish Wilding.

And also, *Mathilda Honeycutt, The Prophesies* also by Hamish Wilding.

Fuck!

"Mathilda." This was a warning from Sebastian.

I ignored him and started for the Ms.

He followed me.

I speeded up.

(Damn his long legs!)

He caught me at the waist and swung me around (no mean feat) and half carrying, half dragging me, started marching toward the door of the library.

There was a little tussle, one, not surprisingly, that I didn't win but did end up thrown on a couch with Sebastian standing over me, breathing kind of hard and staring down with this intense expression on his face.

I stared back at him and was (humiliatingly) downright panting.

Unfortunately, at this point I kinda forgot about the books and got really turned on by Sebastian staring at me like that. So I licked my suddenly very dry lips and tried to think of something else.

Anything else.

But *his* lips.

And the idea of his lips…

On *my* lips.

And on other parts of me.

Yikes.

Ended up staring at his mouth.

He looked away, raked a hand through his (fabulous) dark hair and then muttered, "Fucking hell."

And.

You…will not…*believe* this.

He leaned down, grabbed hold of me and hauled me off the couch.

I thought he was going to toss me over his shoulder and carry me out of the room to chain me up somewhere (mm) and then go tell Mavis on me or something.

But instead he slammed me against his body and *started to kiss me*!

Oh my.

Oh my.

Was not just whisper-soft kiss, but was full-on, open-mouthed, sexual onslaught.

Oh *my*.

Whole body (most especially certain obvious parts) got very, *very* into the kiss.

He wrapped one arm around my waist to hold me close while the other hand went down over my bottom and the back of my thigh. Then he leaned over, hooked his hand behind my knee and pulled it up so jeans did very, *very* pleasant thing at my crotch while he wrapped my leg around his hip.

And then I thought we'd fall back onto the couch and get serious when…

"Oh, darlings. My, my, my…Sebastian. You know it's *far* too early for that."

Ack!

Auntie Mavis.

Instead of jumping away from each other like naughty teenagers, Sebastian's arm tightened (though, he did drop my knee). He kept me where I was and took a deep breath. His eyes were closed.

"Mavis," he said softly with what sounded like a load of regret and not a little bit of impatience, and then he opened his eyes and looked at me, and I kid you not, I thought I was going to have an orgasm just from the way he looked at me!

Sweet goddess, Mother Earth and all things charmed and bewitched.

He looked at me like I look at clotted cream, like it was the divine ambrosia of the gods, and I intended to devour, with extreme pleasure, every last bit of it and then lick the container clean at the end.

Fucking hell indeed.

Then he let me go.

I turned and kinda wobbled and Sebastian caught me by the waistband of my jeans and steadied me until I slowly lowered myself to the arm of the couch.

Then he let go and walked away.

Far away.

All the way across the room to stand behind the desk and stare out the huge arched window there.

Brooding Sebastian was back.

Auntie Mavis trucked in carrying a tray with tea, sandwiches and biscuits on it.

Bless her, she was after this girl's heart with the food but she could have waited at least fifteen (thirty, mm, maybe forty-five, er...) minutes.

She started serving, doing it manually which still surprises me.

Once I found out about the power we had, I mean, who would ever do anything again if they didn't have to?

But Mavis is of the philosophy (not shared by every witch) that the Power of Wicca, like everything natural, is in limited supply and you shouldn't waste it.

She totally ignored the fact that she just walked in on me necking with my bodyguard.

As for me, I was still semi-panting and trying very hard to keep it together and not charge across the room, take a flying leap, land on Sebastian and rip his clothes off.

"How is the boy, my dear?" she asked me as she handed me a plate of sandwiches.

"He's okay, sleeping in the Trunk Room."

She picked up her wand from the tray and drew a circle in the air, lilac and powder-blue pixie dust sprang out, hovering in the air for a moment before Paulina Babcock's (another member of our coven) face filled it.

"I was just cleaning up, Mavis," Paulina told her.

"Before you go, Babs, please check on the boy if you don't mind. He's in the Trunk Room."

"Will do."

Then, *poof*, the pixie dust and Paulina were gone.

Magic is so cool sometimes.

"Pleased to say that Ms. McShane is safe in her hospital bed for tonight. A very strong but short-lived spell will keep her from harm. How long is she supposed to stay there?"

"Who knows, probably a few days so they can—" I started to answer.

"Pish posh." Yes, Mavis talks like this, she's a scream. "We'll have none of that. I know someone…"

At this point I felt something weird in my stomach, something that was creeping downwards with pinpoint accuracy, something that was warm and melty and a little scary.

I looked over at Sebastian and he was not looking out the window anymore but staring at me and…

"Matty, darling, can I please have your attention?"

I jumped when Mavis said my name.

"Oh dear, oh dear," she said shaking her head at me. "Will you be able to keep your mind on your first Spellbound, I wonder?"

In answer to that, I asked, "What's the Mathilda Register?"

Mm.

Her reaction was intriguing. Her head jerked around toward Sebastian who simply shrugged his shoulders and returned to staring out the window.

We went through the whole rigmarole about who told me what and when.

"Well, it would seem we have to have a conversation earlier than I thought," she declared.

Then she settled into one of the couches with the chocolate biscuits in her lap.

～

If getting my first Spellbound then making out with Sebastian wasn't enough to make it a big night, what Mavis was about to tell me was going to put the frosting on the cake.

❧

Mavis then began.

"You see, nearly a millennium ago, there was a coven of thirteen very powerful witches." She turned to Sebastian who had moved around to sit on the desk. "Norman times, yes?"

He nodded.

"I think it was 1069, 1070, something like that," Mavis went on.

"1070," Sebastian clarified.

It was like watching a tennis match.

Mavis continued, "This coven made a lot of waves. It had significant power and influence. They made so many waves that they attracted attention. Unwanted attention." This she said in a dire voice. "The coven needed protection." She stopped, watched me closely then started again, "To protect it, a secret society was born." Another pause for effect. "*Le Société de Mathilde*."

Oh sweet goddess, why me?

Mavis shook her head. "No, my dear, it wasn't named after you but instead after Mathilde de Flambert. A very, very powerful witch and the high priestess of the coven. She was not even a relative of ours, although there were two Honeycutts in that coven."

Humph.

Mavis kept going.

"At first, *Le Société* was formed only to watch over Mathilde and her circle. But over the years, especially through the dark days, it began to work to guard all witches. It grew, expanded and became strong, powerful and even wealthy. The witches it protected worked, and still work I might add, to return the favor of protection. We've managed to be able to transfer bits and pieces of power to our guardians…"

I looked at Sebastian and remembered that night I was out with BecBec and he used the Batman's Cape Invisibility Glamour.

"But it never lasts long," she continued. "These men, and women of course, of *Le Société* often were forced to lay down their homes, their fortunes, their legacies and their very lives to see that we witches were safe."

"Why on earth would they do that?" I asked.

"Why?" Mavis smiled a private, sad smile and took a moment to answer. "Because you protect the ones you love, my darling."

I looked at her. I looked at Sebastian. I looked back at her.

"Hunh?"

"The first of *Le Société* were the husbands of the witches of Mathilde's coven. It grew and built on the sons and lovers of the witches…"

Holy Spousal Unit, Batman!

"No," I breathed.

Oh my, oh my.

"Really?" I asked.

"Oh yes, my dear. Where do you think my Otto is?"

Oh my, oh my.

That means…

"Dad?"

My voice cracked, I couldn't believe it but there she was, nodding her head.

"Granddad?"

More nodding.

Fuckity, fuck, fuck.

"Ash?"

"Who's Ash, darling?"

I pointed at Sebastian and Mavis chuckled.

"But of course. His mother was Isabella Jacobs-Wilding, my dear. A long-time family friend." Mavis smiled somberly at Sebastian, and then she said quietly, "I still miss her."

Fuck.

I watched Sebastian and his face didn't change at all.

Sebastian is the motherless son of a dead witch and I'm the fatherless daughter of a live one.

Fuck.

Then the questions came, "Where's my dad?"

"Deep cover, darling. I cannot say."

"Is Granddad still alive?"

"Of course, dear. He's due for retirement, er…soon."

"What do you mean 'soon.' When is that?"

"I don't know…ten, twenty years."

Ten or twenty years!

"*What?*" I asked, or kinda yelled.

She looked slightly uncomfortable for a second and then cleared her throat.

"My darling Mathilda, my dear girl. You see, we witches…um, your grandmother…my darling child, there is no other way to put it. Matty, you're looking at a one hundred and eleven-year-old woman."

~

There are times in your life when you wish you would pass out and just wake up later when whatever was bothering you is gone.

I remember when I was in gym class and the teacher would announce that we were going to play dodge ball.

I fucking hated dodge ball (I mean, who came up with that idea? It's ridiculous). I wished I could just faint and then be sent to the nurse and have it be over.

Everything Auntie Mavis said felt like one of those plastic, weirdly pink balls hitting me somewhere where it stung.

I didn't want my dad to be a "deep cover" secret society dude.

I didn't want Sebastian's mom to be dead.

And I don't think I wanted to live past one hundred and eleven years old.

Even if I did do it looking no more than fifty, like Mavis.

~

"You're telling me you're one hundred and eleven years old," I said slowly.

"Yes, Matty, I must admit, I'm middle-aged."

As I stared at her with my mouth open she told me about witches and men, and just about everyone else (?) trying to find the fountain of youth. Although witches hadn't found it, they'd certainly perfected a few elixirs ("With the help of the Elves, lovely creatures, BecBec is one, of course…") that helped things along the way.

Then she told me there are dark forces in the world, explaining that few of them were magical:

Your average warlock, but always male and cannot command powers of nature so usually no threat. (Mavis: "Pitiful really");

Some sorcerers and sorceresses who have turned to the dark side;

A few faeries, pixies and imps (mostly naughty) and the brownies, of course;

Mermaids and leprechauns can be annoying by their very nature, but are normally harmless;

Banshees, but that's a whole other story;

Vampires, zombies, werewolves and especially the Abominable Snowmen were usually just misunderstood. (Mavis: "Although, I had a run-in once with the Loch Ness Monster, and I must say she's got what you kids today call an 'attitude.'")

Yes, this was the conversation I had with my aunt. I won't even get into what she said about gremlins, gnomes, trolls, goblins and fucking whirling dervishes (!).

"No," she continued, "these aren't the creatures to fear. The creatures we fear are men. Witches have worked hard on protection, on saving and prolonging life…but they've never found a way to stop an arrow, a dagger, a saber or a bullet from piercing flesh."

Ick.

Ack.

"Mathilde and her coven spent a great deal of energy and expense recording everything that they knew, saw, heard and did. Travels, spells, charms, potions, lore…everything. All witches do. The Witch's Journal, her Book of Shadows, is her most important possession. Over the years, *Le Société* has catalogued these volumes and watched over them."

"*Le Société*," this surprisingly came from Sebastian, "recorded The Prophesies."

Uh-oh.

Here we go.

He carried on, "You aren't the only Prophesied. There are many prophesies, Chosen Ones, some who have done very well, some who have failed."

Uh, what?

And here I was, almost certain to be a Chosen One you had to, a) be One, as in singular, as in *me*, and b) be good at what you did.

How do Chosen Ones fail?

Crazy shades of *The Matrix* sequel. What? Was I part of the Chosen Six? Eight? Two Hundred and Eleven?

Yikes.

Mavis took over. "As for you, my dear, many witches, a few wizards and a sorceress or two have had various prophesies about you. You were prophesied everywhere."

"The enemy heard of you." This was Sebastian again. "Over the centuries, your name was all over the place."

"This scared them." (Mavis)

"You scare them." (Sebastian)

"I scare me!" (Me)

"You scare me too." (Sebastian)

Humph!

Sebastian continued. "In 1772, Algernon Savage was the foremost scholar of The Mathilda Prophesies. He was kidnapped." Ack! "Tortured." Ack! Ack! "And eventually murdered." Oh no. "He gave them what became known as The Mathilda Register." Stupid Algernon. "In other words, a list of all the Spellbinding you would do." Stupid, *stupid* Algernon.

Mavis broke in. "Luckily, dearest Algernon had a healthy imagination and made up most of it so convincingly, even under torture, that they believed him." Clever Algernon. "Unfortunately, he gave away some of the real Prophesies too." Uh-oh. "In the meantime, Sebastian's great-great-great...?" Mavis stopped and looked at Ash.

"Great," he said.

Mavis kept going. "Grandfather, Hamish Wilding, wrote *The Myth of The Mathilda Register* making it clear that *all* of what Algernon told was either made up or not prophesies at all, but history. Furthermore, he printed *Mathilda Honeycutt, The Prophesies*. In turn, his clever wife, Eleanora, put a spell on it."

"Anyone who had a dark heart," it was Sebastian's turn, "read stories of how most of The Prophesies either went unfulfilled or had already happened. That the Mathilda they'd thought was one person was really many Mathildas over the centuries, starting with Mathilde de Flambert and ending in 1698 with Mathilda Winterbottom, one of the Witchfinder General's victims during The Burning Times."

Now Mavis, "For those who didn't have a dark heart, but were pure—"

"And magical," Sebastian cut in.

"They could read The Prophesies in one-heart-stoppingly brilliant volume," Mavis finished.

"It worked," Sebastian added. "Over the years, as it took longer and longer for you to make an appearance and for any of The Prophesies to come true, people began to believe it was all legend, just myth."

"But if that's the case, why are people after me?" I asked.

"Oh, darling, not because they think you are *The* Mathilda, but just that you are *A* Mathilda and therefore, well, I think they believe it's better safe than sorry."

Great.

"How do you know it's me?"

Mavis threw her head back and laughed.

Then she stated, "You, my girl, are unmistakably *The* Mathilda."

I didn't know what this meant but decided to pursue it later.

"But these people who are after Rory," I said. "They mentioned The Mathilda Register in front of Josephine."

Mavis looked at Sebastian who in turn looked at me and said, "That isn't good news."

You're telling me.

18 January

Update:

(Cannot face another marathon writing session.)

Rory:

Is okay.

Living with us, going to school, watches his mom constantly thinking she's going to off herself. Josie (my nickname for Josephine) wants us to let him think that rather than worrying about bad guys trying to off *him*!

He makes me sad so I'm stuffing his face. Mavis says to back off as he will weigh three hundred pounds and be bullied if I don't. (What does Mavis know? The boy needs love and nothing says love like an enormous sugar cookie with lashings of powdered-sugar icing. Especially when he gets to help me make them.)

Cosmo:

Has become potty-trained after massive effort by Mavis, Lucinda, Josephine, Rory and myself (and Ash singlehandedly taught the dog how to sit by saying, sharply in his deep voice, "Sit!" and the dog sat but then so did everyone else in the room).

Josephine:

Just finished the notice she gave on the jobs and is working with us in the café (must admit this is very helpful, as, unlike many of the coven members, she can bake).

Also living with us — Mavis handled her landlord who is a "friend."

Josie, without having to worry constantly about the untimely death of herself and/or her son, has gotten the color in her cheeks, lost the bags under her eyes, put on a pound or two and got the shine back in her hair.

In other words, the bitch is a looker.

Ash says good morning to her every time she comes into the kitchen in the morning wearing a little nightie and short robe.

He never says good morning to me, just reads his paper, or if I'm lucky, looks at me warily like I might mistakenly blow up the kitchen or something.

BecBec:

Is on my shit list (has been since taking me to see Rory and Josephine for what seemed to be no apparent reason other than to upset me).

Keeps zooming around and keeping me awake at night and babbling at me.

I tried to start faerie-speak lessons by walking over to a table and pointing at it and saying, "Table. Table. *Table*." But when I motioned it was BecBec's turn, she said (in high-pitched squeal), "Eek-eeeeek-eek-eek." I don't think they call a table that, but what do I know?

Lucy:

Likes Josephine, dotes on Rory, doesn't have much time for Cosmo. "Bloody dog…why didn't he get a cat?"

Made this fabulous red cake with this luscious, whippy, creamy frosting that may be my new most favorite cake in the whole, wide world.

Mavis:

In hog heaven.

Café seems to be going well, her regulars came back and we have a few new regulars. (Mavis, "Thank the goddess, The Gables, darling, is hell to heat.")

She's pleased with my progress in The Craft.

She gets a real kick out of Rory and gets to mother Josie, who needs her soft touch. Josie may be getting color into her cheeks but she's still pretty jumpy and fragile.

I tried and failed to get more info out of Mavis about Dad, Granddad, *Le Société*, *Mathilda's Register*, being one hundred and eleven, etcetera, but she said we'll have another session later and, "There is only so much a girl can take."

She's telling me?

Aidan:

I called him, no answer.

I stopped by the Plumber Shop (or whatever it's called), and even though his truck was out front, they said he wasn't there. (Summoned a new SuperWitch power and sniffed them…unpleasant…sweating, most likely lying…bastards.)

Josie says she hasn't heard from him in a while. She used to clean the Plumber Shop at night (Plumber Shops are cleaned?) and ran into him a couple of times. She knows nothing else about him except, "He seems nice and he's *really* cute. He looks like that Sawyer guy on *Lost* except, obviously cleaner seeing as Sawyer didn't have a shower most the time because he was a castaway or he was fighting bad guys or running through the jungle or getting shot or tortured or falling out of helicopters and such."

No duh.

(Seems Josie watched *Lost* and took mental notes…hmm.)

I have tried to see him via a variety of sources, my (yay!) new crystal ball being one of them but failed.

Am weirded out that I may have kissed an actual baddie (rather than just an in-my-neurotic-head-baddie) in way of Glenn Close in the *Jagged Edge* (though without the vomiting and hopefully Aidan is not vicious slashing killer but just charming witch hunter (what am I saying?).

The Mathilda Books:

Eleanora Hobbs-Wilding did a number on the books. Her spell means the bad guys read one thing, the good guys read another thing, but when Mathilda Guinevere Honeycutt opens one of them, they say, *Mathilda, it wouldn't be good if you knew your future. Tell Mavis we say hello.*

Fucking Eleanora.

Sebastian:

Does not like nickname.

Ignores me if I use it or gives me dirty look.

I use it a lot.

A lot, a lot.

Got Rory using it. (Hee hee.)

Have not had another incident *à la* making out, etcetera. This is good as Sebastian is a bad, bad man.

He is bad because I started to have many a fantasy after incident in library, but after one particularly, er, *satisfying* evening…came down to breakfast next morning to the surprise of Ash looking at me like a cat who got his cream.

Realized belatedly have mind-meld with him (re: black dragon, etcetera, etcetera).

Fuckity, fuck, fuck.

Had terrible thought that he could see my fantasy!

Drank coffee, ate cranberry orange muffin and watched him surreptitiously.

When he got up to leave, he looked me in the eye…*and grinned*!

Sebastian…does…not…grin.

Bloody cheek.

He can read my mind!

Demanded that Mavis tell me about black dragon gig. She said Black Dragon was Ash's call sign *à la* Val Kilmer as "Iceman" in *Top Gun*. I was to use black dragon as my way of telling him I'm in trouble and need him.

However…

Get this!

He is actually programmed into my mind so no matter what trouble I get into, say, even if I'm drugged and can't think straight, he may have a way of finding me, helping me, etcetera, etcetera.

Do not like this.

At all.

Told Mavis I didn't like it.

She shrugged.

"I could do something about it, I suppose," she muttered. "Since I put the spell on the two of you. But I don't think it would be wise. You could talk to Sebastian about it and see what he says."

Bloody right I would.

I asked where Ash lived, and she hemmed and hawed and finally explained he was staying in The Dungeons.

(FYI: The Dungeons are not *real* dungeons, per se, but Su, Viv and I called them that when we visited. The Dungeons were the two bottom floors of The Gables, which were built into the side of the cliff. It is kind of darker and scarier down there than anywhere else in The Gables. We avoided it as there were too many shadows, which seemed to move when they weren't supposed to and it freaked us out.)

Took windy, twisty route to studded, wooden door that leads into Dungeons and knocked. (Heard loud echoes on other side of door after knocking, creepy, I really hate The Dungeons.)

When Ash arrived at door, he opened it (creakily) and leaned against the jamb with arms crossed on chest (his favorite position to look down his nose at people). Then he looked down his nose at me (could swear he had a little grin on his face).

"Don't eavesdrop into my thoughts anymore. We'll get you a beeper or something," I said, figuring I might scare him into complying with my supreme bossiness and confident demeanor.

"No."

Obviously, it didn't work.

"Some things I think are private. Just meant for, er, me," I told him.

This was embarrassing.

"Mathilda," he said, exuding restrained patience. "You think of me, *any* time you think of me, I'll know. Whatever it is. That's the way it goes, that's how I protect you."

"Well, stop it."

"I can't."

"We'll get Mavis to do something about it," I suggested helpfully.

"I don't want Mavis to do anything about it," he said and then grinned *again*. "I *like* your thoughts about me."

Ack!

Sebastian is most provoking.

(How's that for a thought?)

The Month of February

2 February

Status quo.

Everyone is alive, which I think is good.

Had first month anniversary of re-opening of café as The Witches Dozen. We gave Mavis heart palpitations as Lucy and I gave out mini-cookie and coupon for free coffee drink to everyone who came through the door.

Mavis said with some alarm, "They'll come back expecting a free drink."

To which Lucy replied, "They'll come back."

I think Mavis understands but still thinks we're slightly crazy.

I one-upped Lucy's red cake by unveiling an American angel food cake with my mom's famous whipped cream icing (more like whipped shortening and butter with shitloads of sugar in it, but that's a secret).

Although angel food cake is commonplace in the States, no one has heard of it here (had to get Viv to FedEx an angel food cake tin). I renamed it Hanna Belle Cake after my mom—no one but tourists would know the difference.

Cake was a huge success and even more so since I announced it's fat free (not, of course, if you eat the icing with it, but I explained you could scrape it off (if you're insane)).

Also important to note that Josie introduced me to Jigsaw and found Stila at Space NK and Jimmy Choo at Harvey Nicks in Cabot Circus. I'm surrounded by decent fashion (albeit not with good parking but such is life in England). Now can breathe easier about shopping situation (as in don't have to take the train to London every time I fancy a new sweater or need eye shadow).

YAYAY!

~

3 February

New development.

Was settling in to Movie Night with Lucy and Josie…

Aside: Made the mistake of saying, in all innocence, "I don't get the whole *Taxi Driver*, Martin Scorsese thing. I mean, I prefer the works of Rob Reiner." (Seriously, though, wouldn't you rather watch *This Is Spinal Tap* and see Derek Smalls going on about visionaries than watch Joe Pesci's Tommy DeVito screaming about being funny?)

You would have thought I said, "I don't get the whole fallen chocolate soufflé cake thing. I mean, I prefer boiled rice."

Jeez.

Lucy demanded the next Movie Night be "Dinner with Martin Scorsese." Ack!

Josie came in toting our Indian takeaway and still bitching about the garbage trucks doing collections during rush-hour traffic. She'd been on about this all day, since taking Rory to school that morning (too cold for him to walk, not to mention our fear of bad guys hauling him away).

I told her to shut up and dish up the murgh makhani when she pointed her finger at the TV in a rage.

There was Douglas Addison, prominent American neo-conservative senator for Colorado (in my opinion, the only thing the modifier "neo" was good at being attached to was Keanu Reeves) and some say, next American President. Apparently, he was coming to England for some reason (probably to spread the word of the Lord whilst signing lucrative arms contracts).

"That man, that bloody, *awful* man!" Josie shouted.

Oh no.

Josie was going to go all political again.

Don't get me wrong, I hated to hear my American brethren going on and on and on about God and country. I dig God (don't be surprised, witches are *very* spiritual creatures and respect others of like mind no matter who they worship) and I dig country, but never the twain should meet. (I was living in a country with hundreds of years of history that proved that sad fact.)

But Douglas Addison had something about him.

Sure, he was a scary fascist, but then so was Ralph Fiennes in *Schindler's List*. You wouldn't piss on them if they were on fire (talking about Ralph Fiennes's character of course, I'd definitely piss on Ralph Fiennes if he was on fire, *mama mia*, that man could be in a Brood Off with Sebastian and have a chance at winning!), but you had to admit they had a certain something.

And anyway, Addison dressed like a dream. He'd graced the cover of *GQ* more than once in his political career. The dude was hot (in a tall, dark, dangerous, slim, fit, macho, scary fascist sort of way) and he knew fashion, and I'd sell my soul to the devil for fashion.

"Josie, save it," Lucy said through a mouthful of biryani. "Tell the Council."

"Screw the Council," Josie declared.

Lucy stopped in mid tear of her naan and I (lamentably) dropped a spoonful of pilau rice on the carpet.

Josie didn't say things like that.

"I'm not going to tell them anything," she stated. "They don't *do* anything. I've been writing letters for years."

Then came the *big* announcement.

"If you can't beat 'em, join 'em," she announced pouring the entire contents of her container of lamb pasanda over her rice. "And *then* beat 'em."

Whoa!

Girl Power!

Yee Ha!

A Councilor is born!

Watch out Glenda Jackson…you got company!

~

5 *February*
(Middle of night)
(Little freaked out)

Ran into Aidan at Tesco!

I couldn't sleep (BecBec has disappeared, maybe mad at me, now can't sleep without her whizzing around the room) so went to Tesco to get ingredients for sugar cream pie recipe I looked up on the Internet.

There he was, trying to choose between crunchy or regular chocolate fingers (no contest, crunchy).

I just stood there, staring stupidly at him until he noticed me, and his body kinda jerked when he saw me.

Could be two explanations for jerkage: 1) he was caught or 2) sight of me in my pajama bottoms, a sweatshirt that had seen better days, a five foot long scarf Gran sent me for Yule wrapped around my neck, no makeup and my hair twisted into scary, messy knot on top of head.

"Matty," he greeted and smiled. (Good recovery, dickhead.)

"Aidan," I greeted back (I'm so cool). "Where ya been?"

"Busy…" Mm, yeah right, busy summoning the forces of evil. "I meant to call…"

Ack!

One of a girl's most hated phrases.

I waved my hand dismissing his excuses. "Listen Aidan, I don't know your story but—" I wanted to say, 'I'm onto your game' in a menacing way, but it would seem neither of us was going to let the other finish a sentence because he interrupted me by letting out this huge sigh.

"We can't talk here, but, listen…tomorrow night, midnight, meet me at your tree."

Wha'?!?

What does he know of my tree?

"Excuse me?" I asked, all squinty-eyed.

He looked one way then the other. "I know it sounds strange but just meet me at midnight, tomorrow night."

Is he nuts?

"Alone," he went on.

Yes, he's nuts.

Then he took off, grabbing, I might add, chocolate fingers with caramel (interesting choice, one I must ponder).

I came home without the ingredients I needed for the pie.

And now I don't know what to do.

~

6 February
(Morning)

Woke up early mainly because I didn't sleep.

Mavis was in the kitchen making eggs.

I told her about Aidan.

"Oh, my dear, just go and remember to take your wand. You'll be quite all right. If anything goes awry you'll be able to take on the likes of Aidan."

Then she sniffed as if the strapping, six-foot-tall Aidan with six-pack abs (I have not witnessed his abs with own eyes but figure he *must* have a six-pack) couldn't take me.

Think I need a second opinion (about situation, not abs).

~

(Mid-morning)

Called Su (was middle of night her time but had first showdown with possible baddie on my hands so obviously an emergency—not to mention knowing Su, she had probably just got home from the local Deadhead bar).

Told her the story and asked her what I should do.

She said call her back when it was a decent hour (was wrong about Deadhead bar) then she called me a name and hung up on me.

Decided again that I'm not talking to Su.

~

(Afternoon)

Called Viv.

Told her the story and asked her what I should do.

She said, "What are you, nuts? Don't meet a strange man in the middle of the night."

Told her about Josie connection and possible bad guy status, and he knew about my tree.

She said to go, take my wand and wear my cloak but, "Make sure to take Sebastian."

No way am I taking Sebastian.

Viv doesn't know anything.

I'm clearly on my own.

~

9 February

Am in trouble with Ash.

    Though feel I did the right thing.

    Maybe in the wrong way.

    Still.

~

It was ten to midnight, had my wand, my cloak and I was off to my tree.

    Had been frantically studying freezing spells (Auntie Mavis's cat, Lulubelle, was still frozen halfway across my sitting room by the time I got back).

    Note to self: need to research reversal of freezing spells.

    Checked on Rory, checked on Josie, checked on Mavis…all sleeping soundly.

    Did not check on Sebastian and tried very hard not to think about him.

    There wasn't a cloud in the sky, the moon shone on the channel and the trees were restless.

    And I was scared nearly senseless.

    Though I could tell it was cold. Freezing cold.

    Aidan was standing by my tree.

    I knew one thing for certain, if he hurt my tree, I'd zap him.

    Walked up to the tree and threw back the hood of my cloak.

    "Aidan," I said.

    His body gave a start.

    I could have sworn he was watching me walk up to him, but I surprised him.

    "Jesus," he muttered.

    Clearly he hadn't been watching me walk up to him.

    Mm.

    No wonder Viv said to wear the cloak.

    Before I could say anything else, he said, "Listen, Matty, I don't think it's safe out here, maybe we should go somewhere else to talk."

    Yeah right.

    I think not.

    I leaned against my tree. It was warm.

Hmm.

"I think we can talk right here," I countered.

"I shouldn't be here. Jesus," he repeated. "*You* shouldn't be here." And he looked over my shoulder. "We should go somewhere else. Now."

"Listen, Aidan—" I started then I saw them. The faeries all flew up from their hiding places all at once like hundreds of twinkling lights coming on out of nowhere—and *zing, zang, zoom,* they started whizzing here, there and everywhere.

Holy shit!

It was really cool!

"Let's go!"

That was Aidan, grabbing my arm and pulling me through the wood towards Poet's Walk.

"Aidan, stop!"

That was me trying to pull loose. I didn't know what was going on, and I didn't intend to go anywhere with Aidan.

Then I saw them.

Men.

Three of them lumbering up the Walk, breaking off and heading into the wood…toward us.

A tingle ran up my back when I saw the men—not a good tingle and not a good sign.

Aidan pulled me up to him hard and I slammed against his body (hmm, slamming against men's bodies a lot lately…not bad but would prefer to do it when not on run or in middle of apparent life-threatening situation).

"Go," he whispered in my ear. "Go back to The Gables. Now!" Then he pushed me backward and I went flying, stumbled on my cloak and fell on my ass.

As I was scrambling to get my limbs in order, I saw Aidan charge ahead, duck down and hit one of the men in the stomach on a running tackle. I watched the guy going up, flying over Aidan and landing on his back while I got to my feet.

Holy cow.

Then BecBec whizzed in front of me scaring the bejeezus out of me, so I fell back down on my ass.

"BecBec!" I cried.

She stopped, her wings shuddering, and she looked me up and down as if assessing if I was all right, and then whizzed away faster than I ever saw her whiz before, charging one of the other men.

No way was BecBec gonna be able to take that man.

Damn.

I got to my feet again, pulled out my wand to help as BecBec's whiz became a blur and she disappeared in a rocket of pistachio green pixie dust. The man she was charging came up short, like he'd hit an invisible branch and stumbled backward as she circled him for another pass.

Aidan was grappling with another man while the one he tackled had regained his feet and was charging me.

Ack!

I had to do something.

And fast.

So I pulled out my wand and shouted, *"Freeze!"* and zapped the man coming at me.

Hot pink pixie dust flew out of my wand and slammed him with great velocity right in the gut.

Except it didn't freeze him, instead it seemed to sort of shatter and fly off in bits and hit dozens of faeries that were flying toward him and froze them instead.

"Shit!" I shouted as he carried on toward me.

I tried again.

"Freeze!"

Zap.

Pixie Dust.

Nothing.

It had worked on Lulubelle!

So I tried again.

"Freeze!"

Zap.

Pixie Dust.

Zip.

And again!

"Freeze, dammit!"

Zap.

Pixie Dust.

Nada.

There were faeries frozen in mid-air everywhere, and the rest were avoiding him, me and my wayward spells.

Shit.

He lunged at me. I ducked, slipped, lost control, fell and rolled under him, accidentally taking him down with me.

We wrestled. He seemed huge. He definitely was strong.

I kept hold of my wand and fought as hard as I could and under my breath chanted,

I call the powers of nature, the might of the sea.
Protect all things good and magical in these woods.
As I will, so mote it be.

Over and over again I said it, getting louder and louder as I tried to find an opening to kick the big lout in the balls.

"Shut up, witch!" he hissed at me, his breath smelling of peppermint.

I'm sorry, but a bad guy should not have good breath. I don't know who to complain to about this but I just don't think it's fair. They should be balding, heavy, poorly dressed and smelly.

This should be a rule.

Anyway.

I ignored him (obviously) and carried on chanting, struggling and holding on to my wand.

Then we rolled, rolled again. I managed to get up and I ran with him after me until he tackled me. We rolled again and then I slammed up against something hard.

"Oof," I wheezed.

And then I got my chance, a clear shot, and I used every bit of leverage and strength I had and kicked him right between the legs.

He went down on his knees, and a branch came swinging round as if taken by a huge force of wind and it broadsided him, slamming him completely to the ground.

"Fucking witch," I heard him groan as I looked up at my tree (which was, by the way, the something hard I slammed up against and the branch that hit the baddie belonged to it).

I gave my tree a thumbs up and gestured with my wand (which was safe and sound) and turned to the bad guy.

"Stupid dickhead," I said. (I know, I should be classier, but the guy had me rolling around in the wet leaves in the woods in the middle of the night in the middle of winter for goddess's sake. Not to mention I was wearing my very cool new tweedy hipster slacks that I got from Jigsaw, which were probably now ruined. Jerk.)

The trees were all acting pissed off, the wind was blowing fiercely. I could hear the sea smashing against the cliffs, and the faeries were in what looked like the battle of their little faerie lives, dropping acorns and shit on the baddies and whizzing around them in flashes of salmony-orange, lemon-yellow and pistachio green. And the trees were swinging their branches in scary wide arcs.

It would have been very cool if it wasn't so fucking scary.

Aidan was still struggling with the other guy in what looked like a not-as-amusing-because-it's-real rendition of the Hugh Grant and Colin Firth fight in *Bridget Jones' Diary* (except, of course, Aidan looked hot while struggling, mainly because Aidan *was* hot and he'd look it doing anything, the other guy just looked silly).

It was my turn to charge and I was gearing up for it, still chanting my little ditty to whip the trees into a frenzy, when a tree caught the baddie that Aidan was struggling with and sent him flying into another tree.

"Come on!" he shouted and reached a hand out to me.

Uh-oh.

I had a decision to make.

Baddie behind me was recovering and cutting off escape route to The Gables.

Aidan was in front of me and seemed to have both trees and faeries on his side (or at least not against him).

Hmm.

I had two choices.

Take on bad guy again (and I had kicked bad guy in the crotch so would be slightly more angry at me now, which I guessed would put him off-the-charts-angry).

Or go toward Aidan.

Oh, wait.

Pandora calling me.

~

Later…

Sometimes customers are so annoying, wanting coffee and muffins when I'm writing in my journal.

Anyway, where was I?

Oh…yeah.

I ran toward Aidan.

We took off, the baddies after us, the faeries after them.

Aidan stopped at a car (not any car, a metallic blue BMW Z4 Roadster, oh me, oh my).

He beeped the locks, the lights flashed and as I stood there (half indecisive, half admiring the car) he shouted, "For God's sake, Matty, get in."

I turned and looked back. One of the baddies was closing in on us, faeries rocketing around him like very pretty firework-esque gnats.

I got in the car.

At this point, you would expect me to demand an explanation of midnight rendezvous and plumbers owning £35,000 cars.

But no.

Instead, I kept quiet because Aidan drove like a bat out of hell.

I mean, it was Indy 500 time.

I thought it best to let him concentrate.

When we got on the motorway, he said, "Who *were* those guys?"

I said, "I don't know, I thought you knew."

He said, "Hell, I don't know."

Hmm.

New subject.

"Why did you want to meet at midnight?"

Silence.

I tried another.

"How did you know about my tree?" I asked.

Silence.

Then he sighed.

"Long story," he murmured.

"How about sharing just a little bit," I suggested.

"I can't," he replied.

He looked at me out of the corner of his eye (which I wished he wouldn't do, he should keep his eyes on the road, especially when whizzing up the M5 at over 110 mph).

"Damn, let's get somewhere safe and then we'll talk," he muttered.

That sounded like a plan.

We drove and then drove back and then drove on again. Aidan said he wanted to lose them just in case they were following (?!).

We stopped at one of the few all night gas stations that existed in all of England (my guesstimate, there were three, if you didn't count services, which I wasn't because we weren't at one of those, "Too exposed," Aidan murmured) and he filled up and went inside to pay. He got in the car and handed me a bag of Jelly Babies and a Diet Coke (bless him).

I tore into the Jelly Babies and instantly commenced my search for the orange and green ones (because they were the best) and ignored the dark purple ones (because they were blackcurrant and blackcurrant-flavored candy was the work of Satan).

He watched me bite the heads off Jelly Babies for a minute and then asked, "Did you use magic back there?"

My head shot up and I stared at him. He didn't see? Pixie dust and faeries frozen in mid-air?

"Uh," I answered.

"It didn't work, did it?"

"Er," I answered.

"Just as I thought," he said. Then he said quietly to himself, "Damn."

He drove on. We stopped at a telephone booth and he told me to call Mavis and let her know I was safe. It was nearly three in the morning but she answered the phone, "Hello, darling," sounding wide awake and cheerful then went on to ask, "Having fun?"

Ack!

"Fun? No, I'm with Aidan, we're…somewhere…I don't know where."

"Tell her you'll call her when you're safe," Aidan suggested, all snuggled up in the red phone box with me, smelling all manly-musky and making certain parts of me quiver.

I took a deep breath, ignored the quivering and did as I was instructed.

"I'll call you when I'm somewhere safe."

"Okay, my dear…oh wait, here's—"

The phone clamored and then Ash, sounding wide awake but not so cheerful, "Where are you?"

"Ash, I think there are a couple of bad guys in the wood—"

"Not anymore," he interrupted in a tone that made my quiver turn to a shiver. "Where are you?"

"Hang up." (Aidan)

"Um." (Me)

"Who's that? Where the fuck are you?" (Ash—deep voice very scary now)

"Er." (Me)

"Hang up now, we've got to go!" (Aidan)

"Dammit!" (Ash)

Then Aidan hung up for me and tugged me out of the booth.

"They're here." He pointed at lights far off, coming down the road at us.

We got in the car and off we went, Aidan doing his bat-out-of-hell-in-a-BMW routine and me being quiet.

We drove forever and ever, stopping for Aidan to make a phone call. I played sentry with my hand on my wand inside my cloak, practicing spells under my breath. He seemed very animated and yelled—well, not exactly yelled, too posh for yelling—but he said things loudly like:

"I know I'm not supposed to…" and, "I have nowhere else to take her." (!) And, "What would *you* do?"

Then he hung up looking annoyed and we got in the car.

Aidan definitely didn't seem pleased but he said, "I've got somewhere to go. It's safe."

Oh goodie.

"Or, at least I think it is," he continued.

Ack!

He turned toward me, looked me straight in the eye and said, "You think you could help…do something to put them off?"

Uh-oh.

Magic.

"Er, so…um, you know?"

"That you're a witch?"

I stared.

"Or," he went on, "that you're *the* Witch?"

My mouth dropped open.

(Okay, so I shouldn't play poker.)

"Jesus," he whispered.

I nodded.

"Yes, I know," he said.

Yikes.

I knew that, I guess.

"Just wanted to make sure," I said, trying to sound cool (failing).

"About that help…?" he prompted.

"Okay, yeah. Sure," I said with what I hoped was confidence. I hadn't been doing so well in the magical arena that night.

I got out of the car and stood there.

Aidan got out of the car and stood inside his open door and watched me over the top of the BMW.

Damn, damn, damn. Under the gun. Not good conditions—performing magic in front of the hot, posh, sexy Sawyer-from-*Lost*-like guy.

I cleared my throat.

ACK!

I took a deep breath, concentrated, took my three turns, called to my goddess and:

> *Under cover of darkness,*
> *Through the night,*
> *Cover Aidan and I,*
> *Shadow our flight,*
> *Let our route and destination*
> *Remain a mystery,*
> *As I will, so mote it be.*

(Must admit, that was pretty good.)

I chanted it again and again then brought my wand up and out in a wide arc, scattering Aidan, the Roadster and myself with hot-pink pixie dust, and met both hands above my head with a final splurge of pixie dust raining over us.

Then I got back in the car.

Aidan did too.

"That should do it," I told him.

(I hope.)

Aidan looked at me for a second. Shook his head and started the car (don't know what that was all about).

And then we drove forever and ever again.

I was tired and cranky and the Jelly Babies were wearing off fast.

We needed to get somewhere soon.

I needed breakfast.

And I needed coffee.

~

10 February
(Late Night)

Had to go.

There was a slight flapjack emergency that Nerissa couldn't contain (I was tinkering with a Nigella recipe—should just follow the way of the Goddess of Cookery and not tinker, but I couldn't help myself, it needed chocolate!).

Not to mention we had a bit of a rush, and Pandora still hasn't become quite comfortable with Big Red (Lucy and my nickname for the espresso machine).

Haven't had a moment until now.

Note to self: Nestle Toll House Morsels do not melt very well in microwave.

Another note to self: Use expensive, possibly illegally imported (by Mavis) Toll House Morsels only for cookies, brownies, etcetera.

Another note to self: Don't mess with Nigella recipes! (Except that one that has *way too much* Cointreau in it).

Where was I?

Oh yes, Aidan and I were off to someplace safe.

We rounded a turn, came out of a wood and then I saw nestled in some sloping, gently rolling mini-hills a massive manor house-slash-castle.

It was beautiful, perfect and fucking scary.

"There it is," Aidan said with not a little relief.

"What is it?" I asked with not a little panic.

"The Royal Institute of Psychical Research," he answered as if that explained everything.

"Hunh?" I asked, because that didn't explain *anything*.

Aidan didn't answer, for as we drove toward it a car drove out of it, coming through the raised portcullis in the outer wall right at us. On the one lane road we stopped nose-to-nose with a black Rolls Royce.

"You boys have got some killer cars," I said, to myself apparently as Aidan was getting out.

Four men were getting out of the Rolls too.

All of them were about Mavis's age, except without the Elixir to Look Forever Fifty.

They were *ancient*.

All except one. He looked exactly like I always thought Ichabod Crane would look. Tall, gaunt, with a hooked nose and a receding hairline, hair longish and thin, pulled back in a pipsqueak ponytail.

All of the men were staring curiously...*at me*.

I got out of the car.

No one spoke.

Everyone just stood there.

Staring at me.

"Er…" I said, clearly destined to be a Honeycutt diplomat (not).

Ack!

"Hi," I finally got out.

"Amazing," said one.

"Remarkable," said another.

"Inconceivable," said a third.

I was beginning to get pissed.

What?

They thought witches spoke in tongues or something?

"I don't like it," said Ichabod. He wasn't looking at me curiously; he was looking at me like he wished he wasn't looking at me.

Then everyone started talking all at once.

"Now, Jeremy—" started one.

"We talked about this—" started another.

"I thought we agreed—" started the third.

"There's nothing we can do now—" started Aidan.

"I didn't agree," said Ichabod. "And furthermore, the Directors weren't contacted—"

"There wasn't time!" said one.

"We couldn't stand by—" said another.

"Um…boys?" I tried to interrupt.

Nothing but more genteel interrupting of each other.

"Er…gentleman?" I said, a little louder.

They were beginning…well, not exactly to yell at each other but the conversation was becoming heated.

"*Yo!*" I shouted.

They stopped and stared at me.

"Sorry to interrupt but there are some bad guys after me and I'd rather be…" I looked at the building that made The Gables look homey, "in there." And to myself I finished, *I think*.

"But of course!" said one.

And off we went in the cars, down the lane, one of the ancient dudes backing the Rolls the whole way on the single lane drive while I held my breath—scary!

Then we were out in a courtyard, the more ancient bit of the place looking positively medieval ensconced inside the manor house-slash-castle walls.

"Wow, this place is wicked," I said, not able to stop myself.

Old Dude Number One stepped forward. "Yes, my dear, let's get you inside, where it's safe."

He touched my arm to guide me inside but I cleared my throat awkwardly.

"I, er, have to, um…"

How exactly does one go about this?

"Yes?" Old Dude Number Two asked.

"Um, do you all mind if I put a protection spell on the place? Just a bit of a shadow glamor to hide Aidan and myself."

Gasps all around. Shock and horror on some of the faces, fascination on others.

"If you'd rather not—" I began.

Now a new voice. "By all means, Miss Honeycutt, be our guest."

This was Old Dude Number Four—or New Old Dude—who came out of the medieval castle part and was tottering toward us on a cane and a prayer.

"Uh, hello," I greeted.

He stopped and squinted at me, the new sun playing in his eyes.

"Mathilda Guinevere Honeycutt, standing in the courtyard of the Royal Institute of Psychical Research." He stopped and pinned Aidan with the squint. "I fear there is some grave spinning. Oh yes."

Ack!

What a weird guy.

What the hell is grave spinning?

Then I got it. (Duh!)

"Sir, you obviously know me, may I ask—" I started.

"Of course, Miss Honeycutt. I'm Ambrose Bennett, Executive Director of the Royal Institute of Psychical Research at your service."

Then he bowed, all dramatic.

"Nice to meet you," I said. Sounded lame but what was I supposed to say?

"Your spell, my dear?" he prompted.

So, there I was, being watched by a bunch of old dudes, Ichabod Crane and Aidan.

Ack!

No pressure, right?

I had to focus, breathe deep, open my chakras, find my power source and block out the audience. It was going to take some fierce magic—everything I had—if I had anything at all, or anything left, to protect this big behemoth with me and Aidan in it.

Hmm, very tired.

Must sleep.

~

11 February

(After Herbology with Rhiannon—Mavis has begun to farm me out to the coven for lessons, Rhiannon is our herb chick, she's very cool but constantly trying to put stuff in the muffins. Gotta keep my eye on her.)

Must finish this bit before I head off to Magickal Implements with Nerissa.

Suffice it to say I did a killer spell on The Institute. So much so that Ash had trouble finding me (he was not pleased about that).

The old dudes escorted me to the mediaeval castle portion of the joint and deposited me in a room full of furniture that was so old I was scared to sit on it. They told me breakfast was being prepared (yay!) and then they left me in the room with Aidan but without any promise of coffee (ack!).

In a very Ash-like moment, Aidan stared out the window absorbed in watching something and completely ignoring me.

I cleared my throat.

"Do you think I could get a cup of coffee?"

"Oh God, yes, sorry." He walked to the wall and, if you can believe, pulled a cord. He pulled a fricking cord.

What kind of world was this?

We'd both settled in some impossibly fragile-looking chairs when one of the old guys poked his head in and Aidan asked for coffee.

"So, you were going to explain…?" I prompted when Aidan didn't seem to want to start.

But then he started.

And this is what he said:

Aidan (surprise!) is not a plumber.

He teaches mythology at Trinity College in Cambridge and has been a member of the Royal Institute of Psychical Research for the past three years.

"The Institute," as he calls it, was started in the 1500s by none other than Queen Elizabeth I. The remit of the place was the study of all aspects of the supernatural.

These guys were the people who took their 50s science fiction movie machinery to haunted houses to gauge if there were ghosts, to check the possessed and see if a priest should be brought in, to assess if a palm reader was a charlatan, etcetera.

That is as involved as they got...mostly, for centuries they've just watched and written a shitload of notes (my terminology, not Aidan's).

Aidan was a part-time field researcher at The Institute assigned to me. He'd been watching me since I moved to England months ago. (Not sure how I felt about that.)

Members are not ever, ever, ever (ever) to get involved with the creatures (?!) they are studying.

Never.

Ever.

Aidan had "gotten involved" with me.

This was bad—hence his disappearance after New Year's to answer to "The Directors."

Now, he's brought me to The Institute, which has never had a witch, warlock, pixie, troll, etcetera within its hallowed halls in its nearly five hundred years of existence.

Needless to say, this was a controversial move on Aidan's part.

But I only had one question on my mind:

"What about the bathrooms at the coffee house?"

Aidan explained he only tiled the bathroom and his actual-plumber friend had done all the plumbing, which put my mind at ease (about the toilets, not the tiles).

And then he fell silent and watched me.

Then he watched me more.

I tried not to fidget in the chair as it, if taken on the *Antiques Road Show*, would involve some on-air orgasmic delight from the experts and claims of "priceless."

Then, thank goddess, the old guy came with the coffee.

I took a sip. It was weak and had too much milk, but it also had caffeine, so I started to feel myself again.

Albeit a tired, magicked out, still slightly scared and definitely pissed off at yet another twist in the double-helixed plot that is my life, er...self.

"So..." I started so Aidan wouldn't watch me anymore. "What now?"

He sat back and stretched out his legs, his chair groaned, I held my breath, he crossed his feet at the ankles, arms on his chest, and then he settled, his eyes on me again.

The chair, by some miracle, held.

"Now, you call your bodyguard to come get you."

Ack, he knows about Ash.

He smiled (kinda sexily) at my reaction.

Then he kept talking. "Then we have breakfast."

Yay!

(Though little worried about breakfast cooked by a bevy of Old Dudes.)

He kept going, "And then you go home."

His plan was taking a confusing turn out of the not-exactly-welcoming lap of the League of Vintage Gentleman and into the clutches of Angry Ash.

Hmm, tough choice.

Then he finished, "And then I face The Directors and possible expulsion from The Institute."

Uh-oh.

He laughed before saying, "Don't worry, Matty. It won't be the first time."

Oh…well then.

Before scary-prospect breakfast I had to know a few things first.

"I have a few questions," I told him.

He took a sip of coffee and looked at me under his brows.

Oh my.

If Lucy were here, I think she would confirm that Aidan was flirting with me!

And changing slightly from boy-next-door-possible-baddie plumber to boy-in-the-*mansion*-next-door-not-baddie-but-seriously-sexy professor.

"Fire away," he invited.

Focus, girl, focus.

Um…now, what was I doing?

Oh yes.

I started, "First, you asked about my magic. You look at me funny when I'm done casting a spell. What's the deal?"

"I'm non-magical. I can't see your magic."

Hunh?

"But it was flying all over the place in the wood," I told him. "And then there were the faeries—"

He became a little less relaxed as he watched me.

"Faeries?" he asked. "There were faeries?"

"Yes, hundreds of them."

"Ah." He relaxed again and to himself said, "The acorns." Then back to me. "I thought you were doing that. However, as a mere mortal, I can't see magic. The effects of it, yes. Acorns flying through the air, tree branches swaying and hitting precise targets…that I can see. Faeries, possible but rarely, and only if concentrating and, of course, if they *want* to be seen."

Well, that explained that.

Sort of.

"Why did you want to meet me at midnight?" I asked.

"There was something important I needed to tell you without your shadow present."

Hmm.

"I reckoned you'd be curious if I asked for a midnight meeting and wouldn't tell him."

Hmm. Hmm.

"And because if you told him, he wouldn't have let you come."

Well, I'm sure!

Like Ash controls me!

(Hmm.)

Aidan concluded, "And because I needed to tell you that I have reason to believe that some of the men who are after you have managed to ally themselves with a witch, and I thought you should know."

What!?! my mind screamed.

"*What?*" I my mouth cried.

"Your magic didn't work on them, did it?" he asked.

"No," I answered.

And that would be no as in, not even a little bit.

"They probably had a protection spell."

No!

"How do you know this?" I asked.

He hesitated. Then took a breath and expelled it heavily.

After that, he answered, "Another field researcher, watching another witch, saw the alliance."

This is unbelievable…witches didn't ally themselves with bad guys!

Okay, so, I had to admit, it happened.

Occasionally.

But very, very rarely.

The whole bad witch-slash-dark witch myth was made by man to discredit those who practiced The Craft (not to mention the whole conspiracy against midwives and healers who weren't witches at all).

The vast (as in *vast*) majority of witches are what is now often referred to as "White Witches."

In other words, good. To the core.

A few of them may be dotty, but they wouldn't hurt a fly.

"Who is she?" I asked.

"I don't have that information."

"Can you find out?"

"Maybe."

Getting into Institute territory here, I could see.

"If you find out, will you tell me?" I asked.

"Maybe."

It was my turn to watch him. He wasn't uncomfortable or wary, just cagey.

Men!

I was too tired to push it now.

"How do you know Josephine and Rory?" I asked.

Mention of Josephine and Rory seemed to surprise him. "She cleaned the office at the plumber's. I don't know any Rory."

"That's it?" I asked.

"Is there more?" he asked in response.

Interesting.

"Okay, then, if you're a member of this place and you aren't supposed to get involved, why did you get involved?"

He sat up, set down his coffee cup and massaged his temples for a bit.

When he was done, he dropped his (very nicely formed, very manly, not professorial at all by the way) hands and he said, "There are several reasons, Matty."

Then he stopped.

Men, again!

Why did they make you work so hard for everything?

"Well?" I pressed.

Nothing.

Dammit.

"What are they?"

He watched me again for a bit. This watching me gig was very strange and unsettling and I have to admit (only to my journal) it weirdly excited me (slightly).

Finally, he answered, "Okay, first, I got involved because I believe the real world and the magical world can live in harmony, and The Institute is in the perfect position to facilitate that."

Ha! He obviously hadn't read *Why the Worlds Will Never Live Together in Harmony–A Cautionary Chronicle* by Ulysses Cavanaugh.

Aidan carried on, "Second, I'm not accustomed to inaction. Watching doesn't suit my way of doing things, I'd rather be…doing things."

"You shouldn't have become a member if you didn't agree with the way things were done," I tutted.

He grinned.

Goddess save me from good-looking men who can pull off a grin.

"You sound like Jeremy," he informed me.

"You mean Ichabod Crane?" I asked.

Uh-oh, forgot myself. Maybe they were friends and that was mean.

"That's exactly who I mean," Aidan said.

Oh, there you go. Don't think Aidan likes Ichabod.

Anyway, I didn't want to sound like Jeremy.

Ignoring all that, I went on, "What other reasons do you have?"

More watching.

Then, "Once I saw you, I knew I'd have to get involved."

"Yeah?" I asked.

"Yes, Matty. I couldn't exactly get you in my bed without meeting you."

What!?

Yay!

Oh no!

I had no idea what to think, and then I didn't have to think because an old dude walked into the room to announce breakfast was ready.

Mixed blessing.

After dropping the "get you in my bed" grenade, Aidan conveniently disappeared without a goodbye while I was whisked to a phone by one of the other members.

I called Ash on his mobile. This was the conversation:

"Hi, Ash." (Brightly, to dissipate any bad mood.)

"Where are you?" (Tersely, clearly not in the mood to have bad mood dissipated.)

"The Royal Institute for Psychical Research."
Silence.
Then, "I'll be there in two hours."
Hang up.
Uh-oh.

We had a full, traditional English fry up in the Great Hall (yum-ah-licious! English breakfasts were *the bomb*: fried eggs, fried bread, toast with marmalade, awesome, meaty English bacon, sausages, baked beans, sautéed mushrooms—gut-busting but heaven-on-a-plate, even so, I feared for the cholesterol levels of my companions).

Aidan was out amongst the brethren, as was Jeremy and about twenty-five other Old and Young(ish) Dudes(!).

Members were coming out of the woodwork to get a close-up look at a real, live witch.

I sat at a head table next to Ambrose and another man introduced as Forrest Something-or-Other. I feared I'd never again meet a man by the name of John, Dave or Steve.

Everyone stared at me while they ate their bacon and fried bread.

Conversation was scarce.

And I mean scarce as in *non-existent*.

I had a feeling Aidan was seriously in trouble.

Afterward, Ambrose led me to another room with more ancient furniture. It was a bedroom, and he advised me to rest as I waited for "Mr. Wilding."

He meant Ash.

Everyone knew everything about me except, it would seem, me!

I looked out the window and saw what Aidan had been looking at earlier—dozens of cars in the courtyard. So, he knew I was to be the curious creature at a breakfast of a score of geezers and he didn't warn me.

Men!

Just before the big guy left, I said, "Mr. Bennett?"

"That would be Dr. Bennett, Miss Honeycutt."

Pompous old fart.

"Um…is Aidan in trouble?" I asked.

He studied me (lots and lots of studying around this place—too much, creepy—unless it was Aidan).

"Yes, Miss Honeycutt, Dr. Seymour is 'in trouble.'"

Oo, Aidan's a doctor!

~

I didn't trust the bed, so tried to sit on floor and meditate.

Couldn't meditate after final Aidan announcement and upcoming reunion with my bodyguard, so sent thought waves to Ash repeating, "Don't be mad at me…don't be mad at me…don't be mad at me."

Felt Ash's Jag hit the courtyard before I got up to go to the window and see it.

Had the feeling regardless of thought vibes that he was mad at me anyway.

I ran downstairs and into the entry hall and noticed all the Members had a new curiosity— namely Mr. Wilding, who was striding purposefully toward the door…and me.

Striding, I might add, with a look on his face that could only be described as thunderous.

Uh-oh.

And.

Mm.

"It would seem," a voice came from my side, it was Dr. Bennett, "that you're in trouble too."

He appeared to be correct.

Ash was through the door and steps away from me when I threw all caution to the wind, turned to Dr. Bennett and said, "There's a witch out there that's protecting men who intend to harm me and perhaps my family and Spellbound."

I felt Ash stop beside me.

Dr. Bennett's face looked pained. "And how did you come by that information, Miss Honeycutt?"

I ignored his question. "It would help a lot if you could tell me the name of the witch who's helping them."

Dr. Bennett shook his head. "I'm sorry, but—"

"He can't, of course." This was Ash, and it was said in a really ugly tone.

I mean *really* ugly.

"Let's go," Ash ordered.

As Ash escorted me to the Lush Jag, I thanked my hosts on the trot and we were away.

We drove a bit, and I counted the minutes in hopes of tempers (or perhaps one particular temper) cooling.

Then, "Ash — ?"

"Not now, Mathilda."

I shut up.

From his tone to the muscle twitching in his cheek, it seemed the smart thing to do.

~

12 February

Talked to Mavis about the possible bad witch.

She didn't believe me until I told her Ambrose Bennett had (essentially) confirmed the information.

She's really angry.

"We'll just see about this," she said, and the way she said it scared the bejeezus out of me.

She took off, and I haven't seen her since.

~

15 February

Nothing.

Please note the date, *15 February*.

One-Five *February*.

February as in second month of the New Year.

Day after Valentine's Day.

And…nothing.

Okay, so Ash is mad at me and Aidan may be in the middle of Scary Manor House KP Duty, but what would it hurt?

A card?

A single red rose?

A diamond bracelet?

One kissed me and liked my naughty nighttime fantasies; the other one said straight out he wanted me in his bed. I was thinking they were into me. And Valentine's Day was Valentine's Day, the only day of the year that pretty much demanded you make a gesture if you're into someone.

And these guys own Jags and BMW Roadsters, for goddess's sake!

Now wish I hadn't made four batches of heart-shaped butter cookies. Granted, I didn't exactly present them to their intended (though I saw Ash have one with my own two eyes and I sent the parcel to The Institute (found their address on their website!!) addressed to "The Members," but still, it doesn't take a rocket scientist to figure it out).

How often does a girl get two yummy men at once!? — both of whom clearly fancy her?

Unless you are Julia Roberts…it…just…does…not…happen.

In this dimension (and, I suspect, many others).

I'm putting away my rose quartz.

Fucking men.

On another note, Rory gave me the sweetest Valentine's Card that he made himself (well, he had a little help from Nerissa, but I loosely use the words "help" and "Nerissa" in the same sentence).

~

21 February

I'd had enough.

I mean, how mad at me could he be?

(Ash, that is.)

So, I took off without him on what turned out to be a somewhat (!) dangerous assignation.

I made it.

I'm alive.

Breathing.

Baking.

Making kickass vanilla lattes.

Clattering around in my new, fab, fake crocodile stilettos.

Enough!

I went to the studded Dungeon door and banged on it as hard as I could.

Nothing.

With a mighty heave, I pushed it open and yelled down the steps (because, even though I'd had enough, I wasn't gonna go down there — no way, no how).

"Ash! I want to talk to you!" I shouted.

Nothing.

"Okay then…*Sebastian*, I want to talk to you," I yelled, giving an inch.

Nothing.

I waited.

Then I shouted, "Have it your way!"

Then I humphed off to the library and took down *Mathilda's Register* and slapped it on the desk.

"I'm fed up!" I told the book. "Eleanora, girl, you gotta give me something. Rory seems safe now but I got a renegade witch, a bunch of men immune to magic, a supernatural expert who can't tell me what he knows and a bodyguard who's pissed off at me. How am I to protect my Spellbound?"

Then I opened the book.

It said:

Mathilda, dear, what makes you think Rory is your Spellbound?

What?! I thought.

"What?!" I said.

The letters wiped themselves out.

"Come on! I'm supposed to help someone who's going to do great things in the future. Rory is bright, sweet, young—"

Eleanora interrupted me.

Yes he is, but why wouldn't Josephine be destined to do great things?

Holy Girl Power, Batman!

I wasn't meant to protect Rory, I was meant to protect Josie.

Whoa.

Whole new spin.

"Thanks Elly, you're the greatest," I said to the book.

Don't expect help in the future, and don't call me Elly.

Eleanora had an attitude.

But then, who didn't?

Yay!

Light dawns!

Speaking of attitude, as I closed the *Register* in strolled Ash.

Before I could say anything, he said, "Don't ever do that again."

I wasn't stupid enough to ask what "that" meant.

Instead, I apologized, sincerely and sheepishly, going for cute and abashed.

It worked!

The apology threw him for a loop.

I'd hoped (in my deepest thoughts to myself and my journal) we'd kiss and make up, but no luck.

He recovered quickly and said, "Mathilda, the Members of that Institute stood by throughout the Burning Times. They watched witches burn and drown and endure torture, and they didn't do anything about it. They watched a lot of innocents burn too and they knew it, and they didn't do anything about that either."

Wow, that was a lot of words coming out of Ash all at once.

"Aidan wants to—" I stared.

"What your plumber wants doesn't mean anything. They have a five-hundred-year history of note taking. The Chosen One is coming into her full powers and there's a good possibility that all hell is going to break lose. Don't expect them to be your allies, Mathilda. They're Switzerland. And in the battle between good and evil, Switzerland is useless. Worse than useless, they're cowards."

Wow.

All hell was going to break loose?

Oh shit.

The Month of March

1 March

Let me tell you, a lot has been happening.
First of all, Mom, Gran and Su are all here!
Right now!
In The Gables.
YAY!
Family reunion!!!
And Viv arrives tomorrow.
They're here because we're having a SuperCoven meeting to sniff out the Sinister Evil Bad Villainous Witch, a.k.a. Agatha Darling.

~

This is what happened:

Last Thursday, Auntie Mavis called me into her Magic Room.

In the room with Mavis were, Paulina Babcock, Mavis's Second-in-Command; Octavia Blackwell, if it's Magical, Tavie knows it, she's killer at our Wicca Quiz Nights; and Fay O'Hannigan, who Mavis tells me has the strongest magic in our coven (outside of herself and me) 'cause she's Irish and the Irish have some wicked magic (that is to say, wicked in a *good* way).

So I knew this was a big deal.

Anyhoo.

I sat with them all and they gave me tea (ack!) and Jammie Dodgers (yummy!).

Then they handed me a folder.

In it was a bunch of handwritten notes and photos. The photos were of a woman who looks *exactly*, I kid you not, like the Wicked Witch of the West (except she's kinda heavy, has gray hair and, of course, isn't green).

The file was labeled:

AGATHA BLANCHE DARLING – WITCH, HIGH PRIESTESS, EDWARDS COVEN, WORCESTERSHIRE.

I knew the Darlings. I had read a lot about the Darlings. Most notably, *The Honeycutts and Darlings—The Hatfield and McCoys of the Witch World*.

Darlings didn't like Honeycutts so much.

Honeycutts returned the favor.

It had been a blood feud for years.

Aside: Witches were usually nice ladies, of course, who healed with herbs and could cook and always had a lovely, cozy kitchen, but that doesn't mean we are all like that (read: Darlings) nor that we all have to like each other.

According to Auntie Mavis—and the file, which had a shield on the front of it cut in four sections; one with a dragon in it, one with broomstick, one that was a cross and one with a bat and a banner along the bottom in which was written, NATURALIS, MAGICUS, OBSERVATIO, and in the file was a whole bunch of notes written on The Royal Institute of Psychical Research letterhead—Agatha Darling had turned.

When a witch turns, it's a bad thing (understatement).

The power given to us is from Mother Nature. She allows us to use the power of her lands, winds, fires and seas.

A woman who has any command of those can wreak some serious, fucking havoc.

Not only did Mavis tell us that Agatha Darling had turned, she also told us she'd abandoned her coven.

Agatha was High Priestess of the Edwards Coven, and a coven, especially a particularly powerful one like the Edwards one, without a leader, was ripe pickin's for bad guys.

So, we needed a big-ass coven meeting to find Agatha and learn what she was up to and find a way to stop her.

That meant we needed power.
The Honeycutts were coming.
Yay!

~

12 March

To quote Inigo Montoya from the Rob Reiner Classic, *The Princess Bride*:
"Let me 'splain…no, is too long. Let me sum up."
Su:
Has taken over my sanctuary flat at the top o' The Gables, filled my mini-fridge with organic milk and tofu, covered the lights with scarves, the floor with tie-dyed camisoles (eek!) and gypsy skirts (ack!) and burned enough incense to permeate every article of Ralph, Calvin, Dolce and even Lucky clothing I own.
Viv:
Is also staying in my rooms. Does nothing but complain about the milk, tofu, scarves, scattered clothes and incense while spending lots of time ironing her Liz Claiborne.
Has yet to find *just the right place* for her mini Zen sand and rock garden but has taken over the cupboard space in my wee kitchenette with a variety of teas so huge that even I, a partner in a coffee house, haven't heard of some of the blends.
When Hawkwind isn't blaring from my stereo thanks to Su, Viv inserts her whale song CD.
Yikes!
Gran:
Is taking this opportunity to do a few UK yoga workshops and is pleased as punch that Senator Addison (better known as "That Man") is going to be in-country and is busy (per usual) with plans, plans, more plans and possible political machinations.
Gran is no stranger to *Time* and *Newsweek*—mostly photos of her behind a banner with a bunch of other ladies like Susan Sarandon and Marlo Thomas (although Gran is the only one with stark white dreadlocks) under which captions read, MEMBERS OF (such and such) INCLUDING WELL-KNOWN ACTIVIST MINERVA HONEYCUTT (okay, so maybe they named Sarandon and not Gran) TAKE TO THE STREETS.
Viv, who until recently I thought was a highly sought-after motivational speaker, but is actually is a highly sought-after "How To" book

writer (as in How to Be A Witch), is planning yoga workshops-slash-how to seminars all over England with Gran.

Get this: Greta Maddox (member of our coven) just happens to be an agent who represents people like Gran and Viv.

Why does life work out for Viv, Gran and Greta and I've barely heard from Aidan in a month, and Ash has practically disappeared after the onslaught of femininity to The Gables?

I mean, for two men who have made their intentions pretty clear (ish), they're taking their time. I'm not exactly playing hard to get. For goddess's sake, I live with one of them (okay, so The Gables has more than thirty rooms, but so what!?).

What does a girl have to do to get laid around here?

Ahem.

Mom:

"Look at that garden! It's a mess! You girls!" she said upon driving up to the house.

(By "you girls" she meant "Mathilda," like I don't have enough to do already being savior of world, barista extraordinaire and village fashion-ista, I have to deal with fertilizer as well).

She's out there now, I can see her from my window, wearing a (rather fab, must admit) huge straw hat and attacking some shrubbery with clippers. When not knee deep in compost or elbow deep in homemade granola, she's giving Lucy and Josie candle-making lessons.

Please note that search for Villainous Witch Turned Bad has taken a back seat to career furthering endeavors, political agendas, gardening and candle-making.

Ash:

I walked to Dungeon door yesterday and knocked.

He came up and opened the door, assumed the arms crossed-slash-doorjamb leaning position and lifted an eyebrow.

It was an arrogant look but that didn't mean it wasn't a good look, so I silently told my nether regions to calm down.

His lips twitched suspiciously.

Damn Mavis's mind-meld!

"Yes?" he asked before I could get it together.

"I want to move to The Dungeons," I informed him. "Do you mind sharing your lair?"

"My lair?" he asked, eyebrows knitting.

I nodded my head to The Dungeons.

"You hate it down there. You won't even go down there," he reminded me.

"My sisters are driving me nuts. Two words: Patchouli and Lapsang Souchong." (Okay, that's kinda three words.) "Do you understand me?" I finished, perhaps a little hysterically.

He didn't answer.

"My sanctuary is lost!" I cried.

He didn't look like he cared very much. He seemed far more focused on watching my mouth form the words than helping me with my problems.

"We'll make it less spooky down there," I suggested hopefully.

"Spooky?" he asked, having decided to repeat everything I say.

"Fog lights," I said. "Big ones, like they use in the movies."

He looked me in the eye as if considering that possibility (not).

"And we'll light a sage stick, flush out any ghosts." I was warming to my theme.

"I know a way to make it less spooky." His lips weren't twitching anymore, and he was looking at me in a way that did even more intense things to my nether regions.

"Mathilda!" Mom was shouting from the kitchen. "Where's the lobster pot?"

"What way is that?" I asked, trying to be flirty with my mom shouting at me from the other room. (Not working.)

(Lobster pot?)

"Mathilda!"

Another grin from Ash.

"Your mother's calling you." This was Ash then he stood back as if to let me pass, down the stairs into the dreaded Dungeons. "Would you like to continue this conversation somewhere else?"

I looked at him.

I looked beyond him.

Hmm.

Quandary.

Okay, I know you think I'm insane. But trust me, The Dungeons are scary.

Only people like Ash could live down there. He could probably kill someone with his bare hands. He'd probably seen things that would make my hair curl (egad!). Or worse, done things that would make me wonder about him.

Auntie Mavis had been telling me stories about Sebastian Wilding.

About his years in boarding school (!), his days in the Army (SAS—Special Air Service, some serious English Army dudes *á la* Green Berets, or better example, Russell Crowe in *Proof of Life*), his time "in training" in Asia (*Kill Bill* anyone?).

Anyway.

Weird noises, unexplained breezes, indistinct whispering sounds and strange apparitions would be nothing to him.

I swallowed hard.

They were something to me.

He shook his head and said, "When you're ready," and closed the door in my face.

Bluh.

Apparently, to get laid, a girl has to go to The Dungeon (shiver).

Not ready for that.

Rory:

Thinks Su is a hoot (but then again, she thinks it's okay that he experience beer and has been spending a lot of time introducing him to Led Zeppelin, Jimmy Hendrix, Deep Purple and, of course, Jerry Garcia).

Josie:

Is holed up a lot with Gran, thinks she's fantastic. She's right, although that alliance scares me just a trifle…those two political wildcats may be planning some kind of hijacking of Douglas Addison's visit next week. How am I supposed to protect Josie if she gets in cahoots with Gran?

Agatha Darling:

Apparently, if (rather lame) coven circle by light of the moon last night is anything to go by, has a powerful shadow over herself and whoever she's working with. Members of Edwards Coven are missing; other members aren't talking. Mavis has got the Witchworld grapevine buzzing but nothing has come of it.

Aidan:

Got a package in the mail with a note that said, "Sorry this is late. Thanks for the cookies." With a mobile number. The package held a set of The Faerie Oracle and it was gorgeous.

Mm.

Called the number.

"Dr. Seymour," he answered.

Mm.

Dr. Seymour.

Nice.

"Hi, Aidan," I said.

"Matty?"

"You like the cookies?" I asked.

"Delicious, you've won a few hearts at The Institute with those cookies."

Mm.

I wondered which hearts, exactly.

"Are you still a member?"

"Probation," he answered nonchalantly.

"Thanks for the file," I said.

"What file?" It was his turn to ask.

That Mavis, how did she…?

"What file, Matty?" Aidan sounding slightly more aggressive.

Mm.

"Where's Agatha Darling right now?" I asked.

Silence.

"Aidan?" I prompted.

"Matty, what file?"

"Give up Darling," I said (how cool am I?)

(Or did that sound like 'give up, darling'? Yikes!)

"Matty, I don't think you understand. Probation means—"

I hung up. I thought that was a good way to go.

Probation, shmobation.

Where did Mavis get that file?

And how was my luck bad enough that I'd get an evil nemesis with the name of Darling?

~

15 March

Lucy got me again. She took the battleground out of the sweet into the semi-savory and made some kind of brie, almond, cranberry in-a-puff-pastry thingy with homemade crackers! It even had some braided egg-brushed decoration!

The customers are flipping out for it.

She's not fighting fair.

~

(Later—at The Gables)

Aidan is downstairs in the sitting room waiting for me to get ready for our date.

Date!

Ha!

With Aidan!

Ack!

The professor!

Mm.

Yay!

Ash is in The Dungeon, fuming.

Ha ha!

Or at least I picture him fuming.

Fuming as he runs on his treadmill to work out his frustration.

Shirtless and sweating profusely.

Mm. Mm.

Ack!

Holy Boy Crazy Bitch, Batman!

Gran, Mom, Su and Viv are "entertaining" Aidan.

Ha ha ha!

(Poor Aidan)

~

This is what happened:

Was finishing my shift and leaving the shop with Beatrice, Rhiannon and Pandora as the afternoon crew.

I'd never left the shop without Lucy, Mavis or myself in charge and I was nervous.

Beatrice could hold her own but Rhiannon would have half the village stoned on some kind of herbal concoction, and I think Pandora is genuinely trying to blow up Big Red.

I was fretting and Ash was on some marathon mobile phone conversation, sitting by the fireplace at the café, nursing an espresso while I sucked the last dregs out of my almond mocha latte, obsessively crossing and uncrossing my legs and trying not to jump up and stop Pandora from banging a wooden spoon on Big Red (that spoon came from

Williams Sonoma and I had to sign away my first born to acquire Big Red…was she nuts?).

By the way, Ash had all of a sudden decided that he wanted to escort me everywhere. Mavis, Mom and Gran were adamant I let him, so I had to wait for him to take me home. Ack!

Then, with no warning, Aidan walked in.

"We have to talk," he announced upon arrival at me.

Yay! Aidan!

I wanted to jump up and do a little happy dance but had to remain cool, as he didn't even bother to say hello or give me a kiss on the cheek or anything.

So just said, "Hey," and shot Sebastian a look, mouthing, "I'll just be over there," pointing to a booth.

"Let's grab a booth," I suggested to Aidan.

Aidan took one look at Sebastian, who was still sitting by the fireplace with his legs stretched in front of him, his now empty espresso cup beside him, his mobile at his ear and a carefully blank expression on his face while he watched us.

"No, let's go somewhere private," Aidan said.

(Kinda ballsy, that.)

I leaned toward him and whispered, "He isn't going to shoot you."

Aidan didn't look like he believed me (and I wasn't sure I believed me either).

I put on my supercool, asymmetrical cardie, gestured out the door and mouthed, "I'll be at the museum for just a mo'," to Ash and walked out the door with Aidan.

We walked across the street, up the seafront, into the Victorian pier museum and up the windy stone staircase at the back to the art gallery on the second floor.

As usual, it was deserted.

As safe a place as any.

I looked out the slit window at The Witches Dozen.

Mom had put some lush and plentiful planters out front bursting with flowers, and the dudes had delivered our new New Orleans-at-Disneyland, frenchie, curly, black wrought iron patio furniture a few days ago.

It looked fab.

"Matty?"

"My shop is cool, isn't it?"

He got up next to me and looked out the window then looked at me, his face real close and his blue eyes had this melty warm look in them.

"Yes, Matty, very 'cool,'" he said in a low, gentle, deep, awesome voice.

Ahem.

Steady, girl.

"So, how's this going to go down if Dr. Bennett, Jeremy and The Institute find out you're here?" I asked.

"I'm not worried," Aidan answered without pulling away.

"Why?"

He leaned a shoulder against the wall and crossed his arms on his chest.

I didn't realize I'd put myself in a corner with Aidan fencing me in.

Hmm.

I wasn't worried either. I was something else altogether.

"For one, my great grandfather was a Director. They tend to be more lenient with members who are grandfathered."

Ah.

He went on, "Then, of course, Trevor Whitaker died. That made me the only Mathilda Scholar at The Institute."

But of course!

Aidan is a Mathilda Scholar.

Makes sense.

And I'm Mathilda.

Hmm.

He kept going, "And there's the fact that I have a one hundred and fifty-seven IQ."

What the…!?

Holy Genius, Batman!

Then he finished, "I may be placed on probation, but they won't lose me. Not until they train a new Mathilda Scholar."

Whoa.

Back up.

157 IQ?

Damn!

I didn't know how to process that.

I mean, what did that make him? Was he like Matt Damon in *Good Will Hunting* or Sir Charles Litton in *The Pink Panther*, or Dr. No in *Dr. No*?

Or all three?

He was watching me so I filled the silence.

Be cool…be cool.

"What's up? You got the goods on Darling?"

That's cool.

He smiled.

"What's funny?" I asked.

"You're very cute when you're trying to be The Chosen One."

Humph.

Then, in our little huddle by the window, Aidan cut me a break on the banter and told me he didn't give up Darling's file to Mavis. He also told me as far as The Institute was concerned, that file had never left Darling's "watcher" (very Giles in *Buffy*, in a non-participatory way of course).

Aidan wanted to see the file.

Hmm.

Why not?

I pulled out my mobile with the new ultra-awesome hot pink cover that had retro shapes and the words GLAMOUR GIRL (the new nickname I gave myself the minute I saw the cover) written on it and dialed Mavis.

Of course, in the stone pier museum I had no coverage. So, had to lean a little bit into the slit window and tilt half of myself and twist the other half somewhat awkwardly to get reception.

When Mavis answered, I said, "Auntie Mavis, I'm with Aidan, do we still have the Darling file?"

"Oh no, my dear, that's been replaced, of course. Safe and sound. Tell that young strapping lad I said hello. Toodle-oo," And she disconnected.

I had to let out a little giggle. I mean, "toodle-oo?"

I extricated myself from the window. "Um, I think there was some magic involved with us having that file."

Instead of looking annoyed, Aidan looked impressed.

Then he stated, "I came to see you because I thought the file was a fake and you'd been fed just enough information to get you in trouble."

He obviously didn't know Mavis's watcher very well if he thought that.

Although the "trouble" part seemed to fit me pretty well.

"Why did you think the file was a fake?" I asked.

"Bennett has put down an edict, no more contact with witches."

Considering the edict was put down and he was, like, an inch away from me, and I wasn't only a witch, I was *the* witch, I smiled at him and he smiled back.

Aidan continued, "He also warned us to be on the lookout for any witch antics."

"Witch antics?" I put my hand to my throat and fluttered my eyes. "Well, I never," I flirted.

And flirted well, considering how Aidan's voice dropped a bit lower making it pretty damn sexy.

"So, Mavis must have got in under watcher radar, which is pretty good. Especially Darling's watcher, who is one of our best."

How weird.

I wanted to ask best at what?

Watching?

I cleared my throat and straightened. As much as I was enjoying this, I *had* promised Ash.

Before I could say anything though…

"You and I have unfinished business…" Aidan started, still talking sexy-low.

Uh-oh.

"Aidan, I want to know more about Darling…and to talk…but before that I need—" I needed to let Ash know I was all right.

(Must admit, torn between two-non (not yet?) lovers but not feeling like a fool just feeling…weird.)

"You don't need me for Darling." He was leaning closer, smelling better, raising heart rates faster.

"Aidan," I said.

Black dragon, I thought.

I know, you may think I'm crazy, but would you want to be in trouble with Sebastian Wilding?

No?

Me neither.

"Darling has a shadow protecting her," I informed Aidan. "It's a good one."

Black dragon.

"We can't break it," I went on.

Black dragon.

"Anything you have for us would be helpful," I requested.

Black dragon.

"I'd like to take you out to dinner." Aidan was clearly having a different conversation than the one I was having.

"When?" I liked his conversation better.

"Tonight." Wow. "Without the Black Dragon tagging along."

Ack!

Oh my.

He knows *everything*.

Of course, with a 157 IQ he probably just soaks up information willy-nilly.

"I can't." (I could.)

"You can." (He was right.)

"What do you have against him?" (I meant Ash.)

"I can't tell you." (He knew what I meant.)

Hunh?

"Really? Why?" I asked.

"Because it's a Prophesy, you, me, him…we're destined for—"

"Excuse me."

Oh shit.

It was Ash. He was with us in the pier gallery.

"You know The Prophesies?" I asked Aidan, ignoring Ash.

He sure does take his time, that Ash. Then comes at the wrong moment.

"Mathilda." That was Ash again.

"Sebastian," I retorted, skewering him with a glance and mimicking his tone because I'd regressed to an eight-year-old. "Done with your phone call?" I asked snottily, then I turned to Aidan. "Yes, I'll go out to dinner with you."

A moment of complete silence.

Aidan grinned.

Ash did not.

I finally realized what all those supermodels are constantly moaning about. There may be a lot of interest but it certainly takes a heck of a lot of time and effort to get anyone worked up!

I wanted to know how Aidan knew The Prophesies. He wasn't magical.

And I wanted to know The Prophesies, full stop.

Well, maybe not all of them, but some.

And especially the one that involved me and two superhunks. (Yes, I said, "superhunks," but when there is a lack of vocabulary to describe the deliciousness of said superhunks, one must make do, so superhunks it is.)

So here I am, freaking out with hair half straightened and outfit half chosen, writing in my journal instead of getting ready, and I'm about to go on a date with a doctor.

Yay!

And yet, slightly worried I'm having my first date in England with the wrong guy.

Superhunk or no.

16 March

My life is too...freaking...crazy.

I mean, get this:

I was in my bedroom totally freaking out because I was about to go on my first date in months with a genius professor from Cambridge University who happened to watch witches in his spare time.

And.

I was a witch.

And.

I was supposed to have superwitch powers.

And.

I couldn't figure out what to wear!

Viv and Su showed up being all naggy, annoying sisters, "Aidan's waiting," yadda, yadda, yadda, and half my hair was straight, the other half was out-of-control and I was standing in my underwear amongst a mountain of discarded clothes that was up to my knees while waving around a pair of strappy, champagne satin sandals with rhinestones and shouting (hysterically), "All I know is the shoes!"

They jumped into action.

I mean, they'd seen Aidan—this whole outfit was a delicate maneuver. There weren't many genius doctors out there who looked like movie stars who wanted to go out with me, and this had to be right.

Su took control of my hair and makeup (scary thought) and Viv took control of the wardrobe (even scarier), and believe it or not, they totally kicked in for me.

Su did this part-straight, part-mess, part-braid updo gig with my hair (very Bo Derek meets Demi Moore meets Bob Marley, but blonde) and went heavy on the black eyeliner making me look all 70s flower-child-with-an-attitude.

Viv put me in a pair of low-rise, ass-hugging, black wide-legged trousers, my rhinestone sandals and a filmy black tunic-slash-caftan thingy with a sexy, skimpy black camisole underneath. (Who knew she had it in her?)

I looked *hot*.

~

I know this because when I walked into the lounge, Gran was talking to (raving at?) Aidan, who was nodding, his expression polite.

When he looked at me, well, he didn't look polite anymore.

At all.

In fact, whatever was going on behind his eyes was nowhere near polite.

More like pornographic.

Of course, being the cosmopolitan girl around town, I blushed.

Ulk.

"Ready?" I asked.

~

Get this Part Two:

He took me to the Swank Italian Place on the seafront.

This is proof positive that he is in cahoots with the Queen, because only by Royal Decree could one get a reservation at the Italian place. At short notice, impossible, unless you make a deal with the devil or are in good with Liz.

I tried to be cool—but it was hard.

I was with Aidan.

I looked the shit.

I was with Aidan. (Did I say that already?)

He always looked the shit.

We were at the Swank Italian Place and I had hopes they'd be able to make me a martini.

Aside: England doesn't do martinis. The Land of Bond had forsaken shaken and stirred. It was criminal (but not as criminal as their lack of understanding behind the concept of not parking on double yellow lines. It was *their* rule, why didn't they follow it?).

Aidan left me in a comfy seat on the front patio and went to see to our drinks.

I took the time to take a deep breath, calm myself and get into Glamour Girl Mode by looking at the sea.

I must admit, I spent a lot of time homesick and longing for America's king-size bags of chili cheese Fritos; our entire grocery store aisles dedicated to cake mixes; my book club who spent more time scarfing down brie, tapenade and French bread, drinking wine and dissing the men in our lives than discussing the book; and ready-to-wear Ralph Lauren in any upscale department store; but most of all, a life without cauldrons and prophesies.

But I never longed for home when I looked at the sea.

England may not have king-size bags of chili cheese Fritos but it had some incredible views.

"You smell fantastic," I heard Aidan murmur in my ear.

And England had Aidan.

Shiver.

Mm.

I was in The Zone.

I was all cool, calm, Glamour Girl.

I'd become one with the sea and was ready to hear about Aidan, Sebastian and me, The Prophesies, just how ravishing I smelled (was wearing the scent Mom created for Viv, smelled like gardenia and baby powder on her, smelled like neroli and jasmine on me, magic) and most of all, I was ready for some dedicated flirting—the kind that led to something.

He came with a waitress who handed me my drink.

Ah, a martini.

I couldn't wait.

I was prepared for the chilled, smooth, taste of vodka.

I drank it.

And gagged.

Not a little bit, a lot.

I barely saved myself from spewing it on Aidan's trousers.

Ack!

So much for cool, calm, Glamour Girl.

Hovering waitress spoke in a thick accent, "You don't like?"

Uh.

Duh!

She was Italian, gorgeous, and I hated her on sight.

"What is that?" I asked, still half in gag mode, talking through the sloshing liquid in my mouth.

"Martini," she answered.

"That…is not…a martini," I answered, trying not to drool the sick-sweet liquid on my sexy, see-through tunic and instead allow it to slide down my throat.

"Yes, martini, martini," she said in a panic, grabbing my glass and running away.

"Have some of mine." Aidan offered his drink.

I glugged back a huge gulp of Aidan's drink to wash away gag-martini.

And…

"Mm, yummy."

Yes, that's what I said.

I couldn't help myself, it was divine.

"What *is* that?" I asked.

"Pimm's."

What on earth is Pimm's? And where did I get me some?

I didn't get to ask, as Sophia Loren was back at our table with a bottle that said "Martini" on it.

"See, Martini, martini," she yammered at me.

It may say Martini but I knew martini, I'd spent a lot of time with martini and that Martini was no martini.

Date not starting off on best foot but I did smell "fantastic" with added bonus of being introduced to Pimm's.

~

Get this Part Three:

Was seated in dining area with a Pimm's of my own and all signs of gag-martini whisked away.

I'd ordered halibut in lobster brandy cream sauce.

I'd eat tire in lobster brandy cream sauce.

Date was getting back on track when Aidan settled in across from me looking at me like he'd like to eat *me* for dinner.

Yay!

And then…

"Aidan."

I didn't say it.

No.

In fact, Douglas *Freaking* Addison said it.

Douglas *GQ* Addison stood beside my table at the Swank Italian Place in little seafront town with Victorian pier in England.

I know what you are thinking and no, I didn't enter a new dimension, I was still in my dimension with Douglas Addison standing by my table.

And…

~

Get this Part Four:

Agatha Darling stood next to him.

~

19 March

Had to go—was late for "My Cauldron and Me" classes with Antonia and then got too busy with everything else.

Antonia is helping me stock my Witch Larder—and that means shopping, and one shop leads to another shop, it's a natural progression. Everyone knows that. So now I have some new crystals, more herbs, some lovely glass vials in different shapes with cork tops, some more candles and candlestick holders and a new Lulu Guinness handbag.

Anyway…

Still reeling from genius doctor date.

May also be reeling from the fact that, four days later, Aidan hasn't called me.

It ended on a sweet note, however. I could see in Aidan's mind that note was kinda bittersweet, but still.

This is how the evening progressed:

"Aidan!" Douglas Addison said.

"Doug." Aidan stood and they shook hands.

"This is a small world," Douglas Addison noted.

No duh.

What was *he* doing at Swank Italian Place in Clevedon with Agatha Darling, my arch-nemesis no less?

"What on earth are you doing here?" (Aidan, thankfully asking my question.)

"I could ask you the same." (Addison)

Ha ha—laughter and joviality while I watched Agatha Darling to make sure she wasn't putting some whammy on me.

Aidan turned to me and put an arm light around my waist, pulling me closer (nice). "Let me to introduce you to Mathilda Honeycutt."

Then Addison turned to me.

"Miss Honeycutt," he said quietly.

And I looked into his eyes.

~

I suppose there are bad guys out there who could charm you with a look, no matter how good you are or how bad they are.

I mean, Tony Soprano for one.

I think it would take Tony Soprano approximately five minutes to make me his best friend. It was the eyes, they sparkled. You didn't know if it was mischief, kindness, genuine goodness even with a blackened heart.

I'd been in love with Tony Soprano from the minute I saw my first episode of *The Sopranos*.

It was fucked-up love with a vicious, fictional Mafioso dude, but it was still love.

~

Douglas Addison smiled at me.

The smile reached his eyes.

"I'm delighted to meet you," he said, and I knew he meant it.

From that minute, he had me.

I put my hand out to shake his. He took my hand, turned it, held it gently and kissed it.

Not in a sexy way, but in a sweet, respectful way.

"And I you," I returned, and believe it or not, I meant it too.

Weird.

Too weird.

Gran was gonna disown me.

Addison seemed to remember himself, let me go and introduced us to Darling.

She bobbed her head in a distracted way whilst looking around the restaurant with an attitude and posture that clearly stated she felt she was slumming.

She had little to no interest in me.

Which I thought was super weird.

I, on the other hand, found her fascinating.

The Institute's picture of her didn't do her justice, at all. (She should sue.)

Even though she was average height (and had an unfortunate nose), she was still an imposing and handsome woman. Her clothes were a bit dowdy but of good quality that screamed money.

And the bitch had 'tude.

She wasn't scary in a Wicked Witch of the West kind of way. She was scary in a Nicole Kidman in *The Others* kind of way—uppity and spooky.

Hmm.

"I hate to interrupt you but our party is here," Darling said impatiently.

She nodded to a table across the restaurant that was filled with three suited men.

"Yes, yes, of course," Addison replied, distracted. "I'm in Bristol for an important meeting..." he told Aidan and then went on about getting together for a drink, yadda, yadda, yadda.

I looked at the men.

I looked at Darling.

I looked back at the men.

I looked at Addison.

Shit.

Addison was the devil that Darling had made the deal with. They were in cahoots.

I looked at him, at his supposed genuine friendship with Aidan and his quick, polite glances at me.

What a poser.

I felt cheated.

I felt betrayed.

Why all of this emotion in the expanse of two minutes of knowing the guy?

Yikes!

He left saying something about hoping to see me again and took off for his table.

I felt like I was having a heart attack.

"How do you know him?" I asked Aidan once we were seated again.

"Long time family acquaintance. We go skiing together at Gstaad at Christmas, have for years."

Ack!

"But, he's..." I started then stopped.

"Yes?" Aidan prompted.

"He's, a..." I started again and stopped again.

"Yes?" Aidan prompted again.

"He's a Republican!"

Aidan stared at me and made no reply.

I excused myself after the starters and ran to the bathroom and called Ash.

This was our conversation:

"Yes?" (Ash answering the phone.)

(Who answers the phone like that?)

"It's me." (Me)

(I think I detected a sigh over the line.)

"Mathilda!" (Me)

"I know." (Ash)

"Agatha Darling is here!" (Me)

Silence.

"With Douglas Addison!" (Me again)

More silence.

"Well?" (Me)

"Yes?" (Ash)

"Here, now, in the restaurant." (Me)

Silence.

"Well!?" (Me, getting impatient)

"And?"

"And what? She's the bad guy! Aren't you going to do something?"

"Did she cast an evil spell on you?"

"No."

"Shoot at you with a gun?"

"No."

"Throw food at you in a menacing way?"

"You aren't taking me seriously," I noted irritably.

No answer.

"Ash?" I called.

"It's very American of you to ask for a pre-emptive strike."

How mean!

"Keep an eye on her and get back to me," he ordered, and then he hung up.

Can you believe?

I went back to dinner.

"You okay with Darling being here?" Aidan asked.

"Sure, yeah, no problem," I lied.

No way was I okay.

I was freaking *out*.

Not freaking out enough not to enjoy my fab halibut.

But still freaking.

Freaking so much I didn't even process it when Aidan told me his family held a title (Earl of something-or-other; it'll go to his older brother).

Freaking so much I didn't react at all when he told me about the house he'll inherit from his mother and how, "We let the National Trust open it to the public but..."

Freaking so much I didn't pay a lot of attention when he mentioned Eton, as in, "My years at..."

Too preoccupied to grill Aidan about The Prophesies.

Too preoccupied to think about what came next.

So, when he walked me to the door of The Gables and we stopped, and with a gentle hand he lifted up my chin, just like they do in the movies, I blinked.

"Hi," he said quietly.

It all came rushing back to me.

It was end-of-date-would-you-like-to-come-up-for-a-drink-time.

"Hi," I said back.

And I knew he was going to kiss me.

Yay!

As his head descended, I whispered, "About those Prophesies and you and me and..." (I was teasing, I am Glamour Girl and we're allowed to be a little coquettish).

Then his lips hit mine, and I leaned forward while Aidan leaned into me, putting one arm around me to pull me closer and the other out bracing us against the doorjamb.

It was a nice kiss, a professorial kiss, a kiss one might expect from, say, Stephen Hawkings.

I was standing there, slightly disappointed, expecting something more...

Then his lips opened, my lips opened, his tongue touched mine and…

Yowza!

Super-shivers!

Yay!

Then he really leaned into me and…

Yayayayayay!

Yay!

"Wow," I breathed after he lifted his head.

He grinned.

"Wow," I breathed, this time for the sexy grin.

Then the door opened.

It was, of course, Ash.

Aidan didn't move, didn't let me go, just looked over his shoulder at Ash.

I didn't move either, just peeked over Aidan's arm at Ash.

"Curfew?" Aidan asked.

Ash didn't respond.

He also didn't move.

Thus began a weird display of testosterone as both men held their positions.

One beat.

Two beats.

Yikes!

I held my breath.

Then Aidan looked at me.

"I'll be in touch," he said softly then he kissed my nose, and he was gone.

That was it. He got in his Roadster and took off.

Dinner and a kiss.

Okay, so it was halibut in lobster brandy cream sauce and a fucking great kiss, but still!

Ash grabbed my arm and pulled me inside, closing the door behind me. Then he started walking away, brushing past me.

Uh, what?

Interrupt a kiss like that and then walk away?

I don't think so!

"Hey!" I snapped at his back.

He turned. "Yes?"

Erm.

"Uh…nothing," I muttered.

Okay, maybe he scares me. Just a little.

I started to walk forward.

"You smell…" he muttered when I came abreast of him, and I stopped, "good."

"Good?"

Wha'?

"Yes, good."

"What does that mean?" I asked, hands on hips.

He just looked down at me.

"Well?" I pressed.

"You smell like sex," he answered.

What does sex smell like?

And, is that good?

Yikes.

I mean, I know what sex smells like, but how did I smell like that?

Maybe I shouldn't ask.

He was walking away.

"What does that mean, I smell like sex? I didn't have sex," I informed him.

Okay, perhaps I should have let it alone.

He turned; his lips were twitching now.

He didn't spend the night running his frustrations off on the treadmill.

He didn't spend it slowly getting drunk and pining after me.

He found me amusing.

I amused him.

Now I know how Joe Pesci felt!

"You don't smell like you've had it, you smell like you want it."

My mouth dropped open.

"Don't worry," his voice had dipped low, "that's a good thing," he assured me.

Then he fucking winked at me.

Fucking, *fucking* Sebastian!

And I still didn't know a thing about The Prophesies.

~

22 March

Had to sort Rory out.

I was up in the Tower Room, cleansing my magickal implements as Nerissa taught me to when the phone rang.

And rang.

And rang.

A house full of people and nobody answers the phone.

I grabbed it and it was Rory's headmaster.

Rory had been suspended for three days, fighting in school.

Our little Rory, fighting!

Thank goddess Josie was holed up somewhere joining the Labour Party or Rory would have been in for it.

As I was on Josie's list to pick up Rory when she was unavailable, they told me to come and get him.

He had a busted lip and a face like thunder and said nothing throughout the entire meeting with the headmaster.

On the way home, I tried to get it out of him, but he was having none of it. The minute we got back to The Gables, he thumped through the house toward the Trunk Room like he'd been taking Snotty Kid Lessons from a Disney movie.

Problem is, as he was thumping, he hit one of Mavis's tables and knocked over and broke a Waterford vase.

Not good.

"Best pick that up and then go tell Mavis," I advised, and Rory turned on me, little kid face in full scowl.

Then he grunted with feeling, "Nuh!"

"Nuh?" I asked.

"Yeah! Nuh!"

I know this seems like a weird conversation but I figure it's normal going with a moody eight-year-old.

"What's your problem?" I asked. I could go snotty with the best of them.

"I don't have a problem." Rory trying to out-snot me (no way, I was a master).

"You do have a problem and a busted lip to prove it," I told him.

"Nuh."

"Nuh right back at 'cha!" I snapped.

This is when Su walked in.

"What gives?" she asked.

"You're a hippie," Rory said it like he would say, "You're a loser," to someone he actually thought was a loser.

Su looked at me and then walked out.

I guess I was on my own.

"You better tell me what's going on," I said to Rory.

"And you're a witch."

And he said the word "witch" like it started with a different letter.

Uh-oh.

Then Rory thumped away.

I gave him a while to sulk—it's always good to have a while to sulk—and cleaned up the vase. Then I knocked on the door to the Trunk Room and ignored the "Go away!"

Rory was bouncing a soccer ball against the wall. Mavis would have a conniption.

I caught the ball.

"Rory, honey—"

"I said, go away!"

"Let's talk."

"Doan wanna."

"Well, I don't care if you 'doan wanna,' we're gonna talk."

Rory glared at me with arms crossed on his chest.

Okay…here goes.

"Rory, I'm a witch," I announced.

His glare didn't waver.

I kept going, "And Mavis is a witch. So is Su, Viv, Mom, Gran… we're all witches."

No response.

I continued, "And so are most of the ladies at the café, except Lucy."

Not even a blink of an eye.

I kept speaking.

"Real, honest-to-goodness Sabrinas."

Still no reaction.

I took my wand out of my back pocket, centered myself, focused, took a deep breath and threw up the football.

Then I let fly my magic.

Hot pink pixie dust shot out and shattered against the ball with sparks flying here, there and everywhere, changing the ball to a frog which fell—splat (ack!)—onto the floor and started croaking and jumping around.

I flipped out my wand again—and *bam!*—the frog was a ball again.

That got a response.

And that response was, "Crikey!"

He jumped up and plastered himself against the wall and stared at me like he'd never seen me before.

"This is the story," I said. "I'm a witch and I have power. I use it carefully, for good only and only for people who ask me to help them. Your mom needed my help and asked for it. I'm bound to her by her request, bound to help her and keep her…and you…safe through magic and anything else I dream up. You got that?"

He nodded.

"You got a problem with that?" I asked.

"They say at school you're all lesbians."

"They're all stupid at school. No one's a lesbian and who cares if they are? What's wrong with lesbians?"

"I don't know."

"Well, this is my advice, instead of hitting someone who says something stupid like that, just say, 'So?' or adopt the Pee Wee Defense and say, 'I know you are, but what am I?'"

This cracked the snotty-kid-guard and he started to smile.

"'I know you are but what am I?'" he repeated then asked, "Who's Pee Wee?"

He didn't know Pee Wee!?

"Oh dude, you don't know Pee Wee? Well, we'll have to rectify that," I announced.

And that was me sorting Rory out.

Of course, later Josie sorted him out more.

And even later, I smuggled in *Pee Wee's Big Adventure*. I know I shouldn't have but I'm Cool Mathilda and I have to keep that up.

The Month of April

April 2

It started out as the perfect day.

I should have known it wouldn't last.

~

I woke up early and got on eBay right away, and sometime in the night, I won those Jimmy Choo shoes I'd been bidding on.

(Yay!)

I never, ever win.

(Yay! Yay!)

Since I was so excited to find out about my Jimmy Choos, I had time to do yoga before breakie…so after yoga I felt relaxed and energetic and ready to face the day.

Lunchtime proved my new pizza offering at the Café was a hit.

(Take that Lucy.)

Side note: Sun-dried tomatoes may just be the ambrosia of the gods, and if you put them in the crust *and* in the sauce *and* on the pizza, it can't be beat.

After work, had errands to run. As Ash is still sticking to me like glue (except in *that* way), he had to drive me.

This is not a plus.

Ash is nice to look at (very) and gives me that special feeling (very, very special feeling) but having that all the time is not-so-special (especially since nothing has come of it except a kiss in the library about two gazillion years ago).

So now, Ash-as-bodyguard is sort of Mathilda Torture.

Oh well.

The sacrifices one makes to be Savior of the World.

I do get a reprieve, when in or around The Gables or The Witches Dozen, Ash will leave me alone. Both places have protection spells and pretty strong broomsticks covering their front and rear, so I'm safe.

So...

Off we went on my errands, Ash and I, first to the tip to get rid of the recycling. Then to Brockley Farm Shop so I could buy my lavender (they have the best—they also have pretty great sausages too, so got some of those and some nice, chubby baby carrots and...).

I digress.

And on the way home from Brockley's, I saw Cadbury Garden Centre.

Now, garden centres in England are like little shopping nirvanas tucked here and there all over the country. They have invisible tractor beams that could rival the Death Star. Even if you don't garden or aren't craftsy (like me), you get sucked in and find yourself spending hours flipping through books on perennials and testing knee mats and listening with rapt attention to people explaining the pros and cons of different types of trowels, etcetera.

Ash and I were coming up to Cadbury Garden Centre, otherwise known as the Granddaddy of All Garden Centres, so I shouted, "Turn up there!"

"Where?"

"There!" I pointed.

Ash slowed.

"Why?" he asked, and I think I detected a hint of suspicion.

"I need something." I cast around in my head for an excuse he would buy. "Witch stuff...magickal implements." That sounded good. "It's important!" I added, just in case me shouting wasn't getting through.

"This is an unscheduled stop."

"What? Do you have to report back or something. Turn, turn, turn!!!"

So he turned.

Some time later, as we were walking back to the car, he asked, "You needed pink pots?"

"They aren't pink," I said, changing the subject because I knew I wouldn't ever convince him I needed pots—pink pots, no less.

He looked at me in a way that said he thought I was fibbing.

Then we got into the car.

Not, it is important to mention, the Lush Jag, no.

We were in *my* car.

We were recycling at the tip and it is far easier to recycle in a hatchback (not to mention Su had kinda borrowed the Lush Jag—long story). So we were in my fourth-hand Nissan Micra that used to be the wet dream of a boy racer and now was my daytime nightmare.

∽

Story on how I came to be the not-so-proud owner of the Purple People Eater:

Boy Racer had run out of money and had to unload his Micra.

I was (even then) bidding on Jimmy Choos rather than saving for a decent car.

So.

Boy Racer and I made an unholy alliance that ended up with me owning a partially souped-up Micra, and Boy Racer having, well, nothing but a bit of my money.

To the credit of Boy Racer, he did give the Micra a kickass iridescent green knob on the stick shift and some lights on the undercarriage that would make me hip with all the homeys in the 'hood (ack!). The car also had a paint job that was metallic purple with platinum and green opalescent effects.

Unfortunately, Boy Racer didn't get around to doing anything under the hood.

I understood his priorities, it is first about the way it looks and then you get to the meat of the matter, but engine-wise, the Purple People Eater (as I called it) wasn't much to write home about.

∽

Anyway.

∽

Once buckled into the car, I showed Ash a pot. "See this?"

He looked at the pot then looked at me.

"Yes," he said, with what I suspected was what he considered extreme patience. "It's a pink pot."

"No, it's fuchsia."

Silence.

I pulled out another pot. "See this?"

"Pink," he said.

I shook my head. "No, this is petal."

"Petal?"

"Yes, and this one," I pulled out the third, "anyone can see this isn't pink it's —"

"Brown."

"Truffle!" I snapped.

"You're mad," he announced starting the car (in which, incidentally, he somehow managed still to look cool).

"Yes, I am but at least I'm adorably mad."

Silence for a beat and then, "You don't have any plants to put in the pots," he pointed out.

Oo, I knew I forgot something.

~

This would mark the beginning of the end of my perfect day.

~

From Cadbury Garden Centre, we were off to Junior Poon's on Hill Road.

I'd been looking forward to Junior's for ages. The girls were meeting for drinks and crispy aromatic Peking duck in the wine bar underneath the restaurant. The wine bar looked like spruced up catacombs, complete with low hanging ceilings that, believe you me, could catch you off guard — especially if you'd had one too many.

I loved Junior's.

Junior's rocked!

And crispy aromatic Peking duck was second only to pizza with loads of sun-dried tomatoes in the Ambrosia of the Gods Contest.

I'd been given the mission to get there by six, grab one of the private back alcoves with the comfy couches and order the duck.

Lucy and Josie got off at six thirty and Su was returning the Jag to Ash (under threat of certain death, but that's another story), and we were all going to walk home after lots of Peking duck and wine.

I'd been waiting all day to get my lips around a pancake oozing with hoisin sauce.

I couldn't wait for the duck.

I couldn't wait for the nice pinot noir that I discovered the last time I was at Junior's.

And I couldn't wait for a reprieve from Ash, if only for a few girlie hours.

But, it wasn't to be.

Instead this is what happened:

Ash was driving.

I was holding my pots and thinking about when I could next get to the garden centre to buy some plants to go in the pots.

I was also thinking about Peking duck and how many orders we'd need.

We were close to Junior's, slowing for the Six Ways roundabout…

When…

Smash!

We were rear-ended.

"What the…?" (Me)

Ash didn't slow, he shot through Six Ways, pedal to the metal, the Purple People Eater's engine revving and calling out to Mama, "No more, Mummy, *no more.*"

"Ash, slow down, we were just…"

Smash!

Rammed again.

The car jolted, fish-tailed and Ash downshifted. Ole Purple screeched in protest.

Smash!

Smash!

Smash!

At high speed, Ash took the left angle onto Hill Road.

~

For your information, Hill Road is one of those crazy "chicken roads" that came into being when rich people rode horses, poor people walked, kings chopped people's heads off and the guy who had a premonition of the future existence of automobiles and tried to warn ancestral city-planners was burned at the stake.

In other words, Hill Road was narrow.

Way narrow.

Super narrow.

To a girl from Colorado where you could drive for an hour on the highway between Pueblo and Taos with two whole, big, wide lanes to yourself going eighty-five miles per hour and feeling like you were going sixty and maybe, just maybe, see one dusty pickup…well, to that girl, Hill Road was an eye opener.

These days, Hill Road, like many roads in England, was forced, against its will, to accommodate two lanes of traffic *and* parking *and* scary, aggressive English drivers who were scary, aggressive English drivers precisely *because* of the existence of roads like Hill.

With nothing for it, Hill Road, like many streets in England, protested against all of this and forced all travelers to play chicken in order to get through.

It was a hair-raising experience.

And it was about to get worse.

~

Down Hill Road we went (past Junior's, by the way), the maniac bumping into us again and again, swerving crazily behind us and clipping our fender one side and then the other while *we* were swerving crazily trying to avoid slamming into an upcoming or parked car.

Everyone was honking and tires were screeching, and I counted three drivers who gave us the two-fingered, backhanded "V" (English for "fuck off"), and one of them was a blue-haired old lady who could barely see over the wheel of *her* Micra.

"Do you know how to use a gun?" Ash asked calmly as if we were on a Sunday drive.

Ack!

Guns?

Ack!

I was watching behind us and at Ash's question, my head whipped around so fast my neck cracked (and thus disappeared all benefits of the yoga I did that morning).

"No!" I answered (loudly).

We were making the right turn onto Marine Hill, a forty degree turn you should take at fifteen, twenty miles per hour (tops), and we had to be doing sixty (okay, maybe forty, but still!).

I screamed.

Yes, to my utter mortification, I girlie-Kim-Basinger-in-*Batman* screamed, high-pitched and shrill.

(What can I say? It was terrifying.)

We'd gone the five hundred feet on Marine Hill to Wellington Terrace and managed somewhere during the scream to lose the car behind us for a second.

Ash slammed on the brakes and then cut the wheel to the left, switched gears then *reversed* down Marine Parade.

Yes, he went backwards down Marine Parade.

Holy Mother Earth and all her flowered friends.

Let me explain about Marine Parade.

On a good day…

On Marine Parade…

When you are going forward…

And have plenty of time…

And there is no traffic…

And the sun is shining…

And you are in good health with all your faculties about you…

The angle of Marine Parade to Marine Hill and Wellington Terrace is The Angle of Death.

That junction was where perfect insurance records went to die.

Not to mention, Marine Parade was another "chicken road," but it just happened to have the added heart-attack-inducing sheer wall of granite that held up Marine Hill on one side of the road, and on the other side there was a thirty foot drop onto an access road to the seafront terraced houses.

I didn't scream this time. I was too terrified to move a muscle…even a throat muscle.

The car came after us, screeching tires to make the death angle, and Ash drove backwards down one of the most crazy bits of road in a town full of crazy bits of road.

The whole time he was winding open the window (if you can believe).

Then out came the gun.

Ack!

Blam!

Blam!

Blam!

I don't know if he hit anything because I closed my eyes. I felt like Brenda must have felt in *Highlander* when the Kurgan took her out for a spin.

We were screaming down Marine Parade and Ash cut the wheel at the end and we went careening left into the parking lot of the derelict Royal Pier Hotel.

Screech!

We stopped with a jolt.

Zoom! The car passed us.

Ash pulled the emergency brake and got out of the Micra (gracefully, which is surprising considering he's over six foot and the Micra is called a Micra for a reason). He ran toward the Parade in that manly, loping SWAT jog as-seen-on-TV with the gun held behind his back.

~

Yes, this happened.

~

To me.

~

When he got back to the car he said, "I'm taking you home."

I could think of nothing but…

"What about the Peking duck?"

He looked at me under his brows as he put the car in gear.

I started babbling, "I'm supposed to order the Peking duck. I'm supposed to get the table. In the alcove. At the back. Peking duck is important. I've been looking forward to Peking duck all day…no, all week. The girls are counting on me."

We screeched away from the hotel.

"They'll get over it."

~

He took me to The Gables and the minute I got out of the car, the bag with the pots clutched in one hand, my sausages, lavender and carrots clutched in the other, he skidded out of the driveway without a backward glance…off in the Purple People Eater to track the bad guys.

Needless to say, this turn of events meant Junior Poon's wine bar was out of the question.

Everyone descended on The Gables instead.

After I'd told the story for the five hundredth time and had mellowed out on a Shiraz cabernet blend that was really just an ugly stepsister to the pinot noir, Ash came back.

"Did you find them?" I asked.

"No."

"Did you total my car?"

"No."

"Fuck!" I shouted.

"You can say that again. That car is shite," Lucy said.

"*Fuck!*" I shouted again.

Ash handed me a bag.

"What's this?" I asked.

"It's Peking duck."

After chasing the bad guys in a souped-up Micra, Ash went out and got me some Peking duck.

From Junior's.

How do you like that?

~

3 April

Okay.

I…have got…to get…my shit…together.

I mean, screaming like a girl? I'm a witch, *the* witch for goddesses' sake.

I had my wand on me and I didn't have it together enough to do a spell, even a simple spell, to help out Ash.

I just sat there, silent or screaming.

How embarrassing.

And after that performance, he brought me crispy duck from Junior's.

What am I supposed to make of that?

He must be wondering what he's gotten himself in for, laying his life on the line for the likes of me.

And what is going on with all this nonsense, Darling and Addison at the Italian Place, Mom and Gran and everyone here, without plans to return home anytime soon?

And what is the deal with no one telling me any Prophesies, Ash and Aidan looking and not touching (well, not exactly but almost).

And what exactly is Josie going to do that is so fucking important to the world's future that I have to protect her? Who's after her and why, and where are they now?

Ash is gone, left this morning Mom tells me, to go to London. I'm to stay at The Gables or be taken by Mom, Gran or Mavis to the café.

Ash's Edicts: No Junior Poon's, no Tandoori Nights, no Moon and Sixpence and absolutely no driving around in the Purple People Eater. Ole Purple needs to stay "out of sight."

Okay.

Last but not least…

If I'm The Chosen One, why is my bodyguard giving me orders?

~

17 April

Get this.

If…you…can…believe…this is what just happened!

~

Obviously, slept like the dead (the dead I almost was!).

(Will tell why later…)

Woke up all snuggly, warm, happy, all covered in heavy blankets and tucked in tight.

Sun was shining on my face, very rare of a morning in England.

Felt like staying there forever and ever.

Snuggled deeper into bed and warm thing behind me.

Warm Thing *moved*!

Before I could, like, totally freak out, Warm Thing's arm tensed (not heavy blankets on me—heavy Warm Thing arm on me), and hand that was on my breast tightened with thumb finding just the right spot.

Holy crap!

Oh me.
Oh my.
I maybe made a little noise in my throat.
Just a little one.
(Scared? Or other?)
Warm Thing moved and I heard, "Good Morning," in my ear said in throaty, warm, sexy, sleepy *Ash* voice.
Yowza!
And.
Ack!
What the…?
Felt nuzzling at my neck.
Felt nuzzling other places too.
Body melted.
Mind freaked out.
(Chest hurt like hell but more on that later…)
Hands were moving (not mine).
Lips on neck.
Oh me.
Maybe made another little noise.
Oh my.
Ash gently turned me over to face him and before he kissed me…

~

Okay…maybe I'm one of those people who sabotages their happiness.

I mean, after all these months, I was somehow in bed with Ash all cuddly warm and yummy.

Yesterday, life nearly passed me by and now, here I was all scrumdelicious with the most fantastically handsome, delectably cool man (not to mention fab kisser) I'd ever met.

Yet.
I don't know.
Maybe I should see a shrink.
Maybe I should relax and go with the flow.
Take a few risks.
Live a little.

~

Or maybe…

~

"What are you doing?" I asked.

Nudging close to my ear he said, "I think that's fairly obvious."

Mm.

He would be right.

One of his hands was doing very lovely things around my bottom and toying delicately with my panties.

Er…is it me or is this going fast? (Sabotage)

We haven't even been on a date! (Sabotage)

"Um…" (Sabotage) "Do you think that's a good idea?" I asked. (Sabotage)

"What?" I got the impression that he wasn't paying much attention to me.

Well, he was paying attention to me but he wasn't paying attention to me, if you know what I mean.

"Well, this whole…er…" His hand went somewhere rather nice. "Um…you're my bodyguard."

With some attention to my injury (more on that later…), he pulled up my knee and hooked it over his hip then his thigh slid between mine and he used his hand on my bottom to push me along it and…*oh my*.

I started panting.

"What whole bodyguard thing?" Ash murmured.

"Well, um…won't this…kind of…"

Panting and unable to finish my thought.

Sometime later, doggedly, I went on.

"I mean, yesterday…The Prophesies…The Chosen One gig…er… black dragon…" More panting. "You know…or the fact that we haven't even been out to dinner, or, a…uh…movie…is this the right thing to do?"

Ash didn't even pause with what he was doing, *anything* he was doing.

But he answered.

"Considering The Prophesies say you're to bear me three children, I don't think…"

Ack!

Ackity *ack ack!*

Ack!

Hold on a minute!

I froze.

Then I shouted, "*What?*"

"Two sons and a daughter," he murmured into my neck.

I reared back rather violently (must...ignore...pain...in...chest!), which caught Ash off guard. Instead of going back, my bucking and Ash compensating caused us to roll over...

Ash on his back...

Me on top.

Being the brainiac I am and in my complete panic after hearing future-father-of-my-unborn-children news, I lifted both knees to pull myself away and escape, escape, escape!

I ended up straddling him about ready to push off to leap from the bed when Ash's hands landed on my hips to keep me where I was.

"Hang on," Ash growled.

Two sons...

And...

A daughter.

"What? Do The Prophesies say we're supposed to get married or something?" I asked, kinda flippantly, like that would ever happen.

"Yes," Ash answered.

"*What?*" I shouted again. "What, what, what?"

I tried to push off, somewhat succeeded and got to my feet beside the bed, but he came up after me, caught me and spun me around. I collided with his body ("Careful," he said quietly, trying to hold me still, but again not the time to collide into a gorgeous man's body—not when in   full-on-panic-mode-escape-escape-escape-two-sons-one-daughter-second-degree-burns-on-chest-yikes!).

He shook me gently. "Mathilda, calm down."

"I'm not marrying you," I blurted it out. I couldn't help myself.

"Yes, you are," he answered, completely calm and looking at me somehow amused.

How was this amusing?

Ever?

In the History of Amusing Things, how does this fit?

"Witches get married and then never see their husbands again!" (Me)

"Mm." (Ash, clearly unconcerned at this juncture)

"Their children grow up fatherless." (Me)

"Not exactly." (Ash)

"It's not going to happen." (Me)

"Yes, it is." (Ash)

"No…no…what? Are you asking me to marry you…like, now?" (Me—*ack!*)

"No." (Ash)

"Well then?" (Me)

Ash had one hand at my back, one hand *not* at my back.

"What are you doing?" (Me—hysterical)

"Matty." (Ash)

Wait!

Ash never called me Matty.

By the way, a couple of Ash's fingers had gone renegade from this rather important conversation we were semi-having. And his fingers' antics were causing me to lose track of the conversation.

In fact, losing track was not the way to put it.

We ended up standing there, one of my legs curled around Ash's hip, my hands in his hair and his fingers doing the talking.

It was his turn to avoid my lips but he was just being perverse.

"I wanted to say…" Ash, voice slightly husky, "You were impressive yesterday."

A compliment on my Craft?

From Ash?

I opened my eyes to look at him and he was looking at me in that clotted cream way again, and I have to admit, I lost it.

As in, really lost it.

In a very, *very* nice way.

In other words, an *orgasmic* nice way (literally).

(I lost it so much, I think I might have even bitten him, just a little bit, on the shoulder.)

When I'd pulled it together, still holding on to him, he said, again in that husky voice, "And impressive just now."

Eek!

Of course, he walked out after that.

He didn't leave me standing there but kissed my fucking nose and sat me on the edge of the bed, leaned in close and whispered, "You owe me one."

Then he took off, only wearing the jeans he obviously slept in.

Leaving me in his T-shirt.

Leaving me with the smell of him in his T-shirt.

And the feel of his fingers.

Yowza.

It would seem I owe him at least three.

~

I remember watching *Dynasty* and thinking Joan Collins was the shit with all the drama and lacy peignoir sets, and Blake and Dex and everyone coming out with those sexy one-liners and exiting a room.

Oh, my heart.

I ate it up.

But, no one lives like that.

No one.

But me.

(Without the lacy peignoir sets.)

~

By the way: Ash + Six Pack = Yes.

~

Later:

Okay – backtracking – away from Still Unbelievable Orgasmic Ash Encounter to what happened before – yesterday, which might be slightly more important than Ash-induced orgasm to the history of the world (or, at the very least, to my entry in the *History of Great Wytch Families*).

~

Here we go:

It has begun.

I don't mean to be so dramatic. That sounds like the beginning of an apocalypse movie.

(Booming voice)

IT…HAS…BEGUN!

But, what can I say?

It has.

~

It was one of those spring days when it was warm enough that you could open the windows.

I loved the first day of the year where you could open the windows and let the stale, old dusty air out and let in the crisp spring breeze, which made everything feel fresh.

We had a new syrup in and thus snickerdoodle lattes were the special.

We were playing the Scissor Sisters, loudly, and everyone was filthy *and* gorgeous.

We were jigging from table to table.

We were gliding from fridge to burping, hissing Big Red—the espresso machine.

Our hips swayed.

Our lips hummed.

Ash was in London—no word, no sign, no idea when he'd be back.

His edict was still being enforced by the Triumvirate (as Su called Mavis, Gran and Mom), and I was allowed only at the house and the café and therefore, Josie and Rory were also limited to these places—though Rory was able to go to school (alas).

Life was not happy at Camp Gables.

But on a day like that day, when the sun was shining bright on the channel, the tulips were popping out everywhere and the breeze was easy—nothing mattered.

We were busy at the café, foreshadowing I hoped, for the season to come. I'd been around a bit of the summer last year and our sleepy little seafront had a goodly amount of foot traffic when the weather improved. With as many employees as we had, we needed the business.

It was Lucy, Josie, Antonia and me, and we were a good team. I loved to work with Lucy and Josie especially—the coven was great but Lucy and Josie were my age, my girls and we understood each other.

I'd broken out the flip-flops. I loved the feel of them slap, slap, slapping against the soles of my feet.

My toenails were varnished a pearly mint green.

I had on a little gypsy girl gauzy top and Levi's that I bought at a vintage clothing store that someone (bless their hearts) had worn in well and washed over and over again. They fit in all the good places and were tight in all the better places and, icing on the cake, had a ragged knee.

Sunshine and summer weather meant a whole new wardrobe, and the idea that my skin may, someday soon, lose its pasty winter-white pallor made me want to do cartwheels.

~

Then…

Right down my spine the premonition tickled like a chill.

I stopped to find it…let it in my head…

When the phone rang.

~

Rory.

~

Josie answered the phone and I knew who was on the other end.

Shit.

Josie didn't know but I did. One look at Antonia told me she did too.

"It's the school, they've…*lost* Rory," Josie said, her voice shocked and panicked.

"Let me call Mavis." That was Antonia.

"No time," I said, and there wasn't and Antonia knew it.

My wand was tucked at the small of my back in the waistband of my jeans. I knew this but I checked anyway to make sure it was there.

"Take care of things," I ordered Lucy, and she nodded. "Come on." I grabbed Josie and we headed out.

I didn't think, I just went.

No time.

And no Purple People Eater either.

Shit.

Josie started to blather. "How do you 'lose' a student? Dammit. We've got to go back to The Gables, see if he went home. Maybe he isn't feeling well…maybe he got into another fight…"

I wasn't listening, I was focusing…

On a metallic blue BMW Roadster parked by the seafront.

Aidan was somewhere out there watching me.

I ran toward the Roadster, pulling my wand out and muttering under my breath.

The day before the Junior Poon Ruining Road Chase, Su had been experimenting with the Lush Jag and, one incarcerated evening when we were stuck at The Gables, she'd drunkenly explained the spell she'd perfected.

Grand theft auto, witch-style:

> *Steel, oil, gas, fumes — speed for power, speed to run,*
> *By the force of the moon, the heat of the sun,*
> *Grant me the use of this vehicle — my possession has begun.*
> *Let the power of this spell — in no way reverse,*
> *Or cast upon Josie or me, any curse.*
> *As always and ever, by the strength of my tree*
> *As I will, so mote it be.*

The lights flashed on the Roadster and I knew we were in.

Blessed be, that Su and her criminal mind.

"Go around to the other side." I motioned to Josie as I headed to the driver's side.

"Whose car is this?" she asked.

"Just get in," I murmured.

More muttering and wand action…I was concentrating.

I didn't look up, didn't want to see Aidan racing toward us to stop me from stealing his car, didn't want to lose track of what I was doing.

"Matty." Josie sounded scared.

I stopped and looked at her.

"It's okay, it's Aidan's car, he'll understand." I hoped. "We're going to search The Gables first, see if someone's there to help us. Don't worry, Josie. I promise we'll find Rory."

I was talking smack but she didn't know that.

I had to make up a plan and I needed to get her to The Gables.

After a couple of mistaken incantations and missed bits of the spell (I forgot to rub the "belly of the beast," which meant patting the dashboard) the car roared to life and jumped the curb.

"Whoa, Nelly," I said to the car, jammed her into reverse and rocketed to The Gables.

The car drove like a dream, it made Ole Purple seem like a go-cart.

We skidded to a halt on the gravel outside The Gables, and Josie was out the door before I fully stopped.

She ran in shouting Rory's name.

I ran in too, straight to my Tower Room.

I'd been experimenting with some things and I hoped to the goddess that they worked.

Fumbling through the bottles and vials, the mortars and pestles, cauldrons, candles and messes of incense, I grabbed an amulet that was a vial filled with pulverized carnation and lilac petals, spiked shards of rosemary and a bit of the power of the Glamour Girl.

Muttering to myself and calling to my tree, I ran out of my Tower Room and right into Josie.

"He's not here!" I could hear the panic in her voice.

"I feel him here," I lied as I slipped the vial around her neck. "Keep looking."

She didn't even notice what I'd done, she simply raced away.

I kept up my invocations and I thought it was working; the air was thick with magical energy. I could feel it pressing against my skin and down my throat as I breathed it in.

I raced to the door and found Mom standing there, just outside.

She had her eyes closed, her lips were moving, her arms were raised to the sky, her wand in her right hand, dust dripping from it.

The breeze was blowing her dress and her hair.

She looked scary.

She looked powerful.

She looked kick…fucking…*ass*.

Two burning sage sticks were stuck in the candelabrum on either side of the door, smoking hugely. There was a line of lilac scattered across the doorframe.

As I raced out the door, Mom's eyes popped open and she stared at me. Her eyes were fevered and she was totally freaking me out (in a good way).

"The back door—" I started.

"Covered," Mom said.

"The garden door—"

"Done," Mom said.

"The door to the cliff from The Dungeons?"

"Don't worry about it, Matty," Mom said.

She had it covered.

She'd read my mind.

(Moms are very cool sometimes.)

She grabbed my hand, patted it, looked in my eyes and winked.

We were still holding hands when Josie came tearing toward the front door.

"Josie, don't!" I shouted, and Mom squeezed my hand as Josie rushed toward the door at full speed and slammed into the space in the frame like there was a sheet of clear super-powered glass there.

Butter yellow and gold sparks exploded out from where she hit, and more sparks and pixie dust blasted her back several feet where Josie fell on her ass.

Holy Mom Power, Batman!

"Oops," Mom muttered. "Maybe a little OTT on that."

"Ya think?" I asked.

The look on Josie's face, oh goddess, it made me want to cry.

Instead, I walked into the entryway and looked down at her, trying to stay cool.

"Sorry, Jo Girl, it's for your own good. I need to keep you safe."

She was still on the floor, shaking her head, not understanding that the spell was on the door to keep her in and safe.

"I promise I'll bring Rory back."

Big words.

Man, I hoped I could deliver.

Then I walked quickly out of the house, Josie followed and slammed into the invisible door again.

She was shouting at me, the pain and betrayal in her voice were drifting out like angry, hissing snakes.

I tried to ignore her (didn't work).

I walked to Mom and said, "I want Su and Viv with me...and Ash—"

"Yes, I know. I'll find them, go." And she started toward the shouting Josie who was pounding at the invisible barrier, her face red, her eyes full of tears and yellow and gold sparks flying everywhere.

I started toward the car and saw Aidan leaning against it.

Crap!

"You know, all you had to do was ask," he said.

I pulled out my wand.

I didn't have time for banter. "Get out of the way, Aidan."

He shook his head.

"Out of my way!" I shouted.

"First, I know where Rory is, and second, I'm driving."

"Don't play with me, Aidan. Agatha Darling has Rory somewhere—"

The premonition was clear and not very attractive, and it was all I could think about.

Aidan is cute and all (and a doctor) but Rory was out there with Darling, an unknown entity, and I had to get him back.

Now (I was going to say it) was no time for flirting.

Aidan didn't let me finish. "Yes, she does have him, she's also being watched and I've been watching her watcher. So, get in the car Matty."

Yay!

I wanted to kiss him, but instead I got in the car.

"What will Dr. Bennett think of this?" I asked, trying to sound casual but instead sounding terrified.

"I'll worry about that later," Aidan replied, sounding damnably cool and collected.

I needed to be cool and collected.

I needed to get my shit together.

I didn't pay attention to where we were going. I was opening up the channels of my mind, reaching out to my sisters, calling out to the black dragon at the same time I was gathering my power, every bit of it that I could muster.

In other words, I was breathing deeply and trying to stay calm.

He took me somewhere in the town next over, a once-wealthy seaside resort that had fallen on hard times now that it was cheaper for English folk to find other, warmer beaches on the Continent (where they could bake themselves into unholy, wrinkled messes). Now, for some reason, the town was full of drug rehabilitation centers, which meant it was also full of the drug users who'd dropped out of them and the not-so-lawful flotsam and jetsam that came naturally after that.

I was chanting and rhyming when Aidan pulled up to a hump-topped, dilapidated building with a peeling sign that said, COMMUNITY CENTRE.

I looked at Aidan to ask where the fuck we were but he put a finger up and then pointed to something outside the car.

Across a desolate, muddy field that perhaps was supposed to be a place where kids played but looked like something from a documentary movie about Sarajevo one day post siege, there was a Volvo. Aidan handed me a nifty pair of binoculars, which I put to my eyes and trained on the car.

In the car was Ichabod, better known as Jeremy.

Agatha Darling's Watcher.

Of course.

Shit.

"We're on the roughest council estate in the region," Aidan informed me.

"Is Darling here?" I asked.

"I'm guessing there." He pointed at the Community Centre.

"Why here?" I asked, staring at the building and then looking around.

There were shops across from the Volvo. Not someplace you'd hang out for a latte but somewhere you could buy some fish and chips, place a bet, get a stamp or buy a bottle of booze.

There were houses and blocks of flats also surrounding the field, most of which had debris of some sort resting around it, from old bicycles and dirty mattresses to enormous amounts of cigarette ends and flapping, discarded grocery bags.

Kids were loitering outside the shops, old folks and incredibly young mothers with strollers were hanging at the bus stop.

There were people everywhere.

This wasn't a place to take a kidnapped child.

"On this estate, you don't ask questions *and* you don't answer them. Do you understand what I'm saying to you?" Aidan asked.

I just stared at him.

"No one sees anything here. They don't hear anything…are you understanding me, Matty?"

Shit.

"I'm going in," I announced.

"Alone? No you're not."

I pulled my Glamour Girl pink mobile out of my back pocket and tossed it in his lap. "Call my sisters and get their asses here." Why hadn't I thought of that earlier? "If she's got Rory in there, I'm going in. Now."

I think he said my name but I didn't pay attention.

I heard him get out of the car and slam the other door, exposing himself to Jeremy.

I couldn't worry about Aidan. I just walked to the front doors of the Centre and went in.

The whole time I was walking, I told myself, "I am Glamour Girl. I have mint green toenails and no one will fuck with a woman with mint green toenails. Especially when she's The Chosen One. And if they try, I'll kick their ass."

At least it sounded good in my head.

The inside of the place couldn't have been more different from the outside. A small entry opened to a huge room that had a stage at the far end and a kitchenette to the side. There was local art on the walls, posters promoting events and classes, kids' drawings from a competition, photos of the queen and her court from a fair.

There was some kind of club going on, kids dancing in rows to KC and the Sunshine Band while a gravel-voiced, punk-haired woman shouted encouragement to them.

No Rory.

A soft-spoken woman came up to me just as Aidan caught up with me.

"Alright?" she asked.

This is what people say in England. "Alright?" means anything from, "Hi, how's it going?" to "Can I help you?"

"I'm sorry," I said, still scanning for Rory. "I think I've got the wrong place. I'm looking for a woman with—"

"Some men and a boy?" she asked, her eyes flicking from me to Aidan to the kids in the hall.

Ask no questions, get no lies, my foot.

The woman was petite and pretty. She had great style (fab boots) but you could tell that even though she didn't (couldn't) spend a fortune on her clothes, she was damn well going to make the effort anyway.

I could appreciate that.

She also looked like nothing got by her and if it tried, she'd wrestle it to the fucking ground and then, if she cared enough, she'd spit on it.

At that moment, I could appreciate that too.

This wasn't the kind of place that kept secrets. This was the kind of place that took care of its own…in its own way.

If Darling was looking for something else, she'd made a big, fucking mistake.

I felt hope for the first time since that chill ran down my back.

"Yes, a boy, eight years old, blond, a little skinny," I answered.

The woman sized me up then she sized Aidan up. Thank goddess she came up with the right conclusion.

"Through there." And she pointed.

Thank Aidan…thank the goddess…thank this woman…Rory was here.

She pointed at some sliding double doors at the side of the hall. I thanked her, hurried over and started to push open the doors, but before I could they slammed open against their rails.

Without taking a step, I was pulled in, almost like an enormous invisible cane had wrapped itself around my waist and yanked me through.

At the same time, I heard Aidan's surprised grunt as he was pushed back.

Then the doors slammed shut behind me without benefit of my touch or anyone else's.

And in front of me sat Agatha Darling.

~

Too tired. Drained. Chest hurts regardless of post-orgasmic state.

Must rest.

~

19 April

When I woke up just now, I sensed I wasn't alone.

Not Ash, this time, (in fact, where *is* Ash?) but instead I looked across and Rory was lying there next to me fully dressed, his hands folded over his chest like a dead person in their casket.

It was like he, too, sensed that I was awake because his eyes popped open, he turned his head and looked at me.

"You hungry?" he asked, apropos of nothing.

I wasn't. I felt like shit, tired, cranky. I hadn't seen Ash since the Orgasm (which will heretofore be referred to with a capital "O" for obvious reasons) and, just like yesterday, and the day before, there felt like there was a bleeding, painful hole where my chest used to be.

"As ever, I could eat a horse," I lied.

He knew I was lying, I could tell by the look on his face.

"'Kay, well, Mum is making American pancakes."

I tried to sound thrilled. "Oh, yummy!"

He jumped up and ran out of my room, I don't know if he was scared of my lies or scared of me.

But at least his job was done. He knew I was going to live to see another day.

~

Later…

It still shits me just to think of it.

I feel like hell; Agatha Darling did a real job on me.

The stinking, hateful be-atch.

I still haven't seen Ash.

Aidan has disappeared…again, and isn't answering his mobile…again.

Although, considering the fact that I'm soon-to-be-married to Ash (ack!) *and* his fingers (hmm), perhaps I should have a little conversation with Aidan.

Everyone else is wandering around like zombies as if the before in all of this was a joke.

As if we hadn't prior knowledge that Darling had turned.

Like this is all a surprise.

But, really, what in *the* fuck does she think she's doing?

~

This is how it went down:

I was paralyzed.

Yes, The Chosen One was useless against the powers of Darling.

After the doors slammed shut behind me, she pinned my arms and legs with a swirl of forest and acid green magic. They were locked in position, and I'd have fallen over like a log if she hadn't kept me upright and hovering, my feet dangling a foot off the floor.

Yes, *hovering.*

It was humiliating.

Bitch.

My eyes could move though and I saw Rory. One of the men from that night with Aidan and the faeries in the wood was standing behind him holding him still using an arm across his throat.

Rory didn't look very good. He looked scared—his face and eyes red, wet with tears, his lips trembling.

Man, oh man.

The room was much smaller than the hall, institutional cream-slash-green painted cinder block walls, big windows with wire through them and curtains from the 70s; clean but, against all that is the Law of Interior Design, still hanging. There were comfortable chairs and tables and it looked like a room where you'd have a knitting club. Not at all like the torture chamber it was about to become.

Darling was sitting in an armchair facing me, five or six feet away. She looked refined yet spooky even in the light of a beautiful spring day.

Another man was behind her. Again, I remembered him from that night with Aidan in the woods, mainly because he was the one who I'd kicked in the balls.

He was smirking at me.

Ack!

There was another man off to my left, but I didn't get to take much of him in as once I'd had a look at the lay of the land, she blasted me.

❦

In the movies, they wait to give the hero time to get his bearings. Usually the baddies babble on and on, which gives the hero that time. Time to think of a plan and even an extra moment for him to put it into action.

Definitely time to get in a one-liner.

Harrison Ford doesn't have thirteen guys jumping him all at once… no.

He gets in, the baddie jabbers away and Harrison has time to assess the situation, more time to pull out his firearm or unsheathe his knives or whatever, then he's good to go.

And, when the enemy fires on him, they miss.

And if they don't miss, they hit him where it just glances off. It hurts, of course, and he utters something like, "Yeesh…" and then he's off again, shooting the bad guys like ducks in a barrel.

❦

In real life, I'm sad to say, it doesn't work that way.

❦

I also find it somewhat distressing to report that Agatha Darling has two wands. And what comes out of Agatha Darling's second wand is not

133

charming, sweet-colored pixie dust. Nor is it not-so-charming acid and forest green swirls of magic.

Oh no.

With her second wand pointed straight at my chest, she blasted me with lightning.

Pure, scorching, white-bright lightning.

And it hurt like hell.

~

I didn't say "Yeesh…" I exclaimed, *"Arrrrgh, holy shit, fuck!"*

I was Mel Gibson getting tortured by the little Asian dude in *Lethal Weapon*, except without the water.

And that was when I could talk at all.

~

She didn't need to hold me paralyzed after the lightning died. I fell to my hands and knees, gagging and trying my damnedest not to spew my sun-dried-tomato-laden lunch on the ground.

Her power, from holding me to blasting me, was awesome.

Awesome.

I'd never seen anything of the like—not from Mavis or Gran or all of us put together.

I was in Trouble, with a capital T.

Shit and damn it all to hell.

"Now, Mathilda, we have to talk," she said, her voice posh to the nth degree.

I feared Rs rolling.

I feared ee-ahs included in such words as "here."

I feared that fuckity, fuck, fucking lightning.

I struggled to get up. I didn't go for the wand tucked in my waistband because I couldn't. I barely had the strength to pull myself up to rest on my knees. I was panting, my eyes were unfocused and the pain in my chest was excruciating.

I took the deepest breath I could once I got myself upright and asked, "About what?"

I looked at Rory who looked worse than before, probably not an easy thing to watch, someone getting struck by lightning.

He looked utterly terrified.

Darling continued, "I wanted a chance to explain to you about *tradition*. About the *right* way to do things and the *wrong* way to do things."

Uh, what?

As in, excuse me?

She'd lost me.

I couldn't help myself anymore, I looked away from her to Rory and asked, "You okay?"

Blast!

Again, she hit me with the lightning.

Up in the air and back I went, slamming against the sliding doors, the bolt holding me suspended up there for what seemed like forever.

I heard Aidan on the other side, banging, shouting my name, the doors rattling but they didn't move.

I slithered down when she was done, on all fours again, gagging and this time I was crying and slobbering too. It hurt like hell, the pain was so intense, I thought my arms that were holding me up were going to give way, I was trembling so badly.

"Do not interrupt when I'm speaking," she warned.

I whimpered with pain, too lost in it to be humiliated by the fact that I hadn't even raised a wand to her. I wished with everything I had that Aidan both could and couldn't get those doors open. I needed help, oh goddess, I needed help. But she might be able to make mincemeat of him just as she was making mincemeat of me.

With effort, I pulled up my head and looked to see she was studying me with what seemed like little interest, as little as she showed me in the Swank Italian Place. As if this was some kind of unwelcome duty she had to perform, like the dishes.

This bitch was ice cold.

How on earth could she be a witch?

"I don't think you understand," she went on. "I don't think you *appreciate* the history of witches, my dear."

I heard a noise and looked over at Rory. He was crying like me, gagging against his guard's arm, which had tightened against his throat.

"Do let up, Robert, we don't need the boy anymore," Agatha said to her lackey.

The man let Rory go, and he dropped to his knees too, his eyes wild.

"But!" Darling snapped, both wands swishing through the air like whips as she turned her attention to Rory. "I don't want to hear a thing from you."

Rory went totally still, staring at her in petrified silence as she turned again to me.

I hated her.

Goddess, I hated her like I've never hated anyone.

In fact, I'm not sure I'd ever felt the emotion before because it was nothing like I was feeling then.

"This 'Witches Dozen' business. It won't do," she informed me. "The Prophesies said you'd be…well, obviously…" She gestured with her wand taking in all that was me. "And they weren't wrong. But I never thought…never *dreamed* that Mavis would allow it. That you would herald the beginning of the end of Our World."

She was quiet and I was up again, on my knees, staring at her. It took everything I could to get in that position, and I was scared out of my wits but when she didn't continue, I ventured a question.

"Your World?"

"Not my World, dear, *Our* World. The World of Witches. You are familiar with it, are you not?"

"Uh…" Was this a trick question? "Yes."

"Well, the way it is now, we know what we can do, and they don't." She gestured to one of the men who didn't seem bothered by her in the slightest (bewitched?). "What they don't know *will* hurt them and that has always given us the upper hand."

I was still lost and, even through all the tears and slobber, I must have looked it.

"Oh dear," she sighed like I was the most simple creature she'd ever come across. "I see I'm going to have explain."

Then, she looked at her watch.

What?

She had better things to do?

More people to torture?

More children to kidnap?

More weird lectures to give?

I wish I'd had the courage to say any of that, but I just knelt in front of her.

The Chosen One.

Me.

On my knees.

She kept explaining. "If they don't know what kind of powers we have, they fear them. If they fear them, we keep them…these…" she swished her wand about in a bored way again, indicating the men,

"Creatures, in check. You can't go about being a witch, out in the open, and show them everything. You'll give away our best defense."

"Maybe if they knew, if they understood what we were about, they wouldn't fear us so much." I tried. "They wouldn't —"

Blast!

Me and my mouth.

Another bolt of lightning.

More crying, more snot, more slobber.

Thankfully still no vomit.

But now, I was getting pissed.

I mean, is this all really about tradition?

Scaring the pants off Rory, panicking Josie, blasting me with fucking lightning?

Is it really just about her wanting things to stay the same?

I mean, that's boring.

Where's the plot in that?

Where was the foul, twisted reasoning behind the treachery? Something worthwhile, something you could sink your teeth into, something juicy.

A spurned love — that's got passion.

She's doing it for money — that smacks of greed.

Maybe even envy, I make a better brownie than her or something.

Something sinful, something meaty, something nasty.

This wasn't worth lightning, for goddess's sake!

She was going on and on, not ranting but just explaining, as if to a very small child.

Rory had gotten himself to his feet. The man behind him was sorta glazed over like he'd heard this all before. The guy behind Darling wasn't looking too attentive either. I didn't dare glance at the other one.

My chest hurt like nothing I'd ever known before.

I couldn't hear Aidan behind the door anymore.

I was alone.

I knew I couldn't go for my wand.

And I knew I didn't have a whole lot left in me to do much without my wee twig.

But I also knew that I was The Chosen One.

And I was a Glamour Girl.

And Rory needed me and I'd vowed to keep him safe.

And even though Darling had just looked at me like I'd worn sequins to a funeral, I knew I had style.

So fuck...*her*.

I had to do something.

I'd screamed all girlie-pathetic in the car with Ash—no way was I going to let the side down now.

Not for something as stupid as *tradition*.

I mean, I could get into turkey and stuffing and pumpkin pie, all family get-together, thankful for blessings type of tradition, but this? Telling someone how to live their life because you don't agree?

Fuck that.

So, even if here endeth my chapter in *History of Great Wytch Families*, I was going for it.

I'd seen enough movies to know how it was done.

I didn't even bother with Darling.

Darling was another day.

In all the good movies, during the first run-in with the bad guy, the bad guy always got away.

And anyway, the bitch had lightning.

So I took whatever I had left, visualized it in my fist and ducked, rolled, came up and threw it with everything I had like a baseball straight at the dude behind Rory.

Unbelievably, it came out of my hand like the kickass sphere of magic that it was.

It wasn't bright, white-hot lightning and it wasn't hot pink either.

It was glowing, neon fuchsia pink-purple with gorgeous electric blue sparks flying hither and thither.

It hit him; he went back, his neck snapping his head forward, he slammed against the cinder block wall and then he went down...hard.

Ha!

"Run!" I shouted to Rory, and then ducked, rolled and lobbed another one at the dude behind Darling.

At that point, the doors were kicked through and all hell broke loose.

Aidan was there, coming to my rescue!

But so was Ash!

Yee ha!

I didn't hesitate, my third ball o' vengeance was lacking some of the brilliance in the electric blue department but it didn't matter, the third guy went down too.

Ha ha!

I ducked and rolled again and missed getting hit by lightning by a hairbreadth.

"Tedious," Darling muttered as I stood up, and she tried to hit me with lightning again, ignoring the men and furniture flying about the room.

This time, though, I prayed to my tree with every fiber of my being then waved my arm across my front, visualizing a shield going up. There it went, a pink-purple forcefield with blue sparks flashed out momentarily in front of me, deflecting the bolt, which veered to my left without harming me.

Yee ha!

I saw Ash hesitate while lifting a squirming bad guy to take in what I'd just done before he sent the baddie smashing through the (wired glass!) window.

Aidan was slamming his fist into another guy's nose.

Rory was crawling across the floor to the doors.

Thankfully, the kids in the other room were long gone.

Duck, roll, (whimper a little at the searing pain in chest) and then land a ball of magic, hitting Rory in the back, it exploded and rained hot *and* shell pink pixie dust with silver sparks up and over him.

I allowed myself a short sigh of relief. That last sphere was protection for Rory. (I hoped.)

The woman with the great boots appeared in the doorway. She took one look at the scene and without a word, grabbed Rory and disappeared.

Darling didn't look bored anymore, she actually stood.

"My, my, Mavis has been busy—"

I didn't let her finish, I didn't give a flying fuck what she had to say.

I lifted my arm and Spidey-style, flicked her with some of my brightly hued sparks.

She waved it away like I had with my forcefield and then we were off, me ducking and rolling and throwing orbs of magic while she slapped back with lightning.

Then, with a loud crack, what was left of the doors went flying off their hinges. Viv and Su came charging in, great waves of Viv's glittery turquoise sparkles met with Su's lustrous, grape-colored dust as I sent another sphere of neon across the room.

~

And that's it.

Darling was driven back by Viv, Su and I, disappearing in a sparkling array that camouflaged her for long enough for her to get away.

The men were left as they were, battered and unconscious.

As we all stumbled out (well, it was only me stumbling, everyone else was walking with both Aidan and Ash helping me), the local woman stood with Rory at the front door to the centre. She was smoking a fag and looking like nothing surprised her.

Rory ran and threw himself at me. I winced and whimpered and put my arms around my boy as I caught the woman's eye.

"Alright?" she asked.

I answered the only way I knew how.

"All right."

Then I passed out.

~

Drained, messy with snot, tears and slobber, mortified (not only at the ass-kicking I was given but at the snot, tears and slobber that both Ash and Aidan were seeing), magicked out through body conjuring rather than using my wand and burned to shit by lightning (actual blistered, ugly burns and bruises), I was out like a light.

And you know the rest. I woke up in Ash's arms.

So, like I said.

It has begun.

~

20 April

Middle of the night, my eyes opened.

I felt them coming before I could see them.

Oh well.

Here we go.

I rolled out of bed, thought "black dragon" and grabbed my wand.

I looked at the clock: two a.m.

Couldn't they come at a decent hour, for goddess's sake?

~

My chest was better. Not great: blisters going away, bruising turning that ugly green with hints of yellow. I won't be wearing cleavage anytime soon, but not so painful as before.

Anyhoo.

~

I looked out the window and there they were, silhouetted against the almost-full moon—three of them; pointy hats, ragged skirts, broomsticks and all.

The Witches Council: the hag, the lady and the maiden.

I tucked my wand in the back waistband of my new pajama bottoms (post-duel-with-baddie-get-well-soon gift from Mom with pink and chocolate paisley swirls—lush).

I started down the back stairway only to hear someone coming up. I saw the glint of a flashlight but couldn't see who held it.

I was nowhere near recovered—magic-wise. The last time I checked, I'd drained the source dry during the duel (yesterday, I was trying to conjure a hot fudge sundae once I'd gotten out all the ingredients and was too tired to finish the job manually, but I just managed to explode the cocoa box and get chocolate dust everywhere).

Nevertheless, I shot a warning pulse of shell pink and silver pixie dust (don't know when my magic became all vivid but I dig it).

It illuminated Ash.

"Don't waste it," he ordered.

He's so damn bossy.

Aside: not feeling the Ash Love right now—in *any* way—which could be why I'm not feeling the Ash Love.

I came abreast of him and he shone his flashlight on my bare feet.

"Where are your slippers?" he asked.

"Er," I answered.

The flashlight travelled up my paisley pajamas and pink camisole. "And your dressing gown?"

"Um."

"Wait here."

And he was off.

And, of course, I waited.

~

By the way, I think you get that the Big O has not been repeated. Ash has been persona-non-seena for two days, doing his Mysterious Ash Activities and leaving me wondering how we'll manage to someday get married and have children (unless done in some other dimension where we actually spend time together, go on date, hold hands, talk about politics, argue about who's going to take out the trash and have real, full-blown sex).

~

He came back with my slippers and robe. I should have felt thankful at his gallantry but instead I felt pouty, and who wouldn't? No girl should experience a close encounter of the future-husband kind and then be left to heal from lightning bolt wounds alone.

Once I was properly attired, he held out his hand.

"Give me your wand."

Excuse me? I thought.

"Uh…what?" I asked.

"Your wand," he said.

"Why?" I asked (kinda loud).

No way. I thought.

Mavis and Gran had told me the Witches Council would be investigating. Malevolent witch-on-witch magic was frowned upon. Word got out (Darling's people, no doubt). We were informed that an investigation had been opened and we were to expect a visit.

Of course, I had nothing to worry about. I mean, Darling was clearly a psycho—cavorting with bad guys, kidnapping eight-year-olds and striking people with bolts of lightning.

"You don't know what you're going to meet down there. They could confiscate your wand," Ash told me.

Was he crazy?

"No way!" I snapped. "She kidnapped Rory!"

He sighed, patient as ever (yeah, right). "Mathilda, Prunella Craddock and Endora Eccles are down there—the Crone and the Lady."

This was supposed to explain things?

"Yeah? So?"

"If what you say is true and Agatha Darling has put herself up as the protector of tradition—"

"She kidnapped Rory! He's my Spellbound. I've vowed to keep him safe! Surely they can't—"

Ash stepped close and tipped his chin to look at me. "They've lived their entire lives behind the veil of secrecy. You represent significant change to the Wiccan world, to the way witches practice their Craft, which is to say, the way they live their lives. You can't assume they're going to be on your side."

Oh.

Well, then.

Fuck.

I had to admit that Ash had a point.

I gave him my wand.

~

They were all assembled in the front parlor (the one I called the Plush Parlor because everything was covered in velvet, even the wallpaper was flocked).

Mavis and Gran were already there.

The hag, lady and maiden were wearing the Council uniform, which to be frank needs updating—black crepe silk, ragged hem, lace-up cleavage (under which, thankfully, the crone had added a camisole), pointy hat, chunky shoes and red and white striped stockings.

Jeez.

The crone looked to be about eight hundred years old. The lady was Mavis's age (give or take a hundred years). It was the maiden who surprised me, she was my age.

"I'm Myra Dingle and I'm a proxy," she said, reading my thoughts. "My daughter, the Maiden, is Seraphina and she has school tomorrow. I don't want her up too late."

Well, that explains that.

~

Must say, I was expecting a friendlier interrogation scene. A bunch of kindly witches sitting around commiserating about the state of the witch world today; perhaps while eating steamed syrup sponge with custard and hot cocoa.

Instead, the crone looked cranky, the lady looked bored and the maiden proxy looked like she'd like to be anywhere but there.

And then Dr. Bennett cleared his throat.

Uh…*pardonnez moi*, but what was the fuck was Dr. Bennett doing there?

"What are *you* doing here?" I asked.

Okay, so that wasn't exactly polite, but it was two in the morning, Ash was a jerk, my chest hurt (maybe I was milking that a bit), I didn't have my wand on me and things didn't look like they were going to go to well with the Council.

And there he was, standing by the fireplace, the Head Dude of Psychical Research, standing in, of all places, the Plush Parlor of The Gables.

Dead people somewhere were spinning in their graves, no doubt.

"Dr. Seymour is indisposed," Ambrose Bennett answered. "And, quite *unusually*, he was a firsthand witness to reciprocal malignant Wicca. He's asked me to come in his stead and present evidence on your behalf."

Oh, Aidan.

He's so sweet.

"We," the Crone said, sounding even crankier than she looked, "had a member of *Le Société de Mathilde* at the scene. We hardly need your *watcher's* evidence."

Mm, seems the Crone is in Ash's camp about the Royal Institute.

Dr. Bennett teetered a bit away from the fireplace.

"I'm afraid it isn't testimony Dr. Seymour was intending to share, rather, physical evidence."

And then he whipped out a wand.

I was the only one in the room who gasped. But then, I'd been the only one in the room to feel what Agatha Darling's wand could do.

"That's Darling's wand," I said.

"That it is," Dr. Bennett replied.

The Lady took a step forward. "A watcher in possession of a witch's wand?" She sounded horrified *and* offended. "How…?"

"If you would allow me," Dr. Bennett interrupted her, turned, went to the wall, bent creakily to the floor, fiddled with something and then whipped around with surprising agility.

A bolt of lightning went up and over everyone's head, harmlessly crackling away for a brief moment and then dying.

Five wands were pulled out immediately (not mine, obviously, damn it all).

In the midst of that, Ash strolled casually forward and yanked the wand from Dr. Bennett's unresisting grip.

Then everyone else in the room but me (and Ash) gasped.

With the wand came a long, electrical cord.

"One more moment of your time," Dr. Bennett said and then bent again, rose with some difficulty and then threaded a long cord through the arm of his coat. It ended in a plug.

All of this, he handed to Ash.

"In her *tête-à-tête* with Miss Honeycutt, Mrs. Darling had a little manmade magical assistance," Dr. Bennett declared.

Everyone was stunned speechless, except Ash.

"How did Seymour get this wand?"

"We *are* trained watchers, Mr. Wilding. There isn't much we don't see. Even, perhaps especially, what we aren't *supposed* to see. Dr. Seymour noticed that she hid it before disappearing. No doubt she didn't want to be seen unplugging it or the like. Dr. Seymour went back to get it before she could return to do so."

"Agatha Darling harnessed electricity in that...*thing*...and used it on another witch?" Myra asked in a hushed and disgusted tone.

"Yes," Ash answered.

"Damn tootin'," I muttered.

Now everyone in the room looked horrified and offended.

Except me, I was thrilled Darling didn't have the power to strike me with lightning.

The bitch cheated.

I hadn't.

Woo hoo!

That means I kicked magical ass!

"Well, my work here is done," Dr. Bennett declared and started to the door.

I decided to walk him out, it was the least I could do after my rude greeting. I mean, he did come all the way out here in the middle of the night to present evidence on my behalf, evidence that showed *I kicked magical ass*!

And, (bonus) I could find out how Aidan was doing.

"Sorry to be...well, I wasn't expecting to see you," I told him as we made our way to the front door.

"Please, don't worry, Miss Honeycutt. Your attitude is not a surprise. You're in quite a predicament."

Mm.

He could say that again.

"How's Aidan?" I asked.

"He's well."

"Where *is* Aidan?"

"Family commitments he couldn't avoid." Dr. Bennett stopped, paused, sighed and looked at me (this all took a lot of time). Then he said, "Although, you must know, he very much wished to be here."

Oh, Aidan.

What on earth was I going to do about him?

He kept looking at me for a while—always spooky watching, these watchers. Then he shook his head and started on his slow path to the front door.

Outside was a Rolls Royce with a man standing beside it staring up at The Gables wearing night vision goggles.

What the hell?

These guys were freaks.

"What's he doing?"

Dr. Bennett stopped and looked this way then that.

"Always strange goings-on at The Honeycutt Gables." He paused. "Always."

Er, what? Strange goings-on? Baking cookies? Eating Indian take-away while watching a Coen Brothers marathon? Those weren't strange (to me, of course, they could be strange to an old dude, I was thinking the Coen Brothers were probably not big with old dudes).

Still, minus the serious magical force (natural anyway), it was (relatively) wholesome (not counting Su's criminal tendencies and my lusting after every gorgeous male in the South West (and, er, the South East), and Gran's possible political extremism.

Okay, so not wholesome but still, not strange either.

There was no way around it; Dr. Bennett was the King Freak. How Aidan got caught up with these guys, I would never know.

The other dude opened the back door of the Rolls.

"Wait." I put my hand on the doctor's arm. "What's going to happen to Aidan?"

Again, Dr. Bennett looked at me for a while before he spoke.

"Miss Honeycutt, we are not unaware of what The Prophesies say about you and Dr. Seymour. It isn't as if we didn't have several centuries of forewarning that a member of The Institute would become, let's say, *involved* with a witch."

"What does that mean, '*involved*?'"

Dr. Bennett shook his head again then patted my arm, not unkindly.

"No, no, my dear. Let's just see how it all turns out, shall we?"

Fuck!

He kept speaking. "Needless to say, we can't punish Dr. Seymour for doing what he's destined to do. I, er…that is, we, the Directors, need to minimize the tumult it will cause. Now," he said when I started to say something else, "you take care, Miss Honeycutt. Keep sharp. Study. Read. I daresay we at The Institute would like to see many Valentine's Day tins of cookies coming our way."

Wow.

That was a nice thing to say.

He may be strange but maybe he was a cool strange.

And then he was off.

And I was left wondering—again.

Wonder, wonder, wonder.

Must say, I'm beginning to get sick of wondering. In fact, I wonder if I should bother wondering anymore and just let it all happen. Since it is all going to happen anyway; why not stop wondering and just…

I stopped wondering about stopping wondering when:

A bat.

A big, huge, shiny, scary bat flew through the clearing, following the Rolls down the driveway.

How is that for weird?

And then Mom came out of the bushes, adjusting her clothing.

"What are you doing out here at two a.m.?" I asked, staring at her, I was sure with eyes wide.

"Never you mind, nosey pants. Isn't the Council in there?"

What the heck was going on?

I looked after the Rolls, the bat was nowhere in sight.

Then I looked at Mom.

Then I answered, "Yes."

"We best get you back in then."

All I can say is, I know my Mom's tone and that was that—bat or no bat.

∾

Summing Up:

The Witches Council (with the unfortunate acronym of the W.C.) left not long after Mom and I went back inside.

They took Agatha Darling's wand with them.

They talked about taking mine (apparently, a wand can contain the essence of the magic you perform. Given a certain amount of time, you can trace it. If you catch it in, say a week or so, and the witch doesn't use it too often to override the old magic, you can find out what spells were cast, yadda, yadda, yadda. But since I didn't use my wand, they didn't need to take it).

They expressed some disbelief about my ability (without my wand and as a novice—novice? ha!) to fight off Darling with her wands, both Wiccan and manmade, and all of her thugs.

Instead of waking Rory (who also had school tomorrow and who I didn't want to be freaked out any more than he already was) I was forced to demonstrate by using the miniscule amount of magic I had stored. I threw a glimmery pink and silver baseball-sized sphere that exploded in silver sparks in the fireplace.

(Must say, pretty pleased with that performance, considering.)

"And that's with only a few days recuperation," Gran declared proudly.

The Council all stared in the fireplace then looked at me.

"We'll be investigating further," the Crone announced, sounding resigned and moving toward her broomstick.

"We'll also need to discuss The Witches Dozen," the Lady stated.

"Why?" Mavis asked, somewhat belligerently.

"We've had complaints. Formal complaints," the Lady told her.

"Why?" Mavis asked, again belligerently.

(Was it me or did it seem the Lady and Mavis didn't get on?)

"You know why, Mavis. You also know why we need to inquire about them," the Crone answered.

"Prunella—" Mavis started.

The Crone waved her words away, sighing. "I'm too old for this malarkey."

She grabbed her broomstick. "Endora, Myra...let's go. By the time we get back, Seraphina will be awake and we can fill her in before she goes to school and *then* I can finally get to my bed."

We stood outside, all of us, waiting for them to go (must say, at this point it was good to have slippers and a robe—damn Ash for always being right).

The W.C. were ready, even had the broomsticks between their legs, when Prunella Craddock, the big cheese Council Witch, the Hag, turned to me and said, "One more thing, Mathilda Honeycutt, you're suspended from doing magic until—"

Ack!

Suspended from doing magic?!

"You can't!" That was Mavis.

"You must be joking!" That was Gran.

"I don't believe it!" That was Mom.

"Hear me out!" the Crone snapped. "Until we come back."

"When's that going to be?" I asked (okay, maybe I whined, but what the fuck?).

"Soon. But, if you conjured that," she pointed to the house, "with your magic dwindled then you're far too powerful to be let alone until we assess and report on the extremes of your gift—"

"Bureaucracy," Gran muttered.

"Until we investigate what happened on the Council Estate," the Crone went on.

"Systematic red tape." Gran again.

"And until we locate Agatha Darling and listen to her excuse of why she's..." brief hesitation, "done what she's done," the Crone finished.

"Mathilda's carrying her wand." That was Ash, being bossy again.

"No." Hmm, old Prunella didn't seem to think Ash was all that. "Mavis," she turned to my aunt, "I trust you to take her wand until our return."

"She's carrying her wand." That was Ash again, his tone the teensiest bit sharper.

The Lady turned sharp eyes on him.

"Sebastian Wilding, you have no authority here," she put in her two cents.

"I do, Endora, and you know I do. She's carrying her wand and if she's fired upon, she's going to retaliate."

The Crone butted in. "I'm sorry, young man, but I have to assert the Council's privilege. By your and her account, and our witness, she needs to be assessed. No one with that amount of magic should go about utilizing it until she's registered."

"Oh, for goodness sake, she's The Chosen One! What did you expect?" Mom exclaimed.

"If you tell me, Hanna, that you weren't surprised at the caliber of her Craft, after only, what? Six, seven months of training, then I'll call you a liar," Prunella retorted.

"Okay, so maybe she's a little advanced," Mom allowed.

(Advanced? Yay!!!!)

"Enough of this," Ash interrupted tersely. "You weren't there, Prunella, I was. We don't know what Darling will try next. You never would have expected her to do what she's already done. Admit it."

Silence.

Ash kept talking. "If Darling tries something new, something worse, I can't protect Mathilda against that. You know I can't. Not if she doesn't help. She's already lucky to be alive. I won't have her handicapped by you taking away her wand."

Silence.

(I'm already lucky to be alive? *Ack!*)

"She's carrying her wand," Ash finished.

Silence again.

(Okay, so I knew I was already lucky to be alive, but for Ash to say it, *out loud*. He's like James Bond and The Saint and Shaft all rolled into one, if he couldn't protect me...)

More silence while everyone stared at everyone else.

Then...

"Fine," the Crone gave in, but not good-naturedly. "Mathilda, if you're fired upon, by magic or manmade evil, you are free to do whatever you need to do to keep yourself safe."

"And my Spellbounds," I pushed.

The Crone stared at me, impatience etched in her face.

"And whatever I need to do to keep my Spellbounds safe," I repeated with added detail.

"And your Spellbounds," she allowed.

"And Ash. Whatever I need to do to keep Ash safe."

Ash rolled his eyes heavenward.

"Who's Ash?" Myra whispered to the Lady.

"Sebastian can take care of himself," Prunella said with exasperation.

"Oh," whispered Myra.

"Okay. Well then, anyone else I care about," I said.

"Listen, young woman, you're lucky I relented on you and the Spellbounds," the Crone snapped.

"The coven can take care of themselves, I know. But Lucy at the café is not a witch, and if anyone tries to hurt her or anyone I care about..."

I was kinda thinking of Aidan but didn't want to say it out loud.

"So be it!" shouted Prunella, crankier than ever. She turned to Gran. "Minerva, you can tell she's from your line. Stubborn, too damn stubborn. All right! So be it! But no magic besides that."

She looked at me as if daring me to say anything else.

"Thanks," was all I said.

She glared at me some more and then nodded, then looked from one of us to the other.

"Damn Honeycutts," she grumbled. "You'll be the death of me."

Oh goddess, I hoped not.

(I wish people wouldn't talk like that—too close for comfort.)

Then she finished, "I'll be back."

Great.

I couldn't wait.

And with that, they pushed off, making a path toward the moon.

The Month of May

May 1

I had an old boyfriend who played football (defensive end) who told me the best offense was a good defense.

I think that's a bullshit way of making the boys who were never going to get any of the glory feel better.

This is what I think: If one side of the team sucks then both of them are going to suck because they'll all be losers.

So, okay, I can handle the defensive.

But I'm feeling offensive.

~

Josie:

Not happy with me for magically locking her in the house.

Though she's kinda in the "all's well that ends well" frame of mind.

We discussed Rory, and he's hanging in there but still a little freaked (okay, maybe a lot freaked—have woken up with him beside me doing his casket-training-pose every day for weeks now).

We've talked to Delia, one of our coven who's been a midwife for donkey's years and decided to get a counseling qualification in order to diversify. She's going to have a couple of sessions with Rory, see if she can help.

~

Coven (Defense):

My magic is suspended so will have to gather the troops.

Luckily, I've got the Honeycutt Coven, so the troops are good troops.

I've asked them to put together some protection spells, amulets, etcetera, to cover Rory, Josie, Rory's school, the wood around The Gables and Poet's Walk. I want to be able, at the flick of anyone's wand, to see where either of them is. And, in any of those places, I want any kind of malicious magic to be extinguished the minute it's born.

We consulted Josie and she's cool with it. No one wants a repeat of last month.

The Gables are in an uproar. Protection spells of that strength, that breadth and that distance…well, they require a lot of magic.

Octavia and Fay have set up a command post in the conservatory.

The kitchen's a mess (and it stinks).

The greenhouse looks like a tornado has swept through it.

Paulina, Antonia and Rhiannon have commandeered my Tower Room (and my larder).

Lots of dancing in the moonlight and clandestine meetings around boiling caldrons under cover of darkness in various Wiccan hotspots around the village.

Defense covered.

~

Mavis, Gran, Mom Viv and Su (Offense):

It's time to gather some intelligence.

The Honeycutt women are going on fact-finding tours.

I want Darling and I want her coven, and I want the men who have joined her.

And I want to find out where Douglas Addison fits in with all of this.

Surprisingly, Mom has (eagerly?) volunteered to track and research Addison.

Hmm.

What's up with that?

Mavis's Magic Room is a hive of activity, witches going in, witches going out.

The phones are ringing off the hook.

Barely an hour goes by (day and night) when one of them isn't sweeping in or out wearing their cloaks and (if night) carrying their broomsticks.

Nothing is coming of it, apparently the witch world is folding in on itself, waiting, watching and keeping their mouths shut.

Probably also deciding which side they're on.

Offense commenced.

~

Me:

I went to the library, grabbed the Wiccan White Pages and called everyone in the Edwards Coven — Agatha's girls.

No one answered their freakin' phones.

Except one old bitty who said, "Magic? I'm done with that. I see where it's going and I don't want any part of it!"

Then she hung up.

Went to *Mathilda's Register* and tried Eleanora.

"Elly, you there?"

Nothing.

"Elly, Rory was kidnapped and I was struck by lightning."

Still nothing.

"She used a man-made wand with an electrical cord. Can you believe that?"

Silence.

"The witch world is changing. Elly, I need some answers."

Zip.

"The W.C. has suspended my magic."

Nada.

"Elly, girl, I need you to help me."

Don't call me Elly. The words scripted themselves on the blank page and then vanished.

Finally!

"Elly, honey, do you know what happens next? Do you know where

I can find Agatha Darling? What's her connection with Douglas Addison? Who are her henchmen? Where do they live?"

I'm sorry, Mathilda. I can't help.

"Listen, Elly, I know you aren't supposed to, but I'm in a spot. I don't have magic and the match just got dirty."

I'm sorry.

"Can't you give me anything?"

"Yes, use this time to study, to meditate, to glory in nature."

"That's not help."

It is, Mathilda…you have time, use it wisely.

"I thought I was!"

She ignored me. *And the next time you come to me, ask the right questions.*

Argh!

Ash:

Went to The Dungeon doors and knocked (all right, pounded).

He opened them and stood there, staring down at me, arms crossed on his chest.

Still nothing further after the Big O. He hasn't asked me out on a date, come in and sat by me while I was watching television, given me a good morning kiss when I struggle into the kitchen for coffee.

Nothing.

Everything is back to normal with stalwart Ash—distant as ever.

Fuck him.

I don't have time for that shit.

"You wanted me?" he said.

He wished.

(Well, I kinda did, to be honest, but only because I always pick the wrong guys.)

"We're going up to Worcestershire, you and me. There's a witch, used to be in Darling's coven. I want to talk to her."

"Who is she?"

"Althea Appleton."

He shook his head. "Not a good idea."

So bossy.

"Why?" I asked.

"One, you don't have your magic. Two, Appleton is a member of a coven that we must consider hostile."

"*Was* a member of a coven."

"So she says."

Such a know-it-all.

"And three, Althea Appleton is an oracle."

Hunh?

"A what?"

"Look it up," he advised, and then he went back to The Dungeons.

I couldn't help myself, I stamped my foot.

I'm never marrying you, I thought towards the door.

And, get this.

This is what popped into my head:

Yes you are.

Damn Ash.

~

Martini Night:

Josie, Lucy, Viv, Su and me, and a bunch of fat, green olives, vodka fresh from the freezer, fab stemmed glasses and a stainless-steel shaker (we had vermouth but it was on the kitchen counter, too far away to bother).

The Subject of Martini Night: Sebastian Quincy Wilding and the Big O.

Su's Take: "Why are you worried? An orgasm is an orgasm, is an orgasm. Take them as they come, no pun intended. Be happy that they come, okay, pun intended, and don't ask too many questions or they'll quit coming."

Josie's Take: "I don't know. Sebastian kind of scares me. I think you're better off with Aidan."

Lucy's Take: "Just go to his door, get his ass up here and ask him what he's up to. Seems to me, if Rory's sneaking into your room at night to make sure you're okay, it might be cramping his style. Could be as simple as that."

My favorite; Viv's Take, after everyone else had gone off on new topic of "Where is the craziest place you've done it?" Su, of course, won by doing it in a tree, don't ask me how she managed that feat, but undoubtedly some love spell was involved:

"You know, Matty…" Viv whispered to me about the time Su was explaining the delicate act of balancing one buttock on a tree branch, "I saw the way you were after Darling got through with you—sorry, hon, but you were a mess."

Great.

Then she went on, "It takes a witch's intuition to read a guy like Sebastian, so I'd say he's falling for you."

Hmm, seems to me Viv does not know about future-husband-and-father-of-my-two-boys-and-a-girl part of the story.

She kept talking. "It couldn't have been easy for him to see you in that state. It wasn't easy for any of us."

Try being me!

And she kept right on going.

"I think he's controlling himself, trying to stay cool so he can protect you. After seeing you like that, not to mention seeing how well you'd done protecting your Spellbound, well, as you know, magic like that is seriously seductive."

Er, no, I didn't know.

"Anyway," she forged on, "even the strongest man can lose control in the face of that. You know, the whole glamour of danger, glorying in life, celebrating your victory, seduced by your magic thing. I don't think he intended to move that fast, although I do think he intended to make a move…just not that fast. Now he's backing off. I may be wrong, but that's what I think."

Viv's so clever.

I asked BecBec later before I poured myself into bed, and she just said, "Eee…eeeeeee, eeh, eiyah," then she giggled.

Whatever.

~

4 May

Finally!

They sure have taken their freakin' time.

The Witches Council contacted me, sent a rolled-up piece of lilac-colored, homemade paper wrapped in a black satin ribbon.

Very dramatic.

It said:

On 14 May (the day after my birthday, by the way), at 23:45, Mathilda Guinevere Honeycutt will be tested for Potency of Magical Powers and Craft Integrity. These trials will be conducted at Ladye Bay by Endora Eccles (The Lady) and Seraphina Dingle (The Maiden).

As is custom, The Hag will rule.

Witch Honeycutt can bring her wand or athame (one or the other, not both), her cloak, her broom and one confederate, one familiar and one other.

Kind Regards,

The Witches Council

(Prunella Craddock, The Hag)

~

5 May

Beltane today.

Not too into the festival of fertility, love, union, yadda yadda, yadda.

BecBec is all crazy about it, made me decorate my tree with bright-colored ribbons (seemed to get happy vibes from tree so maybe not a bad idea).

Everyone else did the celebrating as well as the petal action in their sacred circles and then scattered them in the wood, around The Gables, The Dozen and the school, etcetera. (Couldn't do it personally due to magical suspension.)

The petals give a little extra protection.

I guess, every little helps.

~

14 May

My birthday was yesterday.

The Good:

Presents (favorites noted):

Mavis: My own personal flying broomstick decorated with pink, blue and purple ribbons.

Viv (always super gift-giver): Fab, oversized, Jackie O sunglasses.

Lucy: The *Practical Magic* DVD. "Mate," she said, "I'm not stupid."

The Bad:

Josie: St. Jude medallion.

"We have our kind of protection too," she said.

"But he's the Patron Saint of Lost Causes," I said.

She shrugged.

Ack!

The Ugly:

Was sitting under my tree (Beltane decorations looked kinda raggedy so had to get rid of them), taking Eleanora's advice and meditating and communing with nature.

(Really escaping Gables where Nerissa had made a little mistake that caused a big explosion and I made the decision that I should be somewhere where I could breathe.)

Was wearing my birthday present to myself—lush mushroom velour yoga bottoms with powder-blue satin drawstring (low riders) and powder-blue cami with satin ribbon threaded through to tiny bow at the vee in my cleavage (sweet). Plus zippered velour track top and blue ribbed skull-cap (with sequins knitted in—fab!) because warm weather mysteriously gone with April and now only watery-cold-sunlight. Blech.

I felt him before I saw him, but I kept my eyes shut anyway.

When he got close enough, I said, "Well, if it isn't the brilliant Dr. Aidan Knightly Seymour."

"Hey, birthday girl," he said and kissed me on the nose.

A little surprised at the kiss, and felt really nice (as in *really*) but I still didn't open my eyes.

"How did you discover my middle name?" he asked.

"Me and the girls, doing a little bit of research these days."

"Mm," he mumbled.

Yowza.

Him saying "mm" all deep and both approving and disapproving sounded super-sexy.

Best open eyes.

So I did, saw he still looked hot as ever, and I noted, "No longer indisposed, I see."

"No."

He was standing, leaning his back against a tree and staring down his nose at me.

Fancy, schmancy blokes who stare down their nose at you—damn them all the hell.

I stayed still (even though I wanted to get up and kick him on the shin), legs crossed, hands resting on my knees with palms up and fingers relaxed.

Calm and centered. (Ha!)

"Where were you?" I asked.

"Can't say. Sorry, Matty."

"Hmm. Somewhere where your mobile doesn't work."

"Yes."

Oh.

Wasn't expecting that answer.

Or any answer.

"Okay then..."

I closed my eyes again and pretended to ignore him.

He sighed. "I see you're cross with me."

It was my turn to mumble, "Mm."

Silence.

Then.

More silence.

Okay, so I couldn't keep my mouth shut.

Patience is a virtue I just *do not* have. All right?

I opened my eyes and scrambled to my feet.

"The last time I saw you," I said, jabbing my finger in his direction, "I was passing out due to being *struck by lightning*! Three times! Crack! Bang! *Sizzle!* Since then, no word, no call, no get-well card, no checking up on me, no nothing!"

"Matty, I knew you were fine. Dr. Bennett told me, and I do happen to be your watcher."

"Well, do you have to watch so friggin' quietly and from so far away?" I snapped.

He grinned.

Fucking grins.

"Sorry, darling. Unfortunately, most of the time, particularly when you or your Spellbounds aren't in mortal danger, they do prefer me to watch quietly and from far away."

It was the "darling" that got me.

Being called darling is very hot.

Man, oh man.

I'm a slut.

I was lusting after someone else when the father of my children was probably wrapping my present right now (he'd better be or I was never going to speak to him again).

"Listen, Aidan—" I started.

"I've got a birthday surprise for you. But you have to come to my place to get it."

What?

Was he nuts?

"Well, as much as I'd like to pop to Cambridge to get my birthday present, there's a party for me tonight—"

"Your present isn't at my place in Cambridge. It's at my place on Wellington Terrace."

What?

"*What?*" I semi-shrieked.

"I have a place in town." Another grin. "Where do you think I go after a difficult night of following you around?"

He was flirting again.

And he lived in the town.

And he was following me around at night.

Ack!

(I cast my mind back to what I did last night, then remembered it was Karaoke Night at the pub and my choice was "Greased Lightnin'." Ulk!)

Great Goddess, I'll shoot him (if I'm ever able to do magic again).

Though, you must admit, I kinda had to go because a) wanted to scope out where he lived and b) he had a present for me (yay!).

He had "a place on Wellington Terrace" all right.

Georgian detached right on the cliff, lots of happy clematis clinging to the house and the arbor in front, lots of room, somewhat modern and minimalistic decor that was dark and masculine and looked like a page out of a John Lewis catalogue, unrestricted view of the channel—which meant unrestricted view of The Gables on the outcrop—big, probably seriously powerful telescope on patio with which to spy on me at The Gables.

"Nice," was all I would allow myself to say (still kinda peeved).

Really was more than nice, was fucking fabulous.

Man, oh man.

This was hard, knowing I'd spend my life married to Ash but still, somehow, so attracted to Aidan.

Life sucked.

Aidan ordered, "Wait there."

Then he left the room.

I stared at The Gables, and I think I saw a small ball of flame shoot out of one of the windows.

"Nerissa," I whispered.

"What?" It was Aidan, he was back and (I couldn't believe it) carrying a little, fluffy, sweet black kitty with green eyes and a pink satin bow around its neck.

"Kitty!" I shouted and ran across the room.

Somehow, the kitty didn't totally freak at me rushing it and it jumped into my arms, mewing and cuter than buttons.

"Kitty, kitty, kitty!" I cried, cuddling its soft, kitty fur to my face. "You're so cute. I want to eat you up!"

Yay!

I gave it a big nuzzle and kissed its nose.

And then I burst into tears.

(I'm psycho!)

My wet eyes turned to a watery (but still hot) Aidan.

"Oh, Aidan, thank you." And I had to stop because my throat closed and I made that horrible crying gulp you make when you talk and cry at the same time.

"Hey now," he said softly, putting his arms around me and the kitty. "Hey," he whispered. "Every witch needs a familiar. It's just a cat, darling, nothing to get all worked up about."

He called me darling again. (Sob.)

I wish he'd quit calling me darling! (Sob, sob.)

"You don't..." I hiccupped, "understand."

His arms gave me a warm squeeze and his voice was also warm when he said quietly, "Calm down, get to know your new familiar. I'll go get us a drink."

Then he let me go and left the room to go get us a drink.

I petted kitty, immediately named her Daphne (always wanted a fluffy, black cat with green eyes named Daphne and there she was) and wondered how I was going to let Aidan down gently.

He was back with two tall elegant glasses of champagne.

Champagne.

On my birthday.

I loved champagne.

He was so smooth, so handsome, so *everything*.

He handed me a glass and I dropped Daphne so she could explore.

Then he got close and whispered, "Happy Birthday."

Then he kissed my lips softly, saluted me with his glass and I blurted...

(Perhaps stupidly, but I didn't know how to go about it. *You* try being in this situation.)

"I'm getting married to Ash."

His glass stopped halfway to his mouth.

Gone was flirty, charming Aidan.

In the blink of an eye...vanished.

I could swear he looked...

Well...

Dangerous.

"I beg your pardon?" he asked low.

Definitely dangerous.

"Um, well, Ash and I were..." I started.

His eyes narrowed.

Eek!

I kept trying. "That is we, er...had a little conversation, um..."

I trailed off.

And I did this because Aidan had started walking toward me.

Not exactly walking...

More like...

Stalking.

And I started moving backwards.

I tried again. "The thing is, we...he, well...um...he told me that we were prophesied to get married and have three kids."

Aidan stopped stalking.

And then he turned and threw his champagne flute into the fireplace where it shattered into a million pieces.

I stood stock-still and stared in the fireplace.

"Is that so?" he asked.

Eek!

Getting the distinct impression that Aidan didn't like the idea of me married to Ash.

"Yes, er…" I kept looking at the fireplace, "two boys and a girl."

Heavy, awful silence.

Then, he said, "Well, that *is* surprising."

I dared a glance, considering his voice had gone weirdly calm.

Voice may sound calm but his eyes seethed.

~

An aside:

Somehow—due to my scary Bad Choice in Men Gene—Aidan was turning me on now more than he'd ever turned me on before.

And he turned me on a good deal before.

Great.

Lovely.

Just what I bloody-well needed.

~

"I was under the impression it was two girls and a boy," he stated conversationally.

What!?

"*What?!*"

"Oh yes, as the Mathilda Scholar, I'm pretty sure I have it right. Let's see, I remember, and of course I have a photographic memory, it was in 1457 when Baroness Simone de Clare, a great prophetess, said, 'Mathilde will bind herself to an intelligent man who watches and protects her…he will give her three children, one male, two females.'"

He was stalking again.

And, in my retreat, I was running out of room.

I knew this because my back slammed against the wall.

He kept coming.

"Well, if you know then why are you so angry?" I asked softly.

Uh, not the right thing to say.

"And in 1065," he said in a voice that can only be described as glacial, "Althreg of Thanet said, and I'm paraphrasing, no need to get into *Beowulf* territory, 'Three children, The Chosen One called Mathylde will have, two wytches and a protector, sired by a man of great words, a man who sees, a man who guards."

He'd made it to me and put a hand on the wall on either side of me.

"Okay then," I whispered, head tipped up to look at him.

"And it was the Sorceress Gertrude who said —"

"Okay then!" I shouted this time. "I get it. I get it. Two girls and a boy. Jeez."

I mean, this was hard enough already!

Aidan stared at me, clearly pissed off.

"You see, Mathilda," Uh-oh. He never called me Mathilda. "It isn't Ash who will father your children…it's me."

Ack!

Ackity, ack, ack.

Then he stepped in that eensiest bit more so I could feel the heat of his body; his chest brushed mine, his hand came up and he lifted my chin gently so I'd look at him.

"I'm prophesied to marry you and give you three children, two witches and a protector, *Société*-speak that, better known to you as a boy."

I gulped.

How to handle this?

Um.

Um.

Think, Matty, think.

"Um, well, Aidan…" I hoped my voice was sweet, conciliatory, "it kinda sounds like it could be either you *or* Ash."

"Mm," he murmured, so close, I could feel the vibration.

Oh me.

"Yes, that's right." His voice was getting warmer, almost, one could say, *hot*. "It does sound that way."

Oh my.

"But, I prefer to believe it will be me."

At that moment, I kinda did too.

He smiled.

It was a fan-fucking-tastic smile, not because it was Aidan's usual flirty grin, but because it was very scary, very sexy and *very* dangerous.

I was fucked.

"Wilding and I, not to mention the Directors and the Elders, agreed —" he started.

Who?

What?

Agreed?

They agreed!?

"What are you talking about?" I asked.

Somehow, with no space to move in, he managed to get even closer.

"Wilding and I had an agreement before you moved to the UK. The Directors of The Institute and the Elders of *Le Société* arranged it." Yikes! "It was about how he and I would handle you and our involvement with you."

Yikes Part Deux.

Handle me?

Aidan kept speaking. "And Wilding and I agreed to what the Elders and Directors decided."

"Which was?" I prompted when he said no more.

"Well, for one thing, it didn't include telling you what Wilding told you."

Uh-oh.

"So, Ash isn't fighting fair," I concluded.

Sounded like him.

"The operative word, darling…"

Oo, "darling" again. "Darling" in scary, dangerous, sexy voice too.

My.

"Is 'fighting.'"

"Why is that the operative word?"

"Because, before, we'd decided to handle this situation like gentlemen, agreements and working cooperatively through our own particular organizations."

"And now?" I asked.

"Now, I don't feel very cooperative."

Oh…*my.*

"So, um…what now?"

I'd hoped he'd say something like, "This…" and ravish me (yes, I'm a slut, I know I'm a slut, at that delicious point, I didn't care that I was a slut).

But he didn't.

He just stood there, his body pressed against mine, and stared at me, then got his face real close, so close his lips were nearly touching mine.

His eyes dropped to my mouth and he was so…very…close that I could see how thick and lush his lashes were.

Oh me, oh my...ohmeohmyoh.

"Now?" he whispered.

Great Mother Earth, I think I was about to have another Big O just listening to him, and the look in his eyes made my knees buckle.

And my nipples swell.

Yikes!

"Well, now...I take you home and then the games begin."

~

And that was it.

He took Daphne and me home.

No ravishing.

Not even a birthday kiss.

I didn't even get to finish my champagne.

And then he roared off.

In his BMW.

To let the games begin.

How scary is that?

I mean, what does that *mean*?

(I knew what it meant but, um...Yikes!)

~

By the way:

Ash bought me a car.

Yes.

A car.

A red Mini Cooper convertible with the cooler-than-cool COOPER over the back, middle brake light.

It's kickass.

It's really "from the Elders" (okay, excuse me? so who are these Elders all of a sudden?) as I couldn't be seen in Ole Purple after Ash shot at someone with a gun (seriously illegal in the United Kingdom, it's not like this is South Central or even Deer Season Arkansas) while reversing down Marine Parade. The Elders feel Ash may have made a bit of a "scene" (no fucking kidding? —only front page of *The Mercury*) and Ole Purple won't soon be forgotten.

Ash, personally, didn't get me anything.

And, on top of that, he frowned on Daphne.

"The last thing you need is a cat," he declared.

Hmm.

Let the games begin, indeed.

Holy Crap.

~

By the way, the test is tonight.

And I haven't even studied.

~

16 May

Magical suspension lifted.

The W.C. can't find Agatha Darling and since they now consider me "registered," feel it may be too dangerous to my person to interfere with my training. (Great.)

The test wasn't the easiest thing I've ever done (not by a long shot), but no one struck me with lightning either.

But get this:

Am to be registered with the Council as:

Class: Sage, Level: Hazardous.

I mean, what's that supposed to mean? Level: Hazardous?

~

This is unprecedented. Or so Mavis said over and over again to everyone (they were all awake and all at The Gables and all waiting for our return) at about four thirty in the morning—about six hours after I wanted to be in bed.

This is also further proof that I am *The* Mathilda not just *A* Mathilda.

So, even though I don't exactly want the word to get out (as have enough troubles without verified Chosen One status announced to all and sundry), it's to be printed in the monthly W.C. newsletter as a matter of record.

I'm fucked.

In oh so many ways.

Of course, being classed as a Sage was B-I-G, Big.

True Sages were people like Prunella, who were three hundred years old and had seen it, done it and had about three billion T-shirts.

But since my magic was "off the scales" and they didn't have anything else to class me, they put me at Sage.

The Lady didn't seem too happy. (Gotta keep an eye on her.)

The W.C. is going to consider a new ranking system, of course, because even though I was officially a Sage, I was lacking the experience to be a "true Sage."

"Perhaps we can call her a 'Neophyte Sage,'" Endora offered (somewhat sarcastically, if you ask me).

I think I've told you how I feel about the word "Neo"—I certainly didn't want it connected to me.

~

Confused?

Let me help:

Young witches start serious Magical Training somewhere within the year they start their period.

Witch moms know when their daughters are about to "become women" (magic, nature, woman's intuition, etcetera). So they'll plan the training to begin either a few months before or after the first cycle (depending on family tradition).

This meant, that by my age, the Honeycutt tradition and the time my period started, I should have already had 20 years of training.

You start at Tenderfoot. (All witches before their periods are given the class of Tenderfoot—they have powers, even experiment with them, but are not yet taught to harness them in any real way, like being taught to speak but not learning to read until much later.)

Then the Rankings (or Classes) go like this:

Level One: Practitioner (at start of training or at start of your monthly cycle).

Then you move through the upper levels of:

Level Two: Proficient (somewhere in your twenties/thirties).

Advanced Magic (or Magical License—when you're allowed to

create your own spells and use them, or have your own Spellbounds and guard them without guidance).

Level Three: Adept (Su).

Level Four: Mistress (where Viv and Mom were—very advanced for Viv but she was always an over-achiever).

Level Five: Natural (Gran).

Level Six (top level): Sage (Mavis and Me).

So obviously, I am Big Freak.

~

I passed the tests with flying colors.

Mainly they think this happened because I'm The Chosen One, so they think it has always been there, just hibernating.

Not to mention, they said (or Endora did) I wasn't using my magic for twenty years when most witches were, so I had a lot stored up in me.

(Of course, it couldn't be months of reading, studying, reading, practicing, more reading, meditating, reading, communing with nature, reading, ad nauseum and so forth.)

Can't go into detail about the tests. They are very, very secret and had to make blood vow of secrecy (blood vows, by the way, are not real fun) and can't even share it with my Book of Shadows.

~

Anyhoo, just for the record:

Took wand (of course!).

Took Daphne (just so she could have an outing—she was a very good little kitty, minded well and clearly a prodigy mainly because she didn't wander off).

Took my cloak but not my broom (can't fly yet mainly because I'm scared shitless of heights).

My confederate was Mavis.

My other was Lucy (pissed off the W. C. to have a non-magical, non-*Société* person at W.C. Trial, but Lucy totally dug it, even the blood vow business didn't put her off).

~

So now am clear to do what I need to do.
    Though don't know what that is, exactly.
    But am not going to waste time.

The Month of June

3 June

All hell has broken loose.

    Kah-ray-zee.

    I need a vacation. That's what I need. A getaway. Even a long weekend.

Something.

Anything.

Good thing is, have learned to write in journal without actually writing—use magic.

Wish I thought of *that* earlier.

~

So, anyway, what should I tell first?

~

Worcestershire:

Decided to go do a little investigating.

    Some (Ash) would say I was a little cocky after the W.C. Trial went so well.

But I was tired of sitting on my hands.

Am I The Chosen One or what?

I had names, addresses and maps, not to mention a new Mini Cooper.

I wish I could say that the weather was gorgeous, and I could break out my sunnies and put the top down.

Instead, it was cold, misty and miserable and the only thing I dared do was wear flip-flops (in fact, I was going to wear flip-flops even if they killed me, which they very nearly did).

Had the Mini outside The Dozen, my wand in the back waistband of my jeans and my toenails varnished in Ultra-Frost.

Was perfectly willing to go on my own. But, as I was putting my takeaway latte in the cup holder, in my mirror I noticed Lucy straggling down the seafront pavement looking for her morning caffeine fix.

I was just going to poke around in Worcestershire, maybe (just maybe) swing by Althea Appleton's house. No harm bringing Lucy, right?

So, I asked her to come.

As we got Lucy's double espresso installed in her cup holder, Su surprised us by crashing out of the side door of the beat-up VW van parked next to us.

"What're you two up to?" she asked.

Figured, if we could find a toothbrush along the way, having the extra firepower of Su couldn't hurt.

Su left her boy toy snoring in the VW, grabbed a chai and then, as we were about ready to roll, Josie came stalking out of The Dozen.

"Where are you going?" she demanded.

Before any of us could answer, off she was on a tangent about how she was always left out, left behind, everyone thought she was weak, meek little Josephine and couldn't take care of herself.

I was still feeling guilty for the whole scene with Mom's door blast, so Su and I quickly conjured a kickass protection spell bubble (thank goddess for that, it came in handy later) for Josie and Lucy and off we went on our merry way.

To this day I will defend my decision to take Lucy and Josie along. I mean, sure, we were all in danger, but if it weren't for them, Su and I'd be, well…it doesn't bear thinking about.

∽

So, off we went playing tunes on my new pink iSkinned iPod (to go with my new Mini Cooper) blasting away some Guns 'n' Roses ("Take meeee home, yeah, yeah." Axl Rose may be crazy as a jaybird but he's the rockin' shit, and I'm sorry, but you take off that stupid hat and push back Slash's hair, that man's hot.)

~

Anyway.

~

People don't have a lot of good things to say about Birmingham.

I have a one-word retort: Selfridges.

And not the scary, shoulder-to-shoulder shopping nightmare that is the Selfridges on Oxford Street, no—a somewhat sedate, shopping extravaganza.

(Okay, so we were supposed to be investigating in Worcestershire, that isn't far from Birmingham, a girl has to get in the mood. And anyway, Josie needed some new MAC lipglass. And Lucy was going to splash out on that Billy Bag she'd been dithering about for ages. And once I saw that rock and roll, long, thin, fringed scarf—well, it went with the Guns 'n' Roses!)

~

We cruised by Agatha Darling's house.

Not much to say, really. An old manor, tucked in a hillside outside of Worcester. Just stately and such, none of the personality of The Gables.

Had the look about it that said, "No one home."

We popped by the houses of a few of the Edwards Coven.

Knocked on a few doors.

No one around.

Everyone gone.

Probably all out somewhere rigging wands to shoot out acid or something.

Finally, since it all seemed such a dud, decided just to swing round to Althea Appleton's house. Just scope it out…get the lay of the land.

That was it.

I swear (ish).

~

By the way, I do know what an oracle is. I've seen *The Matrix*, as I think I may have already mentioned.

It's just that oracles, in the witch world, are few and far between.

There are loads of seers, prophets, clairvoyants, etcetera.

But oracles are witches that not only see what is happening elsewhere in the present *and* can tell the future, but *also* are prophetesses who are the mouthpieces for the gods and goddesses.

Well, those folks are thin on the ground, let me tell you.

I'm not real certain I wanted to know what the goddesses had to say to me but I figured after lightning from Agatha Darling, Witch Trials at Ladye Bay and being the Object of Whatever in the Battle of Ash and Aidan, I could handle it.

~

Althea Appleton lived in a little, country cottage secluded in a lovely, peaceful glade.

It had its own babbling brook and a riot of beautiful white wisteria climbing all over it. It looked older than time, made of stone that bulged here and there but somehow still held the building together. It even had a thatched roof.

It was the kind of place Sleeping Beauty would dance about gracefully while birds, squirrels and rabbits followed her and stared at her with rapt adoration.

Or it was the kind of place that a crazy old lady would cook a couple of kids in pies.

And it was deserted. No car, no dog, no cat, no movement—no nothing.

Completely still.

So, no harm going up and knocking on the door, right?

Which is what I did.

Su stayed behind with Lucy and Josie, keeping an eye (and wand) out.

I had my wand out too.

And just like in practically every horror film ever made, the moment I knocked on the door, it creaked open, slowly and weirdly.

I looked back at the car.

"Get back here," Josie hissed (the voice of reason, that, in the throes of the temporary lunacy that precedes certain death, no one ever listens to).

"What if the old lady's hurt, passed out, had a stroke?" Lucy asked (ah yes, the somewhat plausible but still completely mad explanation as to why the innocents walk, of their own free will, into the jaws of hell).

Su, being Su, shrugged.

Shit, fuck and everything in between.

~

According to our research, Althea Appleton was two hundred and three years old. She had a "fit" in 1877 and another in 1895, both of which, under modern medicine, could be classed as strokes. She was diagnosed with diabetes in 1941. Under healer's orders, after a heart valve replacement (that caused the cardiac surgeons to ask some uncomfortable questions and sent the Edwards Coven scurrying for some serious document-forging-magic), she retired last year.

Out of the witch business.

Out of the oracle business.

Could be, she was in there, dead or dying.

~

Shit, fuck and everything in between.

~

I took charge.

"You two, get in the car, lock the doors, start the engine and wait for us to come out," I bossed Lucy and Josie. "Su, you come with me."

Su didn't even hesitate (always up for an adventure, my Su).

"What are you, nuts? Get back here," Josie hissed again.

"Don't be such a mom," Su teased as she walked casually to the cottage.

"Don't be stupid!" Josie napped, coming toward us.

"Listen!" I walked back to the car. "Lucy could be right. The woman is two hundred and three years old!"

"Wait," Lucy said, looking around the glade, "I'm changing my mind."

Great.

"So, call the police," Josie suggested logically.

"I can't!" (Me, not logically)

"Why not?" (Josie)

"Because she's a two hundred and three-year-old witch! Just...calm down, get in the car. We'll be out before you know it." (Me)

"I don't like this." (Josie)

"Oh, pipe down, Mom Unit. She's The Chosen One, for goddess's sake. Give her a little credit." (Su, as ever, the diplomat)

We went in, careful, quiet, stealthy.

It was a cottage from a movie. I swear to the goddess, if a hobbit bobbed out of the kitchen smoking a thin pipe, it wouldn't have surprised me.

"This place is cool beans, man. I want to live in a place like this when I grow up."

I could see Su dinging around in a crumbling, flower-covered cottage, smoking pot and making brownies with her male harem.

We checked the downstairs and it was deserted.

There was a rickety, wooden staircase against the front inside of the house that led to the upstairs, and Su and I stood at the base of it, staring up.

"You go first." (Su)

"Why do I have to go first? You go first." (Me)

"You're The Chosen One." (Su)

"Yes, so if something's up there, you can act as my human shield." (Me)

"Nice." (Su)

"Kidding." (Me)

"No you weren't." (Su)

"Yes I was." (Me)

"No—" (Su)

"Shh!" (Me)

We both stared up the stairs.

"Okay, I'll go first. Wand ready?" (Me, looking to my sister)

Su nodded.

Up I went, stair by creaky-ass stair.

I don't know why I went so slowly. The stairs were so damn loud if there was anyone up there they could hear me coming, no sweat.

What we saw at the top was what we'd feared.

Old lady down.

"Shit." (Su)

She was sprawled on the floor, all two hundred pounds of her, just one foot on the bed.

I felt for a pulse but then realized I didn't know how to feel for a pulse.

Su pushed me out of the way and felt for one, then she leaned down and put her ear to the old lady's mouth.

"Pulse is strong and she's breathing okay," she declared.

Su lifted up one of her eyelids.

"Euw," I said.

Then the old lady burped.

Not a pleasant sound.

And an even worse smell.

"She's drunk," Su said, getting out of her crouch position.

Blam! Blam! Blam!

Ack!

Gunshots—right through the window.

Ack!

Su and I dove for cover.

"Crap, crap, crap," said Su.

"Josie and Lucy are out there!" I said.

"Crap, crap, crap," repeated Su.

"Who's shooting at us?" I asked.

"I don't know! How would I know?" Su shouted.

Okay, calm down, Matty, calm down.

W.W.A.D?

What would Ash do?

Not a good question, as Ash wouldn't be there in the first place.

"Su…" I hesitated, still thinking.

"Uh…yeah, I'm here. Where'm I gonna go?"

"You, me, protection spell." I was making those jerky hand motions the Navy Seals do in the movies, like I was guiding a plane in for landing. Soon I was going to be using words like "click" and "vector." "We grab the old woman and we hightail it to the car."

Su stared at me like I'd grown another head.

Then she stated, "Okay, sorry to tell you this, Miss Prodigy, but magic deflecting bullets, not…gonna…happen."

"Yes, but how about an invisibility glamour?" I asked.

"How about, we leave the bitty behind, get our asses to the Mini and get the fuck out of here?" Su shot back.

"They might be after her."

"Why?"

"She's an oracle. She can tell the future, the gods talk to her, why else? Do we want the bad guys to have her? I don't think so!"

~

Okay, so, Su + me x Scary Situation = Disaster.

~

"This is what we do," I declared. "Get Althea down the stairs. I'll go to the window and throw some magic out there to freak them out while you conjure an invisibility glamour and we can hope and pray that Josie and Lucy are okay." And not dead, lying in pools of their own blood, victims of my stupidity.

"I still don't see why we can't leave the old bitty behind," Su bitched.

"We need to take her."

"Why?" she asked.

"Let's just call it intuition."

Su grumbled, I grabbed Althea under her armpits and, giving in, Su grabbed her feet.

~

Ever go down a flight of stairs carrying something heavy, wearing flip-flops?

You know the soft *flip…flop* sound that flip-flops make when you're casually walking down the street?

Well, when you walk down the stairs carrying something heavy, they make more of a *FLIP!…FLOP!* sound—slapping against the soles of your feet, loud enough to wake the dead.

And let the bad guys know exactly where you are.

So, this is how it went:

FLIP! FLOP! FLIP! FLOP!

BLAM! BLAM! BLAM!

(Dust and broken mortar flying hither and yon as bullets slam into the stone outside of house by stairwell.)

FLIP! FLOP! FLIP! FLOP!

BLAM! BLAM! BLAM!

(More dust, more debris—you get the picture.)

"Crap, crap, crap!" Su shouted when we'd finally made it to the bottom of the stairs. She dumped Althea unceremoniously on the floor.

"Careful!" I shouted.

"She's lived for two hundred and three years! This is not gonna hurt her!" Su shouted back.

"Just get the invisibility spell ready!"

Su tore through the cottage, grabbing magickal supplies, tossing herbs this way, seeds that way, wrapping feathers with pentagrams and swinging them around, rubbing oil on her temples, my temples, Althea's temples.

Then she started muttering to herself, mutters turned to rhymes, rhymes turned to chanting.

I did my own bit, threw some magical blobs. There were some explosions, some loud noises, rustling, crackles. The baddies went to investigate.

Then we grabbed Althea and off we went.

Flip-flops, as you may or may not know, have no traction.

They have a smooth sole.

Not exactly the proper footwear to utilize when traversing a wet lawn, carrying a two hundred and three-year-old, two-hundred-pound, drunken oracle, under an invisibility glamour that depends on your partner's magical concentration.

Slip…Slide…

Crash!

And Su, Althea and I went down, ten feet from the Mini.

"We're dead," Su said as the glamour disappeared.

And indeed, it seemed we were as the baddies turned and aimed.

Then, *vroom, vroom!*

The Mini started up in a thunder of revving engine and surged forward, zooming toward the men.

The men stared at the Mini in shock (which to their eyes was uninhabited due to the protection spell Su and I had put on Josie and Lucy). They scattered and ran for their lives as the Mini chased them around the glade.

It then turned, came swooshing, fish-tailing and vrooming back and skidded to a halt close to us.

Get in!" shouted Lucy, throwing open the door.

We managed to shove Althea into the back (she must have been seriously liquored up to go through all that without waking), and I took the wheel from Josie a split second before the guns starting blazing again.

Four women in a Mini was okay (barely).

Five of them, too much.

Way too much.

Miraculously, the bullets missed my Mini, which escaped the scene without a scratch.

~

Needless to say, our arrival home was not heralded with streamers streaming and champagne corks popping.

In fact, this is what happened:

I caught sight of the Lush Jag in my rearview mirror somewhere in Gloucestershire.

Althea had awoken and was kinda pissed off that she'd been kidnapped.

(Understatement.)

And more pissed off that she was squished in the back between Josie and Su.

The Lush Jag kept its distance the entire way home.

A controlled distance.

But I got the impression it was a barely controlled distance.

When we stopped the car in The Gables, my posse and I sat transfixed watching as Ash slowly unfolded himself from the driver's seat of the Jag.

And then, after we got out of the Mini, they deserted me, without a word and without remorse, guiding the teetering Althea into The Gables.

Ash stood, hip resting against the Jag, arms crossed on his chest, adding this time his feet crossed at the ankles.

I was not bamboozled by his casual stance.

I stood my ground, feeling (somewhat) safe with the Mini between us.

After I realized I was going to lose the staring contest, I gave a bit of a wave and said a (damn it all) feeble, "Hey."

"What the fuck did you think you were doing?"

Er, okay, so it was good to know that Ash *was* mad and I had not misjudged the situation.

"Well, I—"

"If you ever even *think* of doing something so fantastically idiotic again, when you get back, I'll find you, drag you somewhere very remote and chain you somewhere very uncomfortable. Do you understand me?"

So…damn…bossy!

And, I'll add, *threatening*.

Me…no…*likey*!

"Don't talk to me like I'm a child!" I stamped my foot, yes, like a child but can you imagine the adrenaline going through my body? Someone shot at me! I couldn't be responsible for my own stupidity at that point. And therefore, being really stupid, I charged around the Mini toward Ash. "I'm fine, they're fine, everything is fine!"

"Stop," he said in a voice that would normally have stopped me but just then, it didn't. "You come any nearer to me, Mathilda, I won't be responsible for what I do."

I finally stopped, crossed my arms (two could play that game) and leaned my torso back.

Then I taunted, "Yeah? What? Are you gonna spank me?"

Bad idea.

He pushed away from the Jag and came toward me.

"Don't tempt me," he warned.

I started toward him again.

"I'm a thirty-four-year-old woman, Ash, with responsibilities."

We stopped, barely a foot apart, Ash's face lethal.

"And you took one of those responsibilities into danger today, Mathilda. You nearly got your Spellbound killed and your sister and your friend *and* yourself. Have you lost your mind?"

"Of course not!"

"You could have fooled me."

"Listen, Ash—"

"Don't do it again."

"Try and stop me."

We were head-to-head by then, him standing angrily over me and me standing belligerently under him.

Another staring contest.

"You're so damn bossy," I said, because I couldn't take it anymore.

"I'm quite serious, Mathilda, you do that again and I won't be responsible for my actions."

With that he walked away.

Gah!

~

And then…

A couple of strong cups of coffee later, I stood in the Plush Parlor talking to Althea with Ash standing (very close) behind me, wearing his broody face.

"Why am I here?" Althea asked.

"We came to your cottage to talk to you then men started shooting at you. We had to get you to a safe place," I said.

"They weren't shooting at me, fool, they were shooting at you." (Althea)

Fool?

Nice.

"Well, even if they were shooting at me, they didn't seem to care who in the house they hit, including you." (Me)

She grumbled but she did it uttering no distinct words.

"And, until we know what's happening, you're safer here." (Me)

Ash's hand settled on the small of my back, his fingers curling into the waistband of my jeans.

"He thinks it's not such a good idea, having a member of the Edwards Coven staying at The Gables." (Althea)

"You're right, I don't." (Ash)

She cackled. Honestly, I swear to the goddess, she *cackled*.

"The Wilding Men. Always been spare of word, abundant of honesty. Bodes well for you, lass." (Althea)

"Not when you're asking if your butt looks big in a pair of jeans, it doesn't." (Me)

She cackled, again.

The cackles were loopy, and I guessed it definitely was a cottage where she cooked kids in pies, not the other sort.

"Do you know where Agatha Darling is?" (Ash)

Humph. Butting in on my interrogation.

"No." (Althea)

"Do you know who made that wand for her?" (Me)

"She got her wand in a ceremony, just as you did." (Althea)

"Not the magical one, the one that plugs into the wall and shoots out electricity." (Me)

Her eyes widened for a brief moment before she smacked her lips together and said, "I need a drink."

"I do too."

I was shocked to hear Ash agree with her but not so shocked when he guided me out of the room by using his hand, my belt and my jeans.

Very seriously horning in on my interrogation.

"I don't like it, her staying here." (Ash)

"I didn't ask you." (Me)

Staring.

Then a deep sigh. (Ash)

"I hope you know what you're doing," he said in a way that stated he thought I didn't.

With that, he walked away.

The next time I saw him, he was back in the Plush Parlor sipping whisky with Althea and she was three sheets gone.

I put Paulina and Octavia on to protecting The Gables against Althea and went to the Tower Room.

The day hadn't been tremendously successful (by a long shot) so there was work to be done.

~

The Dinner Party:

Some ungodly hour the next morning, Viv was shaking my shoulder telling me to get up, *phelf, phlaf, phloof.*

(I didn't hear what she said because I turned over and put a pillow over my head.)

Then, later, Mom was shaking my shoulder.

"Get up! Aidan's been waiting in the sitting room for twenty minutes!"

Aidan?

I looked at the clock.

It was six fifty-two in the bloody morning.

Six.

Fifty.

Two.

In the a.m.

Who came for a visit at that hour?

I got up, ignored my robe, ignored my slippers, ignored my comb *and* brush and stomped down the stone stairs and charged into the sitting room.

Aidan was standing by the fireplace looking like a Kenneth Cole advertisement (without the gayness).

"What?" I snapped.

He turned to me and smiled.

I was wearing the aforementioned defensive end's jersey that he left behind when he dumped me (well, perhaps he didn't *exactly* leave it behind, more like it found itself stuffed behind my chest of drawers until I knew he was well and truly gone, and then I meant to burn it but ended up using it as a nightshirt). It was oversized, over-washed and absolutely comfy.

I ignored the smile and asked, "Do you know what bloody time it is? It's before bloody seven in the bloody morning! I was up until bloody goddess knows when, bloody-well working on saving the world…"

In about two strides, he crossed the room, grabbed me, hauled me into his arms, held me close to his body and kissed me.

Hard.

And wet.

None of the sweet, professorial mucking about, but straight into the juicy, heady, full-on lip and tongue action.

Oh. My. Goddess.

Yum-*mee*.

He lifted his head. "I'll be back tonight at seven. I'm taking you to a dinner party. It's evening dress. Will you be able to do that?"

Er, wha'?

I was still reeling from the kiss; my arms were still around his neck, my fingers still in his hair, my body still flat against his. My jersey was up around my waist and one of his hands was cupping my ass.

Yes, cupping my ass.

And it felt nice.

"Matty?" he prompted.

Ack!

"Evening dress? Like, gowns?" I asked.

"Yes."

I nodded.

Of course I could do evening gowns. I didn't work in retail for twelve years with nothing to show for it.

Then he was off.

What a way to wake up.

~

Fashion Show:

I installed everyone I could find into my little lounge and put on the Versace that took me three months of determined saving, a fifty percent off sale and my twenty-five percent employee discount to afford.

Yays all around (except Althea who shook her head disapprovingly).

Next.

I tried my Ralph Lauren little black dress. It was ready-to-wear but it was fabulous.

Everyone loved it (except Althea who again said not a word but shook her head).

Next.

The Dolce and Gabbana (yes: everyone else, no: Althea, this time with a burp—charming).

Next.

The Vintage Valentino that I'd uncovered at the very back room on the very back rack of a vintage clothing shop. (Yes: everyone else, no: Althea).

Next.

The circa 70s Halston I picked up when my drag queen friend retired (Althea: no).

Gah!

I was running out of evening wear!

It would appear that I would have to pull out all the stops.

I teetered on my vanity stool, pulling the big, shiny box out of the back of the top shelf of the wardrobe.

I unwrapped the layers and layers of tissue and pulled out…
The Chanel.

I'd had to beg, borrow and steal (okay, not steal) to get it. And when I did, I promised myself I'd never wear it. That I would be happy just to own it, just to know it was there.

I didn't want to expose it to the possibility of such common things as sweat, wine spills and snags.

It was too precious for any of that.

But if nothing else would do...

It was matte black, exquisitely heavy, flowing silk. The long skirt was cut on the bias, giving the silk even more personality. Sleeveless with a boat neck, it clung beautifully to the body. At the back, there was a deep V that ended at the base of the spine. There was a simple, not extravagant, gather at the V which flowed down the back of the skirt into the eensy, weensy train.

I swept up my hair and added a tangled choker of slim, sleek, teeny, jet beads.

I put on my black mules that had toes so pointed and heels so stiletto, they could be used as a weapon.

Then I walked into the lounge.

Finally, Althea nodded.

It took the next three hours, eleven phone calls and some hair pulling to find an evening bag that both worked with the dress and held my wand. (Pandora's slim, long, thin beaded number—very posh.)

Sorted.

I opened the door to Aidan when he arrived.

He took one look at me and said, "Nice frock."

Humph.

Nice frock!?

Probably had dinner with Karl Lagerfeld last night or something.

~

The dinner party was in Bath.

Bath is one of the most beautiful cities in the world. It was all built out of this lovely, creamy stone, all of it from the same quarry and its architecture was absolutely regal.

And it had a Prada store.

~

"Aidan!" Douglas Addison said when we'd been admitted into a lovely, large house on Bath's Royal Crescent and escorted into the drawing room.

"Doug," Aidan replied.

All hearty handshakes and me trying to be cool while scanning for Agatha Darling.

"Miss Honeycutt, this is a delightful surprise," Douglas murmured while kissing my fingers. He straightened and turned to Aidan. "Aidan, you didn't tell me you were bringing this ravishing lady." Then his eyes came to me. "You look beautiful."

The last bit was said low and with feeling, for my ears only. Again, not flirty, just a heartfelt compliment.

What was he playing at?

"Let's get you drinks, shall we?" Douglas suggested before I could reply to his compliment and off we went to the bar where I got a real vodka martini in a chilled glass with an olive stuffed with an almond (chic touch).

Aidan and Douglas talked while I continued to try to find her or sense her, whichever worked.

"She's not here and won't be," Aidan whispered in my ear.

I started paying attention to my immediate surroundings to see Douglas was off to welcome more guests, and I turned to Aidan.

"What is this, why are we here?" I asked.

"It's a dinner party," he answered.

"That's lovely, and dinner parties are nice and all, but I've got people shooting at me," I informed him.

"See that person over there?" he asked what I thought was bizarrely while he dipped his head at an Asian dude.

I nodded.

"Chinese Ambassador," Aidan said.

Whoa.

"That lady?" he went on and dipped his head at a woman. "Conservative MP and Foreign Secretary for the Shadow Cabinet."

Holy shit.

"That one?" More dipping of head. "Funded one of the Venezuelan coups of the 90s."

Holy *shit*.

Discreet dip-of-head: "Russian arms dealer."

Another dip-of-head: "Runs an exclusive bordello in Bangkok."

Holy Den of Vipers, Batman!

Last dip-of-head: "Brilliant scientist, or perhaps more interesting to you, someone who could harness enough electricity to shoot a lightning bolt out of what appears to be a wand."

I stared at the little man with a bald patch and a poorly fitting tuxedo.

"You're joking," I breathed.

"No," Aidan replied.

Jeez oh Pete.

What should I do?

Cast a spell?

Zap him to make the rest of his hair fall out?

Or just walk up to him and punch him in the nose?

"Calm down, Matty." Aidan was positioning himself between me and the mad scientist.

I tipped my head back to look up at him. "Okay, I'll ask again, why are we here? Are these your friends?"

"Doug is."

"Is this his house?"

"Leased."

I thought of all the rentals I'd experienced and looked around. I didn't even know you could rent anything this fine. Then I looked back at Aidan.

"Why is Senator Addison here with all these people?" I asked.

"He's a politician, Matty, he's working."

It turned my stomach and excited me, all at the same time.

A gorgeous woman in Gucci sidled up to Aidan and kissed his cheek then she purred, "It's been too long, darling."

I stared.

Fuck me, she was the well-known, anorexic pop princess who'd hit a lull in her career and was cruising on publicity fueled by pictures of her on topless beaches (and other, less savory, photos of her alighting from cars in tight, short skirts with legs spread and no undies, ick).

She didn't say "darling" like Aidan said "darling." To me, her "darling" was far more simpering and fake.

Introductions were made, she and I sized each other up and found each other lacking.

I seriously needed another martini.

Tout de suite.

~

Some rude boyfriend told me this: "Martinis are like nipples, one's not enough and three are too many."

He may have been rude, but it was good advice.

As you may have noticed, I'm not big on taking advice.

~

We eventually went into dinner and Aidan, unfortunately, was seated all the way down the table from me and next to the pop princess. (Grr!)

This, he did not seem to be too bothered about. (Bastard!)

Douglas Addison was at the head of the table, and for some insane reason I was seated to his right. The brilliant scientist dude was across from me.

Okay, so there I was, perfect positioning for anything I wanted to do such as transforming him into a toad or throwing my soup at him.

Instead: introductions, food, wine, small talk, more food, more wine, more small talk, more wine and then more wine.

"So, Mathilda, how are things at your café?" Douglas asked.

"It's a *coffee house* and they're very well, thank you," I answered snottily.

He smiled kindly at me.

Bee-zar.

"Mathilda is a prodigious baker," Douglas told the scientist dude.

"Is that so?" scientist dude said without even attempting to feign interest.

"Oh yes. I've heard her oatmeal cookies are particularly spectacular."

The scientist grunted.

And I thought, perhaps drunkenly, that Addison was taking the mick. I mean, I wasn't an ambassador or an arms dealer or a coup organizer or the madam of a famous brothel, but I could damn well craft a fucking good cookie.

"Are you being funny?" I leaned in to ask. "Because if you are, you aren't."

"No, Mathilda, Aidan told me—"

"Mathilda?" the Scientist dude interrupted as if even after a formal introduction and an hour of conversation my name just seeped into his consciousness. "*Mathilda?*" he repeated.

He was staring at me, the light dawning.

"Yes, 'Mathilda,' that's me," I told him.

His eyes widened, the big dweeb.

Oh hell, I thought, *why not?*

"You're a scientist aren't you? What do you do? Research?"

Martinis are like nipples...

"Er, no."

"Development?"

One is not enough, three too many…

"No…no, I—"

"Oh wait, yes, I've heard about you. Yes, and should I say, your wand worked very well. Congratulations. Very painful." I turned to the man on the other side of me, incidentally, the Russian arms dealer. "That man, with his lovely intellect, used it, not to find a cure for cancer, but instead to make a weapon shaped like a magical wand, but instead it shoots lightning."

The arms dealer looked perhaps a bit too interested.

I turned back to the mad scientist. "You should be proud."

His eyes got bigger.

"I was thinking the other day, I mean, you don't mind suggestions do you?" I asked and didn't wait for an answer. "Anyway," I said, gesturing madly. "Next you should invent one that squirts acid. I think that would be an excellent idea."

His face started to get red.

"Or, wait! How about fire? No, no…bolts of electricity are better than fire, more dramatic. You were smart to go with that. Don't you think?" I asked, turning to the arms dealer.

He spluttered.

"What am I saying? Of course you do."

I then leaned forward to the scientist and drunkenly stage-whispered, "Don't worry, your secret's safe with me." (Hardly, since I'd just told everyone.)

I gave him a big wink and pretended to zip and lock my lips and throw away the key, nearly hitting the dealer with my hand.

I turned to Addison. "Until, that is, the strand of what's left of his hair that I got from his jacket gets into my caldron."

On that, I threw back my head and laughed as insanely as I could muster.

Which was pretty insanely, thank you very much.

Everyone was staring at me.

I didn't care. Mainly because how dirty politicians, flesh peddlers and icky skanks felt about me wasn't high on my priority list.

At this point, I asked a passing server, "Would it be possible if I could I have another martini?"

$\sim$

"Nicely done."

I was alone, having my after-dinner coffee in the back courtyard and wondering if it would act as a magical elixir that would stop me from vomiting when Douglas Addison joined me.

"Mm. Senator Addison," slightly slurring, "as a voting American citizen, may I just say that I'm alarmed at the company you keep."

"Mathilda, my sweet girl, keep your friends close, and your enemies—"

"Closer. I know, but those folks are just, well mostly…um…" At a loss for words I simply said, "Blech."

"Indeed," he agreed on a twitch of his lips.

"What's your association with Agatha Darling?"

Might as well ask.

And anyway, I was shitfaced.

"She's a friend," he answered.

Right.

"Do you know your *friend* kidnapped a young boy who is very close to me, and when I found them, she electrocuted me?"

Okay, I know I was being blunt, but why not? There may be a time to be diplomatic but alone, in a garden, after eating an elegant dinner with some of the dregs of society all wearing designer gear, in other words, proving the world was unfair, and getting blotto was not that time.

And anyway, I'd pulled out *The Chanel.*

For this.

What a disappointment.

I was surprised to see he looked genuinely appalled and maybe a little…could it be…angry?

"No, Mathilda, I didn't know that."

And you know what?

I didn't know whether or not to believe him.

~

Aidan took me home shortly after.

I fell asleep in the car.

Or, perhaps, passed out.

Toe-may-toes, toe-mah-toes.

I awoke just before we arrived and he walked me to the door of The Gables.

"I know I should probably apologize for making a spectacle of myself in front of your friends, but I've got to tell you, your friends leave a lot to be desired."

Maybe I was a tad bit upset because I hadn't particularly enjoyed my second date with a doctor-slash-supernatural watcher-slash-possible future husband and father of my children, and I was definitely still drunk.

I paused, but before he could say anything I continued, "And, if you're trying to woo me, it's not a good idea to try doing it while flirting with a yucky, obvious, fake-tanned skank."

Aidan laughed.

He laughed!

Bastard.

I sure can pick 'em.

"They aren't my friends and you're jealous," Aidan replied.

"If they aren't your friends then why did you take me there?" I asked then added, "And I'm not jealous."

"I took you there because, as The Chosen One, you'll be moving in those circles and you were definitely jealous."

"I will never move in those circles and I...was...not...jealous. Not of that..." I curled a lip, "*thing*. A C-Lister whose next big career move is to be on *Celebrity Big Brother*."

He smiled. "You shouldn't be jealous. Amongst all the people there, you were far and away the most interesting. I think Doug felt the same way."

Mm.

"I don't care what *Doug* thinks. *Doug* is a scary guy."

Aidan smiled. "You don't know the half of it."

Right.

~

By the way, Aidan left after he gave me a kiss on the cheek.

A kiss on the cheek!

Um.

Whatever!

~

18 June

I was walking up Poet's Walk after a morning shift at The Dozen.

I'd passed the turn off to St. Andrew's Church and the creepy-yet-cool-slash-older-than-time graveyard that surrounded it.

I ignored the dog walkers in their wellies, who looked with horror at my high-heeled, cherry-colored go-aheads that click-clacked on the pavement as I walked by.

Lucy had done it again with a walnut and pear salad, with bits of parmesan cheese shaved from hunks freshly chopped from that huge-assed parmesan wheel at the Italian deli on Hill Road.

How was I to compete?

I didn't do salads.

As an update:

Ash, the Numero Uno Grudge Holder, was barely speaking to me.

Aidan had retreated, again.

No sign of Agatha.

No lightning bolts.

No kidnapping.

No new reasons to pull out *The Chanel* (or Versace or Halston, etcetera).

Everyone else was still working on intelligence, protection spells and what had become the hugely popular Witches Dozen Coffee House now that tourist season gripped the seaside.

I walked through the wood thinking of dried cranberries, rocket leaves and gorgonzola and nearly missed my turn off after the donkey's pen into the private footpath to The Gables.

As I made it into the clearing by the greenhouse I saw, sitting on one of Mavis's ornate wicker chairs, Althea, replete with what looked to be one of Gran's famous mint juleps.

"The Chosen One!" she called, lifting her drink to me.

Gluh.

"Anyone shoot at you today?" Althea asked as I approached.

"Not yet," I answered.

And she cackled.

Crazy old coot.

"The day is young," she said.

Great.

Not something you want to hear from someone who sees the future.

"Mint julep?" she asked.

I stopped, my cherry heels sinking into the damp lawn.

The sun was miraculously shining, my shift was done and I had to admit I would never create a salad that would compete with Lucy's.

Further, I hadn't yet had time (or the opportunity since she was mostly drunk) to chat with our loony guest.

What the hell.

"Sure."

Another cackle then she poured me a mint julep.

I sat in the chair beside her, grabbed the drink that was teetering scarily in mid-air (held by her hand), kicked off my go-aheads and put my feet on the little wicker poof that had a yellow and white striped cushion on top.

"How's it hangin'?" I asked Althea.

A slight chuckle came forth but no answer.

"How're you finding it here at The Gables?"

She ignored me, closed her eyes and tipped her face to the sun.

"Enjoying your stay?"

Still nothing.

"Hear from Agatha lately?"

Silence.

"The gods? Goddesses? They talking to you?"

She didn't even move.

"Ring-a-ding ding, 'Hello, this is Hera, the end of the world is nigh.' Anything like that?"

Nothing.

"Have you seen anything interesting, you know, *in your mind*?" I pressed.

She burped.

Then she spoke. "Mm, yes, a fool girl walking the footpaths in high-heeled shoes. You'll wish you didn't when your back goes out on you when you're one hundred and five."

Um, did she see my back go out when I was one hundred and five?

Was I glad that there was an opportunity, maybe, to get to one hundred and five?

I decided to let it go then I asked, "Would you like to go home?"

She opened her eyes and looked at me.

The she muttered, "Home...home, would I like to go home?"

She was so weird.

"Yes, home...you know, the sweet little cottage in the glade..."

where you lure children to their deaths. "Nothing's happened in a while. Maybe you're safe again there."

"I am home, you stupid girl."

I was getting a wee bit tired of the "stupid girl" comments.

"Sorry?"

"I'm always home."

"Listen, Althea, we need to—"

Her face changed and she waved her hand across the distance between us and I fell silent.

But…

Not of my own accord.

Holy Zipped Lips Batman!

No more drunken-and-weird-yet-somehow-benign Althea.

Definitely not benign.

"No, Mathilda, you listen to me." Yowza, her voice was cold. "You leave me to my drink and my sun and my thoughts."

And, right then, I had the terrible urge to get up and clatter away.

But it wasn't my urge.

I even went so far as to put my hands on the chair arms to push myself up.

But I didn't want to get up.

The bitch was trying to control me.

I struggled against her spell and, with some effort, I remained seated and waved my hand just as she did.

To my surprise, the spell fell away.

Now I was pissed.

"Althea, now's the time for you to listen to me."

She resolutely kept her face set and toward the sun.

That pissed me off more.

I snapped my fingers angrily, demanding her attention.

She didn't move but she did say, "Go with the cranberry salad. But with goat's cheese. Strong but not overpowering."

What?

"Althea—"

Still with eyes closed, face tipped to the warmth of the sun, calm as you please, she spoke.

And this is what the crazy old bitch had to say, sounding sober as a judge:

"You are powerful. You've no idea what powers you command. You are not a storm, you are a hurricane. You are not a wave, you are a tsunami. You are not a wind, you are a tornado. You are dangerous because you are foolish, stupid, unprepared. You think you're taking this seriously but you walk up the footpath in high-heeled shoes worried about lettuce leaves. You worry about which man's seed will create your children. You will be the end of the witch world as we know it and you will be the end of your Spellbounds. The gods and goddesses themselves fear your foolhardiness."

Well!

Drama, anyone?

I think I preferred her drunk and slurring.

But, she wasn't done.

"You want to know why they hide your Prophesies? Because they foretell our misfortunes. Because they tell stories of you, Mathilda, The Chosen One, as our Apocalypse. Because they know that you are Disaster. And that, you silly, little fool, is with a capital D."

Holy shit.

She kept going.

"You don't even attempt to read your own feelings, your thoughts. You push away the important and worry about what color to varnish your toenails. Under your roof, you harbor a traitor. A traitor who you ache to touch you, your desire for him blinds you, corrupts you."

Er, what?

Was she talking about Ash?

She didn't elaborate but she kept talking.

"Witches fear you, man is terrified of you, the supernatural and magical worlds wait in horror as you…bake…cookies."

Oh dear Mother Earth and all her fluffy friends.

She kept right on going.

"It might be funny if it wasn't the End of Days."

Oh. My. Goddess.

"Luckily, I'll be dead before it happens. So…cheers!"

And she lifted up her glass and downed the whole thing. Took my glass and downed that too. Then burped. Again.

I left her with that and, of my own volition, went inside and made myself a mojito.

I never much liked mint juleps.

I pulled out my trusty, old recipe box that Mom bought me before I started home ec in seventh grade. It was beaten up and ragged around the edges. I sat at the kitchen table and I sorted through it, card by raggedy-assed card until I found what I was looking for.

Then I walked back out to the garden where Althea looked like she was asleep under the sun.

"Wake up, you old bat," I ordered.

She opened one eye and I shoved the recipe card in her face.

"Catarina's Homemade Bleu Cheese Dressing!" I said, triumphantly, waving the card in her face. "No goat's cheese and dried cranberries. None of that frou frou stuff. Just romaine hearts, homemade croutons and fresh bleu cheese dressing! Maybe some real bacon bits. Voila! A salad to-die-for."

Althea sat up straight and opened her mouth but I interrupted her.

"If you think being mean to me is going to make me scamper off home, then you…and Agatha…have another think coming."

She harrumphed.

"And, just so you know, I can wear high heels, be boy crazy, take your abuse and bake cookies and still kick Agatha's sorry ass all across England and back again. All without the aid of manmade appliances. Or…maybe not entirely without them but only using them in a recreational, stress-relieving capacity."

She had both her eyes open and she was now paying lots of attention.

I kept at her.

"Until I know that no one is going to shoot at you, or me, or until I figure out why I think you should be here, you're stuck. I can promise you, those boys didn't seem to care who they hit with their bullets. And it's highly likely Agatha sent them. So don't be thinking she's loyal to you or anyone who's caught in the crossfire, because she's not. And I won't have the life of a two-hundred-and-three-year-old woman on my hands."

Then I took a big breath and finished.

"And if you say anything mean about Ash again, no more mint juleps and we'll magically lock the liquor cabinet and put a spell on you so that any beverage you touch turns to Kool-Aid. And you can call me a stupid girl as many times as you like, I still look *hot* in these shoes."

And then I walked back into the house to make a batch of homemade bleu cheese dressing.

The Month of July

Yesterday at The Witches Dozen we had big, ole, down and dirty cheeseburgers, homemade macaroni salad, real baked beans, ooey, gooey cream cheesy-chocolaty Better than Robert Redford pudding Fourth of July party.

We even had fireworks.

Granted, they were amateur and fell off the back of one of Mavis's "I know someone's" truck, but they were still great!

It was kickass!

Everyone had a good time.

English folk have gotten over the War of Independence (as they call it) so no hard feelings.

Best part, when Lucy arrived she was waving a copy of the *Bristol Evening Post*. She slapped the paper on the counter right next to the vat of Robert Redford and pointed at an article.

"Check *that* out! We're famous!" she cried.

And there it was, our first review:

Bewitched, Bothered but not Bewildered
   The Witches Dozen
   By Nathan Montgomery
   Food Critic

Rumor has been flying about The Witches Dozen, a small "American" Coffee House right on the seafront in a town not half an hour away from Bristol's city centre.

Some say The Witches Dozen is run by a bevy of true-life, wand-wielding witches.

They say that the goodies are good because they're stuffed with magic.

They also say you can buy yourself a love potion there, if you ask the right witch.

I don't care if it's white magic, black magic or voodoo, just give me more of it.

The Witches Dozen is worth whatever risk you take when you enter through their broomstick-laden door.

As you walk in, running the length of the left side is a carved, polished-to-a-shine, wooden bar connected to a variety of sparkling clean, curved glass display cases filled with mouth-watering selections of sweets and savories.

Behind the bar is a big, shiny, red espresso machine flanked by teetering stacks of a vibrant and eclectic collection of coffee mugs, tea cups and saucers, glasses and ice cream dishes.

Behind that is a huge mirror etched with a scraggly cat, its back arched and its tail straight up.

And above the mirror is a blackboard with stars and moons drawn on in brightly-colored chalk and the flowery, cursive words, Sit long… talk much…eat hearty written across it.

Your invitation.

The Witches Dozen has hipper-than-hip décor that mixes rock 'n' roll with witchy chic and comes out somehow cool and cozy. You can have a latte and an enormous sugar cookie, iced with a thick layer of soft, melt-in-your-mouth lavender-colored icing that is so beautiful and delicious, you want to spend hours savoring every bite.

And you can.

You can stay a minute or most of the day—no one will bother you. In fact, they provide books and games you can read and play if you find you need a diversion or an excuse to stick around.

Best of all, instead of opening at 9:00 and closing at 3:00 like most cafés, it opens at 7:00 in the morning, so you can pop round for a warm, homemade blueberry muffin with demerara crumble and an espresso for breakfast before work. Then it closes at 9:00 in the evening so after your tea you can go out and have a big bowl of "Dozen's Mess" (a take on

Eton Mess but with blackberries instead of raspberries, meringues made of brown sugar rather than caster, and a thin ribbon of custard throughout) and a "Paris on the Platte Café Fantasia" (a tall glass layered with hot cocoa and espresso separated by a thin wedge of orange and topped with a piped mound of whipped cream and sugared orange sprinkles — one of the owners' homages to her favorite coffee house in Denver, Colorado).

The staff is a mish mash. There are old white witches who you fear may not be able to lift that stainless-steel beaker full of milk to be steamed. There are also trendy, young lasses whose stylish clothes and high-heeled clattering give you the impression that the cast of Sex and the City have relocated to the West Country. They also make you wonder if London's fashion elite, in order to get fashion inspiration, may not soon be hanging out on the velvet couches or in the smooth, curved and cushioned wooden booths at the back.

But all the staff work under another American tradition, fine customer service. You always get a smile and a heartfelt "have a nice day" or "y'all come back now." And they mean it. You're made to feel comfortable, welcome and that there's no request you might make that's too taxing.

I've been there many times, the first time Macy Gray was blaring out and everyone, patrons included, were singing out loud, and the last time Billie Holiday was plaintively speaking to our souls. You'd think one or the other would be annoying but the whole vibe of the place suggests you go with the flow...and you do. It could be you're bewitched but why worry?

And the food. A chatty old dame named Nerissa told me the two head cooks/pastry chefs (they both do both) are in a war to see who can make the finest concoction. And the customers benefit greatly from what they call The War of the Wooden Spoons.

If you want delicate flavors and textures, do not go to The Witches Dozen. This is about excess — rich, soulful, comfort food that comes in big (but not overly big) sizes with splashy presentations and bright colors. The "witches" at The Dozen (as it is affectionately known by the regular clientele, which I can say now includes me) are the gorgeous kind of gals that couldn't care less about the calories and they're not embarrassed to ask for seconds and have pudding.

Everything from the furnishings to the music to the staff, to, best of all, the food, indeed says "welcome, sit long, talk much, eat hearty."

Am I bewitched? Maybe.

Bothered, oh yes, but in a good way.

Bewildered about why it's so good?

Not at all.

Witches Dozen, No. 13, The Beach, Opening Hours 7:00 to 9:00 All Week Long.

Woo hoo! How 'bout them apples? Especially like what he said about my fashion sense as obviously he's talking about me (high heels, anyone?).

Dig!

It!

One could say that our Summer Solstice celebration kicked in big time! Ask the gods for success and dance (semi) naked in the moonlight and then let it happen!

∾

19 July

I am now laying in my princess fortress.

My princess fortress that I built in Ash's bed.

My princess fortress that I built in Ash's bed, in Ash's flat, in London.

I'm trying not to think about where Ash is.

If he's dead.

Blown to smithereens.

Shot to bits.

Flayed alive.

Or just being tortured.

And Aidan is also MIA, but not his usual MIA.

The last time I saw him, his BMW Roadster was careening out-of-control.

And now he's probably in intensive care, holding on to the thread of his life and waiting for my dulcet tones to awake him from a coma.

And here I am, surrounded by my princess fortress hoping for the best.

∾

I created the all-powerful princess fortress when I was a little girl.

It had been a long day of Mom forcing us to help her make soap while listening to Simon and Garfunkel.

Then, as if a day of lye, essential oils and "Sound of Silence" isn't bad enough, that evening Gran came over with her little finger cymbals shouting "I'm in the mood to dance!"

That night, the princess fortress was born.

You see, I knew in my heart of hearts that I was really a princess. These weird people who made soap and clanked finger cymbals for fun weren't my real family. No! They kidnapped me when I was a baby.

(What can I say? I was the kind of little girl who lived in those plastic high-heeled shoes, clacking all over the house, the grocery store, everywhere.)

I figured I needed to practice for when the King and Queen of Wherever came to rescue me.

At night, when I was in my real home, that is to say safe in the castle, I would undoubtedly sleep in a princess bed. I would be propped up on at least two pillows (covered in pink satin, of course) behind my head and shoulders with one pillow each running either side of my torso on which to rest my precious princess hands and arms.

Then I would lie still, night after night, waiting for the handsome prince to wake me up and carry me to a new, bigger and better castle.

There he would shower me with Fendi handbags and Tiffany charm bracelets (okay, that last bit came later, when I was a not-so-little girl).

Any time I felt scared or upset, I'd build my princess fortress and it would help me to sleep, help me to cope…just help me.

I hadn't used the fortress in a long, long time.

And now that I was using it, it wasn't working.

BecBec wasn't here to keep me company with her whizzing around and freakish chatter.

And I didn't know where Ash was.

Nor Aidan.

They didn't answer their phones. I'd called The Gables (fifteen times)—no word. I called The Institute of Psychical Research (seven times)—nothing.

I did a lot of pacing.

I searched through Ash's flat looking for an address book or contact list.

Zilch.

I did more pacing.

I took a bath, dressed my scrapes and scratches with antibiotic oint-
ment and I paced some more.

There was nothing else to do but build the princess fortress, climb in
and hope.

~

This is what happened:

The Dozen had been crazed since the review came out. We were up to
six-woman shifts and still everyone was working over their scheduled
hours.

Mavis was in Seventh Heaven.

With all the practice, Pandora seemed to be conquering Big Red and
offering up rather tasty cappuccinos.

Some woman approached Lucy and me about writing a "War of the
Wooden Spoons" cookbook.

It was fantastic.

I had felt very retro that morning so I put on a raspberry-colored,
halter-top sundress with a thin lime-green belt and lime green slingbacks
with a peek-a-boo rounded toe and tapered heel. The *pièce de résistance*
was the raspberry, orange and lime-colored polka-dot bow on the toe.

Fab-you-las.

I was standing at the counter, piping a shitload of chocolate buttercream frosting into a newly fried donut (my latest addition to the menu
and regardless of the 950,000 calories, selling like hotcakes). I was about
to dump it into the enormous bowl of powdered sugar before selling it,
fresh, to the waiting blue-haired lady who was staring at it, drooling.

Then it came on me.

A premonition.

Hole-ee crap.

Shades of Cordelia in *Angel*, there was a pain in my head so intense, I
dropped the donut into the bowl of powdered sugar and with a soft *poof*
the powdered sugar exploded in a tiny, white cloud all over the counter.
Out-of-control, I squeezed the pastry bag filled with buttercream chocolate sending a stream of frosting halfway across the coffee house. I stumbled backwards, clutching at my head, wincing and whimpering as I
crashed into the mugs and cups behind me.

Ash…

And.

Aidan...
In trouble.
Not the normal kind of trouble, which was caused by me.
New trouble.
Bad trouble.
Deadly trouble.

~

The Dozen was in an uproar.

People slipping and sliding across chocolate frosting.

The blue-hair cracking the handle of her umbrella (carried even though there was no sign of rain) against the counter, snapping, "My donut! Look what you did to my donut!"

I didn't say a word, didn't do a thing, I just left.

There was no time, I had to go.

I had to recreate the future.

~

I ran as fast as my lime-colored, raspberry, orange and lime-bowed, cute, 40s-style slingbacks would carry me.

Fuckity, fuck, fuck.

No way was I gonna make it.

And you will appreciate how important this was and how hard it was for me...

I stopped, bent down, took off my sherbet shoes and dropped them where they were.

I pulled my wand out of my cleavage and booked it, barefoot.

I was almost too late.

~

At Campbell's Landing, I ran into the road, waving my arms and chanting the spell.

Cars screeched and honked and careened around me—drivers staring at me with angry faces or giving me the two-fingered salute.

I ignored them.

At the foot of Marine Parade, I leaned over, waving my wand against the asphalt like I was sprinkling carpet freshener in the middle of the street, in broad daylight, in a raspberry dress, and I didn't care who saw.

As I waved, I whispered,

> *Cars do not drive,*
> *Bikes do not ride,*
> *People do not hike,*
> *Their journeys — hold,*
> *Their wanderings — frustrate,*
> *The future has been told,*
> *A future I will not tolerate.*
> *Allow the blast — that I cannot prevent,*
> *Though I will not allow the damage that is meant.*
> *This important spell I cast with a plea,*
> *Calling, with love, to the strength of my tree,*
> *As I will, SO MOTE IT BE!*

Waves of undulating powdery silver magic dust flooded the street from my wand. I would have been pleased with the strength of the spell but I felt the tremor of terror go up my back.

Soon.

Soon.

Soon.

Damn, it was gonna happen soon.

Too much to do, too little time, too much area to cover, not enough magic.

I had to pick…

Ash or Aidan.

Aidan or Ash.

I had a mind-meld with one; I had to count on Mavis's magic to keep Ash safe.

Aidan, unless I stopped it, was going to drive straight into hell.

All around me bikes were skidding, cars were screeching and people were lifted off the ground and gliding eerily away from the silver sparkles sliding out of my wand.

Soon, I'd have to take cover.

But first…

I turned, straightening, and swept out my arm with the wand in my hand and slammed a laser line of hot pink with silver and electric blue sparks at the top of Marine Parade where it exploded in multi-pink-and-violet blast just as a blue BMW Roadster was about to make the turn onto Marine Parade.

The Roadster skidded, slid and started doing spins before I quit looking because I had to get the hell out of Dodge.

I ran toward the railing entry to the footpath that led up the steep incline to Marine Hill. I zig-zagged around it and plunged into the woods.

Please, Ash, don't come! Don't come, don't come, don't come! I thought as cars skidded, bikes plunged and people continued to glide in their weird, bewitched dance to safety.

All of it away from Marine Parade.

≈

Then the bomb exploded.

≈

Yes, *a bomb*.

≈

The sound was immense.

The explosion knocked me off my feet, slamming me into a tree which I slid down and then rolled down the slope slamming into another tree.

Enormous chunks of stone, pavement and dirt flew everywhere, ripping through the canopy of trees that protected me.

Protected me, as in, not a single pebble hit me. Who says nature won't take care of you if you take care of it?

Anyhoo.

People screamed.

Tires squealed.

Amongst it all, I heard the unmistakable noise of debris hitting metal.

"No!" I shouted.

A cloud of dust rolled out behind the explosion.

I pulled myself up and through the trees and I saw Ash's Lush Jag already pummeled by falling debris.

No!

"Ash!" I yelled, running toward the car.

Since my eyes were streaming from trying to see through the dust cloud, I didn't notice that he was already up the footpath where he caught me by the waist, swung me around and half carried, half dragged me through the dust cloud back to the dented Jag, threw me in, got in himself, reversed and we sped away.

~

It was no coincidence that the Roadster and the Lush Jag were headed toward Marine Parade at the same time, only seconds away from when a bomb was about explode.

Someone had arranged it, sent them there to die.

~

So now, I'm lying in Ash's bed in my princess fortress.

Ash had given me ten minutes to pack a bag (not nice, I need thirty minutes just to sort out accessories, even in an extreme situation or maybe *especially* in an extreme situation), leave instructions to the coven for the protection and safety of Josie and Rory (easy, they knew what to do).

Then Ash and I wheeled out of there in my Mini Cooper.

Ash, of course, driving.

He dropped me at his flat and ordered, "Do not open this door for anyone. *Anyone!*"

He actually raised his voice. It was very Daniel Day-Lewis to Madeline Stowe under the waterfall in *The Last of the Mohicans*. Could have been sexy but in the circumstances it totally freaked me out.

And then he took off.

I didn't hear a word from Aidan even though I called him repeatedly on the way to London (a two-hour trip that took Ash one hour and fifteen hair-raising minutes, this drive not filled with conversation mostly because I was still flipping out, and most of that time he was talking tersely on his phone which is against the law in England, but I didn't remind him of that fact at that juncture even if he was flipping me out further by driving like a maniac *and* talking tersely on his phone) and time-and-again from Ash's flat.

Do not *even* ask me why Ash, Aidan and myself weren't at The

Gables, which just happens to be protected by the extraordinarily potent spells cast by sixteen of the world's most powerful witches.

No, don't even ask me that.

No word from Ash since he slammed the door behind himself.

And now I am alone, surrounded by pillows and worried to death about my boys.

~

21 July

Ash and Aidan are okay.

In fact, they're perfectly fine.

But not for long because, pretty soon, I'm going to kill them.

~

The saga continues:

The power of the princess fortress cannot be denied. I fell asleep a little after five o'clock in the morning only to have my mobile ring what seemed like two seconds later.

It was Aidan's ring (the ring tone is called "Moonlit Haze"—I don't know, I just think it suits him) so I snatched it up.

"Aidan! You're alive!" I cried happily.

Okay, so maybe that was a bit dramatic but I'd been working myself up all night.

On the other end of the phone there was chuckling.

Yes, chuckling.

The verbal equivalent of a grin.

"I don't know what's so damn funny, I've been worried sick!" I snapped no-longer-happily.

Then the bed moved.

Ack!

The phone was plucked out of my hand by none other than Ash who was close behind me, up on his elbow, happy-as-you-please, bare-chested, tousle-haired and five-o'clock-shadowed.

"Seymour..." he started, but I didn't hear what else he said because I was too busy staring at him in disbelief.

There he was, laying there, princess fortress be damned, talking normally (okay, not exactly normally, perhaps a little curtly, but still) like bombs weren't exploding, like people hadn't gone missing, like we lay together in bed every night!

(Must say am pleased I chose to bring only good nightgown I owned, made of peachy Lycra/cotton blend that was stretchy and clingy, and so soft it had to be magical. Not to mention it had lovely ecru lace edging. Further mystical quality of being only nightgown in history that didn't shift during sleep to end up exposing my bodacious bosoms with one bodice triangle ending up under my armpit and the other in between my cleavage—instead booby triangles kept position as if guarding priceless jewels (which, kinda, they were). But, I digress.)

I had my back to him and my neck twisted around so I could look at him and then he…

Get this…

No really, you aren't going to believe this…

While he was talking, he rubbed the stubble of his chin ever-so-softly and somewhat absentmindedly on my shoulder.

Er, excuse me?

Hello?

When did my shoulder become available for the absentminded rubbing of someone's morning stubble?

Hunh?

When did that happen?

After our romantic whirlwind courtship full of flowers and presents and beach vacations together, and night after night filled with executing varied positions requiring great flexibility (me) and enormous amounts of stamina (Ash) culminating in many orgasms?

No!

After our engagement and subsequent marriage with me in a custom-made Vera Wang and a Harry Winston ring, carrying a bouquet made entirely of perfect, hand-picked, long-stemmed cream roses and a reception replete with a firework display and beef wellington?

No!

I snatched my shoulder away from his chin (ignoring tingles) and made to exit the bed (in a huff, mind), but I wasn't fast enough.

A steel-like band (better-known-as Ash's arm) encircled me and hauled me back against a rock-hard body (better-known-as Ash).

"We'll be there in an hour," Ash said, and disconnected without a thought that, perhaps, I might want to talk to Aidan.

He then tossed my mobile onto my grass-stained and muddy raspberry sundress that was strewn across the (fabulous, must admit) club chair in the corner.

"Excuse me?" I said sounding exactly as peeved as I was. "Did it occur to you that I might have a thing or two to say to Aidan?"

Silence.

Annoying man!

I let out a pissed-off puff of air then said, "Oh for goddess's sake… let me out of bed."

Get this:

"No," Ash replied.

Fuck that!

I pressed my back against his chest for leverage, my booty pressed against his crotch, and I grabbed on to the edge of the bed and pulled with all my strength, hoping to catapult myself up, out and away.

His arm tightened.

Gah!

Ash: so annoying!

"What happened to my princess fortress?" I snapped, groaning with effort.

More pressing, more pulling, more tightening of arms and a little grunting (on my part) but no answer from Ash.

"Ash, let me go!"

He'd clearly tired of the pressing/pulling bit as, at this point, with very little effort (grr!) he flipped me over and pulled me against his body.

Full frontal.

What the hell he thought he was doing, I…do…*not*…know.

He ignores me for days at a time.

He's never taken me out to a movie.

To dinner.

Whatever…

One orgasm and then he thinks he can slip in bed with me in the middle of the night and he thinks…

He thinks…

Oh my goddess, I think he thought he was gonna kiss me.

His head started to descend and…

"Ash!" I screeched in my best fish wife's voice.

That got his attention.

He winced and jerked his head back.

"For fuck's sake, Mathilda—"

"Don't you curse at me! You miserable," Um? "Cad! Let me go!"
"No." (Ash)
"Yes." (Me)
"No." (Ash)
"Yes." (Me)
"Cad?" (Ash)
Argh!
"I said, let me go!" (Me)
"And I said no." (Ash)

And that was it. I was pushing against his chest with all my strength, he was holding on to me with all of his, and then it came back to me.

The premonition.

The vision flooded my consciousness with the almost Cordelia-like energy of the day before.

Just as clear.

And just as fucking unbelievably, terrifyingly scary.

In reality, I knew it didn't happen as I saw it (thank the goddess and all her god-like friends). That Ash was there in bed with me. That Aidan was out there, able to chuckle over mobile phones and irritate me.

Yes, there was a bomb with debris, rock, dirt, pavement everywhere, people screaming, etcetera, etcetera, and in the end, all was safe.

But, in my mind's eye, the vision of what was supposed to happen was stuck. The vision that included the debris, rock, dirt, pavement everywhere, people screaming, but also in my vision there was big bits of BMW Roadster, Lush Jag and little bits of the two men in my life.

Little gooey, dead bits of my once-gorgeous hunks raining on Marine Parade while I stood in the middle of the bloodbath that used to be my prospective husbands.

What's a girl to do when something so icky, so flipping scary and so just plain horrifyingly awful pops into her head?

What else?

I gave up the fight and burst into tears.

This time, Ash didn't seem surprised by my display or incapable of dealing with it. He rolled onto his back, wrapped one arm around me, tucked my head into his neck and stroked my hair.

"You…were…in…little…bits," I gulped.

He kept stroking my hair.

"Landing on…m-m-Marine Parade," I stammered.

Arms tightened, more stroking.

"Then…you went…away," I blubbered. "And didn't pick up your," hiccup, "phone when I called."

More stroking.

"I was worried!" I wailed, and then I snuggled deeper into him and bawled my eyes out.

I have no idea how long I cried, but once I started to make those mini-catchy breaths and sniffles, Ash moved. He swung his legs off the side of the bed, taking me with him so he was cradling me in his lap and reaching for something on the nightstand.

He then tipped up my chin and started to mop my face with a handkerchief.

When he was done and I had calmed down, I said, "You carry a handkerchief?"

He grinned at me.

"Better now?" he asked.

I nodded.

Pause.

"What's a princess fortress?" he asked.

Oops.

Er, that bit was meant to be kept a secret. No one knew about my princess fortress and no one was supposed to know.

His grin broadened.

"Don't grin at me," I demanded.

"It was the pillow thing, wasn't it?"

Ack!

He was teasing me.

And he was alive and breathing and able to be annoying for another day.

And so was Aidan.

And everything was okay.

At least for right then.

Thank the goddess and all things green and glorious.

And then, because I could, because I wanted to and because who knew what that day would bring…

I kissed him.

I kissed him with the exact amount of happiness I felt that he wasn't in icky, gooey, bloody bits but with all his luscious body parts still were where they were meant to be.

Which means it was a pretty hot kiss.

All of a sudden, I wasn't cradled in his lap but on my back with him on me, his mouth on mine, his tongue in my mouth (and, sometimes, mine in his) and his hands all over me and…

Oo la la…

And…

Me oh my…

"Matty." That was Ash, kinda breathing heavy.

"What?" That was me, definitely breathing heavy.

My hands were roaming his luscious body because I was sure as hell going to do it while his body was still in one piece (not to mention I'd never really explored a washboard stomach, and let me tell you, it felt really, *really* nice).

He sucked in his breath which tensed the muscles in his tummy (*fascinating*).

"Jesus, Matty…stop. We have to get to Harrods."

Er, okay, whoa doggies…Harrods?

He sighed. It was a big sigh filled with big feelings, which sounded to me an awful lot like regret and maybe frustration.

Then he told me, "We have to meet Seymour at Harrods in less than half an hour."

My mind whirled but my mouth didn't move.

Aidan!

Harrods!

(Wish he wouldn't call Aidan "Seymour"—great last name, even better with the word "doctor" in front of it, but not so good alone.)

Oo, wait, just remembered…Harrods has Krispy Kreme.

Mm.

Ash moved and I realized he was taking his weight off me, so I held tight and he sighed and settled on me again.

Yay!

His face said it was only a moment's reprieve.

Boo!

I couldn't stop myself, too much emotion, too little sleep, the promise of Krispy Kreme, I kissed him softly on the lips and asked, "We're never going to have sex, are we? Real, bona fide, man-on-woman action with repeated and prolonged penetration and the exchange of bodily fluids, that kind of sex. We're never gonna have it, are we?"

When I was done, he was looking at me in an entirely differently, me: clotted cream, Ash: starving man, way.

Oh me.

Then he kissed me—hot, hard and long.

Oh my.

There was a promise in that kiss, a promise of future, real, full-blown, fantastic coital relations.

Yay!

Yay!

Yay!

Then in one, smooth movement, he was out of bed and pulled me along with him.

"You've got ten minutes," he said.

Then (can you believe?) he smacked my ass and left the room.

(Ten minutes? I don't think so.)

I know what you're thinking and I'm not so boy crazy or ditzy that I don't realize that someone tried to blow up two men that I care about very much.

The princess fortress isn't just for hiding and worrying.

I do other things in the princess fortress.

Like plotting and planning.

I just hadn't come up with anything yet.

Ash walked me through the sweets section of Harrods (more like dragged, what can I say, we were late, but I was not going to see Aidan, at Harrods (of all places) without at least a coat of mascara and lip gloss and some sheen to my cheeks).

The sweets section of Harrods is one of my most favorite places; a colorful, sugary wonderland that would make Willy Wonka green with envy.

I could spend hours in the marshmallow section alone.

I had no time even to admire, Ash forged through the hustle and bustle like a hot knife through butter.

I followed in his wake with one of my hands curled in his belt so I wouldn't lose him.

Being an American, I wouldn't have made it. I would have been miles back, "Excuse me"-ing and "Pardon me"-ing, and all would be lost.

~

Aside: Do not believe the whole "polite and mannered" English people myth.

English people conduct themselves in public like they have a mission and their mission is the most important thing in the entire world. The fact that you, too, might have a mission does not concern them in the slightest.

So, beware, if you happen to be in a small town grocery store and you can't figure out if you want the organic bio-yogurt with vanilla or the bio-yogurt with peaches and wheat germ and you're standing taking up the precious aisle space in front of the yogurts trying to decide. Beware because an English person will reach right in front of you and grab what they want, breaking your concentration and making you start your deliberations all over again.

If they happen to be walking down the sidewalk with a friend at their side and you're walking up that same sidewalk, don't think that one of the polite and mannered English people will drop back to allow you your own, rightful bit of sidewalk. No, they'd rather run right into you or force you into the street. And they will.

And whatever you do—*whatever you do*—when you approach a queue, study it and ascertain *exactly* where the end is and go there and only there. Do not look like you're confused (they can smell indecision, and if they do, they'll snap). Do not allow your mind to wander to anything else but the queue and your place in it. If you enter the queue anywhere but at the end, you are likely to be beaten to death and no English judge would send your murderers to jail because you deserved it because you *jumped the queue.*

I am not kidding.

And they won't say excuse me or pardon me, there is no concern or remorse.

There is only the mission.

And in the cities, it is far, far worse.

This is not a fault, this is the culture. It's just how it is. It's how *everyone* is. You get used to it and you're supposed to "when in Rome."

Unfortunately for me, consideration is ingrained. Therefore, in busy places, I can't get around very easily because I'm too busy being courteous.

Of course, Ash was a natural.

PS: This rule does not apply to Scots who are very nice and will chat happily with you in elevators.

~

We made it to the Krispy Kreme section, which was shoulder-to-shoulder, a beacon of peace to the world as every color, culture and persuasion were represented waiting harmoniously to get their own hot, glazed donut.

I saw Aidan's head and shoulders rising above a group of Asians chattering and queuing to get their sugar rush, their children already wearing little paper hats.

When I reached him, I threw my arms around him and gave him a happy shake. Then I grabbed his face, kissed his left cheek, his right cheek and then right smack on the lips.

His arms started to slide around me when I felt Ash's hand curl into the waistband of my jeans and he pulled me back.

Not very far back since, due to the crush there wasn't far to go.

So there we were, me caught in the middle of an Aidan-Ash Gorgeous Hunk Sandwich while they did another of their testosterone-induced staring matches.

I sighed.

"Are we gonna get donuts or what? I'm starved," I blurted to interrupt the contest and so I could get my dang donut.

"No," Ash said.

Um.

What?

"What do you mean, 'no?' These are Krispy Kremes!" I gestured to the hundreds of donuts traversing the conveyor belt, floating through the vat of hot fat and being swathed by a solid sheet of liquefied sugar. "I am a lonesome traveler far from home and this is the food of my people!"

I stopped the drama queen tantrum as Ash turned me around and steered me out while Aidan followed us.

No Krispy Kremes.

No reciprocal hug from Aidan.

Not even a moment at the Lalique counter (just to look).

Cruel, cruel world.

I slumped down the pavement through the throngs, dragged along by Ash pulling me by the hand, my disappointment huge that I was turned away from a hot-out-of-the-fat glazed donut and probably toward a fry-up or worse, some health-food crapola.

Ulk.

As I passed, I stared dejectedly into shop windows that I would normally have been noting for future after-breakfast shopping reference.

And then I saw it.

Oh…my…goddess!

I stopped dead (so dead, Ash stopped with me) and pressed my face against the window.

There, in front of me, were rows and rows of mouth-watering pastries: mini-tiramisus, éclairs, thick cream slices, shiny, sugar-glazed fruit tarts, Danishes galore, cakes with fancy, fanned sheets of chocolate that were utter works of art.

And, the most beautiful of all: custard filled donuts that were the size of my hand.

Do not mistake me, not my palm, *my hand*, from the tip of my middle finger to my wrist and then some.

I pressed my nose against the glass hoping it would absorb me so I could fall, face first, into the cream, the chocolate, the…

"Matty?" It was Aidan.

"Here, here. I wanna eat breakfast here," I breathed and pointed at the display.

"We are…come inside so we can get a table."

Patisserie Valerie.

The new love of my life.

I wanted to buy a house across the street so when I wasn't eating there, I could stare at the windows with binoculars.

A short wait and we were at a table (or, more to the point, a table that both Ash and Aidan found acceptable).

Ash sat with his back against one wall, Aidan with is back against the other wall and I faced them.

All I can say is, thank the goddess we didn't live in the Wild West or these two would have gunned each other down in the street long ago.

Okay then.

Coffee.

Check.

Big-ass custard donut.

Check.

There I was, me and my boys and the promise of a huge donut.

Yay!

And.

Ack!

Mm, not the greatest conversationalists, these two.

"Okay," I started. "So…bombs?"

Ash gazed at me, Aidan watched, I waited.

This wasn't going to be easy.

"Obviously, they were trying to take you two out," I noted. "Why would they do that?"

"What makes you think they wanted to take us out?" Ash asked.

"I had a vision…you were coming one way, Aidan the other and… then…er, *kablam*!"

"They weren't trying to take us out. They were trying to take *you* out." Ash, as usual not sugar-coating it, explained.

Um.

"Me?"

"What else would you do after having that vision but run to try to save us and then, there you'd be…" Aidan broke in then trailed off.

"You and the bomb," Ash finished.

Holy fucking shit.

Holy…fucking…*shit*!

"But you two—" I started.

"Just motivation to get you there," Aidan explained.

"And, undoubtedly, a bonus," Ash finished.

Holy fucking shit.

I wanted to cry but it was too late, the coffee and donuts arrived.

Well, not donuts per se, as Ash had a salmon and cream cheese bagel and Aidan had eggs, bacon and toast. I was the only who ordered a donut.

"So, they aren't after Josie? They're after me?" I asked, then I asked more. "I thought Josie and Rory were the targets…why were they after me?"

"With you out of the way, Josie won't be a problem," Aidan explained.

"And, Mathilda, you're *always* the target," Ash added.

Great.

I had, in fact, forgotten that part.

I thought back to crazy Josie who was at her wits end, screaming at Rory, seriously underweight and nearly poisoned by the time I came on the scene.

This was ruining the enjoyment of my donut and that was pissing me off.

"What the hell does she do that it's worth blowing up a fricking street and anyone on it?"

Silence.

Okay, I'd had enough. I mean, bombs were exploding.

"Oh for goddess's sake! Just tell me. I'm tired of this secret prophesies crap. What am I risking my ass, not to mention your asses for here? Hunh?"

More silence.

"Dammit!"

Okay, I shouted, and maybe that isn't the thing to do in Patisserie Valerie as the trendy Londoners (because, make no mistake, this was *not* a tourist trap) started to stare…but tell me, what would you do?

Bombs…were…exploding.

Aidan was the first to speak.

"Josie will one day be Prime Minister. She'll introduce radical and extremely controversial reforms that will shake up industries, economies, entire nations. These reforms will be social, educational and environmental. These reforms will make the rich less rich and will, most frightening to some, work."

Whoa.

Hold on.

Our Josie?

Angry at trash collectors one day and Robin Hood in Parliament the next?

Aidan went on, "Other countries will adopt these reforms, more people will work, more people will go to school, they'll have more, starve less and be healthy. The earth will begin to heal itself. Josephine McShane is going to change the world."

Whoa, part *deux*.

"Fuckin' A Bubba," I muttered.

Sorry, but that was all I could think to say.

"Indeed." Aidan smiled at me. "She'll also be the first leader to recognize the magical and supernatural world in any official public capacity. She'll guide the two worlds into living together in peace."

"Go, Josie, go Josie," I cheered.

My donut was looking good again so I took a big bite.

Please note: this was not a custard donut. This donut was stuffed with crème patisserie. This donut was *divine*. There were probably entire populations on earth that would worship this donut. I knew this for a fact because I was considering being the founding member of the cult.

"That will be after the war, of course," Ash interjected breaking my donut reverie.

I choked on cream and dough.

"Uh, wha'?" I said with my mouth full.

Silence again before Aidan broke it.

"The thing is," Aidan explained, "we're headed to war. Man and witch, mostly, but the sides are blurred."

Man, oh man.

I swallowed passed the lump in my throat.

When I succeeded doing that, I asked, "Why are we here, in London? It has to be safer at home."

"You're safe with me," Ash said. "And I'd been called to London. So you had to come to London."

"I would have been safe at The Gables."

Ash just looked at me.

"There are protection spells…an entire coven with loads of magic," I reminded him.

"I made a vow to keep you alive and I'm going to do that the way I think it should be done. So you're to stay with me."

He said it like that was it.

No discussion.

I had no choice in the matter.

I opened my mouth to say something but Aidan interjected.

"The Directors and Elders wanted to see both Wilding and I, we had to come to London. Things have changed, Matty."

I stopped glaring at Ash and glanced at Aidan. "What things?"

"The Directors and Elders have made an alliance. Controversial but suffice it to say that, right now, the alliance is to be represented through Wilding and myself. We're working together now."

Holy fucking shit.

No way.

I did not think this meant good things for me.

"Working together on what?" I asked.

"On you," Ash answered.

Holy Three-Way, Batman!

"Just a second here…what does that mean 'on me?'"

Ash again answered, "Protecting you, guarding you, helping you… whatever it takes to keep you safe and let you do your work."

I looked at one and then the other.

The world was already changing and I was in the eye of the storm.

"Uh, this is kind of big news isn't it? Isn't The Institute Switzerland?" I said to Aidan.

"What?" Aidan asked.

"As in neutral, non-committal, all that?"

"Not anymore, Mathilda," Ash answered.

"I can't believe —" I started.

"Enough talk, eat. We've got work to do." Of course, that was Ash.

"What work?"

"Eat, we'll fill you in while we work." Ash, being bossy, *again*.

"Aidan?" I asked.

I'm not beneath playing one against the other, especially when I'm being bossed around.

"Just finish your breakfast, Matty. We've got a busy day," Aidan sighed.

Fucking men.

In the taxi to wherever-we-were-going, my mobile rang.

It was Josie.

"You okay?" I asked.

"Kind of," she replied.

"Was anyone hurt?"

"No, thank God," she answered and went on, "The police are here to talk to you."

Wonderful.

"Well, I'm in London," I told her.

"I know that, they know that, they don't like that. When will you be home?"

"Just a sec." I looked at Aidan. "When will I be home?"

"Soon," he said.

That helps.

"Soon," I said to Josie.

"I don't think 'soon' is the answer they're looking for, but leave it to me."

She disconnected and I dropped my phone hand.

I wasn't going to save the world.

Josie was.

Wow.

Try to get your head around that.

Then my mobile rang again.

It was Nerissa.

"Hey, Miss Rissa," I answered.

"Hello, Mathilda, my dear, I'm sorry to say but the police are here for you."

Good goddess and all things leafy and flowery.

"I know, tell them I'm in London and I'll be home soon."

"One other thing, there's a woman here who says she paid for a donut and she's not leaving until she gets it."

Oh for crap's sake.

"Tell her I'll be home soon too."

"All right, dear, take care."

The "take care" was loaded. Poor Nerissa, dealing with blue-haired old ladies and men in blue while bombs exploded in the street.

Good to know, though, that the bomb didn't drive customers away.

But, it was England and they'd had nearly seventy years of bombs exploding.

It was the "Never Mind Mentality" in action.

You know: "The pipes have burst." English person response: "Yes? Oh well then, never mind."

And: "The roof has caved in." English person response: "Really? Never mind."

And: "Someone blew up the road." English person response: "Oh? That's a shame. Never mind."

It may sound crazy, but not only is it true, it's actually quite remarkable. English people make an art of keeping their chin up no matter what the calamity and forging ever onward.

Nothing got them down.

It was freaking cool.

"The police are looking for me," I told Ash and Aidan when they both stared at me expectantly.

They both looked away as if having the police hunting you is no big deal.

Oh well then, never mind.

❧

Normally, when I went to London, I went to the good places, the pretty places, like the parks, shops, palaces, museums and martini bars.

The first place we stopped wasn't pretty except in terms of pretty scary.

I followed Ash and Aidan into a pawn shop and not a very good one. I'd never been in a pawn shop but I still felt qualified to say that. There was lots of new and not-so-new stuff, and a weasel-faced guy with greasy hair sitting behind a counter with bars protecting it.

"No," he said when he saw Ash.

Not exactly welcoming.

I wondered if anyone pawned shampoo because the clerk could use it.

Ash threw a bit of something charred on the counter. It made a black mark as it slid across.

"No," the clerk said to Ash again.

"You know what I want, Jack," Ash said.

"I don't wanna get involved. You weren't here, he wasn't here, she *definitely* wasn't here." He pointed at me.

Well, I am soooo sure!

He continued, "You don't know me, I don't know you. Find someone else."

He pushed the charred bit back at Ash who ignored it but stated, "We'll be back later today."

"Mate, I ain't gonna do it!" he shouted as we walked out.

"You trust him?" Aidan asked Ash.

"Nope," Ash answered.

Great.

"What was that all about?" I asked as we walked down the street.

"Later," Ash said.

"Not later, now." I felt like stamping my foot. "I thought you told me you were going to fill me in."

Aidan hailed a taxi, Ash gave the driver an address, we all climbed in and we were off again.

"About filling me in…" I said.

"I want you to pay attention to where we're going. You need to remember it, it'll be a good source for you," Ash told me (and, incidentally, didn't fill me in).

"A good source of what?" I asked.

"Information. It's called The Hobgoblin. There are other Hobgoblins but not like this Hobgoblin."

"Oh…kay." I said.

Me…no…likey.

Hobgoblin?

"It's a local…as in a *local*. Whenever you go there, you'll have to blend in or there'll be trouble," Aidan added.

~

In Britain, in most pubs, everyone was welcome.

Then there were pubs where most of the clientele were local (as in lived nearby and came in most every night, like "The Vic" in *Eastenders*) but new folks were happily accepted into the collective.

Then there were *locals*. The pubs no one went into but the locals. If you weren't local and you stumbled into a local, trust me, don't be brave, just leave.

~

"Anything else?" I asked.

"Just pay attention, keep quiet and keep your wand at the ready," Ash replied.

Great.

So, if pretty scary described the last place, seriously scary described this one.

The Hobgoblin was a pub and it was a dive. The English equivalent of the place Jodie Foster got gang-raped in *The Accused*.

I didn't like it one bit.

There was practically no one there save two guys at a table, both who clearly hadn't seen the sun shining in quite some time, they were so pale. One was deeply in need of vitamin E lotion as he had stretch marks all over his arms and face (how you get stretch marks on your face, I do not know, especially when you had about half a percent body fat).

There was also a faerie, a boy faerie who looked like he'd seen better days. Let's just say quite a bit of the gossamer had gone from his wings.

"Not you," the bartender said when he saw us.

We weren't very popular today.

Except this guy didn't look scared of Ash, he looked scared of Aidan.

"Derek," Aidan greeted.

"You are not here," Derek returned, still (obviously) unwelcoming and then looked at Ash and me. "And they are definitely not here."

Broken record anyone?

"In fact, you're not all here, together, not in my pub," he declared.

Derek had a posh accent, quite like Aidan's.

Derek also had multiple, what looked like bite marks on his neck and a scar around the left side of his mouth that made him look like a lopsided Joker.

Derek was freaking me out.

"I have nothing to say," he said before anyone asked. "Look around you, mate, no one's coming here anymore. This business is killing me. They know you'd come here."

Aidan just stood there, watching him.

"Mate, I'm telling you, I have nothing to say," Derek repeated.

"You got a faerie? 'Cause if you don't, I'll be your faerie."

I jumped, the little faerie man was floating right by my head, leering at me.

He looked awful, dark circles under his eyes, his little faerie shorts hanging loosely at his waist, his little faerie ribs sticking out.

Yikes.

"Yeah, I have a…" I started but whoa! He wasn't speaking in a high-pitched faerie screech. "Hey wait, I can understand you!"

The faerie's eyes narrowed. Then he pointed at me, threw his head back and laughed.

"Your faerie…they haven't…?" he didn't finish, just more laughter.

So, BecBec was holding out.

I didn't like to be the butt of the joke, I didn't have time to worry about BecBec, and anyway, I was missing out on the Derek interrogation.

"Dude, bugger off," I said to the faerie.

Giggle, giggle and more pointing. Then he swooped in close to my face, all scary faerie and whispered in a spooky, echo-y voice, "I'll take care of you."

Ick!

And.

Yikes!

"I said *bugger off*."

This was not a nice faerie and he wasn't buggering off.

Then, faster than a snap, Ash grabbed the faerie by the legs and yanked him away from my face to hold him an inch from Ash's face.

"What did she say?" Ash asked calmly.

"I'm gone…I'm gone," the faerie said, pushing against Ash's hand, and when Ash let him go, he flew away.

"You saw him?" I whispered. "I thought non-magical people couldn't see?"

Ash took my elbow and pulled me away.

"What makes you think I'm not magical?" Ash whispered back.

"Well I —"

"My mother was a witch, Mathilda, which means I come from a magical line. And I believe in magic. The dark *and* the light."

Hmm.

Interesting.

Just then, Aidan turned and made a sharp head jerk signal to Ash and without another word, we left.

Out on the pavement, Ash asked, "You get anything?"

"Nope," Aidan answered.

"You believe he doesn't know anything?" (Ash)

"Nope." (Aidan)

Ash's mobile rang and he walked away to answer it.

"Who was that guy?" I asked Aidan after Ash walked away.

"Ex-watcher. Banished," Aidan answered.

Ah, that explained the posh accent.

"Why was he banished?"

"He got a little addicted to the underworld."

Yikes.

"You think he knows something, don't you?" I asked.

"A lot of folk go there. Warlocks, exiled faeries. There was a were-wolf and vampire in there just now," Aidan explained. "Derek is a trained watcher. He sees things and hears things others might not."

Whoa.

A werewolf and a vampire?

Holy crap.

"A bomb is a pretty powerful message…I can't imagine no one's been talking about it," Aidan went on.

Ash whistled, he was about twenty feet away and he had a taxi.

Aidan turned toward him.

I guess we were leaving.

I hesitated.

Then I turned toward The Hobgoblin and went back in.

Don't ask me why, I just did.

The werewolf man (stretch marks explained) and vampire looked up when I entered. The faerie was diving into a pint of stout.

I walked up to Derek.

"You know who I am?" I asked.

Derek just looked at me.

I turned to the werewolf man and vampire.

"Do you know who I am?" I asked.

The vampire pushed his chair back, reclined further into it and stretched his legs in front of him, ready for the show.

The werewolf man shrugged.

I pulled my wand out of the back waistband of my jeans and then shoved it back in at the front, making it visible outside my T-shirt.

But I wasn't going to use it.

I heard Aidan and Ash come in as I lifted my hand, palm up and watched as I made a small ball of shell pink form then bands of silver wrapped around it.

"You got something to say to me?" I asked Derek while I watched the sphere form.

I don't know what I was going for…I think Al Pacino in *Serpico*.

It didn't seem to be working as Derek still just stared at me.

The silver disappeared as a violet coating surged up from my palm and wrapped around the orb.

"You're a good witch," Derek said not staring at me but at my palm. "You wouldn't—"

A sparkling electric blue film appeared around the violet, I threw the sphere up and it hovered in mid-air.

I looked questioningly at Derek, raising my brows.

Nothing.

I flicked my fingers and it exploded in a gorgeous firework that was really just for show.

A little fright was all it was meant to be. But it made little silver and shell pink sparks snake lazily around the room. A few exploded near the glasses, taking a couple with them, one overturned a chair.

Derek breathed a sigh of relief.

I lifted up my palm.

"You got something to say to me?" I asked again.

The sphere was creating itself again.

Derek said nothing.

The faerie burped.

I threw up the sphere and the firework was bigger and more brilliant this time. The sparks rocketed around the room much faster. More glasses bit the dust, as did a bottle of whiskey. A chair exploded.

I lifted up my palm again.

"You know who I am too," Derek said. "I know witches…I even know about you. You can't keep that up…even *you* don't have the power without a wand."

The sphere went into triple time, creating itself in seconds before I threw it up and the firework was three times the size, the rockets of sparks were not only silver and shell pink but also violet and brilliant blue and they shot around the room like bullets.

Rows of liquor and glasses exploded with fragments flying everywhere. A table and three chairs blew up, their wood and splinters scattering. More furniture overturned or flew across the room. The faerie dashed under the bar and the vampire and werewolf dove for cover.

I controlled every last spark. Aidan, Ash and myself were untouched. It was taking a lot out of me but I'd be damned if I was going to let on.

Derek had hidden under the bar.

When he straightened up again, there was another sphere in my hand.

"Feel like talking yet?" I asked.

Aidan and Ash had come closer because the werewolf and vampire were up and had brushed the glass and splinters off their clothes. They didn't look just interested anymore, they looked pissed off. The faerie hovered over his overturned glass staring at the dripping stout with despair.

There was silence.

All hell was gonna break loose, any second.

Cripes!

"Okay, okay," Derek said (thank the goddess) as I threw the sphere up and it waited, hovering. "Whatever they're up to, it's too big, no one's talking, like I said."

I flexed my fingers.

"Wait!" Derek shouted. "Bligh's been here. He's been everywhere. Talk to him. He knows something."

Who on this lush, green earth was Bligh?

I kept the sphere hovering when Aidan leaned into my ear and whispered, "Banish it, Matty, we've got what we need. Let's go."

I swept my hand up and around and absorbed the sphere back into my palm.

Still courteous, of course, I said to Derek, "Thank you."

He just stared.

I smiled and nodded to the werewolf and vampire.

"Sorry, guys," I said.

The vampire relaxed and smiled too, nice and slow (must say, he was kinda cute…like, really kinda cute, in a thin, pale, dangerous, sexy David Tennant kind of way).

I hesitated and smiled back then I put my hand on my hip going into my flirty pose when Aidan grabbed my hand and pulled me out the door.

The werewolf man just righted his chair and sat down again.

"You sure you don't need a faerie?" the little guy called while we walked out.

The taxi was waiting, Ash shoved me in.

Nothing.

Not a word.

Total silence.

And then Aidan asked Ash, "You get a confirmation on Islington?"

"Yep," Ash answered.

I may not have expected applause but I did expect something, a "well done," a kiss on the cheek, *something*.

"Um…hello?" I called.

They turned to me.

First, Ash winked.

Then, Aidan grinned.

Fucking men.

~

To sum up:

"Bligh" is Jeremy, as in Ichabod, as in Agatha Darling's watcher.

And Islington is too scary to record in any detail.

Islington is where one of Darling's boys live(d?).

I didn't get to go in, Aidan and Ash left me in the hallway.

The noises that came through the door were enough.

By the time Aidan came out with the all clear and I went in, the bad guy was hog-tied and gagged on the floor.

He didn't look too good.

"They're coming to get him," Ash said as I entered.

The man grunted and strained.

Aidan nodded.

And we left.

The dirty-haired pawn shop dude had closed up shop by the time we got back. We went to a high-rise estate and, without knocking, Ash used his shoulder to break open the door.

We were greeted by the shampoo-deficient boy who was pointing a gun at us while his equally shampoo-neglecting (and also apparently conditioner-shy) girlfriend surveyed us from the sofa, a fag dangling from her mouth.

If you can believe, without hesitation, Ash walked right up to the kid and jerked the gun straight out of his hand.

Oh my goddess, I have to admit, even after my kickass display at The Hobgoblin, that scared the bejeezus out of me, and I let out a little yelp.

"Don't fuck with me, Jack," Ash's voice rumbled.

If Ash ever spoke to me in that tone of voice, I'd pee my pants on the spot.

(I wondered if the kid's name was Jack or if Ash was calling him that to be scary cool. Though, he didn't have to work too hard at being scary…or cool, for that matter.)

The kid stared at him, his expression a mixture of awe, fear and disbelief.

"You have twenty-four hours," Ash warned.

Then we left.

I figured Jack would use his twenty-four hours wisely.

Or, at least, I hoped he would.

Aidan drove me home in my Mini while Ash followed us in a new platinum Audi TT coupe Quattro. Where the hell he got that, I don't know, but it rocked!

The police had been Mavis'ed by the time we got back. They asked me a few questions in the Plush Parlor and after about ten minutes of polite questioning (mostly to do with my welfare, as in, "Are you sure you're all right?") they were on their way, seemingly happy as clams.

The Witches Council wasn't near that happy. After night fell, Aidan went to Wellington Terrace to make some calls to try and track down Ichabod, and Ash retired to The Dungeons.

I was sitting outside with Su, Viv, Josie and Mom drinking martinis and giving them the low down on The Hobgoblin, Patisserie Valerie and my sexual *rompus interruptus* with Ash. Daphne the cat was with us, chasing bugs in the grass. BecBec was nowhere to be found.

At around eleven, we watched a witch-carrying broomstick flit across the moon. When she landed, she gave us a scroll of lilac, hand-made paper wrapped in a black satin ribbon.

We gave her a martini.

> The Witches Council requires the presence of: Mavis Lillian, Minerva Suki, Hanna Belle, Viviana Juliet, Mathilda Guinevere and Ursula Sadie Honeycutt as well as Althea Liza Appleton at a Council Gathering, first August, midnight, at the Avebury Circles.
>
> The Gathering will consist of representatives from:
> The Imperial Order of Elves
> The Vampyre Dominion
> The League of Werewolves
> The Troll and Goblin Union
> The Banshee Nation
> The Magi
> The Guild of Sorcerers & Sorceresses
> The Fellowship of Wizards
> The Elders of Le Société de Mathilde
> The Directors of The Royal Institute of Psychical Research
> The Gathering will be presided over by the Hag and the Unicorn with the Headless Horseman to adjudicate.
> Kind Regards,
> The Witches Council
> (Endora Eccles, The Lady)

~

Headless Horseman?

Great.

~

23 July

I got up early to take care of donut lady and have a look at the devastation.

I had no idea what I was in for that day, but I will say, at least I was getting used to surprises.

Instead of trailing me, Ash said he'd meet me at Aidan's at nine sharp and to keep my wand handy. A good aftereffect of my little demo at The Hobgoblin was that Ash felt a little better about me taking care of myself.

The donut lady seemed mollified after I handed her two chocolate buttercream stuffed donuts and a free Wicked Mocha (a mixture of hot cocoa and espresso poured over a square of Lindt eighty percent cocoa solid chocolate).

Once done, I headed to the bomb site.

They'd already begun to repair Marine Parade.

There were about a half dozen others looking at the hole in the road, mainly morning dog walkers.

The damage seemed small compared to how it sounded and felt. But then, Ash explained later, the bomb wasn't meant to explode the road but instead something on it, namely me.

While I stared at it, a petite woman in a Dorothy Hamill haircut sidled over.

"Um, I'm sorry, could I just bother you a moment?" she asked me.

I looked at her and she blinked back what seemed to be tears.

"I saw it," she whispered. "The silver dust, your silver dust, from your little stick. I saw it and it saved me." She paused. "*You* saved me."

Holy cow.

She must have been from an old Wiccan line and didn't know it to see the magic.

Her voice caught. "I could have been..." She nodded to the hole. "I just wanted to say, thank you." She reached out, hesitated then touched my arm briefly before she hurried away.

I watched her dragging her little Scottie dog behind her, and before I could even react, someone else was talking to me.

"I know who you are." It was a guy who looked like he'd stepped straight out of a diorama depicting Neanderthal man (except, of course, his hair was cut and his beard was trimmed and instead of animal skins, he wore a poorly-fitting Umbro T-shirt), "And I know if it wasn't for you this wouldn't have happened."

Uh-oh.

He kept being a jerk. "If you know what's good for you, you'll close up shop, take your crazy friends and go home. All the way home, if you know what I mean."

I knew what he meant.

He got closer to me but I whipped out my wand.

"You feelin' lucky?" I asked in my best Clint Eastwood.

He looked at my wand with scorn then over my shoulder and his face changed.

Apparently, he wasn't feeling lucky.

I knew Ash was there before I felt the hand at the waistband of my taupe corduroy, OP surfer's shorts. (It had been a crazed morning in the wardrobe, what does one wear when one is hunting baddies? I went with surfer's shorts, a pale pink Miss Sixties rocker cami and a sweet pair of pink suede puma trainers with those golf footies with the little poofy balls on the back — I thought this was a good choice).

(Anyhoo.)

Neanderthal man moved on and Ash and I walked up the footpath to Marine Hill.

The last time we were in these woods, Ash was dragging me through the bomb dust to the now-lost Lush Jag.

"You okay?" he asked.

"Sure," I lied.

He didn't respond except to take hold of my hand and he kept hold, all the way to Aidan's house.

The five-minute walk to Aidan's, holding hands with Ash, wasn't exactly a three-course dinner with champagne or hot, heavy, panting, animal sex.

But it still felt nice.

We were hunting Bligh that day. Somehow Aidan got his hands on a nice Mercedes sedan and we drove back to London in not-exactly-companionable silence (I eventually gave up and listened to my iPod).

Ichabod's flat in London was deserted. No one at his local had seen him in weeks. Aidan had a picture, so we checked a few of the news agents around his flat, some cafés, a couple of takeaways and a few of his reported haunts.

Zip.

So we drove to Cambridge (this time, after a short but not-at-all successful attempt at a game of I Spy, I retreated again to the iPod).

No Ichabod at his Cambridge residence and after short conversations with a variety of colleagues and peers, we learned no one had seen him in a while. We checked around again at the various places, flashing the photo.

Zilch.

Aidan took us to a pub by the river and we sat outside and watched the punters float by.

"About what I expected," he said into his pint.

Ash was silent.

Was I crazy or did these boys seem not to know what they were doing?

"So why—?" I started.

"We'll go out again tonight," Ash interrupted.

(No manners.)

"Yes," Aidan replied.

Tonight?

"Will Mathilda be safe?" Ash asked.

Excuse me?

"Will I be safe from what?" I butted in.

"We're leaving you at The Institute tonight," Aidan explained.

"Uh, no you're not, I'm coming with," I said.

I mean, I seemed to be the only one getting anywhere with my orbs o' magic.

"No," Ash said.

"You're too damn bossy, Sebastian Wilding. I'm coming with you."

"No, Matty, you're not," Aidan said.

That got my attention, Aidan being bossy was new.

"I beg your pardon?"

I got two hard, inflexible stares, one blue-eyed one (Aidan), one brown-eyed one (Ash).

What...eh...ver.

~

I guess Ash didn't feel so much better that I could take care of myself, and Aidan certainly didn't because I found myself left at The Institute, in the waiting, somewhat hesitantly welcoming arms of Dr. Ambrose Bennett and his Team of Antiquities.

"Do you have any idea what they're up to?" I asked Dr. Bennett as we watched the Mercedes drive away.

He shivered as if that was the last thing he'd want to know. "Let's have some sherry, my dear. It'll help us to sleep easier."

~

24 July

Let's just say, Dr. Bennett was wrong. First, sherry sucked. Second, even after drinking the stuff, sleep would escape me, especially in that ancient bed with the curtains drawn around it. It was a bit too disturbing, although it smelled vaguely familiar (in a good way) and the sheets were absolutely sumptuous.

I'd finished recording in my Book of Shadows and was about to nod off when I heard someone come in.

I sat still, listening, ready to lob some magic, but as I listened it sounded like they weren't coming to get me. They were, it seemed, getting undressed.

One shoe dropped.

Then the other.

Ash.

The cad.

Climbing into bed with me in the middle of the night again, ha!

Not this time.

(Especially not since I didn't come prepared to spend the night so I was wearing one of The Institute dude's wife-beater T-shirts and an old pair of pajama bottoms that were about three sizes too big.)

"Don't even think about it," I warned as I reared up on the bed and pulled back the curtain.

Silence.

Darkness.

"Matty?"

Aidan!

The lights flashed on.

And there he was, barefoot and wearing jeans and a tight T-shirt.

"What are you doing in my quarters?" he asked.

"Your...what?"

"My quarters, what are you..." He stopped and watched me for a moment on my knees in his bed. "Damn, Ambrose," he muttered to himself.

Ambrose?

Then he said, "I'll find somewhere else to sleep."

"Wait!" I stopped him and jumped off the bed, completely forgetting my scary sleeping attire. "What did you find out tonight? Anything?"

"Only that Jeremy Bligh has apparently dropped off the face of the earth."

"Shit."

"You can say that again."

"Shit."

"Nice outfit." He smiled, stepping back to take a good look at me.

"Shit." I said it with real feeling that time. "Anything else?" I asked.

"Just that he may be with Darling, so much for him wanting to keep the traditional watcher-witch distance."

Hmm.

"We forgot Jack," I told him.

"We didn't forget Jack. Wilding and I went back to London, tracked him down. The bomb was imported. Not a local job."

"So, Jack used his twenty-four hours wisely."

Aidan shook his head.

"Hardly. Let's just say Wilding can be," Aidan pulled a hand through his hair and finished, "persuasive."

Ack!

He grabbed me by the neck, pulled me forward and kissed my nose. "I have to go find somewhere to sleep. I'm shattered."

"Wait!" I said again.

Aidan hesitated.

I kept talking. "I have to ask you a couple of things. I know you're tired but...I don't know when I'll have time alone with you again."

That got his attention.

~

Okay, so I was going to share some of the things that kept me awake at night.

Might as well, right?

Nothing to lose, right?

Ding ding ding…*wrong answer!*

Believe me, ignorance, my Book of Shadows, is bliss.

∽

He studied me for a bit then walked into the room, sat on the edge of the bed and looked at me.

"Shoot," he said.

Here goes…

"Okay." I hopped on the bed next to him and sat cross-legged. "You're the Mathilda Expert, yes?"

"Yes."

"And you've read The Prophesies, yes?"

"Yes."

"So, way back, when you were telling me who you were, you didn't know Josie. That's bugged me for a while. If you know The Prophesies, why didn't you know Josie when you met her at the plumbers?"

"I study Mathilda, not her Spellbounds."

"So?"

"I'm interested in you, Matty, only you, not your Spellbounds. And anyway, they're rarely named, only described. I knew there was someone in town you'd bind yourself to, but I didn't exactly care who."

"Oh."

Well, that explained that.

And was kinda nice.

Interested in me and only me and all that.

"Is that it?" he asked.

"Yes."

He nodded and then made to get up.

"No," I amended.

He sat back down with a sigh.

Oh man, was I gonna do what I thought I was gonna do?

Yeah, I was.

"Aidan."

He looked at me and then must have seen something in my face because he looked less tired, more concerned and leaned closer. "Yes?"

"Um, Althea Appleton told me…well, uh, she told me that, uh…Ash is a traitor."

He stared at me, all tiredness gone.

Then he pushed off the bed.

I thought, *He's going say yes, if he was going to say no he would have said no already so he's going say yes.*

Oh no. Oh no.

I shouldn't have asked.

How could I even trust Aidan to answer me? They're at war or whatever.

"Don't!" I shouted, "Don't answer that! I don't want to know."

"This is a bit…complicated, Matty."

Ack!

Complicated?

He said no more.

Okay, I was getting annoyed.

Okay, no, I was getting more than annoyed.

So, more than annoyed, I started to have a tantrum. "Why do they keep everything from me? Why? I don't get it." I slammed my fists into the bedclothes. "I know it sounds stupid, but it's…not…fair!"

Aidan walked to the window and looked out.

I wasn't particularly fond of this response.

Therefore, I kept with my tantrum. "I'm a grown woman! I can handle it!"

Well, I couldn't actually. But I wasn't going to tell him that.

"There's a reason, Matty," he finally said.

"Whatever it is, it's stupid," I declared.

"No, actually, it isn't," he said, and I shut up. "You know the vision you had where Wilding and I were caught in the bomb?"

"Of course."

Like I'd ever forget.

"Well, that wasn't planted in your head, that was a real vision. That was meant to happen. You changed the future. It's part of your powers, part of being The Chosen One."

Whoa!

"Really?" I said to his back.

"Yes, really." He sighed and turned to me. "If it wasn't, Josie would be dead by now. Poisoned. That's the point. By saving Josie, in a way, you saved the world."

Whoa!

(Yay me!)

"The Witches Council asked the Directors and Elders, who, in turn, told Wilding and me to keep quiet. They didn't want you to think of The

Prophesies as fixed. They don't want you to know what's prophesied just in case you need to change it."

"So, Ash is a traitor, will I change that?"

Aidan shook his head. "Darling, Wilding isn't a traitor."

"You know that? For certain? Or are you just saying —"

"Yes, I know. For certain. The Prophesies state that you will marry one of us and one of us will…"

He stopped but he didn't start again.

"What? One of you will what?" I prompted.

Pause.

"What?" I pushed.

Big sigh.

"What!?" I was getting kinda louder.

"One of us will father your children and one of us will die for you."

What?!

"*What!?*" I jumped out of bed and started pacing as well as chanting. "Holy crap, holy crap, holy crap. You're joking." Aidan kept his place by the window and watched me while I paced. He looked serious. He didn't speak. He wasn't joking. "Oh shit, you're not joking. Why did you tell me this? Why?"

At that point, I forgot that I pushed him to tell me.

He didn't remind me of this. Instead, he said, "Two reasons, one, because I don't want you thinking Wilding is a traitor. He's a lot of things and one of those is, he's loyal to you."

Thank the goddess for that one.

Aidan kept on. "Althea Appleton is a drunk and she's a meddler, and she's an oracle for God's sake. Never trust one of those."

Great. Never trust an oracle.

So noted.

It made no sense, but whatever.

Aidan continued, "And two, because you might be able to change it."

"Holy crap, holy crap, holy crap," I chanted again, still pacing.

Aidan started toward me, but I put up my hand. He stopped.

"So, you realize that it could be you…that…" I gulped, "dies?"

"I've known since I was a little boy and my grandfather introduced me to the Mathilda Prophesies and explained my part in them. Just as Wilding has known what his destiny was since he was young. We've both grown up knowing we'd either marry you or bleed for you."

"Oh Great Goddess and all things under the moon and the stars," I breathed.

I wanted to cry, I really did, but I was getting sick of crying.

"You're telling me your choice is a lifetime of tantrums, drama and 'does my butt look big in this?' or…death? And you're sticking around?" He made no response so I asked, "Are you nuts?"

He started to grin.

Holy shit.

What if it was him, Aidan, who was going to die?

What if it happened tomorrow?

What if it happened tonight?

I put my hand to my mouth.

"I can't bear this," I told him on a whisper.

His face got gentle. "Yes, you can."

"No, I don't think I can. What if something happens to you, soon, tonight, tomorrow? How will I, we haven't…you and I haven't…but Ash and I…"

I stopped.

Aidan's body went still.

"Ash and you what?" Aidan asked.

"Well, Ash and I at least have…"

I stopped again because his grin was gone.

Oops.

Uh-oh.

"Ash and you have at least what?"

"Aidan, you have to know this is an impossible position for me to be in."

"Ash and you have what?"

His voice was icy and he was coming toward me in that stalky way again.

"Aidan, you're stalking me," I told him as I backed away.

"Damn straight. Ash and you have what?"

I stood my ground and he stopped in front of me. I was a big idiot for saying anything at all.

In my defense, I *had* just learned one of the men in my life was going to die for me and I thought that was a pretty good excuse. But since I did say something, I had no choice (obviously, because he was being stalky and looking broody) but to finish it.

So I stood on tippy-toes and whispered in his ear, as quickly as I could, about the Big O and Ash sleeping in bed with me.

It was only fair.

What were the words? He had a fifty-fifty chance to "bleed" for me.

When I was done, Aidan rocked back on his heels.

"I see."

"I feel like I should apologize," I told him. "But these aren't exactly normal courtships, you know. Neither of you have taken me to a movie or on a picnic or dinner…oh wait, you've taken me to dinner, um…kinda twice…but…"

Shit.

I was babbling.

Shit!

He started stalking me again.

I moved back.

"I thought you were shattered…you were gonna find another bed," I reminded him.

"I'm thinking I might stay in here tonight."

Oh boy.

There we were, me retreating, him advancing.

This man was either going to die for me or give me three babies.

Okay then.

Why was I running away?

I stopped and he covered the distance in two strides, swung me up like I weighed as much as a bag of sugar and tossed me on the bed.

He pulled off his shirt.

Six pack, check!

(Oo, and those nice, sinewy forearms, oh my…)

"I feel stupid in this outfit," I shared because I was nervous and couldn't think of anything else to say. I was staring at his abs like I was going to take a bite out of them and my whole body was shivering.

"Take it off."

Yikes!

"No!"

"Okay, I'll take it off."

Man, oh man.

I fall for them, don't I? Every bossy word out of his mouth made my nether regions quiver. I was ready for him before his knee hit the bed.

Then his knee hit the bed. Then his body hit me. Then his mouth hit mine.

He kissed me, hard, wet, *deep*, ohmygoddess, my insides melted.

He did this for a long time. Then his lips slid down my cheek and with his mouth on my neck, his hands trailing my body, he whispered, "You want me to stop?"

I didn't say anything as his fingers pulled at the multitude of fabric at my waist and his tongue did amazing things to the area around my ear.

"Darling, now is the time to say if you want me to stop," he murmured.

Oo, he called me "darling."

I had no words.

His hand found the drawstring, conquered the fabric, his lips again found my lips...his tongue again found my tongue...

Oh me...oh my.

He broke the kiss but said against my mouth, "Last chance, Mathilda."

"Do...not...stop," I breathed.

I felt his smile against my mouth then his lips slid across my cheek again and, back at my ear, he chuckled and it felt like a million feathers danced from my ear over my entire body.

My nipples turned to rocks and my stomach went molten.

And then I didn't feel anything else for a good long while except the two fingers sliding inside me.

And the thumb on me.

Ohmygoddess, ohmygoddess, ohmygoddess!

Fingers, thumbs, mouth, tongue, oh my!

I arched my hips against his hand right before I moaned his name, real slow.

Yay!

Yayayayay!

Afterward, he kissed me softly, and when I opened my eyes to look at him, I saw he was watching me, and he whispered, "God, you're beautiful."

Yay!

While I recovered, he moved, adjusting my pajamas and stripping to his boxers and he turned out the lights. He slid us both under the covers and pulled me into his arms.

"Um..." I didn't know what to say.

Was that it?

Were we done?

"Shh, darling, I'm exhausted. Go to sleep."

Excuse me?

"Uh, Aidan? Um...sorry, but...what about you?"

"Don't worry about me. I'm good."

Wha'?

"You're…*good?*"

"Yes. Sleep now."

He wasn't good.

He was even.

Fucking men.

~

Will say though, that waking up next to fabulous man who a) will die for me or b) will be my husband and c) calls me beautiful after he makes me climax, is quite lovely.

To say the least.

Ash spoons. Ash pulls you to the warmth of his body and keeps you there, all night, protecting you.

Aidan is not a cuddler. Although I fell asleep in his arms, somewhere in the night I was free to sprawl willy-nilly across my side of the bed. Though, he was not distant. He ended up on his belly, close, with one hand resting possessively on my ass, fingers curling around my hip, the sheets down around his waist and his gorgeous back on view.

Make of that what you will.

So now I sit wrapped up in his robe, in the window seat alternately watching him sleep and writing in my Book of Shadows.

And thinking about my future.

And about Josie, who will save the world.

And about Ash and Aidan and their lifetime of knowing they'll either marry The Chosen One or die protecting her.

And myself, who will have to live without one of them.

The Month of August

3 August

Lots to tell, little time. It's all becoming a blur of work, study, hunt, cast and plot.

Let's see, where did I leave off…?

Oh yes.

I left Aidan in bed, (poor baby, so sleepy). Dressed in my shorts and cami (borrowed one of Aidan's sweaters to go over because it had turned cold, gray and rainy…again) and headed down to the kitchens (had a tour the night before—truly fascinating, The Institute, but too much to tell).

I ended up shooing the cook (who, at a glance, was around nine hundred and eight years old and seriously needed a day off) out of the kitchen.

There were pints and pints of blueberries in the fridge for some reason, so I made the entire membership of The Institute homemade blueberry pancakes with golden syrup and crisp fried, streaky bacon.

I declined to eat in the dining hall (was in clothes from day before and no makeup, so no way was I going to be on show), but instead, ate at the big, wooden table in the kitchen.

Dr. Bennett sat with me, drinking a cup of tea from a delicate china cup and saucer.

Conversation was scarce. Mostly, he watched me.

Once I'd nearly finished, he said, "Did you sleep well, my dear?"

Without thinking, I answered, "I found it tough to settle, but after a while, I slept like a baby."

I had been concentrating on wiping the last bits of syrup with pancake on my plate when I looked up to see a whisper of a smile playing on his lips.

The lights flashed on in my brain.

I'd been had.

Under my breath, I started singing, "Matchmaker" from *Fiddler on the Roof*.

He took a sip of tea but still, he did it grinning.

"You know, Dr. Bennett, I think you are one sly fox," I told him.

"Indeed?" he asked.

"Indeed," I answered.

He nodded then to my surprise said, "And you, Miss Honeycutt, are quite a breath of fresh air."

My mouth dropped open.

How nice!

Just then, one of the members walked (more like hobbled) in.

"Mr. Wilding is here for Miss Honeycutt. He's in the entrance hall."

I jumped up. "Better go, mustn't keep Mr. Wilding waiting."

"I'll escort you," Dr. Bennett offered.

It wasn't exactly him escorting me, I think he forgot his stick and needed to lean on someone. To all appearances, he looked like he was gallantly holding my elbow. The pressure on my arm, though, was more than gallant.

I didn't let on, just walked slowly like I had all day.

"So, Dr. Bennett, do you know where Jeremy Bligh is?"

"I'm sorry to say, Miss Honeycutt, that we have not had a report from Professor Bligh in some time."

Mm.

"Well, Dr. Bennett, would you tell me if you had a report from good ol' Jeremy?" I asked.

He stopped and turned to me.

"Miss Honeycutt, you are a clever woman so I won't bore you with my theories on the cycles of history. Suffice it to say, we have our difficult times, we have our trouble-free times. Unfortunately, fate has settled on me the duty of guiding this Institute through what will be its most complicated time in history. This is a task I do not delight in, but it is my providence to direct The Institute through these rocky waters. I can tell you, Miss Honeycutt, in a time of witches using electric wands, not to mention bombs; I would indeed inform you if I felt there were tidings you needed to know."

I took a moment to process words like "tidings" and "providence," then I kissed his cheek.

"Big changes, eh, Dr. Bennett?" I remarked softly.

"Enormous, Miss Honeycutt," he remarked softly right back.

We eventually made it to the entrance hall in which Ash was standing smack dab in the middle, somehow communicating that he owned the room even though he most definitely did not.

He'd slept elsewhere such was his aversion to The Institute.

"I'll leave you here, Miss Honeycutt," Dr. Bennett said.

I figured that was a wise choice.

"Thanks for everything," I replied.

"Our pleasure." And he smiled, so I smiled back.

Ash had turned at our approach and was watching me leave Dr. Bennett and walk toward him and he did this with his arms crossed on his chest and a not-very-happy look on his face.

I thought it was probably being at The Institute.

Then I thought it was the fact that I was wearing Aidan's sweater.

I wasn't going to worry about it because I knew something about him then that I didn't know before, and now I had a lot more patience with his bad attitude.

I must have looked at him all dewy-eyed because he said, "Jesus, Seymour told you, didn't he?"

Talk about spoiling the mood.

"Told me what?"

He looked me top to bottom.

He knew.

He knew everything.

As in, *everything*.

How did he know?

Holy crap, what did I do in this situation?

"Don't let it change anything, Matty," he ordered, using my nickname, which somehow made the bossy order less bossy.

"Okay," I replied, because what else could I say?

"We ready?" Aidan asked, walking into the room, shrugging into a jacket.

"Yep," Ash answered.

And off we went.

~

We showed the photo here and there, followed a few leads, went back to London, took another trip to The Hobgoblin (Derek, exasperated and throwing up hands: "Not again!") then we went home.

I was busy on my mobile the whole way arranging to get the girls together.

We needed a meeting in the worst way.

I invited Lucy because I figured Lucy was vulnerable, so she should know what she'd gotten herself into by being my friend.

My crazy Lucy sounded excited, saying she'd be there and "couldn't wait."

Love her.

~

Approximately twelve point five seconds after we arrived home (slight exaggeration), the coven, Lucy and Josie clustered in our huge kitchen, sitting around the table, on chairs dragged in, on countertops. I stood at one end, Ash and Aidan flanking me like sentries.

I gave a brief, er, debrief. We handed out copies of photos of Bligh.

Lastly, I warned the witches not to use their magic unless necessary, to keep topped up to their full powers, have their ears and eyes open, communicate frequently and keep their wands with them at all times.

The coven and Lucy left, the Honeycutts and Josie remained.

I asked for a report on the intelligence ops we were performing. Not much going on and surprisingly nothing from Mom about Douglas Addison (although she glanced at Ash after her report, which I thought strange).

We assessed the protection spells and did a little planning and plotting and arranged our next meet to discuss The Gathering.

Ash disappeared after everyone was dismissed.

I walked Aidan to the Merc.

He turned to me before getting in the car and I caught his hand.

"Stay," I urged on a heartfelt whisper. "Go get some of your things and move to The Gables. You'll be safer here."

He laughed like what I said was amusing, cupped the side of my face and ran his thumb down my cheekbone, then his hand dipped to my jaw so his thumb could glide over my bottom lip.

"Matty, you know that won't work. Don't worry about me. I can take care of myself."

Then he kissed me softly, and after I slid my arms around his waist, very, very deeply.

Oh my.

After I watched him drive away, I was walking back to The Gables when I saw a shadow move.

Holy crap.

It was Ash.

Holy crap, part *deux*.

He was walking purposefully toward me while speaking in a growl. "Mathilda, I'm going to warn you I'm not particularly keen on sharing my women."

Great.

"Thanks, Ash, that helps things a lot, like I'm not already confused enough."

Then he arrived at me, and before I knew what he was about, he grabbed me, pulled me to him and kissed me, not softly, but hard, hot and yes, also deep.

Holy crap.

"I find there's a hint of him left on you," he murmured after he was done, "I'm going to erase it. Do you understand what I'm saying to you?"

I nodded, my knees were weak.

He let me go. "Don't say you weren't warned."

Holy crap.

I needed a drink and luckily, when I arrived in the kitchen, Mom was there.

"Martini or mojito?" she asked.

"Margarita," I answered.

It was a tequila night.

I sat at the kitchen window staring at the sun setting across the water.

Mom sat behind me and started twirling my hair like she used to when I was a little girl.

"Do you know which one it is? Which one is going to die?" I asked the Bristol Channel quietly.

She knew exactly what I was talking about.

"Oh, baby, I wish I did, so I could guard your heart like they guard your life."

I sighed.

She sighed too.

Then I turned to my mother. "What's the deal with Addison, Mom? Why'd you look at Ash when —?"

"Don't ask, Matty. It's our secret, Sebastian's and mine. Keeping it from you is protecting you."

I nodded and I did this without hesitation.

In Mom we trust.

~

The next morning, I knocked on Mavis's Magic Room door.

She was crystal gazing when I walked in.

"We've got an unwelcome houseguest," I told her.

"Don't let your emotion override your intuition, diddums," she warned.

Diddums.

Mavis.

Yeesh.

Even with the warning, she got up and we went together to find Althea who was reclining on the couch in the Plush Parlor watching *50 First Dates*.

"That Adam Sandler," she said when we walked in, "he's a charmer."

Oh, for goddess's sakes.

Obviously she hadn't seen *The Longest Yard*.

"Althea, you have a choice." I launched right in. "Either Ash can escort you back to your cottage today or you can sober up and start to work for your keep in The Dozen."

She stared at me, her eyes narrowed.

"Your choice," I said.

Mavis stood next to me, her arms crossed on her ample bosoms.

"I didn't ask to come here," Althea pointed out.

"No, you didn't. My bad. I'm sorry. Now you can go home."

I left, went to the door of The Dungeons and pounded.

Althea joined me in the hall, Mavis trailing her.

"Girl, you're a nutter, you know that?" Althea said to me.

I banged on the doors louder.

"Ash!" I shouted.

"Don't!" Althea stopped me. "Okay, I'll work for my keep."

That surprised me.

"But, you have to get some of my things, clothes, shoes…I'm tired of this borrowed stuff." She pointed to Octavia's castoff sundress that she was wearing, which was, quite rightly, not very attractive.

"You make a list, we'll send someone to get it," I told her. "False alarm!" I shouted at The Dungeon door.

"Why don't you want to go back, Althea?" Mavis asked softly.

See?

Good cop, bad cop.

Or in this case, good witch, bad witch.

I put my hands on my hips and waited.

"Don't pretend you don't know," Althea replied, resignation in her voice. "That one may be a nutter," she jerked a thumb at me (nice), "but Agatha Darling is far loonier."

"And, how exactly is Agatha loonier?" Mavis asked.

The door to The Dungeon opened. Ash came out and stood behind me.

Close behind me.

Althea blanched.

I can't imagine why. I looked at him over my shoulder and he looked better than ever in a white T-shirt and faded jeans.

And he smelled *divine*.

"Girl, you are the most boy-crazy female I've ever met," Althea announced and turned to Ash. "You should bed her so she'll quit running around like a—"

"Don't finish that sentence," Ash warned in a chilly voice.

Althea snapped her mouth shut.

"How is Agatha loonier?" Mavis persevered.

Althea looked at Mavis then she looked at me then at Ash.

Then she sighed.

After that, she spoke. "That witch chose the wrong path years ago. I tried to warn her but she wouldn't listen." She closed her eyes and took in a deep breath, muttering almost as if to herself. "I can't abide a dark witch."

"And the rest of the coven?" Mavis prodded.

"Some chose her path, some didn't, but were afraid to go against the High Priestess of a coven as fierce as Edwards. Her power is fearful, even when she isn't using manmade implements. And her wrath is worse."

"And you? What did you choose?" I asked.

Althea shook her head, clearly struggling with something.

And then, right in front of our eyes, she deflated.

All of her irritating bravado, gone in an instant.

It was a dreadful thing to witness.

"I tried to warn her. She wouldn't listen," Althea admitted softly and leaned against the wall. "And she didn't like it, what I had to say. We rowed, often. I tried to take over the coven. It didn't work. They held the ceremony. I was too old, too weak, too sick. I couldn't fight them."

"What ceremony?" I asked.

Mavis put her hand on Althea's arm.

"They've stripped you of your magic, haven't they?" Mavis whispered.

To my disbelief, tears came to Althea's eyes and she nodded.

What?

Oh Great Goddess.

Stripped of magic, I've never heard of such a thing!

How cruel!

How scary!

How just plain, old mean!

"I thought as much," Mavis muttered.

"And the sight. They took that too," Althea went on.

Holy crap.

"But, the other day, you spoke in my head…you—" I started.

"That wasn't magic, Mathilda. That was mind games. Anyone can do that with enough practice, and I have over a hundred and fifty years of it," Althea answered.

I looked at Ash who looked at me. He raised his brow.

I reckoned I shouldn't believe her but I did.

And I felt sorry for her.

"We'll keep you safe, dear. Don't you worry," Mavis promised and led the old witch away while Ash and I watched.

"Do you believe her?" I asked Ash.

"Yes," he replied, took one last look at the pair of witches as they disappeared and then he went back to The Dungeons.

I headed to my Tower Room. I needed to research this ceremony business.

I also needed to find out if there was a way to get her power back.

I figured we were going to need it.

~

The Gathering:

Unfortunately, I had to fly to The Gathering. It was tradition and not negotiable (and I'd already bucked tradition in so many other ways that I felt I should pick my battles).

The few broomstick lessons I'd had up to that point had not gone so well. But, I must say that Gran was a somewhat impatient teacher.

Viv took over after Gran and she wasn't much better.

It wasn't until lessons with Su that I really caught on.

But I was still a little unsteady doing sidesaddle (would prefer to go with a straddle but that wasn't an option, especially when going to a Gathering).

We flew, all of us, with Althea on the back of Viv's broom, to the standing stones at Avebury.

All the tourists went to Stonehenge.

Spinal Tap even wrote a song about Stonehenge.

But Avebury was much better.

Much bigger.

And far more magical.

And you could walk amongst the stones, touch them and they just hummed with history and power.

I loved Avebury.

Anyhoo.

Some bright spark had built a village smack in the middle of the stone circle centuries ago so The Gatherings had to move out of the circles and down to the end of the Avenue.

By the time we'd landed, everyone was there forming an occult circle and watching us approach.

I must say I was surprised at how unsurprising everyone looked. It was all very...*Hollywood*.

On my first look at the troll and goblin, I had to wonder if Peter Jackson was magical, they were very *Lord of the Rings* (except the troll was shorter and less stupid-looking and the orc-y goblin had little flightless wings).

There was one goateed magus, floating about three feet from the ground on a magic carpet.

The banshee had radiant white hair, and lots of it, with robes so close to the same color you didn't know where the hair stopped and the robes started. The robes and hair flowed so much, even standing still, there had to be magical, invisible fans blowing at her. She also had bright blue eyes just like the freaky school kids in Bonnie Tyler's "Total Eclipse of the Heart" video.

There was a vampire, slightly older than the dude at The Hobgoblin but no less pale and lanky. He leaned against a standing stone, his hands in the pockets of his trousers, watching us (me?) from under his brows. Regardless of his paleness and thinness, he was sexy as hell.

The wizard had dark gray-brown robes and a pointy hat that had flopped over to the side.

The werewolf man had stretch marks and a visible bad attitude.

There were two faerie elves weaving around and leaving lemon and peach contrails.

And the sorcerer's soft, lavender robes shone with sparkly quarter moons and stars.

The sorceress, now she was something. Supermodel gorgeous with long, straighter-than-straight white-blonde hair and pale-blue robes with the sparkly moons and stars. She was wearing this kickass jeweled, large-weave skull cap that had this lush, aquamarine teardrop hanging down the center of her forehead.

Fab.

Dr. Bennett was there and he gave me a little nod, and if I saw correctly, a wink.

There was another man who was older and very handsome and he stared at me, and only me, in a broody way that seemed very familiar. He had to be the Elder from *Le Société de Mathilde*.

Once Althea and the Honeycutts joined The Gathering, Prunella, the Hag, began the proceedings by stepping to the center of our little circle and lifting her wand.

Out of nowhere, a gleaming white unicorn materialized, all beam-me-up Scotty sparkles and My Favorite Pony glitter—immediately touching the point of his horn to Prunella's wand as the two fairies buzzed in like the Red Arrows doing a double flyby and then, *blam*!

The firework exploded, going wide and high, and the pixie dust fell in a perfect circle around us. The ground started rumbling and then huge buried stones rose up, breaking through the turf, grass and dirt flying everywhere and forming a mini-circular amphitheater.

Great Mother Earth, wind and fire, it was cool.

The Hag, the Unicorn and a see-through man in an old-fashioned suit who was surrounded by a weird mist walked into the center of the amphitheater.

The Gathering had begun.

And that was as exciting as it got.

I kid you not.

You know how they show those photos of people at the UN or in Congress having a snooze? Head resting on their hand, elbow resting on the table, mouth open, eyes closed?

Do you want to know why?

Because government is boring.

Boring.

Boring.

Ho-fucking-hum.

Blah, blah and more blah.

Everyone talking a lot.

And no one saying a damn thing.

There I was, past midnight, at the end of a magical avenue of standing stones, sitting in a long-undiscovered, enchanted amphitheater surrounded by supernatural beings, and I fell asleep.

"Mathilda Guinevere Honeycutt!"

My name rang in my ears.

Oops.

Viv, who was sitting beside me, nudged me.

I opened my eyes.

Everyone was staring at me.

"Are you very tired, Mistress Honeycutt?" Endora, the Lady, asked.

"Er…" I answered.

Yikes, shades of yesteryear and chemistry class.

"Is there something else you'd rather be doing, Mistress Honeycutt?" The Lady went on, kinda snottily.

"Um…" I answered.

"Come forward." That was Prunella, the Hag, still standing in the middle with the Unicorn and the ghost of the Headless Horseman. The banshee must have had the floor because she was also in the middle, but at my approach, she floated to the side and sat down (or more like, hovered over a stone seat while her hair and robes blew in non-existent wind).

The Lady was standing on the lowest stone of the circle of seats, staring daggers at me.

I decided that I didn't like Endora Eccles much. She was kind of a bitch.

I walked into the middle.

"Today's proceedings are very important, Mistress Honeycutt," Prunella told me when I arrived. "We haven't had a Gathering—"

"I know," I interrupted. "Since the Vampyre Mutiny of 1962."

Prunella pursed her lips.

"Can I ask," Endora called from her place at the side, "what Mistress Honeycutt *is wearing*?"

I'd expected this. I was supposed to be wearing the witch's uniform, all pointy hats, ripped skirts and red and white striped tights, etcetera.

Not…gonna…happen.

I'd rather be dead, and it took a lot for me to say that in my current life circumstances.

I'd ditched the striped tights and replaced them with fishnets. I cut off the ragged edges of the skirt and the bells of the sleeves and hemmed them. I pulled out the laces of the bodice and added some strategic double-sided tape in the cleavage area. And the *pièce de résistance* was a pair of black, patent-leather Manolo Blahnik mary janes.

I looked like Versace Witch Barbie.

Fab-you-las.

(Don't think I didn't notice the sorceress staring covetously at my mary janes.)

"It's my new and improved uniform," I answered.

I noticed the vampire grinning, but most everyone else was either silent or looked disapproving.

"I hardly think my outfit is—" I started to go on.

"This is exactly—" Endora interrupted me.

"What we should be talking about!" I finished loudly, totally fed up with her diva attitude, not to mention the whole bloody Gathering farce.

I mean, I was The Chosen One so I got to be the diva, thank-you-very-much.

"Okay, I fell asleep," I told The Gathering. "Ex-ka-youse *me!*" I turned to Prunella and the Unicorn. "I'm sorry but I'm the one whose eight-year-old Spellbound was kidnapped thus beginning probably years of counseling."

I whipped around to face Endora.

"I'm the one who was struck by lightning…*three times!*" I jerked my thumb at my chest.

I then whipped around again to face the vampire.

"I'm the one who was shot at while saving an oracle who, incidentally, had her magic and sight stripped in some seriously foul ceremony, that, while we're here, may I say, should be banned."

I turned to the sorceress.

"Last but not least, I'm the one who nearly was blown to smithereens by a fucking bomb!"

There were gasps at my language.

"You brought it on yourself!" Endora retorted from behind me.

I turned back to her and I knew my eyes were wide. "How on earth did I do that?"

"By flying in the face of custom…of ritual…of tradition," Endora answered.

I knew I didn't like her.

"You think it's okay to strike someone with lightning, *three times*, for doing something you don't like?"

"Yes," she answered calmly.

Be-atch.

Totally didn't like her.

"That's like cutting off a child's hand for stealing an Oreo," I replied, disgusted.

"What's an Oreo?" I heard the troll ask the goblin.

The goblin shrugged.

"Hardly," Endora went on. "You're challenging the very laws of nature."

"I believe it's a biscuit, you know, a cookie," the vampire answered the troll.

"Ah," the troll muttered.

I ignored them.

"I don't think so. If I was, the trees wouldn't protect me. If I was, then nature would take away my power. Instead, the Great Goddess has given me *more* power. More than you, more than anyone."

Endora whipped out her wand.

There were more gasps and some uncomfortable shuffling about.

"Oh, please," I snorted. "You don't scare me, there's no place to plug that thing in around here."

Endora's eyes rounded with anger and I turned my back to her. She wouldn't be stupid enough to fire on me in front of my mother or Gran or my sisters.

And certainly not Mavis.

I threw out my arms, looked around at everyone and carried on.

"If I have better things to do…" I whipped back around to Endora, "and make no mistake, my Lady, I do have better things to do…" I again addressed The Gathering, "then you'll have to pardon me so I can do them."

"Mistress Honeycutt," Prunella stopped me, "this Gathering —"

"Begging your pardon, Madame Hag, but this Gathering is taking too much damn time," I declared and then turned back to address everyone around me. "You're here to speak for your people, but don't use a hundred words to say one. The way I see it, you're either with me or against me. You are either traditionalists, or you are modernists."

I was making this up as I went along but I think it sounded okay.

Therefore I kept going. "You either want to live in the closet and hide yourself and your magnificent magic away for the rest of time, or you want to be seen and heard, have a say in how this planet is being governed and, might I add...destroyed."

Everyone was silent and staring.

"My dear girl, if it was that easy —" Prunella began.

"It *is* that easy," I answered.

"Nothing is black and white," the Headless Horseman floated up to me, his arm outstretched and he touched my shoulder.

Of course, I didn't feel anything except a bitter chill.

Spooky.

He looked nice enough, and he definitely had a way about him, but I had to say, he was creepy. I think this had something to do with the way he carried his head like a football half the time.

Ick!

But I digress.

"It *is* just that," I replied. "Black and white. This is the beginning or this is the end. You pick," I said to him, somewhat more ominously and dramatically than I intended, but I'd set the scene and I had to go with it. Then I swung around, throwing out my hand to encompass them all. "You all have to pick."

I looked at each one in turn then I walked on my fabulous shoes right to my broomstick (trying hard not to let the heels sink in to the ground) and I flew (somewhat unsteadily) away.

I knew I was being a drama queen, but I wasn't going to waste all night nor spend another moment with Endora who had to be in cahoots with Agatha Darling, Jeremy Bligh and the rest of them.

The be-atch.

When the rest got home, Mavis reported that the Unicorn had called a vote.

The vampires swore allegiance ("They're always a bit seditious, always up for a little maverick behavior. It's good to have their power on our side, but we must be cautious.")

The wizards and magi were okay either way.

The sorcerers, sorceresses and banshees wanted another Gathering.

The trolls, goblins and werewolves were out, no way, no how. Then again, trolls and goblins didn't exactly fit in with humans should they come out of the closet, and werewolves didn't like humans all that much (to say the least).

"And the witches?" I asked.

Endora was there to cast the witches' vote, so I pretty much knew the answer.

"Endora cast nay," Mavis said.

"So we're on our own," I muttered, dejected.

I wanted to cry, but I'd recently sworn off crying, at least until I was in my bed, in my princess fortress, on my own so no one could see me.

"Well," Mavis said, slowly, "Dr. Bennett explained that he and the Directors and Marcus and the rest of the Elders had formed an allegiance."

"Who's Marcus?" I asked.

"Marcus was the Elder in attendance. Marcus Wilding, Sebastian's father."

Ack!

"Ash's father..." I gulped, "was there?"

Oh goddess, no wonder that dude seemed so familiar.

Ack!

My possible father-in-law was there, and there I was looking like a more stylish Elvira, Mistress of Darkness—double sided tape and all.

Ack!

Now, I really wanted to cry.

"Yes, my dear, he was there and on our side. Both *Le Société* and The Institute are with us, my dear. His announcement made Prunella call a Council meeting. Highly unusual, Endora's not pleased. Normally, the Hag will defer to the Lady at Gatherings. But overturning the Lady's vote and demanding a meeting with the Maiden before casting the Council's binding vote..."

That pleased me no end.

We had some diplomatic work to do. Obviously, this was not going to be my project as I seemed pretty rubbish at diplomacy.

Gran took the assignment to approach, and win over, the wizards and magi and Mavis the sorcerers and sorceresses. They were like my chief Wiccan Whips, if you will.

Kinda cool.

I'd worry about the rest of the supernatural population later.

I called Aidan to let him know how it went, but he already knew.

I was pretty sure Ash already knew, considering his dad was there.

I thought about Marcus Wilding and wondered if Ash would look like him when he grew older.

If he grew older.

Hmm.

Then I went to bed and Daphne curled up in the crook of my knees and purred for a little bit before she fell asleep, and for the rest of the night, I tried to pretend I wasn't scared shitless.

∽

7 August

I figured I was okay.

I'd faced down the folks at The Hobgoblin and an entire Gathering. The Witch World was abuzz with my massive show of *cojones* if the recent newsletter was anything to go by.

So, this should be a piece of cake.

I mean, it was just The Dungeons.

And it was Ash's birthday.

I made him a German Chocolate cake dripping with that yummy, golden icing.

My plan was to carry it down to him, singing happy birthday.

I was The Chosen One with kickass magic—the leader of a revolution, the Che Guevara of the Witch World.

(I picked Che because he was handsome and charismatic and Fidel wasn't, at least not at first, he was scary and eventually became a despot. Incidentally, I was also ignoring the fact that Che ended up gunned down in a hut in Bolivia.)

(Would there one day be T-shirts and coffee mugs with my face on them?)

(Yikes!)

I stood at the door to The Dungeon, luscious cake balanced on one palm, my present tucked under my arm and my other hand ready to open the door.

Which I did.

Then I braced myself.

Nothing.

Whew!

Step one, done.

I stood, staring down the stone steps that led into darkness.

I felt a breeze float up.

It wasn't a pleasant breeze.

It was a malevolent breeze.

A breeze that wanted to hurt me.

Yikes.

I took a deep breath.

It's his birthday surprise, I can do this, I can do this, I told myself.

Nope.

I couldn't do this.

"Mathilda?"

I jumped, nearly dropping the cake.

Ash was walking up behind me.

He wasn't even in The Dungeons.

I'm such a dork.

"Happy birthday!" I cried.

He looked at me, the present, the cake, the open door and then back at me.

"I figured you wouldn't want a big thing made of it, so I thought I'd bring you a cake," I told him. "I was just about to go down…"

That's when the eyebrow went up and the arms crossed the chest, not saying it out loud but his body language screaming, "Liar, liar, pants on fire."

"Okay then," I gave in, exasperated. "I was just psyching myself up to go down but couldn't do it. There! I admit it!"

"May I?" He didn't wait for me to say he could, he took the cake and set it on a small side table. "And?" He took the present and without further ado, ripped off the paper.

I had bought him a fabulous Alexander McQueen shirt. It cost a fortune, but I'd never had a man with that kind of body to dress so I figured I'd go for it. I knew, once he had it on, it would be worth every donut I'd had to stuff with frosting and every cappuccino I'd had to cover with foam in order to afford it.

"It's Alexander McQueen," I said when the thick tissue paper and shiny box fell away and he'd shaken out the shirt and just stared at it.

"He's a very famous designer, or he was, though he still is. It's just that he's dead now. Tragic. He was an artist. A visionary. Anyway, he makes really nice, quality clothes…" I trailed off after realizing I was babbling.

Ash held the shirt out in front of him and then looked around it to me.

I'm so lame.

I bought an Alexander McQueen dress shirt for Sebastian Wilding —man of mystery.

A man who does tai chi in the garden with utter concentration even when Mom is singing Janis Joplin at the top of her lungs while digging in the tulips.

A man who breaks down doors and grabs guns out of shaking criminal hands without blinking an eye.

A man who trades a Jag XJS for an Audi TT coupe without any apparent financial heart attacks.

He probably had a dozen Alexander McQueen shirts and Armani and Hugo Boss…

"I didn't know what to get you. Maybe I should have got you that Burberry umbrella," I muttered, staring at my toes (painted hot, hot, *hot* pink).

Since I was staring at my toes, I didn't notice the hand whipping out until it had a hold of the front of my T-shirt.

One tug and I fell forward, not too far because I collided with the hard wall of Ash's chest and he crushed me in his arms, kissing me.

Deep.

Hot.

Wet.

And *long*.

"I love it," he murmured when he let me go. Then he picked up his cake and walked down the steps to The Dungeon.

Welp, guess that meant he wasn't sharing his cake.

I stared until the darkness swallowed him and then I shut the door.

And I leaned my forehead against it.

And let me tell you, it was right then that I realized I was really, really in trouble.

Really.

Because, I was in love with Sebastian Wilding.

Ack.

And I was pretty certain he liked me too.

A lot.

Worse still, I was in love with Aidan Seymour.

Ack.

I knew it the minute Aidan had grabbed my neck and kissed me on the nose, about to search for another room to sleep in even when he was "shattered."

And he liked me too.

A lot.

The question was…why?

Why did these two fabulous men like me?

Destiny?

Was it as simple as that?

I think not.

I opened the door again, and before I could stop myself, I ran down the steps.

Well, not all of the steps, about half a dozen of them before I had to stop.

"Ash!" I shouted.

Before I could lose (more) of my courage, I went down two more steps then felt something whipping against my ankles.

It felt like a rat's tail.

(Although I've never felt a rat's tail whip against my ankle, I figured that's what it would feel like.)

I whimpered.

"I hate The Dungeon," I whispered to myself. "Hate it, hate it, hate it."

(Pause.)

"Ash!" I shouted.

I stood there then turned back to the door and the precious light of safety and freedom coming from the main house, then I turned to look back down to the dark stairs.

What was I doing? Why was I down there?

I knew why…I had to ask…I had to know.

"Ash!"

There was an ominous creak.

And then, I kid you not, the door slammed behind me.

Gah!

Total darkness and I was (kind of) in The Dungeons.

"Holy fuck, shit, fuck, fuck, fuck." I ran back up the stairs while screeching, "Ash!"

I ran smack into the door, tried the knob, it wouldn't open.

I tried it again.

It still wouldn't open.

Holy fuck, shit, fuck, fuck, fuck!

I started banging on the door with my fists.

"Ash!"

Something settled on my shoulder and I screamed at the top of my lungs like someone straight out of a horror movie.

"Mathilda." Ash turned me, grabbed both arms and shook me gently. "Calm down."

Then he reached across me and opened the door.

What?

I stared at the door.

Oh well, who cared, whatever, the door was open.

Happy light flooded in and I sighed with relief.

I was too relieved to be embarrassed about my scaredy-cat display.

"I hate The Dungeons," I told him.

"You don't say."

I took a good look at him.

Ohmygoddess.

He was wearing the shirt.

He'd changed into the shirt.

And it looked good.

Really good.

"It fits!" I cried.

Ash didn't say anything for a second.

Then he asked, "You tried to go down, didn't you?"

I nodded.

"I think I got down more than five steps," I stated proudly.

"Excellent progress." He grinned. "Why?"

"Why what?"

"Why'd you try to go down?"

Mm.

Well.

After the trauma I'd just endured, I'd lost my nerve.

"Mathilda?" he prompted.

Okay, well, why the hell not?

"Why do you like me?" I asked him.

"What?"

"Why do you like me?"

"Like you?"

"Yeah, like me? Kiss me, touch me, protect me, wanna marry me, give me the big O, you know, *like* me?"

Ash stared at me.

What he didn't do was speak.

So I went on, "I'm nuts. I'm kookier than kooky. I'm materialistic. I'm a klutz. I make stupid decisions. I have a big ass. I'm a designer-label whore." I paused. "By the way, that shirt looks good on you."

He kept staring at me.

I carried on, "I've no idea what I'm doing half the time. I know that high heels are going to ruin my back and my knees one day but I keep wearing them. I don't limit my carbs. I don't count calories. I don't go past six weeks before getting my hair retouched. Ever. Some people take vows of chastity or poverty, I take vows of highlights. I once sold my plasma so I could afford to highlight my hair."

Perhaps I was going too far with these revelations?

He leaned a shoulder against the wall and (yet again!) crossed his arms on his chest.

Stupidly, I kept speaking. "I never leave the house without at least lip gloss. I think Madonna is a genius. I'd rather study a face painted by Kevyn Aucoin than stare at the Mona Lisa. Why? Why on earth do you like me? It doesn't fit."

If he gave me The Chosen One crap or something like, "you make me laugh" I was going to pack it all in and move back to America, I swore to the goddess.

But he didn't say that. He didn't say anything.

"Ash, I really need to know."

And to my surprise, he answered.

"Because your hair is soft and you smell like oranges and jasmine."

Er...what?

"Oranges?" I asked.

"Yes, oranges. And because you're always doing something, trying something or learning something. You never complain of being bored and are always using your mind and your body, even if the results aren't exactly perfect."

That's, um...nice.

I think.

He kept going. "And you have tremendous courage and such a strong personality and sense of compassion that people connect with you instantly."

Oh.

Wow.

He stepped toward me. "And you have the most beautiful smile I've ever seen and I like that, even with everything going on, I see that smile often."

"Mathilda!"

Oh shit!

My mother was shouting at me from the somewhere close, too close.

I can't believe it.

Why?

Why did the gods conspire against me?

"Ash…I can't…"

The fingers of one of his hands slid into my hair while his other hand grabbed my waist and gently brought me forward. "You're extraordinary and I want to…" And then his mouth came to my ear and finished saying what he wanted to do, *exactly* what he wanted to do and he went into some detail.

My belly melted.

"Now, *that* would be a nice birthday gift," I breathed.

"I'll consider it for your next birthday," he said.

Oh my.

"Mathilda!" Mom again.

"So, you like the shirt?" I asked, my fingers toying with a button.

He touched his lips to mine before he said, "No, Mathilda, I love the shirt."

I took in a breath.

"I don't want you to die for me," I blurted.

His thumb traced my ear.

"I don't intend to die for you."

I nodded. "Good."

Finally, we were on the same page!

"But I will if I have to."

Ack!

And he let me go and walked away, back down the steps.

I watched him.

"Mathilda!" Mom screeched.

"Coming!" I screeched back.

Boy, was I in trouble.

~

16 August

Fay was the one who brought me the information. Her faerie had heard it from a vampire who got it from a warlock. Not exactly primo info but we'd had nothing to go on for ages.

Locked tight—the world of the paranormal. No one talking and everyone waiting for war to break out before they picked sides.

(Still not heard from BecBec or why I couldn't understand a word she said and everyone apparently talked loads to their faeries.)

I didn't know what to do with the info because I didn't believe it.

Not.

One.

Word.

Fay didn't want to tell me but she also didn't want me not to know. But we all knew we had to follow every lead, no matter how crazy it sounded.

And this one was Crazy with a capital C.

Althea and I were coming back from our shifts at The Dozen when she helped me make up my mind that I should pursue it.

(Just to prove it wrong.)

Althea was pulling herself out of the Mini when she said, "Tonight's the night, lass."

I was surprised.

"Did Fay tell you?" I asked.

"Nope, had a vision."

"I thought..."

"No, no...years ago, before they took it away. I remember most of my visions and the dates. Yes, even as old as I am," she said waving away the disbelieving look I gave her. "I saw you watching them, both of them...all of them." She paused and looked at me. "I hope you know what you're doing."

I shook my head. "I never know what I'm doing."

We were making our slow way into The Gables. We'd decided to limit Althea's shifts to two hours. She was drinking far less these days and had less of an attitude, but she was still older than the hills and beginning to act it.

"That's what I like about you, girl, your honesty."

"I thought you didn't like me."

"Let's just say, you're growing on me."

"And how's that?"

Her reply was so quiet, I barely heard her. "You're trying to get my magic back, that's how. I don't have a lot of time left on this beautiful earth, girl. But I don't want to die without my magic. They can have the sight, I never had much care for that, but I miss my power."

Well, there you go.

~

The sky was clear, the moon shone brightly and Su and Viv were waiting for me in the wood.

"We're coming," Viv announced.

"This is mine to do. I need you two safe in case something happens to me," I informed her.

The looks on their faces told me they were going to be stubborn.

"Don't make me do this the hard way," I warned.

"You watch too many movies," Su said, and while she was saying it, I whipped out my wand and zapped them.

They both fell to the ground, asleep.

Probably they didn't see that coming.

I looked at them, laying peacefully on the forest floor, and I stumbled to my tree.

"Take care of them," I whispered to it, my hands and forehead pressed against the beloved bark.

I felt an answering jolt of power, nodded, swallowed the tears I wanted to shed for zapping my two siblings with a sleeping spell and what I had to do that night, and off I went.

To Ladye Bay.

It took a while for me to find my hiding spot, but I did. I scratched the shit out of my arms on the brambles where I had to hide but I'd been halfway smart, that is smart enough to wear a pair of jeans so my legs were safe even if my arms weren't.

I wasn't comfortable, at all, but I sat there anyway, and I waited.

Then I waited some more.

Then some more.

After that, I realized that the vampire or warlock was yanking Fay's faerie's chain and it was time for me to go home.

You cannot know how relieved I was.

So relieved I almost cried.

Then, out of nowhere, BecBec appeared before me, and before I could make a sound, she had her finger to her lips and she pointed to the steps that led to Ladye Bay.

I watched Ash and Aidan jog down the steps and walk through the rocks to the water's edge. They didn't speak and their body language was so stiff you could feel the animosity, even where I was, stuck in the bramble on the cliff face looking down on them.

BecBec was under bramble cover, just like me, but then she shot out, just a smidge, to draw my attention to something in the sky.

A bat.

Holy shit.

A bat.

Did I like bats?

No, I don't think I did.

Ack!

Couldn't bats see in the dark?

Could it see me?

Crap…why didn't I bring my cloak?

And then…you will not believe…as it reached the bay, it dipped low, lower, then right before my very eyes it turned into a man.

Poof! Just like that.

And not just any man.

Douglas Fucking Addison.

Holy shit.

Douglas Addison was a vampire.

Ohmygoddess.

And vampires were our allies.

Right?

Okay, okay, I could deal with this.

This was okay, this could even be good.

He walked up to Ash and shook his hand.

They knew each other.

Ash never let on.

Why wouldn't Ash tell me?

Is this what he and Mom knew?

Ash gestured to Aidan and Douglas and Aidan did that man handshake, grab-the-upper-arm-comrade thing.

Aidan clearly was not surprised at the bat-into-man-vampire display.

He knew, too.

Why didn't *he* tell me?

I could normally trust Aidan to tell me everything.

Well, eventually.

The three of them had their heads bowed, talking, looking around furtively.

What were they doing?

What were they saying?

About five minutes later, Aidan turned and left, jogging through the beach stones and up to the steps—somewhat in a hurry.

Ash and Addison remained.

Ten minutes passed, maybe fifteen. My legs were hurting from being in a weird position.

Douglas and Ash had a lot to talk about. Addison did a lot of gesturing; Ash did a lot of listening.

I tried to think of spells to allow me to hear their conversation without letting Ash into my head via our mind-meld and to keep my mind off my palms, which were digging in the underbrush.

Then BecBec burrowed in the crook of my arm, hiding her faerie light.

And I saw the broomstick against moon.

It swooped down and landed.

No.

Yes.

There she was.

The warlock was right.

There was Agatha Darling with Jeremy on the back of her broomstick.

No, no, no.

Please no.

I blinked.

There she was.

I closed one eye and squinted with the other.

It was still her.

Damn.

She walked right up and kissed Addison's cheek.

Jeremy shook his hand.

Then she kissed *Ash's* cheek and Jeremy shook *Ash's* hand.

No, no, no.

Please *no*.

I watched, searching for something, some sign.

But everything seemed kosher.

Even…

Friendly.

Ack!

Of course Aidan would tell me Ash wasn't a traitor.

Because they both were.

No wonder he was so very agitated when I asked.

One would father my children, one would die for me.

Bullshit.

I watched, tears in the back of my throat and stinging my eyes.

How stupid was I?

You could tell they were plotting by the way they stood, talked, looked around. This wasn't the first time they met; there was a familiarity about them.

Then Ash looked toward my hiding spot, and I could swear he was looking right at me.

Shit!

I hadn't controlled Mavis's mind-meld.

I held my breath, cleared my mind and didn't move.

Then Agatha said something and he dipped his head to hear her, respectfully, attentively.

My chest started hurting.

But he didn't raise any alarm.

I still did not breathe easy. Ash was highly trained. BecBec stayed hidden and I didn't move a muscle, I barely breathed.

Not too long later, they all left. Agatha on her broom, Addison turned back into a bat, and Jeremy and Ash went up the steps.

I waited a long time to make sure they were gone before I left my hidey-hole. I wasn't that stupid, I knew Ash would know if I was following him so I wasn't going to try.

I kept BecBec with me.

Ash could see faeries. I didn't want her in trouble.

While I waited, I thought about things and how some of it made sense.

How Aidan and I just happened to be at the Swank Italian Place when Agatha Darling and Douglas Addison showed up. How Aidan took me directly to Agatha at the Community Centre and Ash appeared out of nowhere to help Aidan fight off the baddies in the end (and Agatha got away). How Aidan "found" the electric wand. How both Aidan and Ash were mysteriously lured to the bomb and how Ash knew so damn much about its workings and what it was intended to destroy. How Aidan told me "never to trust an oracle" when Althea drunkenly told me I had a traitor in my home. How, after years of animosity from *Le Société* and neutrality from The Institute, somehow they'd been talked into "working together" by two double agents. How, no matter how hard we looked, we could find hide nor hair of Jeremy Bligh.

But why?

I knew why. Destiny said one of these two men could die for me. I knew that, at least, was no lie by the way my family immediately accepted them.

They never liked my choice in men.

Never.

Especially Viv.

(Then again, most of the men I chose were dicks.)

But why should Aidan and Ash die for me?

Some unknown, loopy American girl stumbles into their life and rocks their world and they have a fifty percent chance to "bleed" for her?

Gluh.

I knew one thing for certain, Sebastian Quincy Wilding and Aidan Knightly Seymour were the type of men who would take destiny in their own hands and manipulate it how *they* saw fit.

I had a beautiful smile and smelled like oranges, my ass.

When I thought it was safe, I walked back to Viv and Su, BecBec with me the whole way, both of us silent and watchful. I held my wand at the ready.

My wand and I shook my sisters awake.

They didn't get angry when they woke up, just took one look at my face and then led me back to The Gables.

They washed my arms and palms while BecBec talked to them in her mile-a-minute, dolphin voice.

Viv understood what she was saying.

"Do you speak Faerie?" I asked.

"Faeries speak English," Viv told me.

I stared at her.

Viv explained, "She speaks ten times faster than normal, like a tape on fast forward. BecBec's a young faerie, she hasn't learned to slow down her speech and you're a young witch and haven't learned to speed up your hearing. It'll all come together one day."

Well at least that was sorted.

Kinda.

They left and I lay in bed staring at the ceiling.

BecBec lay on the pillow next to me, staring too.

Daphne eventually made it to bed when the sun started to rise. She walked right up my belly and lay down on my chest.

I dipped my chin into my throat, looked into her pretty black kitty face and her gorgeous green kitty eyes.

Aidan gave her to me for my birthday.

It was then that I finally started crying.

18 August

Viv and Su told everyone I had flu and I needed to be left alone.

What I really needed was time for the scratches on my arms to heal so no one would see them and wonder.

And time to think.

Su took some of Mom's magical potion and added her own ingredients and put it on my scratches to hasten the healing.

Viv confirmed that what Ash and Aidan told me about Josie was indeed The Prophesy as she understood it, that Josie would change the world for the good.

So at least they hadn't lied about that.

The Prophesies also mentioned Ash and Aidan and that one of them would die for me, one of them would marry me.

Viv went to the library to check with Elly and *Mathilda's Register*.

Elly confirmed it.

One dead dude, one dad dude.

(*And cease calling me Elly!*)

But even Elly couldn't confirm that, in so knowing, one or the other or both could not also change destiny especially with the might of a powerful coven like Edwards behind them.

I spent a lot of time thinking.

I may be somewhat of a ditz and relatively new to this witch business but I wasn't a total lame-ass loser. There was no reason why Ash or Aidan couldn't confide in me that they were playing at double agents.

No reason unless they *were* double agents.

Even if they weren't, I'd had too many twists and turns in the last year to be anything less than cautious.

Not to mention too many secrets kept for no apparent reason.

I finally made my decision and told Su and Viv what I intended to do.

We talked, we argued, we worried, we fretted—none of us wanted to distrust Aidan or Ash and none of us wanted to believe we'd been deceived.

But we had.

The whole thing sucked.

Last night, we cloaked ourselves and went to the Tower Room.

We drew the circle.

We cut the tips of each of our fingers and stood in the sacred circle —arms high, fingers touching, blood mingling.

And we made our vow of secrets and silence.

No one would know of Ash and Aidan's deception. We'd keep even Mom, Gran and Mavis in the dark.

We couldn't trust anyone. Not The Institute, *Le Société*, the Council, the coven, no one. We didn't know who was in on it and the fewer who we actually trusted who knew what we knew, the better; all the easier to keep it quiet.

And in the meantime, we would plan for Josie, Rory and I to be safe so Josie could eventually save the world.

They were my Spellbounds and I was taking them home…

To Denver.

In Denver, I was on *my* turf, and Agatha, Jeremy, Ash and Aidan would have to follow me home.

And fight me there.

But in the meantime, no one must know we suspected.

So we'd have to go on as normal.

I'd have to carry on, besotted and boy-crazy…simultaneously falling in love with two men.

Or, at least, trying to convince them I was.

While Su and Viv quietly planned our get away.

Goddess, help us.

The Month of September

1 September

Of course, deception wasn't as easy as it seemed.

I mean, lying is hard.

Or, it was for Viv and me.

Su seemed to find it easy.

So we gave her most of the hard jobs.

Ash and Aidan both suspected something right away.

I know this because about two days after I resurfaced from my "flu," and after doing a twelve hour shift at The Dozen, I headed straight to Paulina's house for a séance (we were just looking for some lighthearted entertainment and Antonia was pretty certain she could call John Belushi or Richard Pryor, but all we got was someone telling us to, "Fucking leave me alone, you fucking bitches!" which could be practically any dead comedian from the last three decades).

Ash and Aidan were not pleased and both of them were waiting when Josie and I stumbled, exhausted, into The Gables later that night.

"Yo, dudes…later," I said, cool as a cucumber as I passed the Plush Parlor they'd just walked out of.

Ha!

Aidan caught my bicep as I tried to pass, and I looked up into his narrowed, angry blue eyes.

"Where have you been?" he demanded to know in a low voice.

Uh-oh.

I'd never actually seen Aidan angry. Well, not at me anyway. Around me, maybe.

Seemed kinda scary to have his anger actually directed *at* me.

"Séance…we were going for Belushi but I think we got Bruce," I told him.

Aidan's narrowed eyes narrowed more as they roamed my face. "Are you drunk?"

"Kinda, but Josie was driving."

That was a lie. I was dead sober. And Josie's driving was scary, as in scary-slow and granny-like.

"Have you lost your mind? You made your Spellbound your designated driver?" Aidan again demanded to know in a voice that was, again, low.

"Er…" was my answer.

"Why didn't you tell Wilding or me you were out for the night?" he clipped.

"I did," I lied.

"You didn't," Aidan countered.

Mm.

He was right.

I shrugged then stated, "I'm dead on my feet, Aidan, you wanna let go and give me the third degree in the morning?"

He let me go but he did it less in a way that he was doing as I wished and more in a way that if he didn't, he might shake me.

Ash watched me over Aidan's shoulder. He was being annoyed broody (rather than just unhappy broody or broody broody or thoughtful broody—I'd begun to be able to categorize his broodiness) but he didn't say a word.

I looked from one to the other, waved lamely, said, "'Night," and then hightailed it out of there.

See?

Real smooth.

Bluh.

They totally knew something was up.

Lying is not for me.

The only way I could figure to get around it was to avoid them.

Until I worked out how *really* to avoid them.

Because I didn't think I could go through with my part of the plan.

That is, pretend I was still in love with them.

Though I *was* still in love with them but now I was in love with them *and* my heart was breaking.

That was the problem.

It was all too complicated.

So I worked all the time, and when I wasn't working I was creating and researching in my Tower Room, pottering in the greenhouse, trying new recipes in the kitchen, at lessons with one of the coven, sunbathing if there was even the slightest hint of rays to be caught or meditating at my tree.

In the meantime, Su was putting her network of friends to work.

Thank goddess for a quasi-criminal sister.

9 September

Today I was summoned to Mavis's Magic Room.

"What's going on?" she asked even before I could grab a custard cream and sit down.

I tried innocence.

"What?"

She didn't say a word.

"What?" I repeated.

She studied me.

"What?!" This time it was louder.

"You need a vacation. I'll send you and Ash—"

"No!"

Her eyes widened.

"Oh, well that's a surprise…you and Aidan then—"

"No, no, no…I don't need a vacation." I had to think fast. "I need a mini-break." Oo, that's a good idea. "I need a manicure. A facial. A massage. I need a sauna, a Jacuzzi, at least a swimming pool. I need a Johnny Depp marathon starting with *Edward Scissorhands* and ending with *Pirates of the Caribbean*. That's the closest I want to come to testosterone for days."

I'd hit on something believable.

Mavis nodded.

"I see," she said.

"I want time without magic." I was on a roll. "Without incense up my nose and the War of the Supernatural World breathing down my neck. I want to feel safe without someone watching me every second of the day. Can you do that?"

"I think something can be arranged."

"Good."

"Do you want Josie and Rory with you?"

"Of course."

"I'll see to it," she decreed.

I'd bought some time.

Shoo.

But now what do I do?

13 September

Am in a lovely spa on the banks of Loch Lomand outside Glasgow (which happens to be birthplace of delicious Gerard Butler (Glasgow that is, not Loch Lomond) so already happy place, as any birthplace of hot guy had happy aura attached as everyone knew, but hot guy as hot as Gerard Butler meant aura stretched to Loch Lomond and therefore I was rethinking theme of movie marathon I intended to have).

Am also trying to find something for an eight-year-old boy to do and trying to convince myself that not everyone around me was a secret agent here to watch me and report back or worse, kill me and drag my lifeless body into the lake.

Yes, paranoia had set in. If Aidan and Ash could (potentially) betray me, then anyone could be an enemy.

Mavis agreed that I should "spirit away" and not tell Ash or Aidan where I'd gone or they'd want to follow me, so she made this so.

Upon turning on my mobile after arriving at the spa, this is what I got:

First ring (Aidan): "What are you playing at?" (This was said somewhat tersely therefore very, very pissed-offedly.)

Second ring (Ash): "Where the hell are you?" Pause while he read my mind. "I'll be there in two hours."

Ack!

Obviously location popped into my head and communicated itself via mind-meld.

Mavis must have worked her mojo because they both stayed away (so far, now over the two-hour mark and no sign, and I was hoping

Gerard Butler Happy Aura would keep me safe rather than communicate exact position to his hot guy brethren.)

~

Now over three-hour mark.
  Mavis mojo worked.
  Whew.

~

Later…

Had aromatherapy facial — all lavenders and bergamots.
  Then had this wonderful treatment where they put hot stones down my spine.
  Then they took away stones and wrapped me like a mummy in lovely smelling stuff.
  Then they rubbed down my body with gigantic loofahs and lubed me up with creamy body moisturizer.
  Then they sent me back to my room in a terrycloth robe with a towel wrapped around my head, shuffling on my fluffy white slippers like a zombie.
  Found bed, fell face first on it and used magic to record this miraculous instant of pure peace and tranquility in my Book of Shadows.
  Mm.
  Mm.
  Must sleep.

~

14 September

Am free.
  Have had nothing but fruits, vegetables, whole grains and lean proteins since arrival yesterday.
  Did yoga early morning in large class of women who I hope did not notice Rory and his little friend making fun of us outside the arched windows that give a fabulous view of the lake.
  (Rory's made friends with some woman's nine-year-old daughter

who was also hanging about moping. Since then, they've been thick as thieves and causing mayhem wherever they go. Good times.)

Am healthy and happy and thinking I may give up caffeine and refined sugars for good as am sure I have found inner peace and enlightenment through clean and wholesome living.

~

Later...

Have had healthy lunch, a wee trek around the loch and a two-hour massage.

Afterwards, sat in sauna with other women and realized they are not all spies or informants, they are my friends and they love me.

Then sat in my room with Josie.

We drank little bottles of Moët & Chandon through straws and watched *Eastenders* together.

Jack Branning.

Mm.

~

Later...

Am alone in bed after having total Mother of All Breakdowns with Josie.

It was the Moët.

I told her everything about Aidan and Ash and the blood vow of secrecy (secrecy? ha!) and going to Denver.

I told her how I was in love with both men and about their competition and my two Big Os and what Ash said about liking me.

I told her how I was rubbish at lying to them and how it was going to take weeks, maybe months for us to be able to arrange to get out of the country and into a safe place in Colorado, and how I didn't think I could make it.

Ack!

And I cried and cried (and snorted!) and cried and went through nearly half a box of Kleenex.

She just sat next to me and held my hand, then when I kept crying, she held me and when I'd settled down, she popped the top off another mini-bottle of Moët and put in a fresh straw and handed it to me.

She patted my arm and said, "Don't worry, love, I trust you. We'll get through this."

That's it.

Simple faith.

After my meltdown (semi) receded, we snuggled into the couch and watched *A Nightmare on Elm Street* (Gerard Butler DVDs all checked out (humph) but Johnny Depp was no sloppy seconds, still, although I wanted a Johnny Depp-a-thon, that wasn't exactly where I wanted to start).

Now almost asleep and feel better than I have in days.

Love Josie.

15 September

Had granola, blueberries and organic Greek yogurt for breakfast.

Had eyebrow, leg and bikini wax, and brow and lash dye.

Had French pedicure, and manicure with blood red varnish.

Had lunch of blanched asparagus and steamed salmon.

Had highlights retouched and splint ends trimmed.

Did Pilates (not sure I get it, yoga much better).

Beginning to wish women around me were plotting and scheming.

Want big, oozing, yeasty cinnamon roll dripping with sugary-buttery frosting.

Am bored out of my skull.

Am sick of steamed, blanched, salt-less, personality-less food.

Am not cavewoman or lost on deserted island.

Am missing my cauldron, my magical larder and constant threat of death or possible snogging by cute but treacherous boys.

Ack!

Am psychotic but want old life of danger and mayhem back.

16 September

Had mini-drama as Rory left newfound girlfriend who is off to the wilds of Orkney or some such.

Thank goddess (for Rory's sake) for Facebook and Instant Messenger.

We are going home.

Finally.

~

19 September

Progress Report:

Cookbook lady has come back to Lucy and me and said not only does she want cookbook, she has been in talks with some British television channel and they may want cookery show called "War of the Wooden Spoons" filmed in Witches Dozen and beamed out to whole British populace with TV license.

Whoa!

Me: the New Nigella.

(Or Jamie? Pucka!)

Ack!

Su's coven has been hard at work.

They've found a safe house in Baker's Historic District in Denver (Yay! Close to Mom's house!) and started to put protection spells on it (love Baker! close proximity to Mayan Movie Theater. Yay! Independent and foreign films while in hiding. Also close to my old "local" The Hornet. Buffalo chicken salad with bleu cheese dressing. Woo hoo! Oo, how I missed the Mile High City!).

As they do not have the power of the Honeycutt Coven, this could take some time, but at least they've started.

Viv has explained that magic is verboten on flights and in airports and has been for some time (disappointing but understandable).

So, we had a powwow and feel that we need some protection of the muscle-bound type, and if she or he were a little magical, well, all the better.

Had to check with Elly and The Prophesies to make certain-sure there was not third A-named man who would vie for my affections, throwing me into confusion and self-hatred when I find he turns on me in bid to control own destiny.

Elly says only two boys so prophesied so not to worry; could find mercenary without concern of future heartbreak.

But where to find mercenary?

Where else?

23 September

Met Viv in Paddington Station.

She was (allegedly) at meetings somewhere in London to plan a speaking tour of east England up through Yorkshire.

I was (allegedly) locked up in the Tower Room searching for the Magic-Stealing Spell so I could figure out how to reverse Althea's condition.

Get this: Viv was wearing a pink, oxford-cloth, button-down shirt, sand-colored chinos, a pink, naval-style belt, pink (Coach, at least) loafers and a pink Alice band in her hair.

How could this be my sister?

I, on the other hand, was taking full advantage of Indian summer and was wearing my four-inch, stiletto-heeled, T-strap sandals with the big chunks of turquoise imbedded in the T. Added to this were my dark, desert-washed, boot-leg hipster jeans with a wide, stamp-designed tan belt and *giganto* turquoise and rhinestone belt buckle (trust me, it worked). Topped with my gauzy somewhat see-through Indian-inspired tunic with the neckline split *to there* and showing a little curve 'a the breasticle. I'd straightened my hair to within an inch of its life and had on some pretty heavy black eyeliner.

Fab.

Mental Note: Krispy Kreme is taking over London. They have a shop in Paddington (right next to Accessorize, which I had to visit even though they have them in Bristol—am addicted to Accessorize—bought two pairs of sunglasses, which brings my sunnies collection up to sixteen pairs. Yee ha!).

When we opened the door to The Hobgoblin, it was like the scene out of *American Werewolf in London*. Everyone stopped what they were doing and stared at us.

"Way to keep a low profile," I hissed to Viv as we sauntered in.

"What?" she hissed back.

"Your Eighties Soccer Mom getup. Hardly blending in."

"Me? At least I'm not Caucasian Cher looking like, at any moment, I'm going to break into my rendition of 'Gypsies, Tramps and Thieves.'"

She said that like it was an insult.

Derek met us at the bar. "I don't want any trouble."

"Me? Trouble?" I replied.

He rolled his eyes, tugged out a pint of lager for each of us (even though we didn't order lager, quite fancied a cider, but anyway) and walked away.

Scary Faerie was hovering drunkenly at the end of the bar, per usual.

There were far more patrons now than the last time we were here. I scanned the room and saw cute, lean vampire from the Day of Orbs o' Magic walking toward us.

"Uh-oh," I said.

"What?" Then Viv saw him. "No vampires," she said in an undertone.

"I heard that," he said when he arrived, leaning, sanguine, against the bar next to Viv and looking not insulted at all.

Of course.

Vampire hearing is superior to human hearing.

"Where's your posse?" Vampire Guy asked me.

"Er…" I replied.

He raised his brows. "The two tall, somewhat scary-looking blokes?"

"Er…" I muttered.

"One from *GQ*, the other from a Marlboro ad?" he prompted.

Mm, interesting (and accurate) description.

"Um…day off." (Me, being lame)

"I see." He turned to Viv. "You're looking for help."

I bugged my eyes out at Viv.

I mean, how easy was this?

Walk in, pick mercenary and Bob's your uncle.

"Thanks, but no thanks…we need someone who can walk around in daylight. Vampires need not apply." (Viv, kinda being rude and seriously cutting into my London shopping time if she drew this whole gig out.)

He smiled, very cute and seemed not to take offense at Viv's rudeness.

"Human mother," he replied.

Enough said.

Quick lesson:

For the uninitiated, there is quite a bit to learn about vampires.

Firstly, they don't need blood to live.

Well, they do, but only once a month or so and they certainly don't have to kill someone to get it. A good ol' drink will keep them going for weeks. But they don't have to drain someone dry.

In the meantime, they eat and drink like normal folk. Even though undead, their bodies function like a human being's, heart beating, blood flowing through veins and the like.

Secondly, vampires are stronger and faster than humans. They can hear and see better. On average, at least three or four times better than a human. The fitter vampires could be five or six times better than humans. The Muhammed Ali of vampires could kick Superman's ass.

No kidding.

Lastly, vampires die naturally. You could go the stake-to-the-heart, decapitation, silver bullet route, but after two hundred fifty or three hundred years, they die naturally anyway.

Just one day, turn to dust.

Finito.

In the olden days, such as, when they pulled out folks' intestines for public enjoyment, and through the centuries where classes were more established (upstairs, downstairs) vampires didn't worry too much about stopping before the victim died.

They just fed.

They were a superior race, so why not?

But with the end of slavery, industrialization, unionization, civil rights, equal rights, etcetera, they felt some pressure, so killing has been illegal for years (with brief respites in 1895, 1921 and 1962, but don't have time to get into that).

Now, vampires had Blood Covenants which was somewhat like weddings and marriage contracts and feeding rights rolled into one.

They'd find a partner (over a vampire lifetime, they could have three or more, usually women but definitely not unheard of for them to be men, or both) who they bound themselves to (both legally and emotion-ally, the ceremony was supposed to be super-cool in a kind of dark, vampire-y, black velvet, red satin, blood red rose bouquet, big silver goblets filled with pinot noir, rare-to-blue steaks for dinner, Concrete Blond played at reception, type of way) who would let them drink their blood once a month (amongst other things).

No killing, no siring of new vampires (unless "in season" which was a whole other story) and no straying.

Of course, they broke these rules—the first one rarely, the second one every once in a while, and the last one all the time (depending on the vampire).

There are very few female vampires, in fact, females were quite unusual. The life of the vampire doesn't often suit a female, or, at least, most females. And since most vampires aren't the soulless creatures they're made out to be in books, they didn't tend to sire females too often, unless the female wanted it, of course.

They had better things to do with females.

Hmm.

In Blood Covenants it wasn't unusual for the vampire "naturally" to sire a child.

Human/vampire children were very like *Blade* if they were boys. They could walk around in daylight, needed blood but not often (even less than full-blooded vampires, three or four times a year), lived some-what shorter lives (a hundred fifty, two hundred years at most) and were always boys.

Girls produced from human/vampire procreation were invariably human but could be stronger or have excellent eyesight, but usually just plain ole normal.

Don't ask me why this all happened. There is a book I started about vampire DNA (reconfigured at siring or inherited at birth) and the sex chromosomes and all sorts of other stuff that had to do with genetics and the like. But that book was boring so I didn't finish it.

~

"Oh." (Viv)

"I'm Gabriel." (Gabriel)

I bugged my eyes out at Viv again.

Gabriel.

Right.

I took his name as a sign.

We were then at a loss.

How, exactly, did one go about hiring a mercenary?

Gabriel grinned at us. "Let me make this easy for you." Then he laid out his terms and conditions, as if he were selling us a car, but in a very nice French (ish), English, American(?) accent.

Viv and I looked at each other.

"I don't know..." Viv was being unusually indecisive, "are you willing to leave the country?"

"You Mathilda?"

I turned to see a young man in a weird outfit (purple velvet shirt, I didn't even know they made shirts in velvet, but looking at him, I knew they shouldn't) addressing me and standing about five feet away and lastly, for some reason, staring at me belligerently.

What now?

I was minding my own business.

Why me?

"Don't respond," Gabriel said quickly to me.

Seemed like good advice.

I turned away.

"Eh, woman! I said, are you Mathilda?"

"Just ignore him," Gabriel said again. "He's just looking to prove himself against The Mathilda. You've started to get a bit of a reputation, warlocks and other idiots flooding The Hobgoblin in hopes of getting a shot at you. Don't give him the chance."

A reputation?

What reputation?

What was this?

Who was I, Calamity Jane?

Was I now Calamity Mathilda (don't answer that!), the fastest wand in England and open to any moron with an attitude?

"Listen to me, bitch!" the stranger in the bad shirt demanded.

Uh-oh.

I wasn't fond of being called "bitch."

In a flash, Derek was there.

"You said no trouble. Take it outside, as in, the back. We don't need any questions."

I took a deep breath.

I would not sink to his level.

I would not be forced into a confrontation I did not want.

"Hey, dude," I was trying to be patient, "I don't want any..." I started, turning back to the guy, but as I did so, he whipped out a wand (a wand!) and sent this pathetic little wisp of sparkler-esque magic my way.

Without thinking, I just flicked my fingers and a shell pink and violet poof of pixie dust came out and opened, like a parachute, deflecting the sparkles so they ricocheted off and hit the man who dealt them, knocking him on his ass.

Oops.

Not a good idea.

Behind every warlock with bits of magic, there was a witch. And this guy's witch didn't like him to land on his ass in front of all the other bad boys and girls in The Hobgoblin.

"Hey, bitch…what do ya think you're doing, eh?" she asked, storming toward us, belligerent too (and wearing a full-on velvet dress, which was acceptable in most instances, just not the one she was wearing).

Uh-oh, there was that bitch-word again.

"You said no trouble!" Derek shouted.

Too late.

All hell broke loose.

"Who're you calling a bitch?" Viv sneered.

Forgot, Viv hated the word "bitch" more than me.

Wands were pulled out, words were thrown, tables were upended and the tense always up for a mêlée atmosphere of The Hobgoblin exploded into a full-on, Wild West brawl where everyone was invited to join even if they weren't involved in the original beef.

I felt an arm around my waist as I pulled out my wand and then I was flying through the air.

Yes, I said *flying through the air*.

Gabriel had a hold of both Viv and I. We—I kid you *not*—flew through the air while Gabriel nonchalantly leaped over the heads of the crowd to land in front of the door.

Once outside, we started to run but the fracas had spilled out the door (not to mention, not too easy to leg it in turquoise-encrusted T-straps).

The angry witch and her warlock came after us, and Gabriel grabbed us again.

Up in the air, we landed on top of a taxi about five car lengths away.

Up again, we were at the end of the block.

Up, down, up, down, up, down, and before we knew it we were running down the steps of a tube station.

Viv magicked the ticket machine and we were on a train in no time.

Stop, "mind the gap," change trains.

Stop, "mind the gap," change trains.

Stop, "mind the gap," change trains.

Out at Piccadilly, through the Circus, down the street and into the crush of Fortnum and Mason.

We were standing by the counter displaying jars of Goober peanut butter and jelly stripes (just behind the £30 boxes of Fortnum and Mason champagne truffles) and catching our breath when Viv turned to Gabriel and said…

"You're hired."

~

24 September

Listen to this.

Upon arrival at The Dozen this morning, Nerissa charged up to me and shouted, "She was here, yesterday, Girlie Spice!"

Eh?

"What?" (Me)

"Girlie Spice, the one with the nose and the history with Robbie Williams." (Nerissa)

I gave up and looked at Lucy.

"Geri Halliwell. Rissa reckons she stopped by yesterday for one of your new cinnamon rolls."

"Really?" (Me)

(Was currently winning the War of the Wooden Spoons with the introduction of my Cinnabon-esque (little smaller, different frosting with a hint of cream cheese) cinnamon rolls—a whole new concept to English folk and they took to it like ducks to water.)

"Yes, I swear, it was her…Girlie Spice." (Nerissa)

"That's Baby Spice." (Lucy)

"Er, I think she's called Cutie Spice." (This nugget of wisdom from Pandora.)

Oh for goddess's sake.

How soon they forget.

"She's *Ginger* Spice." (Me) "Was she really here?"

"Yes, yes, I swear it was her." (Nerissa)

Lucy shrugged.

Yeah, I could trust that…Nerissa was an expert. I mean, *Girlie Spice*?

Still, could be first celebrity client.

Yay!

Who was next? Jennifer Saunders? Someone told me she lived in Somerset.

Or.

Ohmygoddess.

Madonna?

It could happen.

Yay!

Boo!

I was leaving the country.

I was going to be holed up in a safe house in Baker in about a month's time when the protection spells had reached their full potency.

I would miss Madonna.

My war with Lucy would be lost because I wouldn't be here to fight it.

I wasn't going to get my own TV show!

The Dozens would go back to being another "caff" serving all-day "full English breakfasts" and smelling of grease and bacon with baskets full of pre-wrapped flapjacks and "American" brownies that tasted like cardboard.

Ack!

All I'd worked for…gone.

Damn Agatha, Endora, the Traditionalists and the rest.

They were gonna pay.

The Month of October

5 October

Scary, sad and miserable run-in with potential-father-of-children/life sacrifice/shifty, boy-I-can-pick-'em "Boyfriend" Number One:

~

I was up in my Tower Room.

Over the months I had made it my *Magic* Room.

I replaced the old, battered wooden cupboards, cabinets and work benches.

Delia's husband (one of the few of our coven whose husband was not in *Le Société* but was a furniture craftsman) made me a huge circular, marbled mosaic table for the center of the room (with lovely curlicued wrought iron legs).

(Well, he didn't make them for me, he made them for some rich woman who said she didn't like the marble and he needed to unload them at a cut-rate price that still curled my toes, but they were so very gorgeous I couldn't resist.)

There were matching sets of baker's shelves and some dark-wooded, distressed chests displaying my jars, bottles, bowls, scales, pouches of runes, boxes of tarot, mortars, pestles, knives, pentacles, cauldrons, incense and essence burners, chalices, amulets, crystals, feathers, mirrors and oils.

(Okay, I'd been busy. I shop. I finally found the life-skill that makes my hobby a necessity.)

There were candles, candles and more candles in various colors and assorted (mostly black, iron, curlicued) holders scattered around the room and fixed to the stone walls.

There were huge bunches of herbs and dried flowers hanging from iron racks suspended from the ceiling, and even more on hooks drilled into the walls.

There was a small, round table draped with a sheer, soft pink alter cloth with silver moons and blue and purple stars embroidered in it with my crystal ball sitting on a hot-pink velvet cushion on top with two comfy, upholstered, high-backed chairs around it.

I made a deal with the John Lewis salesmen on the floor model, discontinued chaise lounge and a sleek-lined, armless chair and foot stool, which was surprisingly comfortable even though it looked kickass.

My Magic Room…I loved it and I was going to miss it.

I was in a bit of a panic because I had yet to find the origins, thus be able to prepare a counter-ceremony, of magic-stripping magic.

I felt I had to do that before I left the country. Somehow, I owed it to Althea, and the protection spell in Denver was maturing rapidly and the minute it matured, we were gone.

Su had arranged an escort from DIA (Denver International Airport) that included witches, a couple local vampires and a sorceress with whom Su was friendly.

We'd researched the school in which to enroll Rory and had a work visa in process through a fake engagement of Josie to a multi-media artist and teacher at the Denver Art Institute who had volunteered to be Josie's fake fiancé.

(Where Su finds these folks, I don't know but we were major indebted to this guy who was named, get this: Windspear, I kid you not, Windspear Jones. Un-fucking-believable).

Anyway.

Su was working with the help of a computer chiphead, IT geek to create a trail of years of fake e-mails, fake telephone bills and a bunch of faked photos that would link Josie and Windspear in order to lay testimony for the fiancé visa that we needed for Josie to move to the States.

(Okay, we were breaking the law, but if she worked, she'd pay tax. And she was gonna save the world one day. I mean, give us a break!)

I found out that the magic-stripping magic was so rarely performed that even Mavis, Gran and Mom had exhausted their ideas of where I should search.

I was also in my Tower Room researching ways to sever the mind-meld with Ash.

The mind-meld was more magic that was hard to reverse, especially since I had to cloak my thoughts every once in a while so Ash wouldn't cotton on to the fact I was trying to cut ties with him.

Lastly, I was also in my Tower Room avoiding Aidan.

Because it was his birthday.

Although I was prepared, I didn't think I could handle another birthday. The last one went great (Ash's) and I was already heartbroken enough. I didn't need more reason to be heartbroken.

It was late. I'd fallen asleep on the lounge upside down, my feet over the back and my head at the foot.

My notes and reference books on mind-melds and magic-stripping were in disarray around me.

And my mobile rang.

I jumped, twisted and slid off the lounge into the piles of paper and dangerously delicate tomes o' magic lore.

And I saw before me a pair of legs encased in mushroom-colored corduroy.

I followed the legs up and saw a nicely veined, long-fingered, masculine hand holding out my mobile that said on the front display, GABRIEL CALLING.

Ack!

I grabbed the phone, scrambled to my feet, smiled innocently (I hoped) at the gorgeous head on top of the corduroy and fisherman's sweatered body of Aidan while flipping open the phone and saying a bright, "Hello!"

"You're not alone," Gabriel responded.

Aidan planted his fists into his hips.

"How'd you know that?" I asked.

"You sound bright and cheery, you're never bright and cheery," Gabriel replied.

Cheeky.

"I'm always bright and cheery!"

I cannot believe he said that.

Of course I was bright and cheery.

I was the Queen of Bright and Cheery.

"I'll call back later." And then he disconnected.

"Who's Gabriel?" Aidan asked the minute I disconnected.

Ack!

"Um…"

Ack!

~

Now, I had been a very, very busy girl since my night on the cliff face, but I couldn't avoid Ash and Aidan altogether since we were all on a mission to fight evil (supposedly) and I was expected to be enamored with both of them.

But I'd used my single-minded desire to battle the Traditionalists, not to mention to have as many pairs of shoes and handbags and nice furniture for my Tower Room (thus working extra hard at The Dozen to earn money) as my excuse to steer clear of the Double-Crossing Duo.

I could tell my avoiding them was wearing thin.

Or as Danny Glover would say in *Lethal Weapon*, "Anorexic."

What to do?

Stall.

~

"Wait here! Don't move. I'll be back in two seconds!"

And I ran from the room.

I kinda wished I could run from The Gables, from the town, from the country, but that wasn't in the cards.

Yet.

Instead, I ran to the kitchen and back.

When I arrived, I presented a somewhat-less-tolerant-looking (gah!) Aidan with a bright orange cookie tin wrapped in a hot pink organdie ribbon.

"Happy Birthday!" I shouted, maybe a little too loudly. "Those are oatmeal cookies, just like you like but I changed them. I noticed you like cranberry juice and, later, I saw you dig into Lucy's almond Danish so I experimented and finally put in some dried cranberries…" Yes, I was babbling. "And a bit of ground almond in the mix and added white chocolate for good measure and came up with those…Aidan's Cranberry Almond Oatmeal Cookies with White Chocolate Chunks! Voila!"

Once I'd done a lame little hand flourish with my "voila!" one of his arms snaked out, rounded my waist and he pulled me into a tight hug, burying his face in my hair at the side of my neck.

"Jesus, Matty," he muttered by my ear, relief in his voice.

I felt my throat close as shivers ran down my spine.

Bastard!

Bastard!

Bastard!

"What's the matter, Aidan?" I asked.

I knew exactly what was the matter but I wasn't going to let on.

His arm gave me a squeeze and his lips gave my neck a brush and more shivers ran down my spine.

Then he whispered in my ear, "Nothing, darling."

Darling.

I loved that.

(Bastard.)

"Okay," I whispered back before I pulled away and ran to one of the cabinets. "That isn't all," I said, tearing through cabinets to find what I'd made in a fit of tears and fury but still, it had to be done.

The game had to be played.

I found it, walked back to Aidan and handed him a booklet made of thin strips of hot pink paper held fast at one end by a bright orange, organdie bow.

Then I said, "I asked myself, 'Self? What do you get the man who has everything?' and my Self answered, 'Something money can't buy.' So there it is." Then I gave another lame hand flourish, gesturing to the booklet.

He was leafing through it, no expression on his face.

"It's vouchers," I told him, coming up to his side and pointing as he leafed. "You tear them out and give them to me when you want to redeem them. See, that one is for a night out at the Indian. You know, Monsoon on the High Street?" I explained.

Yikes!

I kept going. "And that one is for, my treat, a movie at the Curzon. You can even have a box of that icky sweet popcorn if you like."

Ack!

I kept on talking. "And that one is for a scalp massage. I have this great copper tool that Su bought me a couple birthdays ago that you scrape on your scalp. I know, it sounds awful but it…is…fucking…

fantastic." I stopped to look at him and then pulled back at the expression on his face.

"You okay?" I asked.

He nodded and turned fully to me.

I retreated.

"Do you like it?" I asked.

He came after me, stalking me again, the look on his face melting my insides.

"Yeah, I like it," he said and tossed the book and tin on the table.

Hmm.

What to do?

He was going to think something was up, why would I move away? He knew I liked him.

There was no reason I'd move away. Especially on his birthday.

We'd slept together.

He'd given me the Big O.

He thought I thought he might die for me.

Yikes!

So I stopped retreating and ran toward him, threw myself at him and kissed him.

Goddess, leaves, twigs and trees, it was, as always, fabulous.

He took over the kiss and all thoughts of betrayal flew from my mind.

This wasn't hard at all.

"Happy birthday," I said (a lot softer this time) when his lips left mine.

"Who's Gabriel?"

Gah!

Single-minded bastard.

He went on, "Is he the vampire you met at The Hobgoblin?"

Ackity ack ack!

Ack!

"You know about that?" (Me)

"Yes." (Aidan)

"How? Derek?" (Me)

"Well, him and half a dozen others who witnessed the brawl." (Aidan)

Oops.

"Why did you hire a vampire?" (Aidan)

"I can't, er…tell you." (Goddess, did I wish I could lie. Okay, I take it back, this *was* hard.)

His arms tightened.

"Matty…" (Aidan, all warning.)

"Aidan, you're just going to have to trust me." (Me)

Ha. Trust! That was a joke.

No response.

"Please?" (Me again, trying to be girlie cute, tipping my head to the side and everything.)

He stared at me.

I stared back.

Boy, did I need to win this staring contest.

Okay, so I couldn't win the staring contest.

So I kissed him instead.

It took a bit.

He fought it.

But I worked hard, giving it my all.

Then with a groan, he gave in, backing me into the lounge, twisting at the last minute and seating himself, taking me with him, not breaking the kiss and lounging back in one smooth move with me on top.

Finally, after my body melted into his due to his superior tongue action, his fingers in my hair fisted gently and tugged even more gently, and he asked, "Do you know what you're doing?"

I gave my stock answer, "I never know what I'm doing."

He twisted me so he was (mostly) on top of me.

I don't know what it is and if other girls feel this way but there is something very nice about the weight of a man on you, especially a man who smelled like wood, vanilla and musk with a hint of citrus (Lalique Le Lion, mm…).

"Matty," he called, his voice lower than normal, a virtual rumble that travelled along my body like a physical thing, "now is not the time to be playing around."

"Aidan," I said in all seriousness as I put my hand on his cheek, "really, you're just going to have to trust me."

He might not think I was doing the right thing.

But I was.

He dipped his head so his face was close to mine and he whispered, "Something isn't right with you."

I rubbed my nose against his.

Then I teased, "You think? I mean, less than a year ago, I was a girl with the simple dream of one day owning a $25,000 Hermes Birkin Bag. Now, look at me, look at this place," I flicked out a hand to encompass my Magic Room, "look at my life. We're on the cusp of war, Aidan, and I'm Che Guevara."

Finally, he grinned. "Che was just the face of the revolution. It was Fidel who was the heart. The reason you see so much of Che is because he was photogenic."

"I know but I don't want to be Fidel. He's hairy, cigar-chomping and icky," I informed him.

Aidan touched his lips to mine then pulled back and stated, "Believe me, you don't want to be Che. Che came to a nasty end in a Bolivian jungle."

Yikes!

I didn't need to be reminded of that.

Aidan went on, "And Fidel lived to subjugate millions."

That sounded better.

Kinda.

I still didn't want to be Fidel.

I decided to change the subject. "Are you going to cut me some slack?"

He kissed me again, I melted again. His kiss grew deeper, I melted more. Things carried on, got a bit out of control. and I must admit, we kinda slid, head first, into second base.

Then he disengaged, rearranged my clothes, kissed my nose and said (clearly convinced by my reaction, which I must admit was a little wanton, can't keep my head on straight when making out with man I adore even if he is probably about to throw me to the wolves), "I'll cut you some slack. But you should remember three things."

I didn't want to remember three things.

Still, I said, "Yeah?"

"One, I'm watching you."

Ack.

"Two, Wilding's watching you."

Yikes.

"And three, we'll do anything to save you, even if it's from yourself."

Great.

~

Scary, sad and miserable run-in with potential-father-of-children/life sacrifice/shifty, boy-I-can-pick-'em "Boyfriend" Number Two:

~

Last night, Aidan redeemed his Curzon voucher.

We went to the movies and he didn't eat the icky, sweet popcorn but instead we shared a bag of Galaxy chocolate Minstrels which I chased with a Diet Coke (of course).

He dropped me at The Gables, backed me against the front door and laid a really good one on me.

Mm.

I was wandering dreamily up the steps to the Tower Room, a long night of browsing through some black magic books (I'd looked every-where else…) when I felt the chill run up my spine and I looked behind me.

It was Ash, stalking me up the stairs.

Holy crap.

I'd forgotten I was caught in their war.

And I'd forgotten Ash's promise.

Clearly he'd seen Aidan drop me off after our date and the episode at the door.

I didn't say anything, just retreated, slowly going up the stairs back-ward with one arm out to ward him off.

My shoulders slammed into the heavy wooden door at the top.

"Ash…" I whispered and there he was.

He didn't utter a word, hardly made a sound. I don't even know how he got there but, within moments, I was lifted up, pressed against the door by his hard torso, both of my legs straddling his hips, one of his hands on my ass, his other hand up my shirt, the cup of my bra pushed aside, his fingers at my breast doing things to my nipple that caused my hoo-hah to *woo hoo*! and his mouth, there is no other word for it, *devouring* mine.

I had one hand in his hair, the other yanking the shirt out of his jeans, and I have to admit I was moaning and whimpering (just a bit).

(Okay, a lot.)

Holy Sexual Prowess Batman!

Everything flew out of my head.

Agatha Darling herself could have opened the door behind us and I would have said, "Just a sec," shut it again and carried on with Ash.

All I could focus on was him, his mouth, his body, his hips (oh me), his fingers (oh my) and how it all felt.

Then I said it, (or moaned it, against his lips, no less), "Please, Ash," all hungry, wanting, semi-begging, my nails digging into the sleek skin of his back under his shirt.

He growled into my mouth.

I felt that in my hoo-hah too.

I dropped my head, nibbled his neck then kissed him there, worried that I'd hurt him then I licked him…

Oh, you get the picture!

I'm a slut.

I admit it.

At that point, I didn't care.

Who knows how I would have humiliated myself if it had gone on one second longer.

But then his fingers stopped, righted my bra and his hand slid down and around my waist. I lifted my head and he just held me, his forehead against mine, his breathing heavy.

"This can't go on much longer," he growled in a tone that scared the bejeezus out of me.

He was right, it couldn't.

"This happens again, you're mine," he declared.

Holy crap.

My stomach plummeted.

In a good way *and* in a bad way.

Yikes!

He lowered me to the ground but I held on to his biceps. I wasn't recovered yet.

"Ash," I whispered.

He made another rumbly growl and kissed me again; laid a big, huge, deep one on me, just when I thought it was over.

"Quiet," he muttered when he was done, resting his chin on top of my head and there we stood for the longest time.

Finally he let me go and backed down a step, hooked his fist in my waistband and pulled me forward until I was eye-to-eye with him.

"I don't know what you're up to but I don't like it," he decreed (again growling).

Great.

He was getting all threatening again and there I was, standing there panting.

He kept growling (and being threatening). "If you carry on and I figure out what you're doing and it's the mess I think it is, I'm putting a stop to it and taking matters into my own hands."

"Why are you always threatening me?" I asked, losing my sexy, making out with Ash vibe. "It isn't necessary to threaten me. I think I've made it clear I'm quite capable of taking care of myself," I reminded him.

"These aren't threats, Mathilda. I'm saying it like it is. You have a couple of days to wrap up whatever it is your cooking up or I intervene, got me?"

I felt, at the look on his face and tone of his voice, that even though he was a big, arrogant, domineering, traitorous bastard, the best thing to do was give up on the bravado and agree.

So I nodded.

He gave me that clotted cream look again.

Man, I hated it when he did that.

Just as much as I loved it.

"And you best not let Seymour redeem any more of your vouchers or I'm ending this détente. Is that clear?"

Détente?

This was détente?

I was screwed when it came down to war.

As in, literally.

Er, hmm.

And, mm.

I shook myself.

"Crystal." I nodded again so he'd understand that I definitely understood and wasn't actually thinking what I was thinking or what I couldn't quit thinking.

Yikes!

"Fuck," he swore, obviously the mind-meld letting him know where my thoughts had wandered and he wrapped his hand around my neck and pulled my head toward him for another shorter but no-less-hotter kiss.

Then he was gone.

I needed to get cracking or I was in some serious trouble.

Or, should I say, more serious trouble.

Ack!

Concentrate.

End the mind-meld.

Get Althea's magic back.
And then home.
Or I "suffer" the consequences.
Bah!

∾

6 October

Found it!
Of course, it was in the black magic books.
"Appropriating Magic."
Icky, dark, horrible magic that was, in practice, actually slicing the magic away from the soul of a witch.
Not nice.
You would not believe some of the bits that went into the ceremony.
I mean, exactly how would one go about gathering "excrement of yale?"
I mean, what the fuck is a "yale?"
Here goes:
Origins: from the Burning Times.
Covens would perform a ceremony to shroud an accused witch's powers in hopes of saving her from the trials that she faced, which most of the time led to death anyway. The trials were nonsense, the witch hunters wouldn't have known what they were looking for if it bit them on the ass.
Which it could do if some magic leaked out of a witch under torture.
Once known as "black," but now referred to as "dark" witches took the shrouding ceremony a bit further. After lots of not-so-nice experimentation, they'd hit on the formula.
By the way, this dark ceremony was borne from witches besotted by men who wished to be warlocks. The witches turned to the darkness in order to hold these men and empower them. Together, they'd trap a witch, usually a young, frail or old one, and strip her magic to convey it onto the new warlock.
This magic was eventually absorbed back into nature as men couldn't hold magic very long.
The same ceremony, with a few more icky components, which included the blood drawn from live animals and more excrement and

some bits of organs and the like, could be used to strip an oracle of her sight.

It was unheard of for a coven to carve the magic from one of their members.

So, Agatha Darling's vile act was unprecedented.

There, I found it.

Now, I had to counteract it.

~

10 October

It was all planned.

I think I knew what I was doing.

Althea had to take us to Agatha's alter and we would have to perform the antidote ceremony there.

I was scared shitless.

It took a powerful coven to pull Althea's power and sight away. We were having a hard time gathering all the ingredients and implements. How we were going to muster the power, I had no earthly clue.

Thank the goddess that Lucy had begun Wicca instruction under Fay. The Honeycutt Coven hadn't taken on the training of a pure adult Tenderfoot since Fay's mother talked Mavis's mother into taking her in over 150 years ago (both were now retired in Spain).

But for Fay's mama, there was a catch; all Irish people had a little bit of magic so you kinda weren't allowed to turn them away.

Lucy was super lucky to be taken on.

(Yay! Glad she asked. Glad Mavis agreed.)

As tradition dictated, as Fay's magic was the youngest, she started Lucy's training.

Even at Tenderfoot, when she didn't have a wand or a spark, we were still gonna have to use Lucy. Feminine power was better than nothing at all.

So that meant we needed Josie too.

And Gabriel, for protection.

(Who, by the way, was expensive. Dratted mercenary vampire was sucking the lifeblood (read: savings for those Me&Ro earrings) out of me, no pun intended.)

We'd need the whole posse if we had the slightest chance to succeed.

~

29 October

The time was right and we finally had our shit together.

We had all the ingredients and the implements for the antidote ceremony. Not to get back Althea's sight (too gross to even contemplate and some of the items were illegal to own, even by Wiccan Law) but to get back her magic.

But even more importantly we had Josie's fiancé visa.

Su, Viv, Josie and Lucy had also managed to send about a dozen boxes of Josie's, Rory's and my stuff to the States without being caught.

The protection spell on the house in Baker was mature and they were expanding it in a nice square from Broadway to Alameda to Santa Fe to Eighth.

The plane tickets were purchased (I could kiss Me&Ro goodbye).

And Viv had conjured cloaking spells for us from Somerset to Dover, across the channel and up to the outskirts of Orly Airport in Paris.

We figured Bristol, Gatwick and Heathrow would all be staked out, so best to leave the country in order to flee the continent.

We were ostensibly having Girl's Night In at Lucy's house.

I knew both Aidan and Ash checked in on us during Girl's Night In.

I considered giving them a sleeping draught but figured I'd rather not suffer the consequences if a) it didn't work or b) it did and I was anywhere near either of them when they woke up.

Viv, Su and I worked together in the bathroom to create the cloaking spell that got us out the back door and into the waiting car that Gabriel was driving.

(Get this: a new, sleek, black Bentley. Yikes! Where did these boys find their cars?)

Althea met us on Castle Road, standing alone in her cloak next to The Corners (a fabulous old house where I would live if I didn't already live in the oldest most fabulous house in town).

"All set?" I asked her when she shoved her way in with the rest of us.

"You know, girl, you could kill me if this doesn't work."

"I know, don't worry Althea, have a little faith," I assured her.

Yeesh!

She grumbled but shut up and thus began the most sinister and alluring night of my life.

Dark Magic is seductive, everyone knows that.

It is warm and enthralling.

It's powerful.

And it's dangerous.

White or Light Magic is from nature, from the earth and seas, the trees and flowers, the winds and rains, the sun and moon. It is night and day. It is a soft summer shower and a fierce hurricane. It is the gazelle and the lion. It comes from the pureness deep within you, your head, heart and womb. It is always good. But it can be perilous if used by those who are foolhardy or unschooled.

Dark Magic is also natural but human-bound.

Dark Magic is made of the things not of the earth or its precious populace. It is made from the weakness of woman and man.

Take Light Magic and twist it with the power of murder, the power of deception, the power of pain, the power of oppression, the power of fanaticism, the power of corruption, the power of greed, the power of decadence, the power of lust, the power of fear—all of which is all around us, all the time and one can succumb to it and let it overwhelm them or one can absorb it into oneself—then harness it and control it.

That is Dark Magic.

And that is what we used to get Althea's magic back.

When we completed the ceremony, we were naked, sweating, panting and spent.

And can I say, a little grossed out yet turned on at the same time.

Ulk.

And we watched in fascinated horror as Althea's body regressed in age to that of a little, wee, innocent, weak babe, before she grew again, in mere moments and she became Althea again.

Then she exploded, or at least her aura did (which is kinda the same thing), shooting violent sparks of lime green and robin egg blue so brutally, we all dove for cover.

Then it was over.

And we pulled ourselves up out of the grass, weakly circling her, depleted of energy and magic while she calmly took out her wand, zapped my cloak, which lay several feet behind me so that it danced through the chill night air and wrapped itself around me, snug and warm. She did that for Viv then Su and with Lucy's fleece and Josie's trench coat.

She helped us to dress, gently, even lovingly. With swift blue and green flashes from her wand, she obliterated our tools and ingredients, our potions and vials, sending them, I've no doubt, to a plane where they will never be used again.

She then led us to the car where Gabriel was waiting (he'd given us privacy to perform the ceremony).

Gabriel and Althea helped us into the car.

When Althea got in last and buckled her belt, she said quietly, "Go gently, lad, you've got some delicate magic in this vehicle."

And we went home.

I led the group to the house as Gabriel left us on Old Church Road for fear Ash or Aidan would see us. He was to take Lucy home.

Viv and Su split from us toward the footpath to come into The Gables from the greenhouse side. Josie and I took the driveway but split so she went in the front door and I headed to the back by the conservatory.

We were trying to divide attention so Ash and Aidan might find one or the other of us, but not all and most importantly not me.

But, as my luck would have it, Aidan was waiting for me in the conservatory.

Not…good…news.

I was exhausted, shattered, spent, drained and just plain old worn out.

I was dead on my feet, physically and emotionally and I didn't have enough magic in me to extinguish a candle.

"Jesus," was Aidan's word when he saw me.

I was pretty sure my makeup had worn off too, but that just proved it.

I offered a weak wave.

"Hey."

But there he was, stalking me again. I couldn't be bothered to back away so I didn't. He grabbed me by my upper arms and it looked a lot like he was trying to stop himself from shaking me or something worse.

"I could just about—" he started, anger in his voice but he stopped himself. "Matty," he whispered crossly, "you've no idea what kind of fool you've been."

Nice.

"We need to get you to bed and you need to stay in bed," he ordered in a terse voice. "And get your mother to give you some of her healing brews."

I nodded, too weak to talk.

He watched me do this then clipped, "Jesus, Matty."

He walked me into the house taking a great deal of my weight most of the time and then eventually all of it as he slid an arm behind my knees and around my back and lifted me up. I draped my arm around his neck and let my head rest on his shoulder as he carried me into my rooms where both Su and Viv were already conked, sleeping the sleep of the dead.

He carefully lowered my feet to the floor, set me slightly to the side and then he opened the door to my bedroom.

And there stood Ash.

There was a little, kinda *zing* sound with a flash.

Followed very closely by this muted, revolting thud noise.

And then Aidan was falling and Ash moved forward quickly, pushing the smoking gun into the back waistband of his jeans.

He bent low as he approached me and, with nothing left in me, I couldn't avoid it when his shoulder hit my belly and he picked me up in a fireman's hold.

And as he walked away, I had just enough energy to lift my head and watch the blood seep out of Aidan and all over the floor.

~

Note on above entry: Derived from residue of the aura of Mathilda Guinevere Honeycutt. Aura read and recorded by Mavis Lillian Honeycutt, 30 October.

~

31 October

This entry written by Josephine McShane.

We've been contacted by High Priestess, Agatha Darling and the Edwards Coven.

This evening at "The Witching Hour" they're performing "The Ceremony" on Mathilda to slice away her power.

After which they will give her, alive, to the Honeycutt Family in exchange for me.

If the Honeycutts do not turn me over, the Edwards Coven will sacrifice her life in a further Dark Ceremony to cement the powers they are transferring to a new Dark Lord.

I've demanded that this exchange go forward.

I've legally transferred custody of Rory to Mathilda.

No one will die for me.

I couldn't raise my son knowing that they did.

My hope is that your next entry will be made by your mistress.

Please, God, answer that prayer.

Hallowe'en

Hallowe'en
(Witches' New Year)
The Night the Veil between the Worlds is Weakest.

~

I didn't cry.

At least I can say I was proud of that.

But that wasn't a lot to hold on to when visions of Aidan's dead body kept popping into my brain.

~

I don't know where they kept me. It didn't have windows or furniture. The floor was wood. The walls were stone. There was an air mattress and a blanket.

Get this: at one point, they gave me half a French stick cut down the middle, smothered in margarine (euw) and tucked with too-cold brie and grapes and a bottle of Cranberry *pressè*.

What kind of prison food was that?

I ate it.

I needed my strength.

Twice, two men (with guns) and two women (with wands) took me from the room down an equally dark hall to a bathroom.

Mostly, my hands were tied behind me and I lay on the mattress.

There was zero noise, nothing to give away where I was.

There was nothing to do either.

It was like being in the Big Brother house without any housemates or any weird and wonky furniture.

I had a fierce caffeine headache caused by the forced cold turkey off lattes.

I was still exhausted and I knew that, although my magic was probably regenerating, without the physical energy or my wand (which was confiscated, of course), I was fucked.

I thought about Aidan.

And I tried not to think about Ash.

Sometime when it was darker and colder and I knew night was coming, the door opened.

The two men with guns and two women with wands came in, and I thought it was bathroom break time.

But then Agatha Darling came in behind them, followed by Ash.

Darling was wearing her cloak and Ash, I swear to the goddess, looked like fucking Darth Vader following the Emperor.

I felt my mouth fill with saliva like I was going to vomit.

I wanted to spit it in his face.

Which, by the way, was still gorgeous and completely void of any emotion.

He was wearing the Alexander McQueen shirt I'd given him.

The bastard.

Then, behind them, in flew a big, black bat.

The bat hovered momentarily before it transformed, and there stood Douglas Fucking Addison.

"Miss Honeycutt," he said, in those smooth, kind tones I'd somewhat gotten used to, which were undoubtedly honed over years of political ass-kissing.

I just stared, trying to look surprised.

('Cause, if you will remember, I wasn't supposed to know he was a vampire.)

He nodded to Ash, and Ash walked forward.

I wanted to back away, but I held my ground, staring daggers at him.

I wished like hell I could use magic, but I couldn't. I figured I had a big night ahead of me. If I had any magic regenerated at all, I had no doubt I'd need it later.

I had no idea it wouldn't matter.

One of the witches came forward, opening a small metal case that carried a vial that was filled with a syringe and some neon pink fluid that looked right out of *X-Men*.

Ash coolly picked up the syringe and vial, pulled the cap off the syringe with his teeth and spit it out then filled it from the vial.

I didn't fight when he grabbed my arm, plunged the syringe into a vein and pushed whatever the fluid was into my bloodstream.

I just stared at him. My eyes (I hope) filled with loathing.

And I thought, *I hate you.*

And the answering thought in my head was, *No, you don't.*

The bastard.

Whatever was in the vial affected me violently. Chills slid across my body so ferociously that I fell to my knees, then my side, curling into a fetal position and shivering uncontrollably.

"What's the matter with her?" Darling asked, standing over me.

"It affects some like that," Ash answered, also staring down at me.

"I thought it was meant to subdue her," Darling carried on.

"She'll calm in a moment, Agatha, not to worry," Addison said.

And I did calm.

I became scary calm.

As in, body comatose, mind not comatose calm.

Ack!

When I did calm, Ash bent down and picked me up in the fireman's hold again. Nothing so intimate as the way Aidan carried me, like a husband carrying his wife over the threshold.

No, with Ash, it was all business.

Goddess, I hated this man.

We left whatever building we were in and they put me in a car.

My body was not my own.

My mind was there, active, I could see everything, hear everything, but I could not move my arms, legs, head—nothing. It was like the whole of my body had gone to sleep, including those annoying and painful tingles.

Why the tingles?

It was dark, it was late and it was Hallowe'en.

I wasn't stupid; the Witching Hour was nearly upon us. I had a feeling I knew what they were up to.

I spent the time in my head calling out to my tree, to find power and strength and to ask it to send a message out through nature that I, The Chosen One, needed help.

What I was thinking, performing a ritual ceremony on Althea when I most needed my magic, I do not know.

A crazy sense of responsibility to Althea as a fellow witch?

She'd been wronged by witches and I was determined that she'd be righted by witches.

And that determination might be the end of me.

~

We arrived.

The glimpses I caught through the darkness were of fields. This time, Ash didn't pick me up, one of the other men did. He carried me up a hill so steep he had to transfer me to another dude halfway up.

At the top the man dumped me on the grass, face up.

Then, out of the corner of my eye, I saw it.

St. Michael's Church.

I was on top of The Tor.

Oh...*crap*!

~

Historians and tourists knew little bits and bobs about Glastonbury's Tor.

Most gruesomely that in the times of Henry VIII, at the dissolution of Glastonbury Abbey (whose ruins now nestled beautifully in the town at the foot of The Tor), the abbey's last abbot was hanged on The Tor, his body quartered, the pieces sent hither and yon with his head staked at the abbey.

But Glastonbury as a whole is a spiritual and mystical place for all faiths from Christianity (legend says Jesus visited when he was a boy) to paganism (mostly Celtic) to Arthurian Legend (the Holy Grail is, indeed, buried at the base of The Tor).

There is a reason for the utter importance and reverence of The Tor and its surrounding lands.

The prehistoric, manmade Tor was the site of Avalon.

Yes, *Avalon*—the mystical island that guards all magicks as well as the gate to the Underworld.

Over time, the sea has receded, Avalon has faded and the magicks have disbursed.

But The Tor remains.

Yes, the myth is true.

You know the Seven Wonders of the World?

The Supernatural World has the Thirty Magical Gates.

And Glastonbury Tor was *Numero Uno*.

This should have soothed me, to be at The Tor, a place of faith and ceremony, of history and power.

A place of immense magic.

The place that could heal me.

But somehow, right at that moment, it didn't.

Wanna know why?

Because there were a lot of people up there.

A *lot*.

My eyes rolled around in my head and I took them all in.

There were witches in cloaks, men in overcoats, bats flying around, sorcerers and sorceresses wandering about.

I noted three magical carpets with Magi floating on them.

Wizards, trolls, goblins, and I even saw a panting whirling dervish.

I also saw Endora Eccles.

And Jeremy Bligh.

And I saw the Scary Faerie from The Hobgoblin zoom in, sober as a judge, and alight on Agatha Darling's shoulder.

Of course, that little shit was Agatha's faerie.

Of course.

I was *so* stupid.

It was a big, freakish Supernatural Hallowe'en Night Come-See-the-Fall-of-The-Chosen-One Party.

Fuck me.

~

They took me into the St. Michael's Church.

St. Michael's Church was small, one "room" if you will. That room was open to the elements, both doorways had no doors and the top had no roof. The church went up, three, maybe four stories—a tall, narrow, imposing stone structure.

In the middle of the "room" there was a large, flat stone that wasn't normally there.

It rose to about waist height.

As I watched, someone spread a black cloth on it.

There you go.

It was an altar and that was where they placed me.

Before, there was chatting, gabbing, general merriment and excitement in the air.

Once one of the men arranged me on the altar, it had gone silent.

The brethren and sisterhood were assembling for the ritual.

Face up on the altar I saw the glistening atmosphere of the sky, which I knew to be a cloak that protected this gathering from any interruption from the surrounding town and its inhabitants.

It undoubtedly protected the gathering from outside magic as well.

Candles were lit around the inside of the church.

I could smell the heavy scent of incense.

And the deep iron stench of fresh blood.

There started a low humming which turned to a chant.

Out of the corner of my eye, I saw Douglas Addison approach and stop by my side. He was wearing a cape lined in blood red satin.

And right then, down from the top of St. Michael's Church, through the long steep, narrow shoot, came a bat, flying straight toward me.

Almost to the bottom, it transformed into a man who gracefully landed behind and to the right of Addison.

"Glad you could make it, son," Addison said with affectionate impatience.

And there stood Gabriel.

Damn.

Yep.

So.

Stupid.

~

It would be irresponsible of me to explain the procedure that sliced away my magic.

And there are not good enough words to describe the pain.

Or to express my emotions when I saw my aura of hot pink, shell pink, violet, silver and electric blue sparks explode straight into the waiting undead bodies of Douglas and Gabriel Addison.

Those paragraphs alone will have to suffice.

I don't even want history to know of the anguish and shame I felt when my magic was stripped.

So I won't tell you.

~

But it was going to get worse.

~

Magic-less, I was no threat.

After the ritual, the celebration had begun.

More chanting, some magical fireworks, and at that point no one paid any attention to me (because I was no longer a threat…huh).

There were champagne corks popping and laughter.

Unbelievable.

Within fifteen, twenty minutes, whatever drug Ash gave me wore off and I could sit up.

"You're not going anywhere," Gabriel said, placing a warning hand on my shoulder. "The night's not over for you yet."

I wanted to say something flip like, "*Et tu*, Gabriel?"

But I just stared at him.

I mean, why would I trust this guy?

My intuition was shit.

Yet somehow, I was really disappointed, not only in myself, but also Gabriel.

And he stood there, his hand on my shoulder, nodding at folks who passed by and drinking a glass of champagne.

Ash walked up.

"Well done," Gabriel told him, he took his hand from me and shook hands with Ash.

I spit on the stone between their two sets of feet.

Ash turned to me and raised a brow.

Gabriel looked at me and laughed.

∾

"She's here."

"They're here."

"Quiet."

"Shh."

"I don't believe it!"

"We've won!"

"This was too easy. Hurrah!"

"Oh no, I was kind of hoping for a human sacrifice." (That from a particularly ugly little goblin, the little fucker.)

I was sitting in the middle of the altar.

Still wearing what I wore to Althea's ceremony, a pair of jeans, my Diesel trainers with all the straps around the top and a heathered-gray cashmere hoodie.

My knees were pulled up to my chest and I was hugging them because I was cold, tired, scared and seriously pissed off.

By this time, Ash and Gabriel were off somewhere probably having the times of their lives hooking up with gorgeous sorceresses.

I was under witch guard. One of the Edwards Coven was standing behind me, her wand at the ready.

And I was waiting for a good time to make a run for it. They may have my magic but that was all they'd take from me that night.

Assholes.

∾

And then I saw Althea (panting heavily) and Josie (helping her) clear the top of The Tor.

"No!" I shouted, unable to control myself. I tried to spring off the slab but a slap of magic from the witch behind me stayed my progress.

Damn!

Everyone turned to look at me.

I wish I'd kept my mouth shut.

There were giggles and titters as people turned away from ineffectual, old me, The Ex-Chosen One, in order to watch Josie and Althea walk into the small clearing.

"I've got this." I heard a familiar French, English, and yes, American accented voice say.

I turned and saw Gabriel relieve the witch from Mathilda watch.

Then Ash positioned himself beside me, leaning his hip against the altar (of all fucking arrogant things to do).

I wanted to push him off.

I wanted to punch him in the face.

I wanted to kick him in the balls.

I wanted to rush forward, grab Josie and Althea and run.

But I had to bide my time and be smart.

For once.

Then something happened.

Agatha Darling walked toward Althea, and Althea unsheathed her wand.

"Back off, woman," Althea warned.

I took in my breath.

Why would they allow a witch, a powerful witch like Althea, to deliver Josie to them?

Why wouldn't they pick Lucy?

Or send someone of their own to collect her?

"Oh, you poor deluded soul," Agatha said, her voice, as usual, serene and bored. "Put that away. You aren't fooling anyone."

My heart jumped.

They didn't know!

They didn't know that Althea had her power back!

I looked up at Ash who was watching the scene, and then I saw his chin dip ever-so-slightly as if he was nodding yes.

My heart leapt.

Ohmygoddess!

Ohmygoddess!

Could it be?

It flooded my head (from the mind-meld, direct from Ash, he gave a quick explanation, too long to go into here) the moment I felt something rough scrape my back and slide into the waistband of my jeans and the tingles came back double time, surging through my body, my limbs…

My magic!

Gabriel was beside me, his hand behind me…

...slipping me my wand!

Agatha turned dismissively from Althea and nodded to a couple henchmen who'd trained guns on Althea and Josie.

"You can kill them now." Then she looked at me, "But leave that one for the sacrifice."

"No!" I screamed, pulled out my wand, and I zapped a killer flash of electric blue, hot pink and sliver magic that hit Agatha Darling slap in the middle of her chest, blew her straight into the air and twenty feet away...to the very edge of The Tor.

Just as Althea lifted her wand straight to the sky and shot an enormous lime green spark that exploded in a mushroom of blue and green pixie dust that covered the entire Tor.

~

That's when it happened.

That's when it really began.

The Supernatural War.

There hadn't been one since recorded time.

And it started that night...on The Tor.

~

The atmosphere exploded in a dazzling and fiery array as Althea's spell broke the magical cloak mere moments before the Modernists flooded the top of The Tor.

There was confusion amongst the Traditionalists. The Chosen One still had her power as did the already stripped Edwards Oracle.

Surprise gave the Modernists the upper hand.

Witches, vampires, sorceresses, wizards, banshees and unicorns flooded the scene.

Faeries flew in, zipping this way and that, flashing white, salmon, pistachio and lemon zaps everywhere.

Vermillion, sunset orange, grass green, bruised peach, Prussian blue, crocus purple—you name it, you saw it—every color known to human and not-so-humankind flooded the arena in flashes and jolts.

There were shouts, screams, stamping, flying...utter mayhem.

"See you later," Gabriel said to Ash.

Then Gabriel grabbed my head roughly, kissed me on the top of my hair (!!!!) and then he jumped over us, landed by Josie and picked her up, jumped again and disappeared over the side of The Tor.

"Get them!" Agatha shouted in her best Cruella De Vil impersonation, pointing at where Gabriel and Josie disappeared.

She was not bored anymore.

She turned to me, wand raised.

But before she could get off a single zing, her wand exploded in a blaze of lilac, powder blue, butter yellow, gold, scarlet and copper—a spell simultaneously cast from the Triumvirate of Mavis, Mom and Gran.

"Let's go." Ash took me by the arm, pulled me from the altar and we ran.

I zapped the offending "human sacrifice" goblin (who was about to hurl a ball of flame at Ash and me) and then I constructed a shield of sparkling pixie dust that twirled unceasingly around Ash and I.

It deflected the spells of two witches and a sorcerer.

We just about made it to the edge of The Tor when I heard Althea shout, "Girl! Watch out!"

I turned in time to see Althea throw herself in front of Ash and I, just as Addison's bat swooped low and transformed.

And then the fuckity, fuck, fucking bullet fired at close range hit Althea and ripped straight through her then lodged into Addison who simply (being undead and it not being a silver bullet or piercing his heart) leapt away, transforming into a bat again.

I didn't scream.

I also didn't hesitate.

I just lifted my wand and zapped the gunman (who was now aiming at us) so violently that he flew through the air and over the side of The Tor.

(I didn't notice that this dramatic event was helped a tiny bit by the bullet that came from Ash's gun.)

I ran to Althea and dropped down to my knees at her side.

"Althea!" I cried as I watched the dark stain spreading across the excruciatingly ugly, pilled oatmeal of her jumper (if I told her once, I told her a million times, she should wear jewel tones). I looked up at Ash. "We have to get her to the hospital."

Althea grabbed my hand. "No, this is my death."

She said it in a quiet, calm voice, and I watched the magical explosions that were filling the air above us reflected in her eyes.

I barely noticed the turquoise, sage green, grape and bronze shield that Viv and Su generated over us.

"Matty, sweetheart, we have to go," Ash said quietly, gently but urgently.

I ignored him and spoke to Althea. "Althea, I can get you down with a levitation spell then we'll get you to the hospital."

She weakly shook her head against the grass. "I've seen enough in my visions, girl, to know my own death. Follow your man."

"Althea."

"Go, child. It was always my destiny. The Chosen One would give me back my most precious gift so I could die with dignity. Then I would help her with her work. Destiny."

"Destiny, shmestiny," I said.

She laughed an icky, shuttering cackle and blood trickled out of her mouth.

Oh goddess!

"Althea!" I exclaimed.

She clutched my hand. "It was an honor to die for you, girl." She looked at Ash then whispered to me, "Choose well, sweet child, and remember to be true only to you."

And that was it.

Then she died.

She didn't close her eyes serenely, but the light went out of them all the same.

My stomach clutched and my throat closed.

"We have to go." Ash was firmly but gently trying to pull me up.

"I can't leave her here!" I cried, struggling against his efforts.

"You won't," Ash whispered.

And I didn't.

All Obi-Wan Kenobi (save with a shitload of lime green and robin egg blue sparks, flashes and pixie dust), Althea disappeared, her beautiful sparks, flashes and pixie dust scattering to the stars, the earth and the wind.

Until nothing remained of her but a soft blue twinkle that seemed to wink at me before it flashed out.

In the midst of battle, it was a beautiful thing to behold.

"Now!" Ash yelled, pulling me up and we were gone.

~

The fight was in full swing on top of The Tor, down its sides and in the skies above it.

Witches were zapping witches.

Vampire bats swooping down and transforming into men, flipping their capes and flashing their teeth.

I couldn't believe my eyes when I saw Lucy kick a baddie in the crotch then link her hands together and nail him one in the face as he bent forward in pain.

"You go girl!" I shouted.

I saw Prunella, the Hag, blaze one of the witches who escorted me to the bathroom.

I saw Mavis and Endora in what looked like a battle to the death, wands slicing through the air, pixie dust shooting out like lasers, shields erecting then exploding.

Ash led, running swiftly, leaping with agility over holes or mounds or prone supernatural beings, all the while holding my hand.

I followed, tripping and skipping, zinging and flaring with my wand here and there to protect Ash and me, and to help any of our allies that I could see.

BecBec zoomed in, trailing us, zipping away in a flash to trip up a baddie or deflect a spell.

Chaos.

~

The whole thing was pretty mind-blowing if you got right down to it.

And kinda all my fault.

It appeared that Ash and I were running *away* from the action rather than participating *in* it, which didn't sit well with me.

It wasn't lost on me that a whole lotta people went out of their way to keep me safe and alive.

And two of them had just put themselves in front of a bullet for me.

I was The Chosen One, SuperWitch and Glamour Girl.

And I wasn't just gonna run away.

~

I skidded to a halt and pulled free of Ash.

"What the fuck are you doing!" he snapped, urgency in his voice.

I put my wand to my lips and winked.

He raised his face to the heavens and said, "Oh, for fuck's sake."

(Not sure which deity would appreciate *that* prayer.)

Then I took three deep breaths.

I turned around three times and stopped at North.

I said out loud to my tree, "Okay, tree. Here goes nothing!"

And I…let…*fly*.

A soft pink laser of pixie dust shot out of my wand, winding swiftly and fully around The Tor looking like the strawberry swirl on a lollipop.

I saw an offshoot of the pink beam strike out, wrap itself around Endora's ankle and knock her off balance so that she dropped her wand and Mavis leapt forward to grab it.

I saw another beam shoot around the waist of the bathroom witch so she was tugged backward; whatever spell she'd thrown going off its mark and missing Prunella.

I saw up above a vampire sliding down the beam like he was surfing a wave, leaping off in a double somersault and landing behind a troll who was about to bring his hammer onto the horn of a unicorn. The vampire kicked the troll in the back of the knee. The troll went down. The unicorn leapt forward, magic surging from its still healthy horn. The vampire transformed into a bat and flew away.

(Don't be too impressed, vampires are known to be show-offs.)

Everywhere my beam touched you could hear screams, cries or cheers.

It was just my little bit.

I put my hand out to Ash and he was watching me with what looked like pride gleaming in his eye (Yes! Pride!).

My fingers closed around his then I declared, "Okay, *now* we can go."

We made it to the bottom of the hill though I didn't see it as I was looking behind me to watch my twirly spell. I kept on going after Ash stopped and ran smack into something solid.

I took a good look at the something solid.

Aidan.

Ohmygoddess!

Yay!

Yay!

Yay!

I shouted for joy and jumped on him, flinging my arms and legs around him and kissing him all over his face.

He gave me a tight squeeze then gently lowered me to the ground, kissing me on the tip of my nose.

It was his turn to hold my hand.

"You ready?" he said to Ash.

"Yes, let's go," Ash replied, not looking at me but behind us, still holding his gun.

"If I could have just one moment."

Jeremy Bligh *and* Scary Faerie appeared from nowhere, "and it was Bligh who was talking.

They had to have had a glamour to shield them because none of us had seen them.

Fucking Agatha.

Bligh was holding a gun pointed at me.

Ash raised his gun and pointed it at Bligh.

Aidan raised *his* (!) gun and pointed it at the Scary Faerie.

I raised my wand and pointed it generally in the direction of the baddies.

But the Faerie was holding an orb o' magic that was much like my orb o' magic but I think all of us standing there knew the difference.

Which meant that BecBec was forced to build an orb of her own.

Holy Mutually-Assured Destruction, Batman!

Yikes!

～

By the way, faeries may be small but they'd been here far longer than humans, their magic was far older and far, *far* more powerful.

So much so, they were not allowed to use their magic near to its full potential in the human realm (only in the faerie realm). If they did, there could be pretty fucking serious consequences when they answered to their higher powers.

One zing from Scary Faerie and we were all toast (and so was half of Glastonbury).

A reciprocal zing from BecBec, even as a young faerie, and there was a good possibility The Tor *and* most of Somerset would explode.

Fuck.

～

Just then, there was a strange but definite rumble in the ground.

What now?

~

Bligh was too intent on aiming to notice the rumble and I felt it best, for once, to keep my mouth shut.

I noticed both Aidan and Ash were steady but Bligh was shaking and looked nervous.

Cocky but nervous.

I didn't like nervous. In moments like that, nervous was not good.

And cocky didn't go well with nervous. In fact, cocky and nervous were a recipe for disaster.

Another rumble came just as Bligh spoke.

"Don't worry, Miss Honeycutt, this won't be like one of your movies where we give you a chance to figure out some ingenious plan to get away. No, instead, I think we'll just kill you."

And then, without further ado, he shot at me just as Scary Faerie threw his orb.

~

The orb should have killed us.

But, you forget.

I *am* The Chosen One.

And we were standing at the base of The Tor.

Which also happened to be the Gate to the Underworld.

~

Not to mention, Ash *was* from magical stock.

So, before Bligh's finger squeezed the trigger, Ash stepped in front of me.

Faster than a speeding bullet?

Not exactly but almost.

And very, *very* unfortunately.

~

At the same moment I used everything I had left to wave a sheet of protective magic up in front of us and it shot forward, toward Bligh and Scary.

~

Simultaneously, with a final rumble and an awful hiss and screech, the Gate opened and out flew a twinkling of multi-colored light, which separated instantaneously and formed into two women.

One was Althea.

The other one, I did not know.

And together, the ghostly spirits absorbed and my shield deflected, the ancient, powerful orb of faerie magic then shot it straight back at Bligh and Scary Faerie, pinpointing them with deadly accuracy.

The blistering burst of mingled otherworldly and SuperWitch power blew them off their feet and backwards to pin them hideously against the side of The Tor. It scorched off their eyebrows and most of their hair and clothes and, icky though it was, quite a bit of their skin as well as a huge spray of the earth around them.

~

I stared in horror at this result and then, without hesitation, Althea and the woman zoomed back into the Gate as if their borrowed time was more than up.

The Gate closed with a resounding whoosh the instant they passed through it and the ground rumbled its last warning.

And in the distance I could just hear the echoing:

"This will be the last time I'm going to tell you, cease calling me Elly or no more help from me!"

~

My spell mixed with the power of the Underworld was extraordinary, unheard of magic.

Beautiful and astonishing.

This fusion of natural and Underworld power would someday fill pages and pages in history books.

The problem was, magic could repel magic.

But faerie, witch, Chosen One or Underworld magic...

None of it…
Could stop bullets.
And Bligh's bullet hit Ash.
Right in the belly.

∾

"Don't worry, baby," I whispered to Ash, whose head was in my lap as he lay across the back seat of Aidan's Mercedes while Aidan drove like his usual madman to the nearest hospital, and BecBec zoomed beside the car, lost in a rocket of color.

We'd jumped into the car, amid dressed and pajamaed townies staring up at the noise and mayhem of the enormous pink lollipop of The Tor. Staring at what they probably thought was a "silly" and annoying Druid ritual or an amateur (but spectacular) fireworks display.

Things such as this were what humans thought, for centuries, to protect their fragile psyches from the likes of the evil and beauty that were just then pouring down from The Tor.

But deep in their bones, they knew.

And although they watched, they made no move to go up, to intervene, to understand.

Their time would come.

∾

"You're gonna be okay," I said to Ash as Aidan pulled to a jarring stop outside a hospital.

Ash opened his mouth to speak.

"If you say you're honored to die for me, I'm gonna hurt you," I told him.

He closed his mouth and grinned.

Then I watched as the light went out of his eyes.

∾

Pain shot through me, excruciating and sharp. Fire burned a searing path from my chest to my throat and my eyes instantly filled with tears.

There would be no beautiful sparkles and flashes from his human death.

Just that extinguished light noting the passing of a magnificent man.

I closed my eyes, the wetness there slid down my cheeks as I bent forward, kissed his forehead and whispered, "I love you, Sebastian."

Aidan yanked the door open (woefully hideously too late), and BecBec zoomed into the car and halted in a glittery dazzle, tears falling from her eyes. I tore my gaze away from Ash and watched as the gossamer from BecBec's wings detached, its ethereal beauty filling the interior of the car, shrouding us, Ash and me, in its glittery light.

She opened her mouth and I watched, silent tears sliding down my cheeks, and I understood, for the first time, the exquisite Elfin words as she sang the timeless Lament of the Elf.

The Month of November

15 November
Baker Historic District
Denver, Colorado
A.K.A. Mathilda's Version of Heaven *and* Hell

~

Su found a huge, six-bedroom Victorian mansion built during Denver's silver boom.

It was built on a rise, so it had from its top story a view over the other houses to the famous purple mountains' majesty.

It had a circular turret that rose two stories further than the rest of the house on the front western corner.

It had a massive, high, wrought iron fence surrounding the property.

The veranda floor was tiled in Italian marble.

There was a two-bedroom carriage house on the side and a one-bedroom mother-in-law house at the back.

It had a ballroom.

It was painted butter yellow with turquoise, pink and grape accents.

It was fan-fucking-tastic.

It was my childhood home.

~

Su's coven was night and day to the Honeycutt Coven.

Everyone was under fifty and nearly everyone was a hippie or Earth Mother.

And all of them dressed very well, for hippies and Earth Mothers, that is.

~

Lucy and Fay were due to arrive in a couple of weeks.

Before she left England, Lucy had to train Antonia, Nerissa, Pandora, Octavia, etcetera in her and my recipes, how to run The Dozen and how to treat Big Red with respect.

~

Mavis was on the hunt for Endora, who got away from what is now known as the Battle of The Tor.

Which, by the way, the Modernists won, forcing the Traditionalists to retreat. We also now control The Tor, which was a damn good thing, strategically, thank the goddess.

Yee ha!

~

Gran was on the hunt for Agatha, who also got away.

~

Scary Faerie and Bligh were both reported missing.

I can't imagine Bligh survived, but Scary Faerie was immortal.

Immortal and pissed off, no doubt.

Not good.

~

The "Real" World couldn't even ignore what happened on The Tor.

Of course, most folks can't see magic. Though, magic has been around a long time. There are lots of bloodlines, "normal folk" that have a latent magical history, a great, great grandma who was a witch, a great, great, great granddad who was a sorcerer, that kind of thing.

Those are normally the folk who "see things" (and don't believe their own eyes) and when they talk about those things, most people think they're crazy (they're not).

Then there are those with open minds, the ones who believe in magic and celebrate (and protect) the earth. They can see magic too (though it doesn't happen often).

But that night, the magical flow tore through the veil. Even those without latent magical blood or those who don't even believe in magic saw *something*.

Lots of discussion and suggestion worldwide about the "phenomena" witnessed by dozens on Hallowe'en night.

"Experts" came forward.

Some of them knew what they were talking about.

Others did not.

One "scholar" was (somewhat hilariously) ripped to shreds by Jeremy Paxman on *News Night*.

Churches issued statements.

Crazies took credit.

After a few days, most dismissed it.

But if you were even a little in touch with nature, you could feel it.

That night, the veil was torn away between the real and magical worlds.

And people were scared.

~

When Aidan and I arrived in Denver, Daphne in tow, Josie, Rory and Cosmo were already at the house, otherwise known as The Acre.

Gabriel was with them.

As was Windspear Jones.

(Oo la la…more like a Native American Indiana Jones. Hoochie mama, he was cute.)

As was Douglas Addison and my mother.

~

I'm sure you've already guessed by now that Douglas Addison is my dad.

Deep cover, indeed.

And Gabriel is my older brother.

I don't credit it, considering that Gabriel is a super-lean, vampire machine and Viv, Su and I all carry our fair share of curves and not a single blood-sucking tendency.

But there you go.

Genetics.

Who understands them?

Mom was in Seven Kinds of Heaven to have "all my babies" for the first time in all our lives under one roof.

Not to mention "Dad" being there (which meant, even though all her babies were under one roof, Mom and Dad spent lots of time in her bedroom—ACK!)

~

You see, the neon pink fluid Ash injected me with was not only a protection against the magic-stripping spell but also a magic-regenerating spell.

While Viv, Su and I had been busy so had Mom, Mavis and Gran.

In Agatha's evil plan, Ash was meant to be injecting me with a drug that would render me motionless.

Instead, he injected me with a brew of potent Honeycutt protection. A spell that simultaneously blocked the severing of my magic, but also, with a good deal of help from the natural magicks that permeated The Tor, regenerated me to full power (and then some).

When my aura "exploded," that was extra magic my body couldn't hold and Dad and Gabe (you know he had to have a nickname) stayed close so they could absorb it and so that no one else would.

That magical spell also simulated pain (unfortunately).

But it had to look real.

~

When Althea's magic was torn away by the Edwards Coven, they gave it to Dad-slash-Douglas in their preparations to make him a "Dark Lord" whatever that was…even Dad didn't get it. He called it the "crazy rantings of a loon" (loon = Agatha).

So when Viv, Su, Lucy, Josie and I took it back, Mom had secluded Dad in my Tower Room so he would be protected from any magical surveillance for when the magic was stripped away again and restored to Althea.

(Oh, forgot to mention…as a vampire, Dad could act as a vessel to store magic. That's why Althea's magic didn't disburse and why Agatha thought that he and Gabe could absorb mine.)

So, at that crucial moment on The Tor, Agatha and the rest didn't know Althea had powers when she marched up that hill with Josie.

~

I could go into a long explanation of how it all worked.

But I won't.

History will dissect it, I've no doubt.

~

I could be pissed off that a lot of folks were keeping a lot of stuff from me all this time, hell, all my life.

But I was alive.

And so was (most) everyone I cared about.

So how mad could you be?

I was classified as a Hazardous Sage.

I was a young witch.

Powerful but unripe.

And I had a lifetime of pretty fucking important work ahead of me.

And anyway, forgiveness is a powerful thing.

And we were at war, there was no time for petty trivialities.

And now it was all in the open, there was no more pussyfooting around.

And all eyes were on me.

I had to keep focus.

I had a war to win.

~

Aidan flew with me to Denver, I slept with my head on his shoulder most of the way.

He was careful to give me space.

Well, not *too* much space.

We spent a lot of time watching movies.

Me with my head in his lap, him stroking my hair (this felt nice, as in, *ultra* nice).

Okay, so we made out a lot and maybe fooled around a bit and I'd kind of, um…made it a practice to sneak into his bedroom at night and sleep next to him (just sleep, after we fooled around a bit, that is).

But, I was happy to be alive.

And I was happy he was alive.

And, well, he's hot.

~

Aidan and I didn't talk much about things.

Like, say, how he and Ash faked Aidan's death.

Or, say, how it was so easy for me to lose trust in him and Ash.

Bottom line, there wasn't a lot to say that wasn't ugly and damaging.

So, we just didn't say it.

Don't judge me, it worked.

~

I hadn't cried, didn't seem much point.

It wouldn't change things.

It wouldn't bring Althea back.

~

Ash was supposed to have recuperated a lot longer than he did before attempting a trans-Atlantic flight.

But yesterday he arrived on the doorstep, leaning on an ebony silver-handled cane, pale as Dad and Gabe, his father Marcus by his side.

He, of course, wasn't going to give Aidan even a hint of the upper hand by staying away too long, and he wasn't stupid enough to think that Aidan wasn't going to take advantage (see entry above).

~

I know what you thought, but I did mention that elfin magic is powerful.

The Lament of the Elf is a magic that has to be performed very shortly after death, before a spirit can leave a body.

The Lament, which consists of magic held in an Elf's gossamer wings mingled with the spell in a song, the physical and audible spells wrap around a "dead" human body, holds the spirit and body intact and restarts the systems. It gives a body only minutes but sometimes minutes make the difference.

They made the difference for Ash.

If we hadn't been outside the hospital, Ash would have really died.

The Lament was known as an Absolute Forbidden Spell amongst the Elves. It has only been performed half a dozen times in the last three to four thousand years.

BecBec was in big time trouble with the Imperial Order of the Elves.

I'd have to go to the Faerie Realm and testify for her soon.

BecBec was in a panic (but that didn't mean she regretted what she did, she didn't—she didn't tell me this, she was in Elf Gaol, but she got a message to me, one I actually understood).

Still, she was in *trouble*.

Poor BecBec.

Dad had come with me to answer the door when Ash arrived (so weird, after thirty-four years, to have a dad…too much to ponder now).

We all walked into the living room where Mom found us.

"Let's leave them to it, shall we?" she said and bustled Marcus and Douglas out of the room.

Ash and I stared at each other for what seemed like a long time (because it was).

It was Ash who broke the silence.

"Seymour got a body slam and a face full of kisses when he arose from the dead." (Ash)

"Could you take a body slam right now?" (Me)

"I can barely stand." (Ash)

"Poor baby." Pause. "You ruined the shirt I gave you." (Me)

"I'm sure you'll find some excuse to buy me another one." (Ash)

I *do* would.

In fact, I already had. There were three of them waiting in my room for him.

"Cheeky." (Me, but I smiled)

I walked to him and gently laid my hands on his face. Then I reached up on tippy-toes and kissed him softly.

"You ever scare me like that again, I'll kill you myself," I warned, tears filling my eyes.

One of his hands settled light on my hip and his face went soft.

"I can't make that promise." (Ash)

"Then *you'll* be the death of *me*." (Me)

"That's one thing I can guarantee won't happen." (Ash)

I smiled through my tears.

He grinned through the pads of his fingers digging in my hip.

I gingerly wrapped my arms around his middle, rested my cheek on his chest and felt him kiss my hair as one of his arms slid to settle around my waist.

Aidan walked in and stopped when he saw us.

For a while, we all stood there together.

"What now?" I asked.

Both of my beautiful boys laughed.

Great.

Ack!

The End

Mathilda will return in…
Mathilda, SuperWitch: The Rise of the Dark Lord

The Month Of December

The Journal of Mathilda also known as My *Book o' Shadows*
(I am SuperWitch, Chosen One, Glamour Girl, and that isn't being braggy. I just am.)
(Even the Glamour Girl part (says me).)

2 December

Okay, so…

Ran out of pages in my last journal, or, as witches call them, *Book of Shadows*, (or also *grimoires*, which is kind of spooky, but also cool, but I digress) so starting a new one.

Mom says should write an introduction in each new journal, just in case the old one gets lost or damaged before *Le Société* can transcribe it into their computer databases or whatever.

So, thankfully, am a witch so can use magic to write so my hand won't hurt because there's lots to say.

Let's see.

I'm Mathilda Guinevere Honeycutt.

I'm a thirty-four-year-old, single, white female. I have blonde hair (helped by chemicals), hazel eyes, long legs, c-cup boobs, a freakishly tiny waist and a big (ish) ass that thankfully is balanced out by boobs and looks really good in jeans, skirts, anything (this could be magical powers but not my own because don't know that spell…yet).

And I'm a witch.

A real witch, wand-wielding, pixie-dust-flying, spells, potions, cauldrons, chanting, so-mote-it-being, the whole enchilada.

I'm not just *a* witch, I'm *the* witch—Mathilda, SuperWitch, The Chosen One, the one prophesied for centuries to save the world.

Sound cool?

It's not.

It's a seriously stressful job, to be the prophesied Savior of the World.

They never show Batman and Superman bitching about always having to go out, night after night, putting their asses on the line, worrying about the people they love.

Bet the Caped Crusader and the Man of Steel have a shed load to bitch about.

Let's just say, being the prophesied Savior of the World is *not* fun.

I'm classified by The British Witches Council as "Sage: Hazardous."

That means I'm super-mega powerful, but I don't have control over my powers.

This, I think, is stupid.

I mean, last Hallowe'en did I *not* kick some ass during the Battle of The Tor?

Yes, I fucking well did.

Anyhoo.

~

I'm American but I spent last year in England at my Auntie Mavis's house, The Gables (that's why the *British* Witches Council classified me).

Went to England because it was time for a change of life, but I had no idea how much of a change of life it would be (or might not have gone and instead continued my career in retail, continued dating men who were no good for me and continued to rack up credit card debt during the sales (also not during the sales, I didn't discriminate when it came to shopping)).

Auntie Mavis is a witch, and so is my entire family (Mom (Hanna), Gran (Minerva), my sisters Viv and Su, and so on—*all* the women in my family are witches).

My dad and brother, Gabe (what I call him, his name is Gabriel), aren't witches (men can't be) but they are vampires (kid you not, real, live(ish), blood-sucking vampires).

Our women come from a powerful coven, one of the oldest and most powerful in the world. The Honeycutt coven could kick ass even if I wasn't in it.

Because of a lot of stuff that's way too much to get into now, learned of my family's and my own witchdom on Hallowe'en night the year before last (let's just say, Hallowe'en has not been good to me lately).

After that, started training, took on my first Spellbound (someone I vow to keep safe, her name is Josephine "Josie" McShane and she has a nine-year-old son, Rory) and in the middle of all that, I kind of started a war.

Yes, *a war* (see above reference to the Battle of The Tor, that's where it all started).

A big old war of the Modernist Sect of the Underworld/ Occult/Supernatural/Magical Folk and the Traditionalist Sect of the same. It doesn't take a brainiac to figure out which believes in what.

I'm a Modernist. I'm kind of de facto Leader of the Modernists since I started it all.

(This is another stressful job I don't really want, by the way.)

When I said I was single, this was not strictly true.

Complicating my life further, there are two men in it.

Two rather luscious men.

They've both vowed to protect me because their lives are entwined with mine through destiny (cah-ray-zee, but true). The Mathilda Prophesies say that one is going to marry me and give me three children (yay!), one is going to die to protect me (not gonna happen, not on my watch!).

I'm in love with both (yes, am a slut—no, have not had sex with either of them (but both have given me the big O, as in Orgasm, just without actual penetration, of, er, the pertinent parts), yes, the Big O's were *good*—no, this situation does not work, yes, they both do *not* like sharing—no, this isn't what dreams are made of, it's pretty confusing and totally stressing me out).

Kinda don't want the last dying bit of The Prophesy to happen to either of them so have decided, even if it kills *me*, I'm going to stop it.

~

First, there's Sebastian "Ash" Quincy Wilding.

Ash is a member of *Le Société de Mathilde*, (not named after me but some old, powerful witch chick from 1070, long story), a secret society that, for nearly a millennia, has sworn to protect witches.

He's the son of a witch (she died, how, I do not know) and an Elder of *Le Société*, named Marcus (he's still alive).

Ash has been assigned by *Le Société* to be my bodyguard.

Ash has got a bit of magic (being the son of a witch), is about six foot two, dark brown hair, dark brown eyes, unbelievable body, doesn't talk much, is a bit scary, has a badass history of military and other training (which is why he's a bit scary), is sexy as hell and is not someone you want to mess with.

Then there's Dr. Aidan Knightly Seymour.

Aidan is a member of the five-hundred-year-old Royal Institute of Psychical Research. In essence, The Institute dudes are ghostbusters, but they also research all things supernatural.

Aidan is a "watcher" for The Institute and is supposed to remain distant and take notes. His assigned subject: me.

He's a maverick, doesn't play by the rules, thinks the magical world and real world can live in harmony (kind of what my war is based on) and gets into trouble *a lot*.

He's about six-foot-one, dark blond hair, bright blue eyes, incredible body, a certified genius (150-plus IQ, no joke), has a posh accent, was educated at Eton and Cambridge, teaches Mythology at Trinity College (when he's not protecting me), is a serious hottie and is also not someone you want to mess with.

Ash got shot saving my life at the Battle of The Tor and nearly died (my faerie, BecBec, saved his life by breaking Elfin Law, so, soon, I'm going to have to go testify for her because she's in Elf Gaol and pretty much screwed, but that's another long story).

While Ash was recovering, Aidan and I, my Spellbounds and family went home to Denver to regroup and figure out what was going to happen next.

'Cause, like I said, we were at war and I was Head Cheese.

Problem is, have no earthly idea what I'm doing.

~

Let's get filled in on the last few weeks.

~

On Hallowe'en night, war began and Ash got shot.

So could be near my Spellbounds and keep them safe ('cause that's my job), Aidan and I took off to Denver.

A couple of weeks later, even though he was still recovering from a belly wound, Ash followed us to Denver.

We were all holed up in my family home, The Acre, a big, Victorian, silver boom mansion in Denver's Baker Historic District.

My sister's coven (that would be Su, blonde dreds, total hippie, wears gypsy shirts and flowing Indian printed skirts with bells that tinkle (loudly), usually barefoot unless it's the dead of winter, wears Birkenstocks with socks in cold weather (fashion murder, if you ask me...Su doesn't ask me)), put a protection spell on The Acre for a square mile so we were in pretty good shape to hole up and plan our War of the Supernatural World strategy.

The night Ash got there my mind wasn't on war strategy.

Not even close.

Was lying in my childhood bedroom, the Turret Room I shared with my sisters (though, they'd moved to their own places ages ago).

I still had the bed I slept in growing up, a four-poster, including canopy, with a pink, frilly, ruffly, super-girlie bedspread and loads of pillows. I had whined about that bed for ages until my mom gave in and bought it for me.

~

As an aside, suffice it to say, am kind of the black sheep of my family.

My gran is all about yoga and politics and not shaving her armpits.

My mom is all about being an Earth Mother and gardening and baking her own granola and making her own candles and stuff like that. She even makes her own cosmetics which would be weird if they didn't work so well.

My sister Viv is all Zen and organized and quiet and serene and always meditating and "one with myself" (who else would she be one with, I'd like to know—she says I don't "get it" and after she explained it, I still don't get it so I decided I'm down with not getting it).

I already described Su.

I'm about designer clothes, martinis and every one of the girls at the MAC Counter at Cherry Creek Shopping Center knew my name. I walk in and I was like Norm in *Cheers*. (That was before I moved to England for more than a year. I was going to have to work on getting my Mall Mojo back.)

Anyhoo.

~

Was staring at the flounced canopy over my bed wondering what I was going to do.

See, for the past couple of weeks, I'd been sneaking out and into Aidan's bed to spend the night with him (no hanky panky, well, no serious, penetrating hanky panky, though we'd gotten to third base).

Did this because Aidan might be my future husband and father to my children.

Also did this because I'd just survived some major, life-changing traumas, not the least of which was Ash getting shot.

But also there was the fact that found out the dad I grew up never knowing was not only deep cover in *Le Société* and a Senator for the great State of Colorado, but also a vampire.

Not only *that*, but also found out that I had a brother I never knew existed.

Then, of course, there was Althea, who I'd dragged into the pre-War of the Supernatural World mess in England by kind of kidnapping her during a shootout (another long story). Althea was an oracle, a tough old bird, a bit of an alcoholic and she could be mean, but she was also someone I'd grown to like.

And she died for me, that is, she put herself in front of a bullet.

For me.

What could I say? With all that, I needed a warm, hard body next to mine.

Believe me, you would too.

(And, as I mentioned, Aidan is hot.)

(And, as I might not have mentioned, I was in love with him.)

(PS: I was in love with Ash too.)

(PPS: Confused much? Me too!)

Newsletter

Would you like advanced notification about Upcoming Releases?
Access to exclusive content? Access to exclusive giveaways? The first to
see a new cover reveal? Sign up for my newsletter to keep up-to-date
with the latest from Kristen Ashley!

Sign up at <u>kristenashley.net</u>

About the Author

Kristen Ashley is the *New York Times* bestselling author of over eighty romance novels including the *Rock Chick*, *Colorado Mountain*, *Dream Man*, *Chaos*, *Unfinished Heroes*, *The 'Burg*, *Magdalene*, *Fantasyland*, *The Three*, *Ghost and Reincarnation*, *The Rising*, *Dream Team*, *Moonlight and Motor Oil*, *River Rain*, *Wild West MC*, *Misted Pines* and *Honey* series along with several standalone novels. She's a hybrid author, publishing titles both independently and traditionally, her books have been translated in fourteen languages and she's sold over five million books.

Kristen's novel, *Law Man*, won the *RT Book Reviews* Reviewer's Choice Award for best Romantic Suspense, her independently published title *Hold On* was nominated for *RT Book Reviews* best Independent Contemporary Romance and her traditionally published title *Breathe* was nominated for best Contemporary Romance. Kristen's titles *Motorcycle Man*, *The Will*, and *Ride Steady* (which won the Reader's Choice award from *Romance Reviews*) all made the final rounds for Goodreads Choice Awards in the Romance category.

Kristen, born in Gary and raised in Brownsburg, Indiana, is a fourth-generation graduate of Purdue University. Since, she's lived in Denver, the West Country of England, and she now resides in Phoenix. She worked as a charity executive for eighteen years prior to beginning her independent publishing career. She now writes full-time.

Although romance is her genre, the prevailing themes running through all of Kristen's novels are friendship, family and a strong sisterhood. To this end, and as a way to thank her readers for their support, Kristen has created the Rock Chick Nation, a series of programs that are designed to give back to her readers and promote a strong female community.

The mission of the Rock Chick Nation is to live your best life, be true to your true self, recognize your beauty, and take your sister's back whether they're at your side as friends and family or if they're thousands of miles away and you don't know who they are.

The programs of the RC Nation include Rock Chick Rendezvous, weekends Kristen organizes full of parties and get-togethers to bring the sisterhood together, Rock Chick Recharges, evenings Kristen arranges for women who have been nominated to receive a special night, and Rock Chick Rewards, an ongoing program that raises funds for nonprofit women's organizations Kristen's readers nominate. Kristen's Rock Chick Rewards have donated hundreds of thousands of dollars to charity and this number continues to rise.

You can read more about Kristen, her titles and the Rock Chick Nation at KristenAshley.net.

facebook.com/kristenashleybooks

instagram.com/kristenashleybooks

pinterest.com/KristenAshleyBooks

goodreads.com/kristenashleybooks

bookbub.com/authors/kristen-ashley

tiktok.com/@kristenashleybooks

ALSO BY KRISTEN ASHLEY

The Colorado Mountain Series:
The Gamble
Sweet Dreams
Lady Luck
Breathe
Jagged
Kaleidoscope
Bounty

Dream Man Series:
Mystery Man
Wild Man
Law Man
Motorcycle Man
Quiet Man

Dream Team Series:
Dream Maker
Dream Chaser
Dream Bites Cookbook
Dream Spinner
Dream Keeper

The Fantasyland Series:
Wildest Dreams
The Golden Dynasty
Fantastical
Broken Dove
Midnight Soul
Gossamer in the Darkness

Ghosts and Reincarnation Series:
Sommersgate House
Lacybourne Manor
Penmort Castle
Fairytale Come Alive
Lucky Stars

The Honey Series:
The Deep End
The Farthest Edge
The Greatest Risk

The Magdalene Series:
The Will
Soaring
The Time in Between

9 781954 680777